D0010754

HOT SHOT

GARY RUFFIN

THE OVERLOOK PRESS
NEW YORK

This edition first published in hardcover in the United States in 2010 by
The Overlook Press, Peter Mayer Publishers, Inc.
141 Wooster Street
New York, NY 10012

Copyright © 2010 by Gary Ruffin

All Rights Reserved. No part of this publication may be reproduced or transmitted in any form or by any means, electronic or mechanical, including photocopy, recording, or any information storage and retrieval system now known or to be invented without permission in writing from the publisher, except by a reviewer who wishes to quote brief passages in connection with a review written for inclusion in a magazine, newspaper, or broadcast.

Cataloging-in-Publication Data is available from the Library of Congress

Book Design and typeformatting by Bernard Schleifer
Manufactured in the United States of America
FIRST EDITION
ISBN 978-1-59020-234-0
10 9 8 7 6 5 4 3 2 1

HOT SHOT

PROLOGUE

SHE COULD SEE THE SHADOW OUTSIDE HER DARKENED BEDROOM, UNDER the door where the crack of light shone. He was back, for the fourth time in two weeks. The first was the night of her ninth birthday, after a gorgeous summer's day, complete with a party and a pony for her and her friends to ride. They had all taken several turns riding the pony, and she had taken the most, being the Birthday Girl.

That seemed like such a long time ago now. She braced herself for what would happen next. Experience had taught her that screaming wouldn't bring anyone to help her. Soon, he would be on her, and *in* her, writhing, grunting and pushing her down, over and over again.

Finally, he would stagger from the dark room, and she would lie awake until morning, wondering what she had done to deserve these terrible nights. Her mother had died a few days after giving her life, and during those long nights she wished she could go to Heaven and be with her.

But she was here in the world, and it was a scary and unforgiving place.

SUMMER 2004

1

MY DOG DIED THIS MORNING.

I awoke to find him struggling to breathe, and cradled his head in my lap as I sat cross-legged on the floor. He was gone within half an hour. Solly was fourteen years old, so it was not unexpected, but it made me sad enough to open Nora's Bar with her at ten A.M. on my day off.

Nora's is three miles north of town, and is the more popular of the two bars within easy driving distance of Gulf Front. I usually only drink for medicinal purposes in the morning, but some events require a toast regardless of the hour. Solly's passing was definitely one of them.

I chose Glenlivet with a drop of water, and drank to my buddy, wishing him cats to chase and a sleeping bag in a warm corner. Nora even gave it to me on the house—something, like Solly's passing, which happens only once in a lifetime. She was methodically cleaning every square inch behind the bar, and left me alone while she went about her business.

There I sat, reflecting on the better points of a Rhodesian Ridgeback mix, when a TV news anchor broke in on Nora's morning movie to announce the suspicious death of a young woman out on the pier at the beach. He turned it over to a reporter interviewing an elderly man who had found the body.

"When did you find her?" the reporter asked.

"Well, I come down here this mornin' about six, 'cause I cain't sleep all 'at good anymore, and I fished the surf 'til about a half hour ago," the old guy said.

"So, it was about ten o'clock when you found her?"

"Yeah, I guess that's about right. See, the whole time I was fishin', they was some gulls flyin' around out at the end of the pier. After I packed up to leave, I walked out there to see what was makin' 'em circle the end of the pier like they was."

"Was she already dead when you found her?"

"'Course she was. What're you tryin' to say?"

"Don't misunderstand, I'm not implying that you had foreknowledge of the event."

The old guy loudly asked, "Four *what?* All I done was find a young half-naked dead lady, and call the cops. That's all there is to it, an' I don't appreciate bein' accused of somethin' I didn't do!"

"No, sir, I'm not implying any misconduct on your part—"

Louder still, the elderly man said, "Well I ain't no killer, an' I ain't gonna be called one on TV!"

The reporter quickly pulled away his microphone and closed the interview, "That's all for now from Gulf Front pier. This is Rick Wade, WFLX Action News . . . back to you in the studio."

Nora drowned out the anchor's finish with several expletives aimed at the news in general, and its impact on her movie in particular. I hardly heard her because I was already thinking about how my day off was going to change.

***

Besides being chief of police in Gulf Front, I'm the only detective on the "force." After graduating from the police academy in Tallahassee, I spent five years there in patrol before making detective in narcotics. Three years later I made detective in homicide, and five weeks short of my third anniversary in that job, I was offered the position of chief. As hard as I had slaved to attain the job in homicide, I just couldn't turn down an opportunity to work in my hometown, and here I am in what has turned out to be my dream job. In my eleven years as chief, there has never been a serious crime in Gulf Front.

Until now.

The remainder of the force consists of two men in their early twenties, and one woman in her mid-thirties. There are two cars for the three of them, all slightly older than they should be. Mine is new, but, I'm the chief. Most of my detecting involves property theft, or teenage vandalism. We are not equipped for anything remotely involving forensics, so I knew we would need outside help, and I don't particularly like outside help. Outsiders in general irritate me if they aren't in town to spend money.

As chief of police, I know just about everybody in this small village, and I had no idea how this young female body got here. I wanted to place her in the tourist category, but this place is so undeveloped and unspoiled that tourism barely leaves a mark. The vast majority of visitors are people in town looking to get a free beach vacation by mooching off relatives. There are no hotels or motels within the city limits, and anybody not visiting family is usually just passing through. That's a good thing in my book, because our beach is one of the most beautiful in the country, and we don't need tourists trashing it.

The town has a bank, two gas stations, three restaurants, a couple of grocery stores, and a hometown newspaper of sorts, *The Gulf Front Observer.* Every other Monday since 1952, the paper has published an edition, and it almost always sells out because everyone in town wants to keep it alive. There are also a few other businesses on Main Street, but no real attractions to speak of. The only things that might attract tourists are the beach, the boardwalk, and the pier. The pier that was now the center of attention as well as a crime scene.

Gulf Front is in the panhandle, somewhere between Panama City Beach, and the Florida-Alabama state line. That's all we ever tell people because we don't want them coming here. This place is quiet and friendly, and we aim to keep it that way.

But, the first apparent murder that had ever happened on my watch as chief took me back to my days in homicide, and my adrenaline began to flow. The calming effect of the Scotch wore off quickly, and I pulled out my breath mints and chewed several in an attempt to at least somewhat soften the stench of morning whisky. I didn't want my troops embarrassed by a chief who'd gotten into the single malt, and I knew reporters and television crews were in my immediate future.

Nora said, "Well, Samuel, I guess you're in for some big fun today. Gonna get to be on TV, and everything. I'll keep my eyes peeled so I don't miss ya on the evening news."

Nora is the only person in town who calls me Samuel. Most people call me Coop, short for Cooper. The only other human I ever allowed to call me Samuel was my mother, and now that she's gone, Nora carries on the tradition of making me flinch for just a second every time I hear the name. My father left us when I was three, and Mom said he used to call me Sammy. To everybody else, I'm Coop.

If someone was asked to describe me, they might say: Average height and weight, broad in the shoulders, green eyes, and brown hair that's just a little too long. Also, my nose is slightly crooked from my days as a running back and safety on the high school football team. I'm a guy who likes to think he's aging gracefully.

Getting up to leave, I thanked her for my drink and said, "Yeah, Nora, this is shaping up to be a jolly good time. I'll check back with you tomorrow, and you can tell me how good I looked on the news."

As I left the cool darkness of Nora's and stepped out into the hot summer sunlight, my cell phone rang. It was Earl Peavey, one of my officers, calling to tell me my services were needed.

"Sorry I didn't call sooner, Coop, but I thought Penny or Adam did, and they thought *I* did, and well, anyway, there's been a young female body found out on the pier."

"Yeah, I heard . . . be there as soon as I can."

"Sorry about your day off."

"That's okay, Earl. I'm on my way."

I got in my patrol car, turned on the seldom-used siren and blue lights, and peeled out of the bar's parking lot, spraying gravel all over the place. It's a good feeling to spray gravel in the line of duty, and since it is rare for me to have the opportunity to do so, I really enjoy it when I get the chance. It's stupid, but that's how I feel about it.

I cruised down the old road that leads to town at seventy miles per, headed for the pier. There was even less traffic than usual, for a soon apparent reason.

When I arrived at the scene, I pulled over and parked on the street a hundred feet or so from the pier, unable to get any closer because there were so many cars and trucks parked in the area. As I got out and headed towards the crime scene, the TV news crews descended upon me, blocking my path. So far it was only the Florida media, out of Pensacola and a few other small towns nearby, so it was relatively easy to make my way through. One of the news vans had been near Gulf Front that morning, and had made it to the scene in record time after hearing Earl's call to headquarters on the police scanner.

I sidestepped them with my best imitation of a police officer who knew what was happening, and for the first time in my forty-four years, got to utter words I've always wanted to say: "No comment." That felt pretty good, and made my day brighter for just a moment. The brightness dimmed when I saw half the town milling around the pier.

Word had spread quickly throughout the community, and it looked like few had stayed home to watch the action unfold on TV. Penny Prevost, my female officer and currently off-again love interest, was losing the struggle to keep everyone back.

"Coop!" she yelled, "Help me get these people outta here!"

"Will do," I said. "Gimme a minute to get my bearings."

I didn't need to get my bearings, but I was enjoying her distress. Unprofessional? Yep. Enjoyable? Somewhat. Worthy behavior for a chief of police? Absolutely not. But I'm not the one who had a date with an insurance salesman from Biloxi last Friday night. Besides, it's good for a person to get a little stirred up before lunch. Helps with the digestion.

My three officers and I work staggered shifts, so that there's always at least one of us on duty at any given time. One of the two guys works the graveyard shift, alternating months. If one of us takes a vacation, I have two part-time deputies at my disposal, and the state sends a trooper by to check up on us almost every day. The seriousness of this particular crime required the involvement of all of us at once. Donny and Melvin, the part-timers, were on the clock together for the first time. Donny was helping people park, and Melvin was on his phone, not doing much of anything.

The aforementioned Earl, and Adam Ingmire, my other male officer, had already put the yellow crime scene tape in position. That was especially good police work, since I didn't even know we *had* yellow crime scene tape.

"Nice tape job," I said.

"Thanks, Chief," they said in unison. Having been roused from a deep sleep by Earl to assist us, Adam was slowly drawing a chalk line around the body, which was barely covered in a very short, revealing pink nightie. When I asked him where he got the chalk, he replied sheepishly, "Two years ago, when I joined the force, I bought it, and I've been carryin' it around in the glove compartment ever since, just in case something like this ever happened. But, now that it has, I sure wish it hadn't."

Adam comes from three generations of cops, and has been called "Twelve" by his father and grandfather since he was born, as in "One-Adam-Twelve," his dad's favorite TV cop show. Adam is slender, with a small head and big teeth, while Earl is a big football lineman type. They make an interesting pair visually, and as long as their jobs don't include anything too heavy, they'll never have a problem in Gulf Front. They wouldn't last very long in a big city, but they're well suited for our little town.

Penny would do very well just about anywhere. She's smart and funny, not to mention beautiful, with long black hair that she wears in a tight bun while on duty. Her eyes are dark brown, and she's built like—well, she's nicely built. With all she has going for her physically, the most attractive thing about her is her voice. It has a sweet, young tone to it, with no sharp edges, and a soft quality that I love. Unless she's yelling at me, of course. I figure if you're going to be around a woman a lot, you need to like the sound of her voice.

Anyway, Penny is completely capable on the job, and performs it with grace and confidence. No one has ever lodged a complaint against her, and I doubt anyone ever will. I told you she was a love interest, but I'm not exaggerating about her competence. She's a good cop, and a better person. I'm still hoping for on-again.

Since the elderly man I had seen talking to the television reporter was one of the few people in town I didn't recognize, I asked Earl, "Where's the old man who found the body?"

"He left as soon as his TV career ended," he said.

"Did anyone question him?"

"No sir, he was gone before I had a chance to talk to 'im. I got his name from the news crew, though. Cecil Harwell, Seabreeze apartments, 7A."

Since there are only eleven hundred and fifty-two souls and four apartment complexes in Gulf Front, there was no need for Earl to say more about Mr. Harwell's location. There are also five housing developments of varying ages and sizes, with the more expensive homes located closer to the ocean. The Seabreeze is a quarter mile from the beach, on Seabreeze Avenue, and houses mostly elderly folks.

"Any word on who the girl is?" I asked.

"Not yet, but we found what we think is the car that brought her here parked by the pier. It's a brand new Caddy with less than three thousand miles on it, white with white leather. I got a call in about the plates right now, so it shouldn't take too long."

"Good," I said. "That's a start."

Earl looked at the crowd, and said, "This is really somethin'. I mean, a murder right here in Gulf Front."

"Let's not jump to conclusions," I said. "There's nothing to indicate it happened here yet." I took one more look at the body, and said, "Tell you what, guys—keep this scene secured and I'll go talk to Mr. Harwell."

"Will do, Chief."

As I made my way back through the crowd, Penny shot me a look that said, *you're a dead man*, and I avoided any more eye contact with her until I was out of sight. The crowd was still interested, but it looked like they knew the show was over. Most had moved off the pier, and the rest had stopped trying to move into position to see the body. I really couldn't blame them for wanting to see what was going on, since news crews in our little town are rare.

I made it to my car, and headed over to the Seabreeze Apartments. I wanted to get talking to old Cecil out of the way. All this activity had my stomach growling, and the one thing I didn't want on top of everything else was to be hungry on my day off. With TV news crews around, and a dead girl on the Gulf Front pier, it looked like I had a real situation on my hands. I didn't want a real situation on my hands.

I wanted lunch.

2

Too busy congratulating himself for his fine performance in front of the camera, Cecil Harwell didn't notice the black van following him home. He smiled at the thought of telling his daughter about his show business debut. Now that he had demonstrated that he was still able to handle himself well in stressful situations, maybe she would stop asking him to move in with her and that dim-witted third husband of hers every time she visited from Panama City.

The van slowed to a stop and parked across the street as Cecil turned into the entrance of his home for the past fifteen years, the last five spent alone after his Millie passed away. Losing her was the worst thing that had ever happened to him, and he still missed her as much as he had on the November day she finally succumbed to her illness.

The old brown Biscayne coughed and sputtered as he turned off the engine. He pulled the bucket of fish from the back seat, walked to his apartment, and savored the air-conditioning that washed over him when he opened the door. Cecil always made sure to turn on the AC before heading to the pier for his early-morning fishing, so the apartment would be nice and cool when he returned. He slept with it turned off, the windows open to the night air, but the days were just too hot for him in the summertime.

He reached in the fridge for his customary strawberry yogurt, and put the kettle on for the day's first cup of green tea. Millie had read some years back about the health benefits of antioxidants found in the tea, and now he couldn't get through the day without four or five cups. It was one of the few bonds he had left, a connection to his wife that he now couldn't let go of even if he tried.

Cecil took a big spoonful of yogurt as he waited for the kettle to come to a boil. Millie had brought the baby blue kettle back from a trip to Bermuda the couple had taken over a decade before, and Cecil intended to use it until it would no longer hold water.

Across the street, the driver started the black van, and circled the block before parking in an open space in front of 7D. Two huge men dressed in suits got out, looked around, and walked towards 7A. The driver knocked and stood on the small porch, his partner behind him on the sidewalk.

When Cecil heard the knock, his initial thought was that reporters had followed him home. Irritated, he walked over and looked through the peephole, and saw the two big men. He couldn't put his finger on it, but something about them made him stop before opening the door. After a moment, he realized why; he recognized the two men, and they weren't reporters.

Earlier, as he fished in the surf, Cecil had noticed them watching, and at the time thought them to be nothing more than casual observers. He'd thought maybe they had been eating breakfast across the street, and were taking in the town's meager sights.

Curious, but still irritated, Cecil called through the door, "Yes? Who's there?"

The man on the porch said, "State attorney's office. We wanna talk about what you seen dis mornin'. You know, over at da pier."

Now fully annoyed, Cecil spoke loudly through the door, "I already said my piece in front'a the TV camera. I didn't see nothin', I don't know nothin', and I ain't got no more to say about it. If you wanna know what I said, talk to them TV folks."

There was silence for a moment, then the man asked, "Could you maybe open da door and talk? I just need a minute of your time, and we'll be on our way."

Cecil said, "I *told* you, mister. I didn't see nothin'. How many ways can I say it?"

The man looked at his partner again, and said, "Sir, don't make dis hard on yourself. You don't understand what I'm sayin' here. Please, sir. Don't make me break dis door down."

His irritation suddenly replaced by alarm, Cecil realized who the men might be. His heart raced like it had the night he found Millie unconscious on the bathroom floor. He said, "You jus' get on outta here! I'll—I'll call the po-leese!"

"Believe me, sir, you don't wanna do dat," the man said, before stepping from the porch to confer with his partner. Cecil started to go over to the phone on the counter by the stove, but stopped when he heard three raps on the door.

"Okay, sir, you win. We'll be goin' now. Sorry we bothered ya."

Cecil's heart was pumping erratically, and in spite of the air conditioning, sweat began to trickle down from under his arms as he tiptoed to the window. He peeked out the window, and watched as they stopped by his car. The partner took out a notepad, and began writing down the license number.

The man who had done the talking smiled as he saw the old man peeking out from behind the curtain, and Cecil reflexively pulled back and wiped the sweat from his upper lip with the back of his hand. When he peeked again, he saw the man open the back of a black van, and pick up something. The man closed the door, put his arm close to his side, and walked back towards the apartment. As he drew within twenty feet, Cecil saw that the man was carrying an axe.

Cecil grabbed the phone from the counter, and quickly shuffled towards the back of the apartment, headed for the sliding glass patio doors that led to the small patch of woods behind the complex. As he frantically tried to unlock the door, he dropped the phone, and bent to retrieve it.

He stood up, unlocked the door with shaking hands, and slid it open. He stepped out on to the tiny patio, right into the grasp of the partner.

Cecil felt his feet leave the concrete as he was manhandled back inside, and he blanched at the strong smell of alcohol on the man's breath. The phone was knocked from his hand and skittered up the hallway linoleum all the way to the kitchen, a part of it breaking away and settling near the front door.

Cecil feared he would pass out as he was hustled to the kitchen, and nearly did as he was thrown to the floor. His captor opened the front door, and in walked the man with the axe, smiling at Cecil as he wielded his weapon. The partner roughly pulled Cecil to his feet, and the old man's fear turned to panic, then shame as he felt wetness run down his leg.

"Look, sir. Me and my friend here don't wanna hurt nobody." The man gently prodded Cecil's stained pants with the axe and said, "Looks like you hadda little accident over here." He and his partner laughed, and Cecil looked at the floor. Axe man continued, "You might get inna much worse accident if you was to talk to somebody about dis mornin'. You hear me?"

Still shaking, Cecil nodded, and his eyes began to water as he kept his head down.

"If anybody comes around wantin' to talk about what you seen, you be sure an' tell 'em you ain't seen nothin', got me?" the man said. "Like I say, you start talkin' and somethin' real bad could happen to you."

His chest so tight he could barely breathe, Cecil wheezed, "Please, I got no reason to talk to nobody. That dead girl don't mean a thing to me. I didn't see nothin' on the pier, and I don't see you here now. I'm tellin' the truth. If you jus' go on, you won't never have no trouble from me. I swear to God you won't."

Cecil hoped the man believed him, because he was telling the truth. He had no intention of risking his life for a girl he had never seen.

Axe man said, "You better be tellin' the truth, or you're a dead man. An old, wet, dead man." The two giants laughed again, and moved to the door. Axe man turned and said to Cecil, "Think of the worst thing I could do to you. Go ahead, think."

Cecil kept his eyes down. After a moment, axe man asked, "Did you think of the worst thing I could do?"

Still looking down, Cecil nodded.

"Whatever you think is the worst thing I *could* do, it ain't half as bad as what I actually *will* do."

Cecil gasped, "Please, I won't never say a word. I swear to God I won't."

Axe man looked Cecil up and down, and said, "I believe you, mister. I really do. Just remember what I said. Now, I feel better, don't you? I'm glad we had dis little talk."

The man handed the axe to his partner, and extended his hand for Cecil to shake. Cecil relaxed and let out a heavy sigh just before the man grabbed him by the throat and dragged him back to the bedroom. There, the enormous man dispensed of Cecil with one savage twist of the old man's neck, and let him drop to the floor.

He shoved the patio door closed with his elbow, and walked back towards the front of the apartment. His partner picked up a kitchen towel that was draped over the faucet, and used it to cover his fingers as he turned off the gas burner under the now-whistling teakettle. He picked up the damaged phone, wiped it clean, and tossed it in the sink. He wiped the doorknobs clean as they left, and kept the towel.

The two coolly strolled to the van, and, seeing no one but an old lady squinting at them in the harsh sunlight from across the complex, drove off. It had been less than ten minutes since they'd pulled into the Seabreeze parking lot.

As they headed back through Gulf Front on their way to the interstate, no one in the dwindling crowd near the pier gave them more than a glance. The sight of a black van slowly motoring along the oceanside highway couldn't begin to compare with a dead girl in a pink nightie.

Just past the pier, a small boy broke away from his mother and bolted into the path of the van, causing the driver to slam on his brakes and swerve to the left.

He missed a Gulf Front police car by less than a foot.

3

When I pulled into the Seabreeze, I parked near 7A, and walked to the front door. I knocked and waited for thirty seconds before trying the doorbell, which didn't seem to work. I knocked again, louder this time, and when I still got no answer, tried the door. It was unlocked, so I stepped inside and called, "Mr. Harwell? Anybody home?"

No sign of anyone in the kitchen, and feeling uneasy, I stood still and listened. Nothing. Only the loud hum of the old refrigerator, obviously on its last legs. There was a cordless telephone in the sink, which seemed odd, but I didn't stop to consider it. Feeling more uneasy by the second, I slowly moved down the hall towards the back of the small apartment, and there he was.

Cecil Harwell was lying face up on the bedroom floor, his neck grotesquely twisted. I checked his pulse to see if he was dead, and found that he most definitely was. I stood over the body for a few moments, planning my first move, before slowly walking back to the kitchen.

After lying dormant for so many years, my adrenaline was cranked up, and really had me on edge. After a few deep breaths, I got an operator to put me through to the Florida Department of Law Enforcement over in Pensacola. After a few minutes on hold, by chance I was put through to Al Haulbrook, an old friend from my days in homicide.

"Al Haulbrook here," he said.

"Well, well, look who's takin' my call. Hey, Haulbrook, you fat drunk. Coop here. How's that cushy job goin?"

"The job's not so cushy today, pal. I'm supposed to be out on a deep-sea charter, pounding a twelve-pack. Instead, I'm here filling in for a friend, repaying a huge favor. *Huge*. But enough about my problems—I hear you have one of your own. In fact, I thought you'd be calling soon. I was just talking about you."

"Yeah? What were you talkin' about?" I said.

"I just got off the horn with Pensacola FBI. They're getting a forensic team together to send your way. Seems there's a female corpse on your pier?"

"Yeah, but we haven't heard a word from the feds."

"You won't. They don't worry about good manners—especially nowadays. They just show up."

"Well, there's definitely a dead girl on our pier, but unfortunately, that's not the whole story. I just found another corpse, only this one's an old guy who was a citizen of Gulf. That's the reason for my call—I need you to send some help over here. Or should I say, more help."

"You figure there's a connection?"

"Has to be. This guy was on TV less than an hour ago, telling about how he found the dead girl. So, right after we have a body dump on the pier, the citizen who found the body turns up dead as a hammer on his bedroom floor. Sound like a connection? You tell me."

"Okay, I will. There's a connection," Haulbrook said.

"What else did you hear?"

"That the girl's from Louisiana, and she's the daughter of a Senator. Somebody made an anonymous call to the FBI and identified her. The feds will be knocking down your door very soon, Coop. I bet they'll want to take over your citizen's case, too. And as far as I'm concerned, they're welcome to it. We're spread thin right now."

"They'll get no argument from me," I said.

If the anonymous caller was telling the truth, federal involvement was definitely called for, since the vehicle had crossed state lines with the body on board.

Al knew what I was thinking, and said, "The agent I talked to said they're convinced that the call is legit. The girl was missing."

"Well, I can't handle all this without outside help. *Lots* of outside help. Do me a favor, Al. And it's not a huge one. Call the FBI back and tell 'em what's up, and to send another forensic team over here pronto. Seabreeze Apartments, Seabreeze Avenue."

"Seabreeze on Seabreeze. Got it. Okay, I'll call right now. Listen, I'm sorry to hear about all this, but it was great to hear from you, man. Call me if you need anything else."

My second move was to call Penny to come help question the neighbors. I decided to keep the news of Cecil's Harwell's murder to myself for the time being because I wanted to tell my team face to face. Somebody would have to stay with the body at the pier, so I told Penny to leave Earl—whose size might intimidate the little old folks at the Seabreeze—and bring Adam.

I didn't want to upset the neighbors, who seemingly had no idea what had taken place; the parking lot was empty and I saw no one peeking out of windows. Considering the normal sight and hearing loss among oldsters, it was likely there would be no point in asking if anyone had seen or heard anything, but it had to be done.

It was unnerving, two murders in a town where hardly anybody could remember *one*. While I waited outside on the porch, Earl called to say that the Cadillac was registered to a building contractor from New Orleans and had been stolen there. He also said that a couple of FBI agents had arrived at the pier, and had taken over watch duty.

That was fast, I thought. I had some experience with the FBI in my Tallahassee days, but hadn't worked closely enough with them to form an opinion. Now I was the chief, and sure to be working closely with them soon. The stories of the tension they cause, and meddling on their part, are legendary among state and local cops, so I mentally braced for conflict.

I was also victimized by a monster headache, and wished that I had waited until evening to toast Solly. I was beginning to feel like a character in a Raymond Chandler novel, and thinking up possible titles like: "Scotch with a Double Twist of Murder."

Okay, it was a terrible title. I needed lunch.

***

Penny and Adam pulled into the Seabreeze, and came over to me, curious as to the reason of my call. I took another deep breath and gave them the news.

"Okay, here goes," I said. "Mr. Harwell is dead, lying on his bedroom floor with a broken neck. I'm sorry as I can be about that, but we've got work to do."

They expressed their shock differently: Penny's eyes blazed as her right hand lowered to her Glock .40, while Adam looked stunned and disbelieving. Neither of them had ever been involved with such brutality, so I gave them a minute to take it all in.

"You guys okay?" I asked.

Penny looked at Adam, then back at me, and said, "I knew something like this would happen someday. We've been real lucky for a long time."

Adam said, "Yeah, we've been mighty spoiled. I guess it's about time we had some trouble around here. Pop told me it always comes sooner or later."

"Your pop's right," I said.

The three of us stood quietly for a moment, as if honoring old Cecil. I outlined the plan of action, "Okay, listen up. You guys go door to door and see if anybody saw or heard, et cetera. Any questions?"

Adam said, "Just one. What's goin' on, Coop?"

I shrugged and said, "Obviously, Gulf Front is the new murder capital of the United States."

As they went to question the residents, my growing hunger made it impossible to wait for lunch any longer. I called Frankie's Pizza Palace, Gulf Front's doorway to the world of international cuisine, and ordered two large pepperonis—one with extra sauce for Penny out of habit—and three bottled waters. As I sat on the porch waiting for my crew to go about their duties, my headache eased somewhat, and I mentally ran through what we knew so far.

We had a stolen New Orleans Cadillac, a pretty young female corpse dumped on the town pier, and an elderly guy with a snapped neck who might have been a witness. Or somebody *thought* he might have been a witness. The poor old guy didn't matter to the killer, he was just in the way.

My first train of thought took me to organized crime: the possibly pointless murder of Cecil Harwell, the cliché of a Cadillac stolen in New Orleans, the body dump. It all sounded like the actions of real live Mafia types.

But I could think of no good reason why Gulf Front should suddenly become the center of gangland activity. If The Boys really were the perpetrators, then I figured the girl was the key.

"Outstanding work, Sherlock," I said to myself, and waited for lunch to magically appear.

***

I had already finished more than my share of the pizzas by the time my team had taken care of their duties. I wondered how the murders would affect them later, since they're so green in such matters, but they seemed to be taking it in stride. They came over and dove into the boxes, and I gave them a minute to swallow before asking what information they had acquired.

Penny said, "Zip, zero, nada—that's the extent of my valuable information. Mmm, extra sauce."

Adam read from his notes, "Mrs. Airth, a senior citizen living in 3C, saw two *very* large, unidentified males coming out of Mr. Harwell's apartment. Both males were dressed in suit and tie, and both were Caucasian. She noticed them because they were quote, 'so well dressed and all.' When I asked if the men looked suspicious, she said that they 'couldn't be bad because they weren't in a hurry.' Then I asked if she had seen what kind of car they were driving, and she replied, no, she had been in a hurry to get to the market because 'if she didn't get back with the Miracle Whip right away, she'd have to listen to Arthur mumbling under his breath all day.' "

Mrs. Airth's comical testimony gave us at least two suspects at the scene, and men in suits figured to be something other than Gulf Front residents. I doubt if you could find a dozen men wearing suits in Gulf on any given day, even a Sunday.

Everything was now in order, at least as good as we could make it, and somebody else would do the actual detective work. I just hoped I hadn't inadvertently screwed up the crime scene.

I said to Penny, "It's been a long time since I wrote a murder report."

"I'll take care of it, Coop. I could use the experience. You just concentrate on finding out who did this."

"Thanks. I'll make it up to you."

She smiled and said, "Damn straight you will."

When the pizza was gone, Adam went behind the apartment office to throw the trash in a dumpster. Penny and I stood in awkward silence for a moment, and then she said, "Doreen told me to remind you that no matter what's goin' on in Gulf Front, her wedding's in six days, and you still have to give her away."

"Oh, yeah."

I had nearly forgotten about my secretary's impending nuptials. Doreen was getting married at sunrise on the beach to a wealthy businessman she'd met when his car broke down in front of the police station. He had come inside to cool off, and they hit it off immediately. But I didn't have time to think about that.

Since it looked like this day was going to be longer than most, I started to call Mrs. Wiley, my landlady, to ask her to feed Solly. I caught myself three digits into dialing the number, stopped, and felt the sadness again for a moment.

The county had already disposed of Solly's body as a favor to me, and I was going to have to stop worrying about him, and start worrying about getting some answers. But I wasn't even sure what questions to ask, or who to ask.

My monster headache returned, and I wanted to talk to my dog.

4

The interrogations over, Adam kept watch at the Seabreeze, and I followed Penny back to the pier. On the way, I thought about how to approach the Feds.

Should I play dumb, be standoffish, or come right out and admit that I had no idea what was going on, and beg for help? None of those options felt right, except maybe the standoffish one. I considered the old saying, "Say nothing and be thought a fool, or open your mouth and remove all doubt." Mouth closed.

We parked in the now-empty lot, and headed towards the pier. Except for a few stragglers, the crowd had moved on. The body was still lying safely behind the yellow tape in the scorching midday sun. National news crews had arrived and were busy taping their versions of the situation. I waved them off, and they left us alone as we made our way on to the pier.

Earl joined us, having turned over the watch duty to the FBI. Penny glanced at me, nodded, and took Earl off to one side and told him about Cecil Harwell.

Out at the end of the pier, two male agents in sunglasses and dark suits were standing guard over the corpse, scanning the surrounding area, including the water. They made no move to meet us halfway or acknowledge our arrival, and I felt better about my plan to keep silent. I couldn't wait for the first guy to speak to me, so I could take a long, meaningful pause before I said word one.

"Chief Cooper?" a female voice asked, and we stopped and turned to see a very attractive woman heading towards us. She was absolutely gorgeous, even in her severe navy blue suit. Natural blonde hair pulled back, legs that were fit and shapely, and blue, blue eyes that stopped my mind from working just long enough to make me seem extremely rude, stupid, or—I hoped—standoffish. One look from Penny confirmed that I merely looked stupid.

"Yes, I'm Chief Cooper," I managed to say, looking at her as if I'd never seen a woman before. "Uh, you people sure don't waste time. How'd you get here so fast?"

"Chopper from Pensacola. We were down here for a seminar. Our home office is in D.C," she said in a voice that could only come from below the Mason-Dixon line.

She continued, "We've identified the victim. She's Caroline Quitman, the daughter and only child of United States Senator Harry James Quitman of Louisiana. She's been missing for a little over twenty-four hours. An agent talked to the owner of the Cadillac in New Orleans, but he doesn't seem to be involved. He claims he was on a fishing trip all last week, and returned to find his car stolen. He had notified the NOPD, and they feel he's telling the truth. So, we came here, to get a look at the crime scene, and to meet you and your force."

She turned to a young, black man in a dark gray suit standing behind her. "This is Special Agent Bradford Clay, my associate. Agent Clay will be in charge of our team 'til I get back. I'm sure there won't be any problems."

I was still staring at her, having drifted off halfway through her monologue. "That sounds right," I said, which I figured was an adequate reply to anything she might have said.

My immediate and powerful attraction put me at a decided disadvantage. She could have said, "You killed her, Chief Cooper, and I can prove it," and I would have said, "That sounds right."

I've never behaved so unprofessionally in my career. Well, except for a few times when Penny and I were on, and on duty. But even then, I was somewhat lucid. This woman had me in a daze, and I felt like a schoolboy. This day was all over the map, emotionally: First Solly, then the dead girl, then old Cecil, and now *this* creature.

"I'm Special Agent Shelley Brooke, by the way," she said, extending her hand for me to shake. I took it, and mumbled how nice it was to meet her.

After we all shook hands and exchanged business cards and cell phone numbers, Agent Brooke said, "On the way over, we got word of a secondary site nearby. Do you have anything on that?"

"Oh, yeah," I said. "Sorry I didn't mention that. I called it in to the FDLE office in Pensacola."

"Yes, I know," she said with a smile.

"Right," I mumbled. I looked towards the yellow tape, and said, "I knew the girl was a daughter."

When Penny and Earl looked at me as if I'd lost my mind, I realized just how discombobulated I was. Before I could stick my foot deeper in my mouth, Agent Brooke said, "Let's have a look at the crime scene."

We all moved towards the end of the pier. Penny took the lead, as though reestablishing her territory, and Agent Brooke and I followed closely behind. Earl and Clay brought up the rear, talking about how hot it was as we walked.

We reached the tape and the young agents who had been watching over the scene shook hands with Agents Brooke and Clay, and nodded to Penny, Earl, and me. I thought how hot they must all be, dressed in their dark suits. My people wear lightweight, tan gear year round, and I dress in whatever I have that's clean. It being my day off, I happened to be dressed even more casually than usual. My white Florida State University tee shirt and khaki shorts didn't seem to register with the FBI agents. They were all business.

Agent Brooke said, "The forensic folks should be here in about forty-five minutes. I hope this hot sun doesn't compromise the site too much."

"Me, too," I said, still feeling foggy. "I've had enough experience to know not to move her or touch anything," I blathered after a moment.

"I thought as much," she said, and smiled a megawatt smile.

Then I pictured myself opening the front door of Cecil Harwell's apartment, but kept that little gem to myself. I should have confessed, but I was toast. I was in trouble with Penny, I missed my dog, and I was beginning to miss Nora's liquor more with each passing minute.

5

THE FORENSIC TEAM ARRIVED AND TOOK CONTROL OF THE PIER SITUATION. Seven feds of differing genders, sizes, and colors buzzed around the site, while Penny and I stood off to one side with Agent Brooke. Penny stared at the agents and their actions, transfixed.

I was looking out of the corner of my eye at Shelley—I was already planning my life with her, and had decided to use her first name as often as possible, in my mind at least—while also trying to appear interested in what was taking place.

She caught me looking at her, and smiled slightly, and I smiled slightly back, hoping I looked cool. I certainly didn't *feel* cool. I felt like I was back in high school, staring at Mona Herzog across the aisle in Miss Strickland's English class.

Agent Brooke broke my reverie, "Well, Chief, I've got to catch the chopper, so I can make my flight back to D.C. I have one quick meeting there, but I'll be back tonight around suppertime, and I'll get in touch with you tomorrow mornin'."

Suppertime. Yep, this one was definitely Southern. Nobody eats "supper" in Washington.

"Do you need a ride back to the chopper?" I asked, a little too quickly.

"No thanks, I've got it covered. But thanks for askin'."

Askin'. Droppin' Gs. A Southern beauty with brains and a gun, I thought. What could be better?

***

I was watching a sailboat out in the gulf, trying to judge how far it was from shore, when Penny said, "Agent Brooke seems to be a very competent type, don'tcha think?"

I asked, "Type of what?"

"You know, a competent agent. A take-charge type."

"Oh, yeah . . . very take-charge. You don't have a problem with that, do you?"

"No," she said, "But I thought *you* might. 'Big Chief take orders from squaw woman.' Might get a little crowded on the reservation."

"Stop already with the 'Injun' references," I said, thinking about the happy water I swallowed earlier, and praying that my breath mints had worked. "She's just doin' her job, and so am I."

Penny smiled, and asked, "What do you think is really going on here?"

"I'm leaning towards some kind of Mob connection, but it's only a guess at this point. The stolen New Orleans Caddy, a body dumped here, the way Cecil Harwell was handled in broad daylight. Just a hunch."

Penny said, "Yeah, that all makes sense. I should've thought of that right off, but I guess I'm so used to local punks and rednecks committing all the crimes around here, I didn't even think about big-timers comin' to town. And I hate to say it, but she was the daughter of a senator, and the way politics are today, anything's possible. You never know what's gonna happen next with those clowns in Washington, not to mention Louisiana. Powerful people have powerful enemies as well as friends. I think I'm gonna ask these forensic people if they've heard anything."

With that she sidled up to the youngest, best looking male agent at the scene, and gave him the Prevost smile, the one that has served her and her Cajun family so well over the years. Penny is one beautimous female, as the Cajuns say, and I had no doubt that she would know everything the Feds did within a matter of minutes.

Her background might even help somewhat since it looked like the trail did indeed lead to Louisiana. She has family and other contacts there, but she's not a detective. Fortunately, I had a contact over there, too.

Watching the agents work reminded me of the old days, and I decided then and there that I was going to get in on the action somehow. The feds might find some prints or DNA at Cecil Harwell's apartment, but I doubted there was any need for me and mine to be there. New Orleans looked like the place to be, and I had no problem leaving Penny in charge to deal with the FBI—she could use the experience. And I could use the freedom.

And since Agent Shelley Brooke was from D.C., and a United States Senator's daughter was involved, it was quite possible that she might end up working the case. Cecil Harwell's murder was reason enough to head over to New Orleans, but there was another reason I wanted to go.

A blonde FBI agent.

I turned my gaze back to the sailboat, and my thoughts back to Shelley. I wondered what she likes for breakfast.

After a few minutes, I walked over and asked Agent Clay where we stood as far as his crew was concerned.

He said, "Chief, I don't think they'll find anything here. It looks like pros did this."

I said, "I agree. Two very large white men in suits were sighted at the secondary site. My obvious guess is that Mr. Harwell—the other victim—saw somethin' while he was fishin' near the pier, or at least the bad guys thought he did. Either way, they couldn't just leave town without making sure the old guy never talked."

Clay nodded, and said, "I've already contacted our OC unit in New Orleans, and I'm betting they'll know who to go after."

***

The rest of the afternoon dragged by as the FBI did its work, and I kept out of the sun as much as possible. Most of my time was spent answering questions from news crews and feds, and going back and forth between the two crime scenes. I helped the FBI agents in any way I could, even arranging lunch delivery for some of them. My day off was turning out to be a day on, even though I spent some of the time daydreaming about Agent Brooke. At four o'clock, I drove back over to the Seabreeze apartments and double-parked in front of 7A. Adam was standing out front talking to a tall, thin, clean-cut man dressed in yet another dark suit. Adam said, "Chief, meet the man in charge."

"Special Agent David Torras, Pensacola office," the man said as we shook hands. He looked to be around thirty-five, and seemed friendly enough.

"Nice to meet you, Agent," I said. "I should tell you—your people will find my prints on the front doorknob. I'm the one who found the body."

We swapped cards and numbers, and after a minute of small talk, Agent Torras excused himself and went inside.

Adam said, "He's a pretty nice guy. Looks like this won't be so bad—havin' the feds around, I mean."

"Yeah, he seems okay. Let's hope it stays that way."

By five o'clock, I was more than ready to hang it up. The FBI had indeed taken over both crime scenes, and the agents assigned to the cases had turned out to be competent, polite, and very efficient. There wasn't a hint of tension between us, and when I left the Seabreeze, I felt good about how things had gone.

I drove east along the coast highway, not quite ready to face my empty apartment. The sun was low, but the ocean still shimmered under a cloudless blue sky. My headache had finally succumbed to the aspirin I had been chewing most of the day, and I finally had time to slow down and think.

I was thinking about puppies: whether to get one, what kind, pound pup or pedigree, male or female, what to name him or her, anything to keep my mind off the day's happenings. I knew that soon I was going to have more than enough to keep me occupied, so this ride might be my last chance to relax for a while.

I had felt pressure in varying degrees on a daily basis as a detective in Tallahassee, but stress in Gulf Front is almost nonexistent. So the heightened level of stress I was feeling as chief was new to me, feds in Gulf Front were new to me, and driving alongside the ocean to avoid going home was new to me. Then there was the old feeling of being smitten, something I haven't felt since I met Penny eight years ago when she interviewed for her job.

I drove for over an hour, and had just turned around to head back when Mrs. Wiley called to make sure that I would be home soon. She had followed the old Southern—and Northern too, I guess—tradition of cooking for someone who has recently buried a loved one. Technically, it was supposed to be done when a *human* died, but I said nothing except thanks, and, yes, I was on my way home. Mrs. Wiley's a peach among women.

Traffic was heavier on the way back, due to a fender bender, and I arrived at my place a few minutes before eight, just as it was getting dark. The phone rang as I put my keys on the kitchen bar. I took the first three calls, all from local citizens wanting to know if I had seen myself on the local news, and if the town would survive. No, I hadn't seen myself on the news, as I was late in coming home, and yes, I was fairly certain the town would still be standing tomorrow.

When the phone rang a fourth time, I unplugged it, and turned off my cell as well. Penny has been trying for years to convince me that an answering machine is essential to life, but I am steadfast in my refusal to own one. The way I see it, I have the right to be at home, *and* unavailable. Besides, the damnable cell phone is a bad enough intrusion on my time away from the job.

I looked in the fridge, and found a seafood casserole with salad, homemade rolls, peach cobbler, and a note that read: *"Solly is in Heaven now . . . don't you worry about him no more."* It made me smile, and so did the delicious food. Mrs. Wiley is a magnificent cook.

I drank a beer after supper, toasting my landlady this time. Then I cranked up the air conditioning, sat back on the couch, and checked the cable news. Sure enough, at eight minutes after nine, there I was in my short pants talking to a reporter as if I knew whereof I spoke. My voice sounded alien to me, and it was clear that a haircut was in order. I suffered through one more pass at eight minutes after the half-hour, and then looked for something interesting to watch.

I finally found an old movie, "The Searchers," starring John Wayne. I love The Duke, and watch him whenever I get the chance.

I hit the bed at eleven-thirty, and dreamed of cats swimming in the ocean.

6

When I woke up, I showered, brushed my teeth, and dressed in clean jeans and a short-sleeved white shirt. I packed my suitcase and a bag, and was ready to see what I could uncover in New Orleans.

I put the luggage in the back seat of my patrol car, and headed downtown. I was less hungry than usual after a night of Mrs. Wiley's cooking, but definitely in need of coffee and the sports page. And, with good reason, I never go without breakfast.

In 1993, in my second month as chief of police, I tried to arrest Tom Conway by myself at a ramshackle bar called The Gator Trap, out in the sticks ten miles northeast of town. Tom weighs about three hundred pounds, and punches like every bit of it. The call had come in about some trouble at The Trap a little after eleven on a Saturday night, and since the only other officer on duty was out on a call, I had to serve and protect the good people of Gulf Front alone.

The first thing I saw as I entered the bar was a man suspended in the air, spinning wildly above ol' Tom's head before being hurled into the jukebox, which was playing George Jones as I recall. Tom looked around, eyes ablaze, searching the suddenly silent room for anybody else that wanted flying lessons.

As any moron would do, I walked right up to him, got in his face, and told him in no uncertain terms that he was under arrest. Tom saw things differently, and before I could read him his rights, he gave *me* one. The punch broke my jaw, and it had to be wired shut. I was on a liquid diet, sipping through a straw for quite some time. When you can't eat, you appreciate eating more than people who can, and I've never forgotten what it feels like to go without solid food. So, I never miss a chance to start the day with solid food for breakfast, and hopefully, I never will again.

***

Penny had the day off and was up bright and early, driving her red Miata convertible to Pensacola to shop for some new running shoes at the big mall on the north side of town. Her current pair was over six months old, and definitely had to go. She usually ran on the beach every day but Sunday; when she had troubles, running was the only thing that helped her solve her problems and feel better.

The problem this time was the look she'd seen on Coop's face when he first laid eyes on Agent Brooke. She had never seen him lose his cool like he had when the two were introduced out on the pier. Penny wanted Coop back, and the last thing she needed was competition.

Especially blonde, intelligent, beautiful competition.

Agent Brooke didn't seem to be particularly interested in Coop, but Penny was worried that the FBI agent might become more interested. When Penny met Coop, at first glance she found his looks to be nothing special, but she felt differently now. She found him more attractive by the minute as she worked with him. Even though his reluctance to commit to their relationship drove her crazy, in her mind he was the personification of a diamond in the rough. She was afraid that Agent Brooke would soon feel the same thing if the two of them were thrown together, and it worried her.

It worried her enough to drive to a stupid mall on her day off and spend the precious time shopping, which was something she hated with a passion. Coop always teased her about it, saying she was the only woman he had ever known who didn't possess the shopping gene. She loved his teasing her, and missed teasing him back. She always gave as good as she got, and the fun they had together was what she missed the most since their latest break-up. The sex had always been great, but the fun times they shared were what made the relationship so special in her eyes. If shopping for shoes so she could run and think would help her get him back, then shopping for shoes was what she'd do.

But did there have to be so many idiots shopping every time she went?

***

The only decent breakfast chow to be found in Gulf Front is at Matthews Cafeteria, a great old spot on Main Street. One of the oldest businesses in town, it's been owned and operated by the Matthews family since the early Fifties, and looks like something straight out of Mayberry. Red-checked oilcloth on the tables, off-white linoleum flooring that's cracked and worn, and a delicious array of cholesterol-laden Southern food: Grits, bacon, sausage, toast, biscuits, gravy, eggs, hash browns, cinnamon rolls, and the best coffee in America.

It serves breakfast and lunch, and opens at 5:30 A.M., when all decent folk are up and hungry. I have been having breakfast at Matthews since I took the job as chief, and now I can't imagine a day without it. The clientele consists mainly of a bunch of older men who hold court at a long table that's unofficially reserved for them. They are loud, and funny, and have an opinion on everything.

The guys ribbed me about how I looked on the news, and then wanted my take on the events of yesterday. I turned the tables and asked what *they* thought, and they quickly let me and everyone within earshot know. Each had his own take on the situation, and as usual the conversation was entertaining and informative. Well, sort of.

"They ain't been a murder in Gulf since '51 when Leonard Heath come back from Korea, an' caught Miz Heath with ol' Ed Womack," said C.L. Bugg, a retired construction boss and leader of the bunch. "I was fifteen then, but I remember it like it was today. They fried Leonard about a year and a half later, an' Miz Heath didn't even go to the prison for the burial. She had already married a preacher from Kissimmee, an' had dropped another kid by then. That was a big scandal, but a dead senator's daughter on the pier makes that look like nothin'. They's gonna be all *kinda* news people and whatnot comin' here fer this. Shoot, I might even shave."

This made all the old boys laugh, and for the next thirty seconds or so the conversation was impossible to follow, as everybody was going all at once, at top volume. I listened for a few more minutes, finished my bacon and eggs, said my goodbyes, and headed to the office.

The Gulf Front police station is housed in a freestanding one-story building on an asphalt lot a half-mile east of the pier. It's on the beach side of the road, and my office in the back has big windows that show off the beautiful ocean view.

I arrived at my usual time, eight o'clock on the dot. Doreen stopped filing her nails, popped up from behind her desk and said, "Hello there, TV star and father of the bride!"

Doreen is fifty-nine, petite, and wears a beehive hairdo, with eyeglasses and clothes that are stuck in a Fifties time warp. A lifelong spinster, she was here my first day on the job, and is the actual chief of the station.

"Hello there, yourself," I said. "Would your sprightly greeting have anything to do with your upcoming wedding to one Mr. J. D. Fields of Montgomery?"

She beamed, "Why, yes it does, boss man. Since daddy is no longer with us, you're the man entrusted with the responsibility of giving me away and making me the happiest girl in the world."

I ignored the "girl" remark, and said, "Well, you're half right, but Mr. Fields is responsible for your happiness after you leave me high and dry, without a rudder, at the mercy of the criminal element. You know I'm happy for you, but not for me and this police force."

"You'll be fine, and the station will survive." She paused and added with a grin, "Maybe."

I said, "I know it's romantic and all, but does the wedding have to be at sunrise?"

Doreen looked me over, and said, "Are you just playing dumb, or are you really dumb? *Hello*—Gulf Front after noon in late July? Do you know how many of my friends and family would keel over from the heat, not to mention the bride and groom? And sunset would be just about as bad. No sir, if I'm gonna have a beach wedding this time of year, it has to be at sunrise, or after dark, and I choose sunrise. This will be my only wedding, and I'm the bride, so everybody has to do what I say. Now, that's the plan, so get over it, or get used to it."

"Well, okay, if you're scared of a little heat," I said, actually thankful not to be part of an outdoor ceremony in ninety-degree weather.

It was as good a time as any to tell her about *my* plan, so I said, "Just so you'll know—I'm going over to New Orleans to see if I can help out with these cases. It looks like Mr. Harwell's killers—and the girl's—were some bad guys from over there, and the first forty-eight hours can make or break a homicide investigation. So, if I get caught up in it, I might not make it back for the wedding. *Might* not, I'm sayin'."

Doreen put her hands on her tiny hips, and said, "Coop, you listen to me, and listen good. I didn't work in homicide, but I watch TV, and I'm well aware that forty-eight hours can make or break a case. I'm also well aware that you'll have almost three times that many hours before the wedding. The FBI can surely do without you for one day so you can give away your favorite secretary and mother figure. I know it's a terrible thing, Mr. Harwell gettin' killed and all, but do you think he would want you to miss my wedding because of it? No, he wouldn't. Now, you be back here on time, or you'll answer to me."

I looked her right in those steely gray eyes of hers, and backed down. The best way to handle Doreen is to let her think she's won, and then do whatever you wanted in the first place. And along with Penny, she's the closest thing I have to family in Gulf Front, so I caved, "I guess I better be back here on time then."

Doreen nodded in triumph, and said, "And get a haircut." With that, she sat back down at her desk, and resumed filing her nails. My secretary can be bossy at times, and a little ornery, but she's always had my back.

Even so, there would be no haircut.

I had just settled into my desk chair when my cell rang. It was Agent Clay, ready to tell me what he had gotten from forensics.

"It was a heroin overdose that killed Ms. Quitman, and since there were no signs of a struggle, they can't rule out suicide. She had needle tracks in several places on her body, indicating that this was not her first time using. The most recent track, and the fatal one, was found in her left foot between her big toe and the second one. There was also significant damage in her nasal passages that, as you know, could mean sniffing or snorting drugs. The main thing found in her blood was a large amount of 85 percent pure heroin, enough to kill two or three big men."

I said, "Another mob specialty—nearly pure stuff."

"Exactly. There were also traces of several other things, including cocaine. Most of the needle tracks were in places that could not be easily seen, such as between her toes, and behind her knees. Looks like she was practiced in the art of hiding her habit, but still, it could have been a homicide, they can't know for sure. Oh, and one other thing: She was two months pregnant. So, if someone didn't want her to have the child, that gives us motive for murder. And it gives us a reason for suicide if *she* didn't want to have the child. It's all pretty much up in the air at this point. I'll be in touch again as soon as we know more."

"Thanks, Agent. You guys do good work. Has there been any progress on Mr. Harwell's case?"

"No word yet."

"Okay. Well, thanks again. By the way—have you heard from Agent Brooke?"

"No sir, but I expect a call within the hour."

"Good," I said. "Would you ask her to call me when you hear from her?"

"Sure," he said.

"Thank you, and thanks for the report."

"All part of our friendly FBI service," he said.

We hung up and I called to Doreen, "See if you can get me Neal over in New Orleans, please ma'am."

"Will do," she chirped, happily back in charge.

I met Detective Neal Feagin (rhymes with President Reagan), on our first day of training at the police academy in Tallahassee. Our names were close enough alphabetically to place us in most of the same classes, and, like me, he's around five-ten, so we were regularly paired in physical training against one another. We were born in the same month in the same year, me on New Year's Day, and Neal on January thirteenth.

We hit it off immediately, and got an apartment together, where we stayed throughout our training. We were wild in those days, two young maniacs sporting firearms, and it's a wonder that we both managed to avoid prison. Well, maybe that's an exaggeration, but we did raise quite a lot of sand.

We still see each other several times a year, fishing here in Gulf, or fishing and camping in the southern part of Louisiana whenever I visit him and his family in New Orleans. I spent a wild night during Mardi Gras once with Neal, my first and last time doing that. We also gamble on occasion at Harrah's, where we usually drop a few dollars playing poker, blackjack, or shooting craps.

I've spent many a Thanksgiving Day eating Susan Feagin's turkey and cornbread dressing, and staying over for the weekend—their three daughters are as close to having my own children as I'm ever going to get. I also spend Christmas with them every year, and am treated like a member of the family. Neal is my best and oldest friend, and I wanted to know what he knew about the Quitman family, and Caroline in particular. Heroin could mean all sorts of things, the Mob among them, and I wanted his take on them, too.

"Detective Feagin on one," Doreen called from her reception area.

"Thanks," I called back, picking up and asking, "Neal—how's the humidity?" my typical question of anyone suffering through a New Orleans summer.

"Wonderful, couldn't be wetter. How's the fishing in Gulf?"

"Haven't been even once this month, and now it looks like I won't be goin' anytime soon," I said.

"I know. I heard about the girl on the pier and your first homicide over there. Feds have been callin' here all mornin'. Did you know the old guy?"

"No," I said. "One of the few I've never met."

"You know, I don't get shocked anymore, even when it's a Senator's daughter, but I couldn't believe it when I heard that her body was found in your town," Neal said. "That's just weird. But anyway, welcome back to the club, bud, and I'm sorry you're a member again."

"Me, too. I always thought I'd make it through to retirement without ever working another homicide, but to tell the truth, it got the juices flowing a little. You also probably heard the girl wasn't done here, and Mr. Harwell was collateral damage, which is why I called. I'm looking for information on the bad guys in New Orleans," I said.

"I'm guessin' you also want some info on the Quitman girl."

"That would be correct. Man, you are some kind of detector."

Neal replied, "I get paid giant dollars to know all things, and this is pretty interesting stuff, I must admit. It appears that Ms. Quitman was running with a pretty rough crowd. One of our drug informants says she's well known at a place just off The Quarter, a hangout for pimps and dealers and all sorts of really nice folks. Her daddy couldn't control her anymore it seems. Our guy says she's been known to try just about everything, including a little light hooking. And evidently, she would do any drug with anybody. The Senator is said to be so used to her behavior that he didn't even bother to report her missing. His housekeeper was the one who called in and said Caroline was nowhere to be found, after checking all her usual hangouts. In fact, Senator Q seems to be taking things in stride, according to all reports. Chesnut over in Vice said the Senator didn't even blink last month when they told him about her alleged contacts in drugs and prostitution. Said he just stared at him, as if he had already heard all of the allegations and knew them to be true."

"Maybe he did," I said. "I'm gonna come see you and take in the sights, including one Senator Quitman. Do you know if he's in town?"

"Yeah, he's holed up inside his mansion over in the Garden District, avoiding the press and us as best he can. Caroline's funeral is set for tomorrow."

"Man, that's a real shame, a young girl being buried like that. Speaking of funerals, guess who's getting married?"

"Don't tell me Penny finally wised up and dumped you."

"Not likely."

"No way it's you gettin' hitched, so—who?" he asked.

"Doreen."

"You don't mean it. Well, bless her heart. I guess you're never too old."

"Guess not. I've never seen her so happy."

Neal said, "I'm sure you're happy for Doreen, too—I know how close y'all are—but it's a shame she won't be workin' with you anymore. How are you gonna stay in business without her around?"

"It will definitely be a big adjustment. After the walls fall down around me, I guess I'll find somebody to take her place."

"Well, good luck with *that*. Now—come on over and we'll see if we can't find us some killers. And while we're at it, we can eat Susan's cooking and gamble, and you can talk to a Senator. Harrah's tonight after I get off work, for sure. How's that sound?"

"That sounds great," I said, visions of Agent Brooke leaning over a craps table appearing in my head. "Let me tie up a few loose ends here, and I'll get back to ya."

"I'll be right here. And tell Doreen congratulations, or whatever it is you say to a bride."

I went out and promised Doreen I'd be back in time to give her away if she would let me skip rehearsals, since all I had to do was walk her down to the beach and stand there. She agreed, and I went back and dug out my gun cleaning kit from the bottom desk drawer.

I still carry the same piece I got a week before I started in patrol, a .38 Smith & Wesson. When I took the job as chief in Gulf Front, I dutifully wore it for the first year. But after seeing what the job entails, I hardly ever bother anymore, choosing instead to keep it locked in the glove compartment of my patrol car while on duty.

My officers all carry their weapons, however, and Penny regularly practices with hers at a shooting range in Pensacola. I tag along once or twice a year, and those are the only times my old revolver sees the light of day, so I was sure it needed a good cleaning. I might not need it in Gulf Front, but it could come in handy in the big city. As I oiled and cleaned it, I planned my next moves.

A trip to New Orleans—with Agent Brooke—seemed like a good idea, but my good ideas aren't always so good. Yet I was willing to give it a shot if it meant spending time with her, and I was ready to do whatever it took to make it happen. I started to plot ways to wheedle my way into the FBI investigation that I hoped would include her.

I even sent up a selfish prayer, and sat back to wait for an answer.

7

DON CARRABBA WAS NOT HAPPY, BUT HIS FACE SHOWED NOTHING. A man of honor, among the last of that dying breed, he was still fit enough to be feared for his strength. He certainly did not need displays of anger to make his desires known. His soft words carried the clout that came from being the unquestioned leader of all Mob activity in New Orleans for as long as anyone could remember.

"Could you not have been more careful? It's bad enough that you had to kill the man, but you should have at least removed the body. You know how I hate to leave things to chance. What made you do such a foolish thing?"

"I'm sorry about involvin' the old man, Don Carmine, an' I'm not tryin' to make excuses, but we was movin' as fast as we could, maybe too fast, and got a little sloppy. Me and Alberto was up all night, didn't even take time to change clothes. Then we seen the old guy when we was leavin' da pier, and hadda wait around an' deal wit' him. I couldn't just let da guy be a problem later, is what I was thinkin'. We had no choice but to do what we done."

Vinnie, a captain in the Carrabba family, was not known for his guile. He was a brute who was thought to enjoy the pain and suffering he inflicted. His reputation as a sadistic killer had been forged over twenty years in the Don's service. If someone needed killing, Vinnie was the guy, and he was also ruthlessly efficient as a torturer or arsonist.

The most frightening thing about him was the joy he found in his work—the most interesting thing about him was his love of fine clothing. His street name was "Vinnie Shoes," as he seemingly had a pair for each day of the year, obsessively cleaned and polished.

While most of his crew wore much more casual attire, Vinnie's suits were hand-made, and fit him perfectly, which was not an easy thing to accomplish since his three hundred twenty-five pound body was oddly shaped. A giant chest and stomach rested on short, tree-trunk legs. He wore his thick black hair combed straight back, heavily oiled, and had it cut two or three times a week.

Alberto Prizzi, Vinnie's partner in crime, was not quite as big. At two hundred forty pounds, he was less imposing, but he also dressed sharper than the average hood. He had thinning brown hair which he also greased straight back, and deep acne scars on his cheeks and nose. The top soldier in Vinnie's crew, he rarely spoke, and never said a word in the Don's presence unless directly addressed. Like the Don, Alberto was from Sicily, and still had a thick accent, even after being stateside for thirteen years. He avoided eye contact with both his superiors, preferring to keep his head down.

Don Carrabba said, "Lucky for you—and more important, lucky for *me*— I know what I am doing. Your handling of the old man was no good, but it will not ruin my plans completely. You will do your part to make this right, and we will discuss the matter no more. There are other things you must do now." Seeing the relief in Vinnie's face, he added, "It will all work out in the end. Go now, and be ready for your next assignment."

"Yes, Don Carrabba," Vinnie replied. He knew what his boss meant about the next assignment. Just last week, Don Carrabba had been indicted for racketeering under the RICO statutes, and there would be jobs that had to be done before the trial started. He also knew better than to comment on the indictments or the assignments. Bowing slightly, he nodded at Alberto, and they backed out of the room, leaving Carrabba in his study.

As Vinnie and Alberto left the Don's office, another man was seated in the large foyer, waiting to step in. Vinnie shook hands with him, and said, "Good to see you, been a long time. He's waitin' for ya." With that, Vinnie and Alberto walked over to the front door and left.

The man knocked on the office door, and heard, "Come." As he entered, Don Carmine greeted him, "Hello, my old friend, a pleasure to see you, as always. Please, take your seat."

The man did as he was told, as he had for over twenty years, and sat in the chair opposite the large oak desk. He looked around, and as always, was impressed with the beauty of the Don's surroundings.

The large antique Oriental rug, the Renaissance oil paintings in their gold frames, the Leonardo line drawings encased in glass, and his favorite piece, the first-century Roman marble bust of Nero. It struck him again: how could such a crude man as Carrabba come to possess such exquisite things?

The new world had its place in the room, too. A large flat screen TV sat on a stand in the corner, next to a DVD player and a VCR with a perpetually blinking 12:00. An opera CD played softly, a woman's voice soaring from hidden speakers.

Don Carmine smiled at his visitor and said, "After what has happened, I have been expecting you. We do not see each other as much as we once did, but I was sure we would be talking soon. Gianna is in Key Biscayne, so feel free to speak your mind."

"Okay, I'll get right to the point, Don Carmine. I'm sure you'll agree that what happened changes everything."

Don Carmine took a cigar from the humidor on his desk, and clipped the end before lighting it. He took a deep draw, blew smoke across the desk, and said, "This changes nothing. Everything will remain the same; you will still do as you are told, and I will still do the telling."

The man lightly hiccoughed, and tasted the bourbon that had recently substituted for breakfast. After a moment, he said, "So . . . when *do* things change? When does it all end?"

"It will never end, unless something terrible happens to you. And that, of course is completely in your hands. We have an agreement that has changed, but your debt remains unpaid. We just need to make different arrangements," Don Carmine said.

"What if I refuse?"

The old crime boss stood. "That would not be wise. You do not want to find out what happens when a man refuses to pay his debt to me. It is not a good way to live your life. That which will remain of your life, I mean."

The conversation was over, and Don Carmine stared until the man left the beautifully appointed room and the magnificent old house.

8

FIFTEEN MINUTES AFTER I SPOKE WITH NEAL, DOREEN CALLED OUT again, "Coop, Agent Brooke on line two."

"Thanks," I said, and pushed the button to answer. "Agent Brooke," I said in what I hoped was a business-like tone.

"Hello, Chief Cooper. I'm so rushed, I'll get right to the point. Agent Clay and I are convinced that organized crime is behind all this, and he informed me that you agree."

"I'd bet my badge on it," I said.

"That leads me to another point. I understand you were with homicide in Tallahassee? We could definitely use your take on all this. Are you free to come to New Orleans with us for a few days and help in the investigations of Caroline Quitman and Cecil Harwell?"

Prayer answered. "I've been planning a trip over there myself, Agent—to look into Mr. Harwell's murder." Then a small lie: "I hadn't thought about teaming up with you folks on the Quitman case, but since you brought it up—I think I could be of help."

"I know you could, Chief," she said. "The more experienced hands involved these first days, the better, as I'm sure you know."

"Exactly my thought. So, what do I need to do?"

"Just pack a bag, and we'll have someone pick you up at the station in about thirty minutes to drive you over to the chopper. Does that work for you?"

Did that work for me...

"Yes, Agent Brooke, that works for me. I can be ready in thirty minutes." I left out the part about already having my bag packed.

"Great. See you then."

"Fine," I said, and meant it. I had my suitcase, my marching orders, and Special Agent Shelley Brooke as a traveling companion. It was hard to keep the idiotic smile off my face as I waited for my

FBI escort. Doreen came in and out of my office several times, once mentioning that Penny had told her all about Agent Brooke. I barely acknowledged the comment, and knitted my brow as if I was in deep deliberation. I was in deep deliberation all right, but it was along the lines of casino gambling and a certain lady FBI agent, not Penny or police business.

Doreen, like everybody else, is on Penny's side when it comes to our romantic situation. But luckily for me, even though Doreen can do anything around an office, she can't read minds.

***

The chopper ride to New Orleans was my first, and a difficult experience for me, since I don't enjoy flying. I found out that liftoff is sudden in a helicopter, and it took my stomach about thirty seconds to catch up with the rest of me. Conversation was limited to the weather and identification of the sights by Shelley or the pilot. The headsets weren't conducive to serious discussion of the case, or small talk about New Orleans, so I mainly listened, nodding and smiling whenever I was addressed.

The view was spectacular, and the ride eventually became more pleasant. It was over before I knew it, and after a landing far smoother than the takeoff we were driven to a hotel about a mile from the Superdome. We checked in, and agreed to meet in the lobby in ten minutes.

My room was nice, and I unpacked quickly, envisioning Shelley sitting on my bed, enchanted by my grasp of the situation. The only problem was that I had no grasp of the situation, so the fantasy ended quickly. I would have to dazzle her in some other way, and at that moment, I had no idea what that way would be. I washed my face and walked out to take the elevator down to the lobby.

Shelley was already there waiting for me, and I realized that I was going to have to stop fantasizing and get serious, or she would leave me in her dust. Our first destination was Neal's office, where I was to introduce Neal to Shelley, and obtain a copy of the coroner's report. Our driver was waiting for us outside in the turnaround, and Agent Brooke took the front seat. I got in the back, glad to be behind her where I could look at her as much as possible without her catching me.

***

I saw Neal before he noticed us, standing by the water cooler in the glass-paneled Detective's Division, talking to a male uniformed officer. When he saw me, he motioned for us to wait in his office, a small room filled to capacity with clutter and debris. I've been in Neal's office twenty times at a minimum, and it's always a wreck. Shelley and I took seats in front of the desk, and I said, "Neal looks as busy as he always does." Not a great opener, but at least I said it without stammering.

"Yeah, these big city police departments are amazing. How they get anything done is beyond me, but I hear only good things about detective Feagin," she said.

"Neal is the greatest, and my best friend. We've known each other for years, went through training together. Fishing buddies in Gulf and out on the bayou, and gamblin' partners here in town. Small time gamblers though, I must admit."

Shelley laughed lightly and said, "Well, I'm glad to know you guys are small-timers. I don't need any more bad guys to chase. Changing the subject, the Cadillac was clean. She was already dead when placed in the trunk, and since the car was stolen, it isn't goin' to tell us much anyway. We need to find out more about Senator Quitman. His reputation in Washington is a little on the shady side. Allegations of handing out favors, organized crime connections, accepting payoffs, sex stuff. Typical Washington scandal material. And from what I've heard, it's also standard fare in Louisiana politics."

Sex stuff. I tried to get my mind on the case at hand, but all I could think about was Shelley and sex stuff.

I was wondering if I was going to be any help to the investigation when Neal blew into the room, sat on the corner of his desk, and said, "Sorry to keep y'all waiting. This place is out of control today, what with the Quitman case and all. How are you, bud?"

"Doin' great. Even flew on a helicopter."

"You gotta be kiddin' me—you? Flying? Wonders never cease."

"Tell me about it. Now, let me introduce you. Neal, this is Special Agent Shelley Brooke of the FBI," I said.

"Good to meet you, Agent."

"Nice to meet you too, detective," Shelley said, displaying her mighty smile again. I figured Neal could handle it, since he's been happily married for over twenty years, and has three beautiful daughters living with him. We couldn't both be walking around in a daze. "Chief Cooper tells me you two know each other well. I won't reveal what else he said, his secrets are safe with me."

Another Hollywood smile. I swear I was trying not to notice, but it was impossible. Adolescent dumbass Panhandle police chief—*ridiculous*. I was suddenly very thirsty, and excused myself to go find a water cooler in the hall. Neal looked at me with a small grin as I left, and I knew he knew what my problem was.

When I returned, Neal was saying, "We're tryin' right this minute to get our Mob informants down here for questioning. No word yet on how that's goin'. Should know pretty soon if any of them have information about Caroline's whereabouts the last few days. Anything else I can do for you?"

"I'd like to see the coroner's report," Shelley said. "If it's ready."

"Not a problem." He picked up the phone, punched a number, and said, "Jeffers? I need a copy of the coroner's report on the Quitman girl. Yeah. For the lady. Okay, thanks." He hung up, and said, "On the way. Coop? Any questions?"

"Nah, nothing that can't wait. We just came by to let you two meet and get our feet wet."

"Good deal, I'll catch up with you later. Your cell number the same?" I nodded, and he said, "Why don't you two go have brunch and wait for me to call when I get the info from our snitches?"

Neal. My man. Helping me through life's troubled waters.

Shelley said, "Good idea, I'm famished." With that, we stood up to go. Shelley and Neal shook hands, and Neal grinned at me behind Shelley's back as we left the office. I rolled my eyes at him, and gave him my best "I don't know what the hell you're grinning about" look. A young female officer handed Shelley a copy of the coroner's report as we headed to the car.

9

We started to sit down to brunch in our hotel, but decided to graze instead of ordering from the menu. Brunch in New Orleans is a real treat, and our hotel had an especially nice spread. The trip was starting out very nicely.

Shelley's cell phone rang as we walked through the buffet line. She put her plate down and stepped away from the line, listened for about twenty seconds, and replied, "That's fine sir. Thank you. Goodbye." She turned to me and said, "We have an appointment with Senator Quitman at three. That'll give me time to read the coroner's report, and see if there's anything in it that seems unusual or unexplained. I don't expect the senator to be very forthcoming, so maybe I can find something that will help us. I'm wondering about the pregnancy. You think he knew?"

"My gut feeling is that he *did* know, but I have no real reason to think that. Just a feeling I have."

"Well, I'm one who believes that first impressions are quite often right. I'm not a big believer in psychics, but I do think police officers are unusually sensitive concerning their cases, and the people involved in them."

Thousand-watt smile again. She was making a difficult situation next to impossible for me. I resolved then and there to stop acting like a dog in heat, figuratively humping her leg every few minutes. From that moment on, nothing but complete, focused attention to my duties as a detective and chief of police. She was not going to see me act in any way except completely profess—

"Chief?" she asked." Are you goin' to stare at the beignets all day, or are you gonna take one?"

"Umm, I'm gonna take a couple. Want one?"

"No thanks," she said, frowning slightly, "I'm watching my hips this month."

Oh, brother, what an opening. Luckily, I was able to restrain myself and mumble, "I should watch what I eat, too. But I can't come to New Orleans without havin' a few beignets."

She nodded, and we walked back to our table, a nice sunny one right next to the ceiling-to-floor windows. It was in a corner of the building, on the third floor, overlooking an intersection. There were about a dozen men in hardhats working to restore an old brick building across the street, and they gave me an excuse to keep my eyes in a proper place. Shelley, like most striking women I have known, seemed unaware of her effect on every man in the room, but I wasn't. Every male between twelve and ninety was stealing glances at her, some openly staring.

She ate delicately, seemingly unfazed. I was just glad we weren't up on the hotel roof by the swimming pool. Or rather, I was glad we weren't up by the swimming pool yet. I ate slowly, in the same deliberate rhythm that she did, rather than wolfing everything down like I usually do. We had a very enjoyable brunch, making small talk about the city, and the helicopter ride, and how much she enjoyed her job with the Bureau.

I told her about Solly, and she displayed a love for animals that made me appreciate her even more. Among other things, Ms. Brooke described herself as a bird fancier. Her home in McLean, Virginia, sits on two acres, and she has feeders and houses and birdbaths scattered all around her large backyard.

She told me that her mother had died just hours after delivering her, and that her father still lived in McLean in the same house she had lived in until she was accepted at Quantico.

Knowing these things about her, I felt even more at ease in her presence. She signed the check, and we rose and stood at the window, taking one more look out at the sunny street.

"Chief?" she asked, "Do you have plans for this evening?"

"Yes, as a matter of fact I do. I'm goin' over to Harrah's with Detective Feagin when we finish today's business, and maybe lose a few bucks."

"Mind if I tag along?"

I regained control of my jaw, and said, "You're more than welcome to join us, Agent Brooke. Neal's meeting me here after we both take care of our duties. Not sure what time, but I'll ring your room when we're ready."

"Great. Would you do me a favor?"

I nodded dumbly.

"Would you please call me Shelley?"

"Yes—Shelley—if you'll call me Coop."

"Deal."

Best deal I'd made in years.

***

We had a while to wait before our driver came to take us to our meeting with the Senator, so we both went to our rooms. I turned on the TV to a local station, took a Coke from the small fridge, and lay back on the bed to watch. The news had preempted whatever was usually on at that time of day, and the report centered on Senator Quitman's association with the city and the outpouring of sympathy from the public at large. There were interviews with city residents, tourists, and the mayor, who all seemed truly saddened by the news.

No confession from Caroline Quitman's murderer, so I used the remote to turn off the tube, and used the time to think about what to ask the senator. Maybe an indirect approach: "Senator, what's your favorite, chicken, or seafood gumbo, and by the way, do you know why your daughter was killed or did you hire two hit men to do it?"

Or, play the sympathetic role: "Senator, I'm so sorry for your loss, but, didyouhaveyourdaughterkilledandwhy?"

Or I could let Shelley take the lead when the time came. As if I had a choice. The Feds were in charge, whether I liked it or not. I was stuffed from brunch, and made the mistake of closing my eyes while still in a prone position on the bed. I was out like a light within seconds.

The annoying jangle of the ringing phone jarred me awake. Damn, hotel phones can be loud. I looked at my watch as I reached for the phone, and figured it would be Shelley calling to tell me I was late.

"Hi Coop," she said. "I'm just callin' to give you a heads up. I fell asleep, but luckily our driver called and said he'll be here in fifteen minutes. Are you about ready?"

"Yeah, I was just waiting for your call. Fell asleep, hunh? Well, that can happen after a big brunch. I was just about to call and ask what time I should be ready. I'll meet you in the lobby in say…ten minutes?"

"I'll be there," she said, and we hung up.

As I was pulling my room door closed on the way out, my cell rang. "Hello? Oh, hi Neal. Yes, she is. Really? I didn't notice. You think? No, I would say smaller than—look, will you shut the hell up, and quit laughin'? Yes, I'll call you after—no, I haven't forgotten. I'll be waiting. Will you shut the hell up? Bye, Kojak, you imbecile." I laughed as I hung up, and walked to the elevator.

Feagin can be so immature at times.

10

WHILE WE RODE TO THE SENATOR'S MANSION, SHELLEY INFORMED ME that the coroner's report told her little that we didn't already know. Twenty-two year-old Caucasian female, in reasonably good health, approximately two months pregnant, and a massive level of heroin in her bloodstream as the cause of death. A hot shot, as the junkies say, a large enough dose to insure death. But was it Caroline or someone else who administered it? Senator Quitman might be able to shed some light on the subject. Agreeing that neither of us should try to alienate him, we decided to both play nice during the interrogation. The ride in the air-conditioned SUV was pleasant, the sun shining down through the trees that lined a lot of the streets, a pale blue sky overhead.

As we came closer to the Senator's home, we saw that the local TV stations and a few national crews were strung out along the sidewalk and halfway into the street in front of the mansion. They turned as one animal when we slowed to enter the half-moon drive, their video and still cameras trained on our vehicle.

There were considerably more of them than had been at the pier, but it was not yet a full-blown frenzy. They were actually well-behaved, considering that a senator's daughter was dead, and the circumstances could easily be sensationalized. I felt sure that the situation would change after Caroline's burial.

As the car stopped, Shelley said, "This might turn out to be very enlightening. Or, not."

I smiled and said, "Maybe we'll get lucky here today—and tonight at the casino."

With that we thanked our driver, got out of the government-issue Suburban, and walked up the brick path to the front door of the mansion. It was white, and huge, and had those columns that big old Southern houses have. Two stories and a big front porch, just the kind of place a Louisiana Senator should own. I knocked loudly with the brass doorknocker, and we waited for someone to open the huge wooden door.

The door opened, and a lovely young woman in a gray maid's outfit asked with a trace of an accent, "Are you from the police?"

"Yes and no," Shelley said, "I'm Special Agent Brooke of the FBI, and he is police, Chief Cooper of the Gulf Front police department. Is the Senator ready to see us?"

"Yes, ma'am, he will be right down. Please follow me and wait for him in the parlor."

We entered, and I was struck by the beauty of the foyer, especially the wide grand staircase. Dark wood was everywhere, and the floors were covered in places with beautiful antique rugs. Immaculately clean, the interior looked like it might have looked a hundred and fifty years ago. Portraits of what I assumed were long-dead Quitmans lined the wide hall leading to the parlor.

Caroline had grown up in this impressive old house, and I wondered what could make a young woman want to leave a place like this to hang out in seedy dope bars. I always think of the wealthy as happy, healthy, and above it all, but that was clearly not true in Caroline's case. She was a very troubled young lady, and I hoped we would learn something in our meeting with her father that would help us to understand what had made her so unhappy.

The maid led us into the parlor and said, "Please have a seat and I will tell the senator that you are here."

The room was painted a soft yellow, with a silver-gray patterned rug over dark wood floors, high ceilings, and large sunlit windows with the drapes pulled back. On the left in front of the windows stood a wet bar stocked with top-notch booze of every flavor. We sat in beautiful old chairs with tall backs and soft seats, covered in luxurious mahogany leather. They were on either side of the huge stone fireplace, and faced each other. The room was dripping with the romance of the Old South, and luckily, Senator Q arrived before I blurted out a marriage proposal.

A strong baritone voice boomed, "Good afternoon. I'm Harry James Quitman. Welcome to my home."

He quickly strode across the room, and as we rose, took each of our hands and shook them vigorously, as if he was out on the campaign trail. It was a strong entrance, maybe a little too strong. He certainly didn't act like a man who was to bury his only child tomorrow, and was facing a viewing of her body tonight.

"A pleasure to meet you, Senator," Shelley said as she graced him with one of her most radiant smiles. Then seriously, she added, "We're both so sorry for your loss. We won't take up too much of your time; we just want to ask a few questions. I'm Agent Brooke, and this is Police Chief Cooper."

"Glad to know you Agent—Chief—thank you for your kind condolences, they mean a lot in this sad time. As to your questions, feel free to ask anything you'd like," he replied, and gave a pretty good smile of his own in return.

The Senator is a short man, but his personality is such that you don't really notice. He was dressed in an orange golf shirt over white linen slacks and a pair of brown sandals. The longish silver hair framing his ruddy face was perfectly coiffed, and his posture was excellent. He made a grand first impression. Casual, but powerful.

"I know y'all cain't have one, but I'm goin' to make myself a drink. It's a bit early, but I need a little somethin' to settle my tummy. Please, have a seat."

I hate it when grown men use the word "tummy." Stomach, belly, gut, pie safe; these are all acceptable, but not "tummy." Besides, judging from Harry James' florid complexion, it was never too early for him to hoist a cocktail.

"Don't mind us, go right ahead," Shelley said, and with that, we sat back down in our chairs, and he moved to the bar in front of the big windows that faced the street. He opened the ice bucket, put two cubes in a crystal tumbler, and reached for the bottle of Wild Turkey. All that high-end stuff for the taking, and he chose Wild Turkey. To each his own, I guess. He opened the bottle, lifted it by the neck, and started to pour himself a drink.

The windows behind the senator suddenly exploded into the room, sending glass flying in every direction.

"*Down!*" I yelled, but he was frozen. I made it to him in a flash, and knocked him to the floor behind the bar, covering him. Even at my somewhat advanced age, I can still motor when the adrenaline allows.

The gunfire from an automatic weapon of some sort ended

quickly, and I heard the squealing sound of a vehicle accelerating away from the front of the mansion.

Shelley had drawn her gun, and was peering around the corner of the window, making sure the danger had passed, and checking on Donald, the young agent who was serving as our driver.

She said, "Donald's halfway under the Suburban, but he waved at me. Looks like he's okay. The news crews are scattered all over the yard and street, but there don't seem to be any casualties. None that I can see, anyway."

I pulled myself off the Senator, and saw there was blood on him. His eyes looked like cue balls, and he was clutching what was left of the neck of the whiskey bottle in one hand, and his now empty tumbler in the other.

He had smashed the bottle onto the back of the bar as we went down in a heap, and the blood was from his hand where he had cut himself. The Wild Turkey had drenched his pants and the carpet, and splattered the wall next to him. The scent was overpowering, and I became slightly dizzy for a moment. I could have used what was soaking into the carpet to calm my nerves, which buzzed through me like a chainsaw.

The housekeeper came running in, screaming hysterically in a language I couldn't identify.

Trying to soothe her, Harry James said, "Now, Marina, everything and everybody are okay." He started to take her hands, realized he was bloody, and pulled them back saying, "Calm yourself, darlin', it's all over now, and we have these nice folks here to protect us."

Marina looked at us as if she wasn't so sure about that, but she quieted herself, and assumed the collected look of a professional problem solver. She started to leave, telling the senator she would go get the other servants to come clean up the mess.

"No, Marina, please don't do that," Shelley said. "We need to leave the room just as it is so as not to disturb any evidence."

Marina looked at her boss, and he said, "She's right, darlin', we'll worry about all that later."

She looked at the whiskey-stained carpet, sighed deeply, and silently left the parlor.

Shelley was calling for FBI assistance, and I got on the phone with the 911 operator, to tell her what the situation was. The place would soon be crawling with armed officers and agents, and I knew our opportunity to interview the senator was fading fast. I saw that Shelley was thinking the same thing when she caught my eye and shrugged her shoulders in an attitude of resignation.

Great minds.

The operator assured me that help was on the way, and as I hung up, I heard her already taking another call. I put my cell in my pocket, and took a seat in one of the big chairs, shaking slightly from the excitement of it all. My mind was humming, and I needed to slow it down before it exploded like the windows had.

11

THE POLICE AND FBI PERSONNEL STARTED ARRIVING NO MORE THAN five minutes after the last bullet entered the parlor. Ten minutes later, the place was full of law officers. Shelley took control, and I looked around the parlor.

The first thing I noticed was that the bullets had struck the top of the windows, and had lodged in the opposite wall, high above where Harry James' head and body could have possibly been. Obviously, the "hit" was intended as a warning, and not a murder attempt.

Two FBI guys and three NOPD officers were standing under the bullet holes in the wall, discussing that same thing. They were pointing and gesturing, and looking back and forth between the window and the wall. I heard one of them say that the bullets lodged in the holes were of a high caliber, and that they would have them identified quickly.

I'm no ballistics expert, so I left it all in their capable hands. The gunfire had come from a late-model gray sedan according to the witnesses, and several of the video camera people had taken shots that clearly showed the license plate. The opinion among all of us was that the car must be stolen, but it was a lead that some unlucky officer would have to follow, before coming to the same conclusion eventually.

According to the same witnesses, the shooter and driver were in the mandatory ski masks. I almost felt sorry for the hoods. Driving around New Orleans in the summer wearing ski masks? That would be hotter than Hell on a Saturday night. I wondered if they could apply for hazardous duty pay.

I also thought about going up to the most beleaguered-looking FBI guy I could find, and suggesting that we put out an all-points bulletin on a gray sedan containing two really, really, sweaty-headed guys.

I decided against it.

Two young paramedics were treating the Senator, who seemed to have gone into shock. The swagger was gone. Agents were trying to question him, but he was almost non-responsive. They soon gave up, and left him to the medics. I motioned to Shelley, and we walked outside to a corner of the front porch, out of earshot.

I said, "Well, there goes our, uh, shot at ol' Harry James."

Shelley chuckled, and said, "Yep, but I didn't really think he'd talk to us. I was just hopin' we might catch him off-guard, maybe get him to say somethin' before he had time to think. I imagine we never really had that much of a chance anyway. He seems pretty slick, or at least he did before they shot up his windows."

"I guess you noticed the trajectory of the bullets was all wrong if you were aimin' to hit Harry James," I said. "Pretty easy to call that a warning. Question is, who wanted to warn our Senator, and beyond that, why would Harry James need a warning?"

"That's what you and I are gonna find out, Coop. I have a feeling though, that the only way we'll get to talk to Quitman again is through his attorneys. No doubt he'll clam up as soon as they get their hands on him. I'm sure that Neal and his guys are our best chance now. What do you think?

"I agree. Maybe Neal will have somethin' for us tonight, and we can mix business with pain."

"Business with pain?"

"Yeah, the business of trying to solve this crime, and the pain of losin' our hard-earned bucks gambling in a casino."

"Well then," she said, "I'm all for a little pain. Roulette's my game of choice, and besides, I could use a night out with two handsome guys, even if one of them *is* married."

A two-thousand megawatt smile this time, and the failed interrogation of Harry James Quitman became a small blip on my radar screen, as I shamelessly imagined winning at roulette and at Shelley.

The only question was: What would I do with her if I did?

12

BACK IN MY ROOM AT THE HOTEL, I TURNED ON THE TV AND FOUND that every local station was broadcasting live from the Quitman mansion. CNN and Fox News were also there, and after a few minutes I decided to forget the case, and concentrate on having a good time. All the problems and questions would still be there in the morning, and I was pretty sure that the Feds could make it through one night without me and Shelley.

I turned off my cell phone, to make sure nobody from Gulf Front could find me. Actually, I turned it off so Penny couldn't find me.

I showered and dressed in the best set of clothes that I had with me: Fairly new blue jeans, light blue button-down cotton Oxford shirt, and the black cowboy boots that Penny had given me for Christmas last year when she was still tolerating me.

I pondered using the cologne supplied by the hotel, but since I never use the stuff, I pondered why I was pondering. Being smitten is getting more difficult for me these days, and I could just imagine Neal sniffing me and howling with laughter at my manly scent. The bottle remained unopened.

Neal called on the hotel phone as I was giving my boots a last minute buffing with a sock, and said he was five minutes from the front door. He asked why my cell wasn't on, and I told him I accidentally turned it off. He didn't need to know that I had designs on Agent Brooke just yet.

I called Shelley and relayed the message, thinking that I would beat her to the lobby, as her room was one floor above mine. I was wrong, and found her standing by the revolving door that led to the street, dressed for a night out. Simple low-cut black dress, a length I would almost call short, her blonde hair loose and falling down onto her bare shoulders.

She was facing away as I approached, and I got an eyeful of her stunning backside. Her legs looked even better than they had on the pier, and her hair made me even crazier. She turned, showing just the right amount of cleavage. When she saw me, Shelley smiled, her full lips painted a bright red. This was going to be a night to remember, at least for me.

"Why, Coop," she purred. "You clean up real nice."

"Thanks, Shelley, you look pretty good yourself," I said, the king of understatement.

Out of the corner of my eye, I recognized Neal's giant Ford pickup pulling into the hotel turnaround. His wife Susan became an overnight millionaire several years ago when her parents were killed in a plane crash, and she had bought the truck as a gift for Neal a year earlier. The pickup was big, red, and loud.

The doorman scowled at it, and reluctantly opened the door for Shelley and me. I handed him a buck to initiate the hilarity, winning laughs and hoots for my largesse from Neal and Shelley as we climbed up into the belly of the beast.

I was seated close to Shelley, our thighs and knees touching. Her perfume was light and clean, and I was glad that I wasn't competing with her in the scent department. She smelled delicious. Detective Feagin was dressed in the same manner as me, only his oxford was white, and his boots were tan.

Neal gunned the engine once for emphasis, and we laughed again at the poor doorman as he stalked angrily back to his post, screwing up his face in disgust. Neal pulled out of the turnaround slowly so we could all watch the guy's tortured expression. It was a good start to what I hoped would be a great night.

After a drive through typically heavy traffic, Neal pulled into Harrah's, and turned the truck over to the parking attendant as I helped Shelley down from the truck. We walked behind the Ford and went in with Neal as a trio, Shelley taking an arm from each of us. We were still laughing about the doorman, and made quite an entrance, several people turning to see who was having such a good time.

The casino was humming as usual, and we stopped in the lobby so Shelley could use the ladies room. As she walked away, Neal said, "Damn, bud, that is *definitely* not your typical FBI agent. She's not even your typical Hollywood movie babe. Basically, she's not even typical."

I nodded. "I was hoping you wouldn't notice. She's already got me approaching uselessness, and I was prayin' that you would pick up the slack. One of us is goin' to have to be a professional around her, and all I've been able to do is *act* like one. You've gotta help me, man."

We both laughed, and looked around the casino, looking for trouble where most likely there was none—typical cop behavior. On the occasions I've gambled legally, I've noticed that casino crowds are democratic. They were a mixture of well-dressed and casual, black, white, and all the shades between, old and young, pretty and not so pretty, serious and devil-may-care.

I always enjoy my casino experiences, mainly because I expect to lose, so it doesn't bother me when I do. Neal feels the same way, and we always have a good time throwing away our money together. Susan usually gives Neal a few hundred extra, and like the good bud he is, he shares some of it with me. We're a happy pair of losers, and fishing is the same way. Sitting in the boat drinking beer, daydreaming and laughing with your buddy is what it's all about. Catch a fish, that's pure gravy.

Satisfied that the area was safe, I turned to see Shelley walking toward us, her hair swinging gently, her eyes locked with mine. Somehow I was able to keep my eyes on her without turning away, something I would not have bet on before that moment. The games had begun, and my odds of winning seemed to be improving.

"Well, boys," she said, still looking directly at me, "Shall we enter this den of thieves?"

Neal figured me for a goner, and spoke for me, "Yes, Agent Brooke, it would be our pleasure, wouldn't it Chief Cooper?"

"Sure would," I said, and unlocked my gaze. To Neal: "Lead on, and let's see if we can lose your lovely wife's money."

Shelley looked at Neal quizzically, but let the comment pass. We walked down into the main room, and Shelley took my hand and led me in the direction of the roulette tables, saying, "It's the wheel for me, Coop—okay by you?"

"Roulette is my favorite sport," I said, and felt a rush from holding her hand. She could have led me anywhere at that particular moment. Things were looking rosier by the minute, and I became suddenly aware of how much I enjoy the fact that casinos have no clocks. The night was young, and I really didn't care how old it got, or how much it cost Susan and me. I definitely did not care that roulette is my least favorite game of chance. The woman wants roulette, the woman *gets* roulette.

Neal said, "I'm goin' to the craps table, I'll catch up with y'all later," and winking at me, strolled off to roll some bones.

Shelley and I took two adjacent chairs at the roulette table—the only empty ones on our side of the board. As I almost always do, I forgot and tried to hand my two fifty dollar bills directly to the lady behind the wheel. She shook her head and motioned for me to put them on the table, which I did, and she took them and slid a small stack of baby blue chips toward me. As we were at a five-dollar minimum table, my stack was not too impressive, but with my limited knowledge and interest in the game, I was planning on a conservative approach. Not Agent Brooke, however.

Shelley coolly laid down ten Ben Franklins, and the roulette lady counted out and slid a large grouping of yellow chips towards her. She noted my slightly slackened jaw, made a mock stern face, and said, "Coop, it's time we get serious . . . I'm just getting warmed up here. Later, it's the 'big kids' table." She laughed, and I laughed with her, happy to be at *any* table with my favorite Fed.

13

I KNOW VERY LITTLE ABOUT ROULETTE, AND CARE EVEN LESS, SO MY first ten bets were confined to red or black. Not so for Shelley. She placed chips all over the table, and her chip stack gradually grew. After the first few bets, I too became more adventurous, with different results. Within about half an hour, I was broke, so I watched Shelley and the other players go at it.

I learned that roulette can be a convivial activity, and I talked with several of the players. One little old Asian lady, who couldn't speak a word of English, was placing huge bets, and raking in the chips at a steady rate. She smiled at me as she laid down her wagers, and I smiled too, hoping to make sense of her strategy. But I couldn't decode her secrets, so I talked and laughed with our other tablemates, and watched as Special Agent Brooke of the FBI played and won at roulette like a gangster's moll.

"Coop," Shelley said quietly, leaning close to my ear, "You wanna stay on here for a while when Neal's ready to go? I thought we could get a cab back to the hotel, maybe stop someplace nice for a little late night snack?"

I was surprised, but recovered quickly, and said in the smoothest voice I could muster, "Shelley, I would love to stay on and go out." I took a chance, and added, "It would be a pleasure to spend more time with you tonight."

"Oh, you have no idea, Chief."

My mind spun like the wheel I was watching. Roulette was turning out to be a wonderful pastime after all. I smiled at the Asian lady, and started planning my big move. Once again, Shelley was way ahead of me. I turned back to see Shelley rake in some more winnings and she looked me in the eye, and opened her red lips to speak.

"Let's talk to the concierge, and find a nice, quiet place with some mellow jazz and a dance floor. After that, we should retire to my room and improve federal and state relations, have a sleepover, and forget the case until tomorrow. Whatcha think, Chief Cooper?"

After a short pause, I replied, "I think I'm all in favor of improving relations, Agent Brooke. In fact, on that note, I think I'll play some more. The way my luck's runnin', seems to me I'd be a fool to give up so soon."

I laid a hundred dollar bill down on the table, and was given more chips. Two hours later, I had actually broken even. Shelley was up over two thousand dollars, and we talked and laughed the whole time. It was the most fun I'd had in quite a while.

Neal's voice boomed from behind me, "Hey guys, I won thirty five hundred and fifty clams shootin' craps! I've *never* had a night like this!"

I wanted to say, "Neither have I bud, neither have I," but I just absorbed his pounding of my back and grinned along with him, saying what a great thing it was that he was such a big winner. Shelley congratulated him too, and winked at me when Neal turned to follow a particularly curvy cocktail waitress with his professionally trained eyes. As Neal likes to say, he's married, but he ain't dead.

When he turned back around, Shelley said, "Detective Feagin, Chief Cooper has graciously offered to stay here with me, and continue playin'. I'm on a little hot streak here, and I'd like to stay a while longer. You don't mind do you? We can catch a cab back to the hotel."

"No, of course not, Agent Brooke. I'd wait for y'all, but Susan gave me a curfew, and I know better than to miss it. You kids stay here and have a ball. That's the most important thing to do in New Orleans. Y'all let the good times roll. I'm sure I'll see you both tomorrow."

Neal shook my hand, nodded at Shelley, said good night, and left without making a single crack. I love that man, I really do.

Shelley played for five more minutes before she said, "Well, I guess we can move out safely now, Coop. What say we cash in our chips, and find that concierge?"

"Excellent plan, Agent. But you're the only one who'll be cashin' in."

"I wouldn't say that, Chief. I know a game or two that you might be winning real soon."

As Shelley exchanged her stacks for larger chips, thoughts of a night in bed with her entered the adolescent part of my brain. Looking around the casino, I wondered how many other liaisons were being planned.

I watched a young couple in their wedding clothes walk into the casino. The bride was still in her gown, the pudgy groom in his tuxedo. For some reason he was wearing a gray fedora. Frank Sinatra, he wasn't. I thought about how sad he would be if he knew the size of the gap between how cool he *thought* he looked, and how cool he *actually* looked. There was no gap concerning *my* coolness, however.

I was with the hottest FBI agent in the world—my coolness was unquestioned.

As we walked toward the cashier's lair, Shelley took my hand and gave it a squeeze, looking me in the eyes. I pulled her gently closer, and we slowed our pace a little.

She said, "Why don't you go to the front desk, and find that concierge, while I go cash us out. The rest of the night's on me."

I handed her my chips, and reluctantly let go, but still held her gaze.

"At your service, ma'am. I'll find us a nice, dark, quiet place where we can get a bite to eat and dance a few slow dances."

"Perfect. Meetcha at the desk in five."

She kissed me softly and turned to walk away, her hair once again swaying to the rhythm of her hips. I was reminded of a line from some movie I saw: "I hate to see you go, but I love to watch you leave."

Still keeping my eyes on her, I started to walk to the front desk, and slammed straight into one of the biggest guys I have ever encountered.

He was a mountain, dressed to the nines, with thick oily black hair combed straight back. He had on a beautiful dark blue pinstriped suit, and a really sharp red silk tie over a blindingly white shirt. His black shoes were so perfectly shined that they gleamed.

"Excuse me, sir," I said as we untangled. "Wasn't lookin' where I was goin'."

"Not a problem," he said in what sounded like a New York or Jersey accent. "I woulda been watching her as long as I coulda, too.

You're a lucky man." He nodded, and I nodded back, and he went toward the blackjack tables while I headed for the front desk.

The concierge gave me a choice of two clubs that fit our plans, and I chose the one closest to our hotel. No use spending any more time away from Shelley's room than was absolutely necessary, I reasoned.

I'm an excellent reasoner.

14

We spent the cab ride leaning against each other and rarely speaking. Shelley stroked my hand and arm in a gentle way, scratching softly and massaging my fingers. We both looked out at the summer night, neon and streetlights blazing in the old city. I enjoyed the quiet, and I sensed Shelley felt the same.

She kissed me softly, and smiled as she leaned her head onto my shoulder as the cab stopped in front of the nightclub. I reached for my wallet, but she said, "Nope, the casino's payin' for the rest of the night, I told you that. You're out with a rich Fed, mister. Sit back and enjoy the ride."

Smiling, she paid the driver a fifty, and his face beamed when she told him to keep the change. I knew we were both thinking the same thing: "My kinda woman."

The club was dark, and soft jazz was being played by a quintet that included a baby grand piano, sax, electric guitar, stand-up bass, and drums.

At my request, the hostess led us to a table off to the side, away from the dance floor and the bright blue stage lights. The candle on the table set the perfect mood. She gave us menus, and asked if we would like cocktails with our food. Shelley ordered a Sazerac, and I chose a draft beer. As she left to get our drinks, a waiter came over and we ordered an appetizer tray with a little of everything on it.

"You're sure that's all you want? I'm buyin', Chief. Anything your heart desires."

"My heart desires a slow dance with you right this minute," I said. "I don't wanna waste this tune, it's one of my all-time favorites. May I have this dance, Agent Brooke?"

"Yes you may. I've been waitin' all day to get my paws on you."

She gave me her hand, and we rose and walked to the small dance floor, where we joined three other couples moving to the sultry music. The song was "Harlem Nocturne," a shadowy, seductive tune if ever there was one. The sax took the lead, and the guy was really good, playing in and out and around the melody.

In the darkness, Shelley came into my arms, and laid her head on my shoulder as I held her close. We moved to the music well together, and I added dancing to her ever-growing list of talents. She was about three inches shorter than me in her heels, and I couldn't wait for the moment when she took them off, and I became even taller. I'm a little over five-foot ten, so I guessed her height to be five three or four—perfect as far as I'm concerned.

"Mmm," she murmured, taking the sounds right out of my mouth. "This is really nice, Coop. I'm so glad we have some time alone."

"Shelley, please don't take this the wrong way, but I've been dyin' to do this since we met on the pier."

"I know," she laughed. "It was kinda easy to tell, the way you kept lookin' at me." She leaned her head back, and said, "I'm guessin' you didn't know I felt the same way, though, am I right? I've learned to be—careful when I'm on duty, as far as my emotions are concerned. I don't want people to know what I'm feelin,' good or bad. But, I've never found myself so strongly attracted to a man while on the job before."

"Wow. I was completely unaware that I had any kind of a chance with you. I gotta tell you, you're the most exciting woman I've ever met—as you can probably feel," I said as I brought our lower bodies together.

"Yeah . . . I feel what you mean there, Chief."

The music was sexy and slow, and I was in another world, my eyes closed, oblivious to everything but the sounds of the band and the smell and feel of this beautiful woman. We moved together as if we had been doing it for years.

When the song ended, we stayed close together a moment longer, then returned to our table where our food and drinks were already waiting.

"Let's get outta here," Shelley said, leaving another fifty on the table. "I'm ready to dance back in my room."

***

When we got back to the hotel, I turned my cell back on as we got out of the cab. We kept our distance as we walked across the lobby of the hotel to the bank of elevators, nodding hello to the desk clerk. The door opened, we entered the empty elevator, waited for the doors to close, and immediately embraced, my face nuzzling her neck. She kissed my cheek, and whispered, "Almost home, Chief Cooper. You sure about this?"

"Yes, Agent Brooke, I'm sure about this. Please don't tell me you're having second thoughts."

She leaned back, and looked me in the eyes, and said, "My thoughts are on firsts, Coop. Like the first time we undress, and the first time I see you naked, and the first time you touch me where I want to be touched. No second thoughts allowed."

"I like the way you think, Shelley. In fact, I like the way you do everything."

When the elevator stopped at Shelley's floor, we separated and walked directly to her room without speaking or looking at one another. Anyone passing would have seen a couple that could've been on a first date, or a brother and sister, or an old married couple.

The only other person we saw was a bellhop three doors down, his back to us as he rolled a room service cart down the hall. Shelley put her key-card in the door, and turned to me and said, "Come in and check out the mini-bar while I go in the bathroom and freshen up a little. I'd like a bourbon with no ice and help yourself."

"Yes, ma'am," I said, and headed to the bar. I set up two bourbons neat, and placed them on the dresser across from the bed, tossing the little bottles into the trashcan. There was a small lamp on in the corner, and it gave a nice warm glow to the room. I turned on the radio in the wall, and found more jazz. I walked to the window, and looked down on the city nine stories below. It was just after midnight, and as I watched the traffic, my cell phone rang; I answered it thinking it was Neal.

"Hey," I said.

It was Penny.

"Where in the hell *are* you?" she said.

"I'm in my room, where else would I be?" I said, looking back towards the bathroom to make sure Shelley wasn't watching or listening. "Why are you callin' so late? What's the matter? Did the feds find something at Cecil Harwell's place?"

"No, nothing yet, as far as I know."

Trying to move things along, I said a little too quickly, "What is it, then?"

Penny said, "Well, I've been calling and leaving messages all night. I thought you would've called by now and let me know what's goin' on. The shooting at the Senator's house has been all over the local and national news, and we were all worried about you. Where did you go tonight?"

"Well, first of all, if I had been hurt or shot, you woulda heard about it on the news by now. Second of all, what's this '*we*' were all worried. Don't you mean *you* were worried? And third, Neal and I went to Harrah's for a gamblin' spree where I broke even and the detective won thirty-five hundred bucks and change. Enough information, Officer Prevost?"

"I guess so. And yeah, *we* were all worried, not just me. And just where was Agent Brooke this whole time? She go out with you boys?"

I had only seconds to decide how to play this one, and I chose the old fashioned way: I lied through my teeth. Neal grinning at me flashed through my mind as I said, "I guess she was in her room, or out with some other Fed. How should I know where Agent Brooke goes in a strange city at night? FBI folks aren't exactly known for their wild and wooly ways, ya know."

I could feel the web I was weaving tangle as Shelley walked out of the bathroom wearing the skimpiest, sexiest, black lace something-or-other I had ever seen.

I gulped, and said into the phone, "I'll call you tomorrow if there's anything to report. G'night."

Penny was saying something as I hung up, but I couldn't make out the words. The gist, however, was clear. No doubt about it, Officer Penny Prevost was going to gun me down the next time she saw me. I switched off my cell again, this time in self-defense, and beheld Agent Brooke.

"Some news about the case?" she asked as she picked up a glass of bourbon.

"No, no, that was Adam, one of my officers, callin' to see if he could have the day off tomorrow. He wants to play golf," I lied, wondering if lingerie was standard issue for federal agents on the road. She read my mind, a quick read under the circumstances.

Placing her hand on the black lace covering her breast, she said, "I bought this on vacation at a little shop in Paris last spring. You like?"

I looked at her barely-covered breasts and whistled a slow, low, wolf whistle. My heartbeat was loud in my ears as I looked her over, up, and down.

She pulled her hair up on top of her head, turned left, then right, and asked, "Do you want my hair up, or down?"

"Down," I said. "I want my hands in it."

"Mmm," she said, letting it fall back to her shoulders. "I want your hands in it, too. I want you to pull it from behind."

"I think I better have that drink now and try to calm down a little."

I moved over to take my bourbon, but she blocked my way, putting her arms on my shoulders, and clasping her hands together behind my neck.

She said, "You can have a drink later, if you're a good boy. Go wash up, and I'll phone the desk and leave a wake-up call. Five-thirty be alright?"

"Yes ma'am. That'll give me plenty of time to get up and out of here. I suppose you want to keep this quiet?"

"We should be quiet in the daytime, but let's not have any boundaries in here. But I feel that discretion should be the order of the day. The workday, I mean. Do you agree?"

"I do, and please know that what we do in here, stays in here. I don't want either of us to have problems because of this, Shelley. Especially you."

"Don't worry. It'll be more fun if we keep it to ourselves. Secret glances and clandestine meetings make for a hotter time in my book, Coop. Makes me all warm just thinkin' about it."

She gave me a peck on the lips, and slowly removed her hands from behind my neck. I went into the bathroom, and washed my face and hands, looking in the mirror at a middle-aged cop who had to be the luckiest guy in New Orleans, roulette wheels notwithstanding.

When I came out, Shelley was standing naked by the bed. The

Parisian garment was now in her hands. She giggled at the expression on my face, and threw the lingerie at me. It fell to the floor at my feet, a pile of black silk and lace. She pulled back the covers, and sat on the bed, her back against the headboard, and stretched out her perfect legs. I honestly don't recall a more beautiful sight. As I walked toward the small lamp in the corner to turn it off, Shelley said, "No, Coop, please leave it on. I want to see everything."

I undressed and joined her on the bed.

15

After Coop abruptly ended their conversation, Penny turned off her cell phone downstairs in the hotel lobby. She had rented a car in Pensacola, so Coop wouldn't spot her Miata. Then she'd driven to New Orleans, without telling anyone about her trip, and followed Coop and Shelley and Neal to the casino.

She'd watched the roulette table from a slot machine about forty feet away, with a good view of the action. She even won a few dollars. But she could tell that Coop and Shelley were talking about more than gambling and police work, and it hurt.

She followed as they took the cab to the nightclub, and sat in her rented car across the street. Later she saw them leave and stayed a few cars back as they headed for the hotel. When she called Coop's room, she let it ring a dozen times before finally hanging up.

Then, using her police ID, she talked the young male desk clerk into giving her Coop's room number. She went up and pressed her ear to the door, and hearing nothing, knocked lightly, then more forcefully. When Coop didn't answer, she put one and one together, and came up with two law officers in Shelley's room.

She had tried calling Coop on his cell phone throughout the evening, and had never gotten through. When he finally answered his cell, she knew the score, and who was winning.

Penny was now faced with a long, lonely drive home, and a full day at work with little or no sleep. The thing that hurt most was the fact that Coop had been lying to her. Or that was what *almost* hurt the most.

Knowing that she had lost him to Shelley was made even more painful by the knowledge that it had been her idea to break it off this time with Coop.

That stupid bastard Chief Samuel Cooper, the only man who

could make her laugh, or cry, which she started to do as she walked out of the hotel lobby into the late-night drizzle.

***

I was wide awake when the front desk called at five-thirty, so the unmercifully jangling phone was not such a shock to my satisfied system.

Shelley was asleep with her left leg lying across me. Her full breasts rested on my chest. She stirred as I took the wake-up call, and turned away, pulling the pillow over her head. I thanked the clerk, and sat up on my side of the bed, not yet willing to leave.

I was drained. The thought crossed my mind that I might have a future with Shelley, but I didn't have time for a daydream so I stretched and got moving.

Walking to the bathroom, I remembered her saying my name in my ear over and over, but shook it off as I threw some water on my face. As I came out, I picked up and put on my clothes as I found them. At one point, Shelley had slipped into my cowboy boots, and I found them in the corner where she had flung them after taking a ride.

After I was dressed, I sat next to her on the bed, and removed the pillow from her head. She smiled lazily, her eyes still closed, and asked, "Excuse me, sir, did you get the number of that truck?"

I gently pushed her hair from her eyes, and she opened them halfway. She said, "Officer, I wanna report a man who followed me here last night, and had his way with me—and my way, too. I want him arrested and charged with making me crazy."

***

I left Shelley's room after kissing her sleepy head, and took the elevator down to my floor. Back in my room, I undressed, and soaped and sang through a nice, hot, fifteen-minute shower.

Songs of my youth were the order of the day: "You Are The Sunshine Of My Life," by Stevie Wonder, and that Elton John song that starts out: "It's a little bit funny, this feelin' inside," and a rousing rendition of "Burnin' Love" by The King. I hoped the people in the next room were heavy sleepers, but I really didn't care. It had been quite some time since a woman had made me feel like singing. In fact, the last thing a woman had made me feel was crappy. Penny was that woman, and I had deserved it, but that was all behind me now.

My cell phone rang as I was tying my tie, already dressed in the only suit I own and ready to attend Caroline's funeral. It was Neal, calling to hear about last night.

"Well? Did you and the Agent make a memory last night?" he asked.

"Yeah . . . but not the kind *you* wanna hear about so early this mornin'. We had a nice late supper at a little jazz club called Pearl's Place, and made it back here safe and sound."

"You're tellin' me that all you two did was eat, listen to jazz, and go *home*?"

"Yep, that's all there was to it. Good band, though. Got a really great sax player. Name's Erv Hinkle. You really oughta take Susan over there some night. I think she'd really enjoy that."

"Yeah, maybe I will." After a pause, he said, "You holdin' out on me, bud? You sayin' you didn't even *try* to put a move on her?"

"Detective Feagin, do you really think I have a shot at someone like Agent Brooke? You saw what she looks like. With her brainpower and sense of humor, she must have at least a dozen guys on a string. She's reasonable, and very polite, but I seriously doubt that she's looking for a graying police Chief from Gulf Front, Florida."

"Hmm. Let me see. Come to think of it, you're right. You ain't got a chance in hell."

"Exactly," I said, and quickly changed the subject. "What are you and me gonna do tonight, copper?"

"We're gonna go see a pimp near the Quarter, and try and learn about Ms. Quitman. An informant gave us the name of the scum ball that turned Caroline out last year. The CI said this dude is a pretty heavy hitter down there, and if we look under the right rock, we might find some connection that will lead us to a motive."

"Great. What time should I be downstairs ready to go? I'll be attending the funeral today, but I should be back here by five at the latest," I said.

"I'll be there at ten or ten-fifteen. Will that give you enough time to eat and do whatever it is you Florida tourists do?"

"Yes sir, Cap'n. I'll be waiting at the entrance. How many guys you got workin' the funeral?"

"We have twelve, and the FBI informs me that they have an indeterminate amount of agents who will be in attendance. No shit, that's what the guy I talked to said: 'An indeterminate amount of agents who will be in attendance.' What a douche bag."

"Well, Shelley and Agent Clay seem alright to me. Maybe you got a jerk because of your attitude, you degenerate gambler. How did Susan like the fact that you won for a change?"

"*We* made a memory, loser."

16

I HAD BREAKFAST ALONE IN THE HOTEL COFFEE SHOP, READING THE sports page and lingering over my coffee. It was another hot, muggy day in southern Louisiana, and I wasn't looking forward to the funeral and wearing my navy blue suit in the New Orleans summer sun.

I was going out of respect for Caroline, and on the outside chance that I might learn something or see somebody that aroused suspicion. Most likely, nothing would come of it, but at least the senator would appreciate it, which might come in handy down the road.

A young woman being buried for no good reason, steamy hot weather, and a media extravaganza all added up to a really lousy day.

Shelley called and said that she would not be able to be with me until early evening, so I decided to go see Neal and prep for our excursion into the seedy side of town. The French Quarter is not unknown to me, but I've never been in any of its dark, dangerous places. As I sat there killing time, I was excited and bored at the same time. Usually, boredom is all I know in Gulf, so it was kind of appealing to be anticipating a little danger.

Since I only had a minor part in this play, I didn't have access to wheels, so I called Neal and he sent a rookie patrolman over to pick me up at nine a.m. When I got to Neal's office, he was on the phone, and waved me to a seat, giving the phone the finger and scowling. He said, "yes sir," about eighteen times, and hung up, blowing out a big breath.

"Lord, give me strength," he said as he reached for his paper coffee cup. "That was Donaldson, the biggest a-hole of what I am forced by law to call my superiors. He ripped me a new one, screamin' about drive-bys and television reporters and how I better get this case solved and—wait, I'm sorry, you don't wanna hear all this."

"Actually, I enjoy hearing about your suffering. It makes me feel better about my pathetic life."

"Well, I'm glad I can help, pitiful man who spent the night with Agent Goodbody out on the town and has no story to tell. Come on now, you can tell your ol' bud. Didn't you even try to make a move on that?"

"I told you. Nothin' happened, detective. And please don't refer to my future bride as 'that.'"

"'Future bride' my newly reamed butt," Neal said. "But it's a nice dream, wouldn't you say?"

"Yeah. Now, what's the plan for tonight?"

Neal's phone rang again, and he answered it and said, "Can you please hold for a second, sir?" To me: "Another call from upstairs. I've gotta take it. How 'bout we make our plans for tonight after the funeral?"

"Okay, detective, you sit here and take it like a man, and I'll go get you some Preparation H at the hotel gift shop."

"Hilarious. Get outta here, and I'll see you at the funeral."

I could hear the shouting through the phone, and thought again what a great place Gulf Front is.

***

The funeral mass was scheduled for noon at Saint Louis Cathedral, the church the Quitman family had attended since Harry James was a pup, and where Caroline was baptized or christened, or whatever you call it.

It towers over the French Quarter. I had seen it before on a trip to the city to meet Penny's mom and dad who live about forty-five minutes outside of town.

Having a little time to kill, I called Earl to cover my tracks, and told him that he was playing golf today at the Scenic Hills Country Club in Pensacola, and that he would shoot a ninety-three. He asked me why he was doing this, of course, and I told him that it was police business, and only to mention it if someone ever asked him about it. Earl's a good cop and like a son to me, so he agreed, and asked if everything was okay.

"Yeah, everything's fine. I'm in kind of a hurry right now, but I'll explain when I get back. There's nothin' for you to worry about."

"Okay. Good deal. Have a good time, and stay outta trouble."

"Will do. See ya."

My backside now covered—though I knew it was ridiculous to worry about Shelley ever asking Earl about his golf game—I turned on the TV and dialed up the local news.

The reporter in front of the cathedral was a young Hispanic woman, and she delivered her account of the events calmly. Media and onlookers already surrounded the church. I wondered what the crowd would be like when the service actually began. She finished with a promise to tell all about Caroline's personal saga at five o'clock.

The next story up was a piece on an outbreak of food poisoning at a famous upscale eatery in the city, which didn't affect me since I never eat at fancy restaurants. But I was hungry, and since lunch would have to wait until after the service, I raided my mini-fridge and ate a couple of candy bars and drank a bottle of water.

Neal surprised me at eleven-fifteen with a knock on my door.

"Hey, bud, there's been a change of plans. Guess who's takin' you to the church?" he asked as he walked in and headed for the bathroom. He checked himself in the mirror to make sure his holster wasn't noticeable under his well-tailored charcoal-gray suit. It was obviously expensive, and Neal looked like he was about as comfortable as I had been talking to Penny last night. The striped tie was loose, but he still looked like he was choking.

"Wow, detective, you look good enough to be buried yourself," I said, reaching over and feeling the material of his suit. "Susan obviously forced you to stand still long enough to buy *this* set of threads. I know from seeing you dress yourself for work that you didn't have anything to do with it."

"If I don't get outta this thing soon, I may *need* buryin'. Susan threatened to cut off my gambling money and truck payments if I don't look good for the cameras. She saw me on the news last night in my usual clothes, no jacket and my tie undone, and went upstairs without a word and laid out all this crap for me on the guest room bed. This mornin', when I came out of the shower, she ordered me to wear it. And when I balked, she let me have it with both barrels. I'm sure I'll be the talk of the station house for a few days. Let's get movin . . . I wanna get outta these clothes as soon as possible."

***

Onlookers and media types both national and local surrounded the cathedral—officers and agents manning the barricades held back the crowd and formed a walkway to the front doors. We made our way in, and took seats at the back of the large church. I looked around for Shelley, but didn't see her.

I did see several faces that I recognized, including Senators, Congressmen, the Mayor of New Orleans, and even the Vice President and his wife. The crowd was standing room only, and I wondered how many of them were aware of Caroline's double life. There were a few TV cameras and news people, but they didn't intrude, and were barely noticeable.

Harry James and his brother and sister were seated on the left in the front row, and a small, white-haired woman Neal identified as the matriarch of the family, Mamie Jewell Quitman, sat weeping next to the Senator.

I said, "Look at the senator. No emotion at all. It sure doesn't look like he just lost his only child."

"I've seen all kinds of reactions to tragedy, bud. His lack of emotion might not be significant."

I took another long look at Harry James, and couldn't shake the feeling that it somehow was.

The service was long, but beautiful. The rituals of the church soothed me, and made me think again what a shame it was that such a young life had ended so abruptly. I think Caroline would have been pleased at all the nice things that were said about her. I hope somebody remembers me in such a fine way when my time comes.

The burial was to take place at Saint Louis Cemetery Number One, the oldest in New Orleans, dating back to the seventeen sixties. The Queen of Voodoo, Marie Laveau, reputedly is buried there. The neighborhood is rough and dangerous, and I had a feeling Harry James would rarely visit, if ever. On the way over, Neal and I finally got to discuss our upcoming evening raid on the seamier fringes of the French Quarter.

"Well, our slime ball informant, one Mr. T-Bone Walker, says the man we wanna see hangs out at a blues club called 'Blind Willie's.' He runs his business out of the back room, since he supposedly owns the joint. His given name is Jerome Raymond Nickerson, but his street name is Ray-Ray. Has a stable of twelve to fifteen girls, depending on who's in or out of jail. He also deals cocaine and heroin in large quantities, and is reported to be connected to the Mob. Of course, in New Orleans, 'The Mob' means the Carrabba Family."

I said, "Every good drug-dealing pimp should have the love and support of a family."

"I couldn't agree more. Ray-Ray bein' cozy with them helps to explain how he's been able to operate without too much trouble from the law. That, and his alleged ability to pay off the right people inside City Hall. T-Bone says Ray-Ray's as mean as they come, and a little over seven feet tall. He also has a small army of bodyguards, but he'll talk to us—if the price is right. Headquarters gave me a bankroll to grease palms that need greasin'. Ray-Ray's also known for being able to fulfill even the kinkiest sexual request, and believe me, this town has a *huge* appetite for the bizarre where sex is concerned. The guys in Vice tell stories about—well, let's just say this town is full of two-legged creatures who howl at the moon."

17

An interment in New Orleans is unusual, since they all take place above ground. The town is below sea level, and the caskets might pop up and float around in large floods. At least that's what Neal told me, and he usually doesn't kid about such matters. One thing for sure, Caroline was interred above ground, in the Quitman family mausoleum.

As we were leaving, I finally saw Shelley standing with a group of Feds near the entrance to the cemetery. She glanced at our car, and gave no indication that she saw me, but I gave a small wave just in case. Neal didn't see me wave, and a few seconds later pointed her out.

To change the subject, I asked him if he could breathe. He said something about his collar being tight, but I didn't respond, watching Shelley for as long as I could see her, even following her in the passenger's side rear view mirror. Finally, I agreed with Neal that ties and collars are evil, and we pulled out into the street, joining the slowly moving traffic.

I usually think of my mother when I attend a funeral, and today was no exception. I wondered how our lives might have turned out if my father stayed. Mom never talked about him much, and I never asked, figuring she'd tell me about him someday. That someday never came, and I'm not sure even now if that's good or bad.

I know that I got my green eyes from my father, since Mom's were brown, but other than that I don't have a lot of information. Mom's the one who instilled a sense of fairness in me, something that led to my becoming a police officer, and I'll always be grateful for that.

Neal noticed that I'd grown quiet, and asked if I was feeling okay. I said that I was just thinking about tonight, and we talked about pimps, whores, and cops on the take until he dropped me off back at my hotel.

It was nice and cool in my room after the blistering Louisiana sun and the stuffy cathedral, and it felt good to sit down and relax. I ordered a club sandwich with fries from room service, and looked out the window to see that it had started to rain.

When my food arrived, I watched part of a movie on cable while I ate.

It had that redhead from Australia in it, whose name I can never recall, and the guy from a doctor show on TV. It was pretty bad, but at least I was able to escape the news for a while.

Mindlessness has its place, I always say, especially when it keeps me from thinking about things beyond my control. Thinking of the night ahead was making me anxious, and the diversion was welcome. A good bad movie was just what I needed, and this flick delivered.

When the time finally came, I put on my windbreaker and met Neal in the hotel turnaround, ready to get moving after an afternoon of monotony. Neal was driving a dark blue sedan instead of the big red pickup. It screamed "cop," but I thought maybe that was a good thing. We were heading into a world underneath the radar of polite society, and perhaps it was best to broadcast who we were.

A light rain was still falling, and as I got in, I looked at Neal's seersucker sport coat and asked, "Did Susan dress you again?"

"Nope. Picked this out all by myself."

As we drove through rainy streets, the neon lights of the bars and strip joints in the Quarter glowed in the mist. There couldn't have been a spookier feel to the night—muggy, dark, and mysterious, the streets reflecting the lights like a dirty mirror.

I could almost hear the voodoo drums of rituals being performed nearby, and the voices of fortunetellers reading crystal balls and the palms of the faithful. What I actually heard, coming from the streets and every doorway, were the crowds—mostly young—noisy and reveling in their boozing and sinning, drunkenly shouting and laughing. It was a world away from Gulf Front, but my anxiety had turned to a feeling of excitement now that we were actually in the trenches.

I knew we didn't have long to wait, and I was definitely now ready to see what the city's backside had to tell us about Caroline's other life.

***

The rain had stopped by the time we turned a corner a few blocks out of the Quarter, and saw Blind Willie's, a blues and juke joint with a big blue neon alligator in the front window. We parked in the poorly lit, muddy lot next to a gorgeous red 1959 Cadillac El Dorado Biarritz convertible.

The top was up, and I couldn't help wishing that it was down. That model was the last Caddy with giant fins, and it's my all-time favorite car. It was in absolute mint condition, and the white leather interior was spotless.

I considered pimping as a career change, since I knew I would never be able to afford such a magnificent automobile on a police chief 's salary, but the fantasy quickly ended when I saw one of the girls working the street, dressed in the shortest shorts I've ever seen.

At least I think it was a girl. The mammal in question could have been anything. Man, woman, or something in between. He-she-it looked us over, made us as cops immediately, and sashayed across the street. I don't use the expression "sashayed" lightly. This was the definition of the word in living color.

There was a massive black man at the door, and Neal shouted our names in his ear over the loud, driving music of a blues band. The bandstand and dance floor were along the entire right side of the long, narrow room. The doorman sent a young guy to announce our arrival.

The singer and featured performer was a four-hundred-pound black gentleman called "Po' Fatty'." He and "The Bone Daddies" were in the middle of "Let The Good Times Roll," a perfect choice for the crowd on the dance floor. The dancers were a mix of college students, tourists, and locals of all ages and colors, and they were sweating and grooving together happily. The club was dimly lit, and a fog of smoke floated through and above it all. Blind Willie's looked as if it had been there for at least a hundred years.

There was a bar that ran almost the entire length of the left side of the room, and at the end of it, an arched opening that led to a restaurant. The yellow neon lettering over the archway read: "Cajun Heaven" and a small banner underneath said: "Sunday Jazz Brunch." The place was larger than I had expected, and I wondered what it would be like to have to keep watch over such a place in Gulf Front.

At that moment, a beautiful young Creole woman with a flawless café au lait complexion and straight, shoulder-length glossy black hair turned and made eye contact, and beckoned me to follow her into the back room. I yelled to Neal over the blaring music that we had our invitation, and he nodded and followed me through the crowd.

The woman waited until we caught up with her, and opened the door into a small waiting area. She introduced herself as Lucy, and asked us if we wanted a drink while we waited. Her red dress was one of those Chinese silky deals, and fit her like a snake's skin. Her black high heels were open-toed, and thin straps wrapped around her ankles. We declined her offer of a drink, and she said she'd tell Ray-Ray that we had arrived.

She disappeared through long strings of colorful Mardi Gras beads hanging from the top of a doorway, into the blackness of another room where she went through yet another door. Neal and I sat on an old beat-up lime-green Naugahyde sofa, and waited for our audience with the mighty Ray-Ray.

18

"I CAN'T WAIT TO SEE THIS DUDE," NEAL SAID. "FIVE BUCKS SAYS HE'S wearin' an endangered species somewhere on his body. Fur, or alligator, or maybe an eagle feather or two. You want in on the action?"

"Nope. Too easy. I think we should bet on the *color* of his attire. My money's on pink, maybe yellow. And I got five says he wears a big pimp hat indoors. You cover *that* bet?"

"Okay, I'll take that one . . . no hat, you lose. If he has on any—"

"Gentleman," our lovely hostess suddenly said, having silently returned, "Follow me, please."

We were led through the dark room and into the warm glow of recessed lighting, in a tastefully decorated backroom. Especially nice for the back of what was essentially a dive. It was sparse in the Japanese style, or at least Asian, with shades of gray and black predominately, dim lighting, and a lot of dark wood. Lucy looked right at home, almost as if she was a part of the décor. To our left, two gargantuan black men, one of them wearing mirrored sunglasses, stood by a small, glossy table.

As we stopped in the middle of the room, the guy not wearing shades picked up a silver tray from the table, walked over to Neal, and held it in front of him.

Neal asked, "What's that for?"

"Dass for you to put yo' weapons on, if you carryin' any. Ray-Ray don't like no weapons up in here," the man said.

Neal showed his badge, "Guess you didn't get the memo. We're not here to do the usual business."

The man looked at me, and asked, "You carryin'?"

I flashed my badge, and he took the tray back over to the side table and put it down.

I was glad to be armed, but if those men had wanted to hurt us, having guns wouldn't have done much good. They would have been on us before we even had a chance to draw. In Tallahassee, I had a lot of contact with addicts and small-time dealers during my days in narcotics, but they were like rats and cats in an alley compared to this setup. We were in the lion's den, and I must say, it was very impressive and a little intimidating.

Lucy stood behind what I assumed was Ray-Ray's desk, and checked her manicure. A small black guy with a shaved head came in and stood next to Tray Carrier and Sunglasses. The trio watched us coolly as we stood there waiting for their boss, and after a long moment, the new guy said, "I can get y'all a drink or a girl if you want. Have 'em here, or take 'em witchoo if you rather do dat."

"Thanks, but no thanks," said Neal. "Just wanna see the boss."

"Have it yo' way. But you missin' out on a good thang," he said, inclining his shiny head in Lucy's direction.

A door to our left opened, and a slim, seven-foot-tall black man entered through the gap. He was wearing no fur, no hat, no gaudy colors, but instead, a tan summer suit. He undid the collar of his white shirt, pulled off his mustard-colored tie, and handed it to Lucy, who folded it neatly and placed it on the desk. There was no big gold chain or any other stereotypical jewelry that you would expect a pimp to display. Ray-Ray looked like any other seven-foot black businessman after a hard day at the office.

"Good evening, gentlemen," he said in a scratchy voice that sounded as if he smoked three packs a day. "I understand you want information about CQ—that's the name she used down here in Hell." He smiled coldly, and took his seat behind the large desk, motioning us to sit in the two chairs in front of it.

"Yeah, we want to know if you have any idea who might have killed her," Neal said, as we took our seats.

"So, you think it was homicide?" Ray-Ray said in a voice with no discernible accent. In fact, he sounded more like a college professor than a pimp. This dude was nothing like I had expected. I made a mental note to reserve judgment on pimps in the future.

"We're leaning in that direction," Neal said. "Do you think Caroline Quitman would commit suicide? Did she ever seem to be depressed or scared in any way?"

"Well," Ray-Ray said. "Let's see how much information you're prepared to buy."

With that, Neal pulled out a roll of hundreds, peeled off ten bills, and laid them on the desk. Ray-Ray leaned forward, picked them up, and handed them to Lucy. She walked over to the door Ray-Ray had used to enter, and left through it.

Neal said, "So? What's your take on Caroline?"

"Honestly detective, Caroline Quitman was the happiest drug-addicted whore I've ever known," Ray-Ray said with a straight face. His henchmen snickered and grinned, turning their faces away from us. He continued, "CQ was a joy to know, not your typical street-walker. She had a great sense of humor, and really only came down here for the thrill, and the danger. Money was not a problem for her, she had no need of the *work*. She just took it a little too far, and found herself in over her head with the dope. I've seen it a hundred times, but I felt bad when I heard of her death. She was a good kid, and I'm sorry about what happened. Whatever that might have been."

Neal asked, "Can you steer me in a direction that might help us find out what *did* happen to her?"

"I'll tell you, Detective, I don't have any way of knowing for sure. But I personally feel she insulted this nut job that wanted her for his own, and when she said no, he made it look like a suicide by shooting her full of dope. The nut in question is a white pimp named Slippy Menard who's wanted her to join his stable ever since she came down here. She never gave him the time of day, and I think he decided CQ had disrespected him one too many times. She even tossed a drink in his face here one night about two weeks back when he was making his standard pitch. That's just a gut feeling, you understand. I don't know of anyone else who would want to hurt her. Do you know about Menard?"

Neal said, "Yeah, his name has come up, and I'll definitely move him to the top of our list. What can you tell me about the Carrabba family? Do you have any contacts in the organization?"

Everyone in the room knew he had contacts with them, but his answer was no surprise.

"I see them around town on occasion, and I've met a couple soldiers in here, but I have no contacts that would help in this case."

"Oh, I see," said Neal, meeting Ray-Ray's neutral expression with one of his own. "So, for a grand I get a white pimp that gives you a 'feelin'.' I had hoped for more than that, Mr. Nickerson. A lot more."

"I can only give what I have, detective. Tell you what, though. If I hear anything, I'll be in touch."

I could see Neal's jaw working as he struggled to keep himself from leaping across the desk and getting his money's worth by throttling Ray-Ray for a thousand minutes, but he kept his cop face on, and said nothing.

"Well," the pimp said, "Unless you have any more questions, I need to get moving."

"One more thing, please," Neal said through clenched teeth. "Do you have any idea who may have gotten Caroline pregnant?"

Ray-Ray looked at Neal blankly for a moment, then said, "Pregnant, hunh? That's too bad. Didn't know about that. It's probably for the best that the kid never made it into this world, though. It would've had a bad start. A lot of people I know should have never been born. Maybe this kid was lucky. Just remember one thing: You heard nothing about any of this from me. Mr. Menard and I are on good terms. I don't want him to find out that I talked to you about him, and get his feelings hurt."

This brought more snickers and grins from his men, who probably got paid by the chortle.

"Don't worry, *Jerome*," Neal said in a tone that made Ray-Ray's eyes flash. "I won't say a word to Slippy Menard about our little chat. If there's one thing I'd like to avoid at all costs, it's a pimp-slappin' contest."

19

NEAL AND I MADE OUR WAY DOWN A HALL AND OUT THE BACK DOOR, escorted by Ray-Ray's three thugs. They all seemed to be a little mad at us because of Neal's treatment of their boss, and there were no more offers of booze or sex, just glares that said we were lucky to be alive. The bald guy pulled the door closed behind us, and the deadbolt clicked.

As we walked away from the guards and headed to our ride, Neal said, "Well, *that* was a big waste of time. And money."

I nodded, keeping my eyes on the ground, and noticed that the rain had left plenty of mud puddles for us to try to avoid. Despite my efforts, I stepped right in one just as I heard Lucy's voice calling for us to stop and wait for her.

"Take me some place where we can talk," she said as she quickly moved toward our car, glancing at the backdoor of the club nervously.

Neal opened the rear door for her, and she jumped in the back seat as if the devil himself was after her, lying down on the seat so Ray-Ray's men couldn't see her.

We got in the front, and Neal started the car, asking where she wanted to go.

"Take a right outta here, and go to the next four-way stop, then turn left and go 'til I tell you to stop."

Neal did as he was told, and ten minutes later Lucy said, "Pull into that church parking lot."

I guess if hellhounds are on your trail, a Lutheran church is as good a place as any to talk to the cops.

Neal stopped the car, and we both turned to see Lucy try to light a cigarette. Her hands were shaking so violently that Neal took her lighter and held it, and her face glowed in the light as she took a deep drag and exhaled smoke into the air above her head.

"Anybody find out I'm talkin' to y'all, an' I'm a dead girl."

"They won't hear it from us," Neal said. I nodded in agreement.

"I just wanted to tell y'all that Caroline would *never* have killed herself. She was all the time talkin' 'bout how she was gonna be gettin' back on the right path. Said she was gonna go to college, make somethin' of herself. I know how she feel, 'cause I feel like that myself sometimes. This life can break you down."

Lucy became silent for a moment, and then said, "Somethin' else I know, is that Caroline had been involved with them gangsters y'all axed about. Them Carrabbas. She tol' me she was pregnant, and I think one of them was the baby daddy. She was with that big guy a lot lately, the one who wears all them shiny shoes."

"Do you know his name?" asked Neal.

"Yeah. Vinnie somethin'. He been comin' around the club a lot lately, and I saw her leave with him a buncha times. She told me he was spending all kindsa money on her, said he even took her to Vegas a coupla times. She said he was real nice to her, even though she was a little scared of him on account of his work, and everything. She also said she spent quite a bit of time at that Don Carrabba's meetin' house with Vinnie, partyin' and entertainin' businessmen and all kindsa guys, even cops and politicians. She said she didn't always use protection, and that sometimes things got wild, but she was too far gone to care. Caroline done a lotta crazy stuff, but I just don't think she killed herself, I really don't. They was so many people who coulda had her killed, and that crowd coulda made it *look* like suicide. Shoot, they could kill her and pay everybody off, and never get caught, understand?"

"I understand," Neal said.

Lucy continued, "The main reason I'm here though, is I turned twenty-two in June, and I made a promise to myself that as soon as I could get a little money saved up, I was outta this town. I been with Ray-Ray since I was seventeen, and all the good things he told me was gonna happen, well, they ain't. When I heard what happened to Caroline, I decided it was time for me to go, even if I ain't have no money. I was gonna wait 'til Sunday, but when I seen y'all talkin' with Ray-Ray, I thought it was a sign from God, or somebody. Two cops showin' up like that, jus' when I need help? Anyway, this ain't nothin' new, girls come and go down here all the time, dead or alive, but this was the lass straw. It coulda just as easy been me all chopped up like that."

We were all silent for a while. I looked at Neal, and could tell he was as surprised as I was by what Lucy had told us.

Neal finally said, "Well, Lucy, Caroline's death is a terrible thing, but if you turn your life around because of it, at least she won't have died in vain." He changed gears, "You know, if you wanna testify against Ray-Ray and the Carrabba family, we could get you some protection."

"I wish I could. I really do. But them gangsters own this town, and Ray-ray tight with 'em. Only hope I got is to make a clean break, and get clear outta New Orleans."

"I understand," Neal said. "But if you change your mind, you know who to call."

"Mmm-hmmm," Lucy said.

"Would you like us to take you home?"

"Lord, no. I stay with Ray-Ray. I ain't the only one, neither. Any'a them girls see me come home with a cop, and I'm dead like Caroline. The less time I'm in yo' car, the better. Ray-Ray got peoples all *over* this town. If they was to see me . . ." She shook her head slowly, staring out at the blackness.

"Got it. Is there someplace else we can take you?"

"Naw, I'm gonna call my sister to come get me. Ray-Ray don't know nothin' 'bout her. I kept her a secret all these years. I'll jus' get out here, and call her."

"Okay, if you're sure. Listen, Lucy, thanks again for all your help. We really appreciate it, and you may have helped us find Caroline's killer. "

"I sure do hope so. Somebody need to stop them bastards. You catch 'im, okay?"

"We'll do our damndest," Neal said. "And, Lucy? Good luck on your new life. You made the right decision."

"You sure did," I agreed. "Best of luck to you."

"Thank y'all."

Neal looked in the outside rear-view mirror and said, "All right then, I didn't see anyone on our tail. You have a cell phone?"

"Yeah. Don't worry 'bout me, you jus' worry about Caroline. She was a friend, and I don't have a whole lotta of friends. Y'all go on and find the son-of-a-whore who killed her."

Neal chuckled at her choice of words, and said, "Okay, Lucy. You be careful, and thanks again."

"You welcome," she said, and opened the car door, looking all around the dark lot as she got out. She waved as she quickly made her way to the side of the building and stepped into the shadows.

"Well," I said, "I never saw *that* comin'. She sure didn't look like she was planning to leave Ray-Ray and New Orleans earlier. Of course, she couldn't exactly broadcast that while we were in the club. Think she was tellin' the truth?"

"Hard to say, but she seemed to be on the level. I hope for her sake she's leaving Ray-Ray's sorry ass, but sometimes working girls aren't exactly mentally stable. The important question is whether she's tellin' the truth about Caroline or not. Did she know Caroline well enough to have inside knowledge of *her* state of mind. The Vinnie she was takin' about is a well-known Carrabba capo, so that gives her story a little credibility. But, as far as Caroline's state of mind goes, you know as well as I do from doing this job that nobody really knows anybody. People are constantly doin' stuff that no one saw comin'. On the other hand, maybe everything Lucy said is true, and I'm just bein' too cynical. I mean—if you think about it—hookers never lie to cops," he said, and rolled his eyes.

"Well, Detective Feagin, if I had to bet, I'd say she's not lyin'. The change of heart seemed genuine to me, and I think she knew Caroline well enough to be right about her, too. But then again, my dealings with whores are all from long ago, so maybe I'm not up to speed. The only whore I know in Gulf Front is Peggy Hilton, and she's been givin' it away for free since high school, really more of a slut than a whore. I bow to your extensive state-of-the-art knowledge in these matters."

"Thank you," Neal said, and started the car. "You should bow to my knowledge more often. You might learn how to become a real peace officer."

"Great. Let's get outta here before Ray-Ray's buddies find us. Get me to my mini-bar."

***

Neal dropped me off at my hotel, and as I was passing the front desk, the young male clerk called to me, "Sir?"

"Yes?" I said as I walked over to him.

"You're Chief Cooper, aren't you?"

"That's me."

"An Agent Brooke left you this," he said, and handed me a sealed envelope.

"Thanks."

"My pleasure, sir."

I headed for the elevators, note in hand, and pushed the "up" button. I decided to wait until I got to my room before opening it. Something made me think it wasn't the invitation to meet her for another clandestine free-for-all that I hoped it was.

Back in my room, I opened the bar, fixed a bourbon neat in Shelley's honor, and opened the envelope. The handwriting was feminine, clearly legible, and beautiful. Just like Shelley.

"Coop . . . got called back to D.C . . . will phone you tomorrow evening at six New Orleans time . . . sorry we can't tango tonight . . . don't go out looking for loose women, I have agents stationed all over the hotel to follow you (this job has its perks)...love, Shelley."

I was disappointed, but figured that it might be for the best. Another night with Agent Brooke at the helm might have killed me. Besides, my French Quarter adventure had me thinking so much, it would have been difficult to enjoy another dance with Shelley.

I made a mental note to be sure I was in my room at six o'clock tomorrow evening. I was most definitely not going to miss her call. I swilled my drink, went into the bathroom, and turned on the shower. After dealing with Mr. Nickerson and his world all night, I needed a good scouring.

20

LUCY'S SISTER WAS RELUCTANT TO GET OUT OF BED ON A SWELTERING, soggy New Orleans night and drive halfway across town to pick up her younger sibling. But when she heard Lucy say that she was finally leaving Ray-Ray, Wanda Ellis became ecstatic and more than willing.

The Ellis sisters were not close, due to Lucy's occupation, but they looked out for one another whenever the need arose. Lucy hung up feeling better about her safety. Wanda was the kind of big sister you might not always like, but you had to respect for her decency and strength. She was raising twin six year-old girls alone, their father having run off when he learned that Wanda was pregnant. She was a large woman, toughened by her hard life, and unlike Lucy, afraid of nothing.

Lucy put her cell back in her small purse when they hung up, and lit another cigarette, taking deep draws on it as she prayed for Wanda to arrive quickly. A dog barked from the neighborhood behind the church, and she was relieved when the sound faded away as the animal ran after something in the other direction.

As she waited, Lucy thought of how hard it would be to leave her sister and nieces, but was resigned to the fact that there was no other option. She only saw them rarely, but they were the only semblance of family life she knew. Maybe she could fix the twins' hair up nice, and take them to the park that was near Wanda's place one last time before leaving New Orleans. Wanda never had time to take the girls to the park, so it was a real treat for them when their pretty young aunt took them.

Lucy was thinking how cute her nieces would look in pigtails as the black van pulled into the parking lot, its lights off, and her street-walker instincts told her to move.

She turned to run, but her shoes and tight dress made running impossible. The most she could manage was an awkward trot, and her heart raced wildly as she made her way across the wet lawn beside the brick building, desperate to find shelter behind the church.

The van slammed to a stop at the spot Lucy had just vacated, and Richie Fratello, a young protégé of Vincenzo Mandola, bolted from the front passenger's door, and chased the terrified woman.

Lucy made it around the back corner of the church, and found herself trapped in a fenced-in loading area. She tried to hide between two small dumpsters by wedging herself in, but her dress caught on a sharp front edge, and she whimpered curses as she tugged at it. She almost had it free when she saw a man sprint around the corner.

Fratello ran up, grabbed her by the hair, and screamed, "Where you runnin', bitch? Hunh? Where you runnin'?"

Hearing the commotion, the dog resumed barking, louder this time.

The man slapped Lucy hard, and she slumped, ripping her dress as she went down to her knees. Fratello gripped her arm, and pulled her to her feet just as the van came around the corner and stopped ten feet away.

Lucy was frozen when she recognized Alberto Prizzi. The sound of the frenzied barking faded in her ears as Prizzi roughly marched her over to the van and pushed her into the middle seat.

Vinnie Mandola took her arm, smiling at her mute terror. He looked at her as if she were a brand new pair of Ferragamos. One of the only things Vinnie loved more than exquisite footwear was the look of horror in his playthings' eyes when they realized that there was no place to hide. He was not a religious man, but sometimes at those moments, Vinnie felt as though he could actually see their spirits leaving their bodies.

***

I was downstairs in the coffee shop bright and early the next morning, reading *The Times-Picayune* while I enjoyed my usual big breakfast. I had just finished eating and was figuring the tip when my cell phone rang. I picked it up off of the table and said, "Hello?"

Neal asked, "Guess who was found dead this morning in front of Slippy Menard's townhouse?"

I didn't want to. "Lucy."

He sighed heavily, and said, "Yep. They left her naked on the front steps for the entire world to see. She was unrecognizable. No part of her body was unmarked, in fact some parts were missing. Nobody around here has ever seen anything like it. I thank God she was taken away before I got there. I'm not sure I could've handled seeing her up close. The report is real horror-story stuff. The medical examiner, Brougham, said she doesn't wanna go to sleep tonight—afraid she'll dream about it. Those animals musta followed us from Blind Willie's, or got a call from someone who did. I can't *believe* I didn't pick up the tail followin' us last night. Has to be Vinnie Mandola, from what the Organized Crime Unit said. The guy Lucy mentioned? The one she saw with Caroline? All the signs point to him and some guy named 'Prizzi.' We got people lookin' for 'em, but so far, nothin'. The OCU says this pair heads up the Carrabba Family's number one execution and torture crew. They also said this killing was over the top, even for these guys. And I led those pricks right to her."

I sighed heavily, and said, "Guess they left her at that white pimp's door to send him a message to stay outta this."

"Most likely," Neal said. "Maggots like Mandola hardly ever leave their handiwork where it can be found, unless they *are* leavin' a message. Mr. Slippy Menard is nowhere to be found. I doubt that he'll be seen around here any time soon, if ever. I'm not worried about him . . . but . . . I feel like I got that girl killed by not doin' my job. Here she was, wanting to get away from that life, just tryin' to help, reaching out to us. Damn, man, Lucy was no cherub, but she didn't deserve to be sliced and diced."

I paused, trying to think of anything good to say about the young Creole woman's death. "Well, at least she died tryin' to do somethin' good." After a pause, "Screw that, she shouldn't have had to die for any reason. And by the way, detective, I didn't spot the tail either, so don't feel like it's all on you. We share the credit equally for this one."

"Yeah, maybe, but this is my town, and I should've been able to recognize a tail following us. If only I had..."

"If—Dog—Rabbit," I said.

"What?" Neal asked.

"Nothin', just somethin' an old guy I know always says when

we're playin' poker. It's short for 'if that dog had kept runnin,' he woulda caught that rabbit.' He says it whenever a player says 'if I had stayed in, I woulda won that pot.' Basically, it means it's too late for 'ifs.'"

"Well, it's definitely too late for Lucy. Caroline, too."

"Look, we'll find out who did these women, Neal. You're the best detective in New Orleans, and I'm the best detective in Gulf Front."

"You're the only detective in Gulf Front."

"Yeah, well, that makes me the best detective, too.

"I gotta go, you're killin' me," Neal said.

"Seriously, you have to leave this one behind. These animals will make a wrong move one of these days, and we'll be right there to take 'em down when they do."

We hung up, and I wished I felt as confident as I sounded.

***

I spent the rest of the morning walking around the Quarter—browsing in a voodoo store, listening to the street musicians, and watching the painters. At lunchtime, I asked a cab driver for a recommendation, and he took me to Central Grocery, saying they have the best muffeletas in the city. Being a big fan of Dixie beer, I drank one with the huge "half " sandwich, but only one. I wanted to be wide-awake when Shelley called, because I had resolved to never be caught napping by her again. At least, not until the case was solved.

As I stepped outside, my cell rang. "Hello?"

"Chief Cooper?"

"Yes?"

"This is agent Torras. We met Monday when I took charge of the Cecil Harwell case?"

"Right. Hello again, Agent Torras. I guess you've got some news for me."

"Sure do. Sorry it took so long. There was nothing found at Cecil Harwell's apartment—well, almost nothing. We did manage to find another set of prints other than yours and Mr. Harwell's, belonging to his daughter. She got a DUI over in Panama City last year, so she popped up. No other trace though, and we went over the place from top to bottom. Chief, I'm sorry to say this, but it looks like this one's gonna go cold, and probably stay that way."

"Well, if the FBI can't find anything, the Gulf Front police sure aren't going to. Thanks for the information and the call, Agent."

"You're welcome, Chief. I'll be in touch if things change."

The rest of the afternoon crawled by, and I took another cab back to my hotel, leaving myself an hour and fifteen minutes to take my second shower of the day and relax a while. New Orleans in summer is like a sauna much of the time, and I needed cool water on my overheated body.

I flipped on the local five o'clock evening news as I was toweling off, dripping on the carpet. Lucy's murder was the lead story. It bled, so it led.

A perfectly coiffed young blonde announced: "Our top story, the shocking, sadistic murder of a young New Orleans woman. Area police are calling it one of the most vicious killings they've ever seen. WNOL's Lorraine Langley is live at the scene. Lorraine?"

Silence, as Lorraine spoke earnestly into the camera, but wasn't heard. There was a problem with the sound, so the blonde anchorwoman cut her off, explaining that we would be going back to Lorraine as soon as the difficulty was under control.

I opted not to wait, and turned off the tube, knowing that I would be seeing and hearing more than I needed to know about Lucy's death soon enough. I wondered what Nora was watching on the tube in her bar back in Gulf Front.

Dialing up the jazz station on the radio again, I got dressed in my last clean shirt and boxers, and put back on the jeans I had worn all day. It was definitely time for a laundry run, and I called down to get someone to come take care of it. I now had a little under an hour 'til Shelley was due to call, so I sat down in the chair by the window and looked at the hotel brochure, trying to think about anything besides Lucy.

21

At five fifty-five, my room phone rang, loud and unnerving as ever. She was early. More points for the Lady Lawman.

"Hello there," I said in my manliest manner.

"Coop?" Penny asked in a puzzled tone. "That you?"

"Uh, yeah, Penny, it's me."

"What's with the voice?"

"Um, Neal was supposed to call, I thought it was him. Just foolin' around."

"Oh," she said. "Good one."

"What's up? Everything okay back home?"

"Well, almost everything. Adam got punched out last night, tryin' to break up a fight."

"Damn. Is he okay?" I asked.

"Yeah, last night at the station, he tried to stop a brawl between a married couple from Alabama who were tryin' to kill each other, and the wife broke Adam's nose with a roundhouse right that was meant for hubby. He'd brought 'em in on a drunk drivin' charge, and they went at it while he was tryin' to fingerprint the husband. He's fine, Doc took care of it. He's just takin' a whole lotta ribbin' from the guys at Matthews. We were there for breakfast this mornin', and lemme tell ya, it was brutal. Adam's bein' a good sport, though. He even thinks it's kinda funny."

"It is, a little," I said.

"I know. Did you talk with Agent Torras? About Mr. Harwell?"

"Yeah. Too bad there's nothin' there."

"Sure is." She paused, and then said, "Listen, the reason I called is—I still worry about you, Coop, and you never call me, so I'm checkin' to see how you're doin', and if there's any news, you know, on the girl. "

"I'm sorry, I was goin' to call you later tonight," I lied. "There really isn't anything worth telling yet. We're no closer to solving this deal than we were when I left," I lied again. Penny was turning me into quite the prevaricator.

She said, "And how's Miss FBI?"

That was the real reason for her call. Penny and I hadn't really let go of each other yet.

"Agent Brooke? Haven't seen her. I think she went back to Washington. I'm waiting for Neal to come get me. We're goin' to the Quarter tonight and have a look around. He thinks he has a line on some low-life pimp who may have known Caroline."

That wasn't really a lie. I just changed the time and date a little bit. I wasn't under oath, for cryin' out loud.

"Good," she said. "Well, you be careful okay? And another thing. You know you need to be here for Doreen, right?"

It took a second to register. "Oh. Right. The wedding. Yeah, I remember. I'll catch a bus tomorrow night, unless something big happens when we, uh, go talk to the pimp. I'll keep you posted on any new developments," I said. "You just take care of Adam, and be careful. I don't wanna hear about you getting a broken nose."

"All right. Call me soon, okay?" she asked in that sweet tone she uses when we're on again.

"I will. You take it easy, Penny," I said, and hung up before she could keep me away from Shelley another minute. It was six o'clock on the dot, and I wanted to hear that Fed's voice again.

Less than five seconds after I hung it up, the phone ran again. I picked it up and answered in my usual tone. "Hello?"

"Chief Cooper, how's everything in New Orleans?" Shelley asked.

"Why, hello Agent Brooke, things are great. Even better now that I'm talkin' to my favorite Federal employee."

"Sweet talker. You boys find out anything new while I've been gone that I should know?"

"I'll tell you when I see you," I said. "By the way, when *will* I see you?"

"Tomorrow afternoon, I'll be in another seminar in Pensacola. And then I'll see you at your hotel tomorrow night about eight-thirty. Hold on...I'm gonna put you on speakerphone. I just got out of the shower, and I need to put on some clothes. There. Can you hear me okay?" she asked, her voice sounding as if it was coming from a cave.

"Yes ma'am, I hear you loud and clear. And I see you loud and clear in my mind's eye."

"Why Chief, you have me blushing all over. Can you see *that* in your one-track-mind's eye?"

"Ohhh yeah," I said. "I wish I could see you in person, though. I never thought I'd miss having an FBI agent around."

"You better be missin' me. All I could think about all day long was our little party in my room."

"I don't think you could've missed me as much as I've missed you. That's not possible. You know how long I've been waiting for a woman like you to come into my life?"

Silence.

I thought maybe the line had gone dead.

"Shelley? You there?"

"Shhh," she whispered. "I think I heard something downstairs."

I held my breath, waiting for her to speak again.

Still whispering, she said, "Coop. I'll be right back. I'm gonna go down and check—"

She let out a muffled scream as what sounded like a lamp crashed to the floor, and a man's voice growled, "*Shut the fuck up!*" I heard the sounds of a violent struggle. Shelley tried to scream again, drowned out by glass breaking, and wood splintering.

Then suddenly, the line went dead. Probably cut, or jerked from the wall. My heart was pounding so hard I thought it was going to burst in my chest.

What should I do first? Was she hurt badly, or even dead? How do I reach 911 in Washington? Who the hell was attacking Shelley in her own home?

I came to my senses, still holding the hotel phone in a death grip. I threw it to the floor, grabbed my cell from where it lay on the bed, and dialed Neal's number as fast as I could.

22

I WAITED IN MY ROOM FOR THIRTY MINUTES AFTER CALLING NEAL, AND when I still hadn't heard back from him, I took the elevator down to the lobby where I could pace back and forth more freely. The desk clerk smiled slightly as I made my way back and forth across the lobby. I thought he probably had his finger on some kind of emergency call button behind the desk, because with each pass I made he looked a little more apprehensive. I probably should have reassured him that he had nothing to fear from me, but then I thought maybe a little apprehension would help him pass the time.

I had finally decided to walk outside and pace some more when my cell phone rang.

"Yeah?" I said.

"Hey, bud," Neal said. "I got the scoop for you. It's not good news, but at least it's somethin'."

My heart rate increased as I asked, "Whatta-ya mean?"

"I talked with a Sergeant Sisk in D.C. He went out on the 911 call, and found no sign of Shelley. There were indications of a break-in, and the upstairs bedroom was pretty trashed from what he said. I also got in touch with Agent Clay, and he said the FBI was keeping everything under wraps, and they weren't goin' to report it to the press. It seems they've been contacted with a ransom demand for five million bucks, and they don't want the media screwin' it all up. Nobody could give me a good reason why Agent Brooke should be the target of kidnappers, but since they were doin' me a favor talkin' to me at all, I let it slide. The main thing is, you don't know anything about this, okay, bud?"

"Okay," I said. "So they really don't even know if she's dead or alive, right?"

"Well, I guess that's right. But she seemed like she can take care of herself. If any woman can handle this type of situation, it's her."

"That's for sure," I said, trying to strike the proper balance between professionalism and normal concern. "And, with the Feds workin' the case, she'll be back on the job in no time." I hoped my voice didn't give me away. I had a lump in my throat the size of a baseball.

"Exactly," Neal said reassuringly. "I betcha they find her long before we figure out who killed Caroline Quitman. We'll all have a big laugh about it when this is all over. Maybe we can all go and hit the casino again."

"Absolutely," I said with much more conviction than I felt at that moment.

Another mystery had been dropped in my lap, but this one hit much closer to home.

***

Back upstairs, I had room service bring me up a cheeseburger for supper. It took all my strength just to pick it up. I gave up on it after two bites, lay back on the bed, and closed my eyes.

Everything was buzzing through my head without stopping long enough for me to form a cohesive thought. Shelley, Caroline, Cecil Harwell, amoral mobsters, pimps and whores, all passed through my overloaded skull. How the hell did I end up here in New Orleans with all this trouble in my life in only a couple of days? I was feeling big-time sorry for myself.

Then the thought of Shelley and her situation entered my mind, and the pity party ended.

I tried to sleep, but after two hours of tossing and turning on the bed, I decided to do the one thing that always helps when I feel this way: Go to a bar, where I could be with other lost people, and drink enough to slow down my speeding brain. It was almost ten when I left my room.

The hotel had a lounge down a hall off the lobby, and as I approached the entrance I saw a sign with an eight-by-ten headshot of an eye-catching brunette. Her name was Sharon Staley, and she performed from nine 'til one, singing and playing the piano.

The barroom could have been anywhere in the country, and I instantly felt comfortable. It was almost empty, so I had my choice of places to sit. I chose the bar, and pulled out a stool and sat down. A young guy with a nametag that read "Ben" came over and asked me what I wanted to drink. I ordered a single-malt, and looked around the room while I waited for it.

Ms. Staley was playing the black grand piano in the corner and singing in a sexy, dark voice that put me at ease. Her sleeveless white dress added a note of elegant sophistication to the otherwise commonplace bar scene.

She was singing and playing "Crazy," and I thought what a perfect soundtrack that was for my life, considering the past few days. I listened and watched as Ben brought me my drink.

"Wanna start a tab?" he asked.

"Yes sir, I most certainly do," I said, reaching for the booze a little too hastily. Ben watched me take it, then walked back to his end of the bar, knowing a desperate man when he saw one.

I couldn't get the sound of Shelley's muted screams out of my head. The first jolt of whiskey did nothing. I swallowed the rest, and signaled Ben for another. He brought it, I slammed it, and asked for a third. He calmly poured, and waited to see if I would slam it back, too.

I said, "I think I'll actually taste this one. I won't need you for a while."

"I'll be here when you do," he said, and moved to the other end of the bar again, where he began washing glasses in the sink behind the bar.

The Scotch began to work its typical magic, and Shelley's screams moved to the back of my mind. I concentrated on the music, listening again to the piano and the warm, plaintive voice.

Sharon finished her tune and acknowledged the polite applause of the seven or eight patrons by smiling and saying, "Thank y'all so much…I'll be back after a short break. Don't forget to tip Ben and Katie."

Katie, the waitress, a big blonde with a ponytail, said in a comically loud voice, "YEAH, Y'ALL DON'T FORGET TO TIP ME AND BEN!" This got a laugh from the small crowd, and I knew I'd made the right decision in coming downstairs.

***

Ms. Staley walked across the room to a seat three down from me at the bar, and asked Ben for a Perrier and lime. Ben brought it to her, and she took a drink and glanced in my direction. I asked her if she minded if I sat with her, and she said, "No, I don't mind at all."

I moved over and said, "You play and sing great. Good songs, too."

"Thanks."

An uncomfortable moment passed, and then she asked, "Are you a local? I don't remember seeing you in here before."

"No, I'm from Florida. Here on business."

"Yeah? What's your business, if you don't mind me asking?"

"I'm Chief of police in Gulf Front, Florida. Harry James Quitman's daughter was found dead on our pier a few days back. I'm in New Orleans workin' with the FBI on the case. So far, it's been a little crazy, which explains my presence in the lounge and this scotch in my hand."

"Oh yes," she said, "I know Harry James well. I've run into him around town many times. I knew Caroline also. I played the Sunday jazz brunch at Blind Willie's for the last six months. She was there for almost all of them, and we became friendly. I really liked her, but you could tell she was in trouble of some kind. She was always high, and seemed as if she'd never come down from the night before. And the crowd she was running with, well, lemme tell ya, they were no churchgoers. That place gave me the creeps—I never felt safe there. I was glad when my contract was up, and I could leave that joint behind. In fact, Sunday a week ago was my last day there."

"Did you ever meet the owner?" I asked.

"No. Never did. But from what I heard about him, maybe that was for the best."

"Believe me, it was definitely for the best. The less you know about Mr. Nickerson, the safer you'll be."

"You know," Sharon said, "I'm sure that Harry James must have known all those folks pretty well. I saw him there three or four times, going into the back, and not coming out again, at least not that I saw. I guess he could've gone out the back door, but from what Caroline told me, there were rooms and offices that only special friends of the owner got to see. She said that a lot of parties went on in those rooms. Caroline was not really a pro, but she told me she turned a few tricks in those rooms. I always wondered if she ever saw her dad partying back there—that might've been a bit awkward, to say the least. Harry James was known to use the girls quite a bit, and the word was that he gambled heavily. I could never figure out why he just didn't go to the casinos."

I said, "Well, the casinos won't let you play on credit like the bad guys will. In fact, it's better for them to have you always owin' them money. The initial loan rarely gets paid. They then collect a weekly percentage fee, and that keeps you in debt to them forever. Also, if you gamble with the Mob, there's the beauty of not having to pay taxes on your winnings. And on top of all that, a senator doesn't wanna get a reputation as a degenerate gambler. Illicit sex is forgiven nowadays, it seems, but most people still get mad about their politicians avoiding taxes or being involved with dirty money."

"That's true," she said. "I never really thought about it that way. All I know is that he was well known for his sexual appetites, and that he was said to be spending the family fortune like Monopoly money. Caroline told me that she was resigned to the fact that there would probably be nothing left for her when it came time to inherit her share. Maybe that's why she felt like her future didn't matter. She told me several times that she fully expected to die young, and that she didn't care what happened tomorrow. It was all about living for the moment as far as she was concerned."

I looked her in the eye, and said, "That's strange. A young woman we talked to who was close to her said that Caroline was looking forward to the future, that she was talkin' about goin' to school and getting her life back on track."

"Really? That's the opposite of the impression she gave me. Of course, it's quite possible that she was putting on an act for me. Or putting on an act for her friend. One thing I've learned is that you can't always believe what people say in a bar," she said with a smile.

I smiled back, and asked, "You mean to tell me that people lie when they drink?"

She didn't answer, but looked over my shoulder towards the door and said, "Oh, no. My ex-husband just walked in—you should be ready for anything."

I turned to look, and saw a short, stout man in a rumpled gray suit and loosened tie weaving toward us with a quizzical look on his drunken face. He seemed to be trying to focus as he staggered toward us, and my guard went up immediately. I've seen that look dozens of times right before trouble started.

He shouted, "Sharon! Who you talkin' to here? Romeo? Can't you go *one night* without whorin' in public?"

"Hank! Shut up and get the hell out of here!" Sharon spat. "This man is a policeman!"

He shouted, "Is that so?" He turned to me. "What's yer name, copper?"

"Coop. And I think it would be a good idea if you lowered your voice a little," I said, standing up.

"Coop? What the hell kinda name is *COOP*? Sounds like a name for a queer!" he yelled.

Sharon jumped in, "Hank, just shut up and leave us alone! You've got no business checking up on me. The restraining order took effect this morning. Now get out of my face before I call security!"

"Se-*curity*? Security's *ASS*!" he yelled as he spun around, looking at the small crowd, daring them to stop him.

"Look, Hank," I said calmly, "Sharon doesn't want your company, and if you're here unlawfully, it's my du-"

POW! Right in my kisser! Hank cold-cocked me with a roundhouse right that buckled my knees, and quickly threw another punch that caught me in the left eye. Then he grabbed Sharon's arm, but she threw her water in his face, and he let go of her with a stunned look.

I struggled to stand up straight, and Hank started to throw another right hand at me.

One thing I remember from my police training days is that most guys lead with their right, unlike the professionals, so I blocked the punch with my left forearm, and smashed my right fist into Hank's face with all the force I could muster. He fell back, caught himself on a barstool, and lit into me like a windmill, arms and fists flying, striking out at me as if my punch hadn't even slightly affected him.

As I was being pummeled, I managed to grab his lapels and throw him off of me, sending him on to a glass table. Hank crashed into it and destroyed it without cutting himself to shreds somehow, and was up and on his feet again faster than any drunk I'd ever seen.

His face now a bright red, Hank howled, flew at me again, and threw another barrage of wild punches. I grabbed his tie and jerked down hard, pulling him to his knees. My eye was watering from the first blow he had landed, but I managed to violently bring *my* knee into direct contact with his mouth.

Normally, that would've been that, but Hank was on such an adrenaline high that he kept coming and attacking, blood gushing from his broken teeth. He hit me so hard in the jaw that I saw stars, and slammed me into the row of barstools, knocking down several on our way to the floor.

By now, Ben had called security, and the patrons were backing off, or yelling at me to kill the guy. Sharon had moved behind the bar, and picked up a magnum of champagne.

She was heading for us when Hank grabbed my hair and head-butted me with such force that I felt the skin of my forehead split open. Blood poured down over my eyes, and I began to lose consciousness. The last thing I saw before blacking out was Sharon raising the bottle and slamming it into the back of Hank's head.

23

When I came to, I sat up to find two of the Crescent City's finest standing over me, looking down and frowning. Another officer was down on one knee behind me making sure that my handcuffs were secure. Yet another was talking to Ben and Katie and Sharon. The bar patrons were nowhere to be seen, and Hank was on his back, handcuffed to a leg of the piano. Through his bleeding teeth, he screamed obscenities and threatened litigation in a shrill voice that could probably be heard on the top floor of the hotel.

I had blood all over my face and the front of my now bare chest. Someone had removed my shirt, and tied it around my forehead to stop the blood flow. My left eye was almost completely closed, and my forehead throbbed rhythmically. Things looked bad for the good guy, and I had to move quickly, or this was gonna be a major embarrassment.

I turned my head and said to the young officer checking my cuffs, "I don't know if this'll make any difference, but I'm the chief of police over in Gulf Front, Florida."

"Well, then you should know better than to get into a barroom brawl, shouldn't you, Chief?" he said, looking up at his fellow lawmen and laughing. They laughed too.

I didn't.

I said, "May I ask what the charges are, officer?"

"Sure, you may ask," he smirked. He stood over me, and said, "Let's start with destruction of property, move on to reckless endangerment, maybe throw in a little disturbing the peace, add a smidgen of drunk and disorderly, and toss in assault and battery just for laughs."

I read his nametag, and said, "Whoa, officer Blanchard, this is a clear case of self-defense. You can ask anybody who was here."

"Sir, we're doin' that as we speak, but being a police officer yourself, you must be aware that you can't get drunk and fight in public, destroy property, and expect to just walk away. We can sort it all out back at the station. I'm sure you know the old saying—tell it to the judge."

I said, "I'm telling *you*, I didn't start this, and I'm not even close to being drunk, if you'll—"

"Look, I talked to the bartender. He says he served you three drinks in less than thirty minutes. We can step outside to my car, and you can take a Breathalyzer test right this minute. Wanna do that?"

He had me there, and he knew it. I had barely touched my third drink, but if I took the test at that moment, the fact that I had been drinking only a short time ago would have made it much more difficult to pass. The longer I had to let the alcohol pass through my system, the better.

"I'll wait," I said.

He smirked again, and said, "That's a good boy. Now, you just relax and let us take care of everything. If what you're sayin' is true, you'll be out on the streets again before ya know it." He left me and walked over to Hank, pulling out and brandishing his nightstick.

Hank became quiet immediately, and shut his bloody mouth. I looked bad, but I got a perverse sense of fulfillment seeing how badly Hank was bruised and bleeding.

Score one for the good guys.

***

The paramedics arrived fifteen minutes later. Two took care of me, and two went over to Hank. A female medic knelt down in front of me, carefully took my shirt off my head, and said, "That's a pretty nasty head wound you have there. You're gonna need stitches."

She cleaned me up and bandaged my forehead, and when she finished, Blanchard pulled me to my feet and tied my shirt around my neck like a yuppie wears a sweater, except they don't usually have bloodstains all over their designer duds. As he started to lead me outside, Sharon hustled across the room and asked him if she could have a quick word with me. Blanchard looked at her approvingly, and said, "Sure, ma'am, but make it quick," and walked over to Hank.

"Coop, is there anyone you want me to call? I've told the officers a million times it wasn't your fault, but they say you have to go to jail anyway. I'm so sorry about all this."

"That's okay, it's nothing to worry about. Just write down these numbers."

She raced to the bar and got a pen from Ben, and grabbed a napkin from the bar.

"Shoot," she said.

I knew that I would get a phone call in jail, but I wanted Neal to start pulling strings as fast as possible. I gave Sharon Neal's cell number, and she promised to call him. Blanchard came back with the now-silent Hank in his grip, and led us out through the lobby to the police cars.

A small number of people watched the parade of me, Hank, the police, and the paramedics. The desk clerk's jaw dropped when he recognized me. It's the only time I remember actually wanting to go to jail, if only to get away from the humiliation of being nabbed by the gendarmes after a bar fight.

Years ago, an over-the-hill boxer was talking to reporters after a bout in which he had taken a particularly bad beating. He was asked what he should have done differently. The boxer said: "I shoulda stayed in bed."

I shoulda stayed in my room.

24

When we reached the jail, I turned over the contents of my pockets to a bored, old sergeant, and then Blanchard took me in a room where he gave me a Breathalyzer. I blew softly, and he said, "C'mon, you know better than that. Gimme a real blow this time."

I did, and I could tell by his disappointed expression that I passed. "Point-oh-six. Under."

"Gosh, I sure am sorry," I said.

He took me to another room where I was fingerprinted and had my mug shots taken. I must have looked like one of those clowns on "Cops," except for the shirt that was still tied around my neck. Those guys are usually shirtless. And shoeless. And brainless.

Bad boys, bad boys.

After my session with the photographer, my handcuffs were removed, and I untied my shirt and put it on, blood and all. I was then told that since I was a police officer, I would be going to my own cell instead of being placed in the drunk tank.

Hank was put in the tank, with three unconscious gentlemen, and had found his voice again. He was yelling about police brutality and malfeasance, and how he was going to rain down litigation on the heads of his tormentors.

Blanchard took my arm to escort me, and we walked down a hallway to a door that led into a small cellblock containing five or six cells. He unlocked the first cell and said, "Enjoy your stay."

"I'm sure I will, Officer Blanchard. Everybody's just so *nice* here," I said as I entered.

He smirked one last time, slid the cell door closed, and left the way he had come.

A thick wall separated the cells, and mine had a toilet with no lid, a two-tiered bunk bed, a sink, and a metal mirror. Directly across from the front of the cell was a row of barred windows, with a heavy metal screen covering the glass. All you could tell from looking out the window was that it was dark outside. I rubbed my raw wrists and sat down on the bottom bed, relieved to be able to finally relax.

I didn't get the chance.

My next-door cellmate asked in a slurred, loud, completely inebriated voice, "Hey . . . hey . . . hey! Hey buddy, what'd you do to get in here?"

"I killed a drunk who was talkin' too loud, and botherin' me."

"Good for you!" he said enthusiastically. "I cain't stand damn loudmouth drunks who cain't hold their liquor. You got a cigarette?"

"No, I don't. I smoked my last one right after I killed the drunk."

"Damn, 'at's too bad. I can understand why you done it, though. A man needs a good smoke after he kills a man. And it's only right that you had the last one."

"Yeah. It ain't nothin' to me to kill a man, but not havin' a smoke right afterwards, that's a different proposition entirely," I said.

He said, "You know what? My foot's bleedin' real bad over here. I think one of them sumbitches musta cut me on the way over here, 'cause I don't carry my knife no more. Looky here."

He stuck his foot out through the bars in front of his cell, about three or four feet in the air. I stood up and stuck my head out through my bars so I could see.

He had wrapped his bare foot in about thirty feet of toilet paper, and there was a spot of blood on the bottom of the paper approximately the size of a dime. I encouraged him to call for medical attention at once, and he began to shout in the direction of the door.

"Hey out there! Help! I'm bleedin' like a stuck pig in here! Heyyyyyyy! You sumbitches better come help me, or somebody's ass is gonna get whupped!"

"Louder," I said. "They won't come unless you get their attention."

"*Heyyyyyyy*! Some of you damn sumbitches better damn well get y'all's damn asses in here! And I mean NOW!"

A huge redheaded officer unlocked the door leading to our small block, and walked over to my neighbor's cell.

"Bean, what the hell's the matter now? Put your damn foot back inside, and stop all this yellin'. If I hear one more word outta you, I'm gonna put *my* foot so far up your ass, it'll take'a archaeologist to find it."

Bean whined, "Hell, Bobby, I'm hurt here. This guy next door said y'all would fix me up if I yelled loud enough."

Bobby looked at me curiously, and I silently shook my head "no."

The officer turned back and said, "Bean, do us all a favor, and just shut up and go to sleep. I'll make sure you get some help in the mornin'. I believe you ain't gonna bleed to death before daybreak."

He grinned at me, shook his big red head, and disappeared through the cellblock door.

Bean said, "They just don't care about people in here." After a moment, he asked, "You got a cigarette?"

"No, I don't smoke, sorry." I paused for effect. "Hey. Maybe if you yell loud enough, they'll bring you a pack."

"Yeah! 'At's a damn good idea! You got a head on you like a lizard. By God, I'll yell till them chicken-shit bastards bring me a whole pack! You watch!"

At that moment, the cellblock door opened again, and Neal and Bobby walked through.

Neal saw me and said, "Damn, bud, they told me you were in pretty rough shape, but *damn*. You look like you were run over by a beer truck. You okay?"

"I'm fine, just a little sore. Can I get outta here now?"

"Yes sir. I called in a few favors and you're a free man. I even made sure there'll be no record of your involvement in this little altercation. It might take a while to lose the mug shots, but I know who to call to take care of that. Right now, we can drop by your hotel, and you can shower and put on some clean clothes. The dried blood clashes with your puffy purple eyelid."

"Comical," I said.

"After we get you all clean, we'll go to my house, and you can get a good night's sleep in our guest room. When you wake up, we can get Susan to make us some breakfast. She'll love havin' another kid around the house to take care of. She's always wanted a little boy," he said.

"That's funny, Detective," I said. "You're a regular riot."

Spending the night at Neal's was the best idea I'd heard in weeks. The last thing I needed was to be alone in my hotel room with Shelley's muffled screams in my head.

I just hoped I didn't scare Susan and the girls with my new look.

25

As we were driving out of the jail parking lot, I remembered that the paramedic had said I needed stitches, and told Neal.

"No problem, we're five minutes from the best ER in town. Now tell me what the hell you got yourself into tonight."

"Okay, but the fight can wait. Lemme tell you what the singer in the lounge told me about Harry James and Caroline."

"The one who called me?" he asked.

"That's the one."

"Go, man," he said.

"Well, it turns out that the Senator has a taste for mob gambling and mob hookers. Sharon, the singer, said she witnessed him going in the back of Ray-Ray's place several times, and not returning. Seems that Caroline turned tricks back there, and told Sharon there was a whole bunch of secret rooms and offices where she worked, and where Harry James partied. Caroline also told Sharon a very different story about how her life was going than the one Lucy told us. Sharon said that Caroline had told her that the way Harry James was spendin' the family fortune, she never expected to see a dime of it. Caroline also said she expected to die young, and didn't much care. She never mentioned makin' a new life for herself. It's just the opposite of what she told Lucy. I tell ya, I'm at a loss as to how we proceed."

"Wow," Neal said. "I've known about Harry's carousing and sex scandals. Hell, everybody knows, but this stuff about Mob gamblin' and hookers is news to me. There have been allegations of mob ties over the years, but nothin's ever come of it. If anyone has the goods on him, he must be payin' 'em off to keep outta trouble. The accusations have always centered on favors. Harry James pushing through legislation that's favorable to Don Carrabba, like getting him zoning clearance or permits to drill for oil. I don't know if he's ever even been inside a casino down here. There have been attempts to catch him doing somethin' under the table politically, but nothin's ever stuck as far as the law's concerned. According to the courts, the Senator is clean."

"Not according to Sharon," I said.

"Hmmm. Well, I'm sure she has a pretty good perspective on that kinda stuff if she worked at Blind Willie's. I don't doubt for a minute that Harry is cozy with Carrabba. And, for whatever reason, I'm leaning toward believin' her description of Caroline's mindset over Lucy's. This really puts us back to square one."

"I know. We need to look into Harry James's activities in Washington, and see if it leads us back here. Then there's the matter of Caroline telling two completely different versions of her life story. Man, this is like sloshin' through the swamp blindfolded."

"Really. Tell ya what. I'll get in touch with Agent Clay, and ask him to keep an eye on Senator Quitman in Washington. Maybe somethin' will come of that. Obviously, we can forget about Ray-Ray as a source of info. I'm still gettin' my butt chewed on for that fiasco."

I said, "Agent Clay is a good choice. He can keep us up to speed on Agent Brooke's kidnapping, too. I'd like to help with that, but I'm sure they want us to keep out of their way."

My heart skipped a beat at the thought of Shelley's circumstances, but that was confidential. I said, "Bud, we need some good news right about now. These last few days have been one slap in the face after another—don't even say it."

Neal chuckled and said, "Speaking of news, I almost forgot. I just got some that you might find interesting. I got in touch with a good fishin' buddy of mine while you were out partying, and we may have struck gold."

"You have another fishin' buddy? You're just another two-timing man."

He said, "Naw, it's nothing like that, sweetheart. He means nothing to me."

"A likely story."

"Anyway, his name is Ron Ferguson, and he's pretty high up the ladder with the Federal Marshals. There's a young woman they just placed in witness protection that might be a huge help to us. It's a stroke of luck like you won't believe."

"Give," I said.

"It seems that one Ms. Angeline Devereaux of Baton Rouge was engaged to be married to the only son of a man we both know better all the time, Don Carmine Carrabba. She was going to have the finest society wedding New Orleans has ever seen. All the bluebloods were in Heaven, a real-life Mob boss's son and heir marrying one of their own. Unlike most other society spots, this town has a soft spot for pirates and shady characters, especially if they've got the big bucks. Anyway, a little problem came to light, somethin' that changed everything. The Don's baby boy found another young debutante that was more to his likin,' and dumped Ms. Devereaux three days before the big event. She went nuts, shot up his car, and decided to get her revenge by tellin' the Feds all she knows about big daddy and sonny boy. Ron said the whole unit is frothin' at the mouth. A while back, they charged Don Carrabba with several counts of racketeering based on what she's told them. There are some things that he said he'd tell me about later, too. Things that he couldn't discuss on the phone. He says she's gonna sing like Aretha Franklin at the trial, and they're all making room on their office walls for the commendations they'll receive when they bring the old man down."

"Yeah, so how does this help us?"

"I'm gettin' there," Neal said. "Ron said he can get us an interview with Angeline while she's in custody. She may be able to blow this thing wide open for us."

"Yeah, man. This could be a big deal if she knows anything about Harry James and Caroline. How in the hell did you manage to get us access to her?"

Neal looked at me like the cat that swallowed the canary. "I promised Ron that I'd pony up for boat rentals the rest of the season."

Payola in the Deep South—boat rentals.

26

We pulled into the hospital lot and Neal parked in a space reserved for emergencies. We went in and I gave the desk nurse my insurance information, and then an intern took me to the non-emergency section of the ER. After a wait of ten minutes or so, a tall young man came in with a nurse and introduced himself as Doctor Roth.

He checked me for a possible concussion, and said, "No concussion. You have a pretty hard head."

"I could've told you that," I said.

The nurse gently removed the bandage from my forehead, and they had me sewn up in less than thirty minutes. Before he left, the doctor asked, "Do you have pain anywhere else?"

"I'm sore pretty much all over, but I'll live."

He turned to the nurse, and said, "Margaret, bring him a week's worth of Extra Strength Tylenol, please."

She said, "Be right back," and left.

Dr. Roth said, "Take a couple now, and follow the directions on the package. And—do us all a favor—stay out of bars for a while."

I shook his hand, and said, "Liquor will never pass my lips again. At least not tonight."

As he was walking out, Margaret returned with a small sack of Tylenol samples. "Thanks for everything, Margaret," I said.

She smiled. "You're very welcome. Now, get outta here, and behave yourself."

I've been in emergency rooms a few times in my life, spent probably ten or twelve days in the hospital for various reasons, and I have a real soft spot for nurses. You run into a doctor now and again who's full of himself—and other stuff—but I'd say 99% of nurses are actual angels.

Back in the truck, we headed for my hotel, where Neal waited in the lobby while I went up to take a quick shower. The same desk clerk that had been there earlier gave me a small salute as I walked to the elevators in my bloody shirt. I returned the salute, and took the elevator upstairs, thanking God that there were no other guests who were going up with me.

Opening the room door, I saw my freshly laundered clothes that had been left for me by the valet service neatly folded on the bed. I was glad that I had had the foresight to get the laundry done, especially my boxers.

I didn't realize until I undressed just how much I had bled. I got in the shower and rinsed off wearing my shirt and boxers for the first few minutes in an effort to try to clean them. The bloody water swirling in the drain reminded me of the shower scene in "Psycho."

I dressed slowly, my head throbbing considerably. After packing the wet shirt and shorts in a plastic swimsuit bag the hotel provided, I pulled the door closed on my way out, and rode the elevator down to the lobby.

I went ahead and checked out early, since I wouldn't need the room for a while, if at all. I planned to take a bus back to Gulf in the morning after a night at Neal's, because I wanted a day to relax and heal a little before Doreen's wedding. I just couldn't ask Penny to come get me, and I didn't have the energy to deal with renting a car, so it was a bus, or walk. Thinking about all that made me tired, and I could hardly wait to hit the sack and forget it all.

***

As I got in Neal's ride, I said, "I've decided to go home first thing tomorrow morning. That way, I can rest up for the wedding."

"How are you gonna get home?"

"You can take me to the bus station, or I'll call a cab."

He studied me for a moment, "Whatever you say. Just so long as you come right back after the wedding."

The ride to the Feagin residence took about forty minutes, and the conversation was mainly about baseball and old times, nothing that involved the Quitman case or Shelley's kidnapping. I think Neal instinctively knew to keep things light. It seemed that whenever Shelley would come to the front of my mind, he would say something that would help me gently push her back so I could think about something else.

I had my first good laugh in quite a while when he brought up the time we went Christmas shopping, drunk out of our minds.

We had graduated from the Academy the previous summer, and Neal met Susan a few weeks before Thanksgiving. Back in her hometown of Atlanta, she had been in her high school marching band, and she was in the marching band at Florida State that season. We were looking to buy her a guitar because she wanted to learn how to play something other than the clarinet.

So, on Christmas Eve, Neal decided to go to the biggest music store in Tallahassee and find a guitar to buy for her big present. The only problem was that he decided to do this while we were finishing a fifth of Jack Daniel's in the apartment we shared.

We were barely conscious and in no shape to walk, let alone drive. The plan for the evening was to stay home and celebrate the holiday by drinking bourbon and eating pizza. Susan was coming over for Christmas Day, and we were going to open presents and have a dinner that she was going to cook and bring over.

We should have been searching for a TV program to watch, but when Neal said that we should go get a guitar, I remember saying, "Yeah, that's a really good idea. While we're there, I can get a harmonica."

Since I have no musical talent whatsoever, Neal should have seen that *maybe it wasn't such a good idea to go out after all.* But the booze had us in the holiday spirit, and we stumbled out to Neal's beat-up 1965 MGB convertible.

Because it was Christmas Eve, the stores were open a little later than usual. As best as I can recall, it was about seven-thirty. I do remember that it was dark and a little chillier than the typical December night in Florida.

Neal behind the wheel, we somehow made it through the heavy traffic, and bought the guitar without too much trouble... except for the unlucky woman who was looking to buy a guitar in the same part of the store as Neal when he puked into the back of an amplifier.

I thought she was going to heave-ho herself, but she managed to make it out of the store, dragging her little boy with one hand, and covering her mouth with the other. I always wondered about the poor soul who had to make that amplifier presentable after Neal's gastronomic assault.

Season's Greetings.

Back in the MGB with the guitar sort of safely in the trunk—Neal hadn't been able to afford a case for it—we headed for home. The traffic had worsened while we were shopping, and was bumper-to bumper in both directions for miles.

We hadn't moved an inch in five or ten minutes, the car idling in neutral, when Neal suddenly put the car in gear, switched off the ignition, and passed out in his bucket seat. I tried to wake him for what seemed like several minutes, but was probably in reality only thirty seconds.

He was out cold, and the line of cars in front of us was beginning to move. I had no choice but to get out on my side, stagger over to his in front of a hundred cars filling four lanes, and push him over into my seat in the small car, while horns blared and people cursed me.

It was one of the few moments other than my wanting a harmonica and Neal's barfing in the music store that I am able to remember from that Christmas jaunt. The honking horns were unbearable, especially since I was drunk as nine hoot owls.

I managed to drive us back to the apartment, though I have no memory of actually doing it. It's a miracle that I didn't kill anybody, and that we weren't stopped by one of our fellow cops.

On Christmas morning, Susan came over and found Neal still asleep in the car, the apartment door wide open, me passed out naked in the empty bathtub, and the guitar lying on the kitchen floor.

Merry Christmas!

When she started belly laughing instead of shooting us both with our own guns, I knew Neal had found his soul mate. He knew it, too, and Susan's Christmas turkey dinner sealed the deal.

***

We arrived at Neal's house at a little after two a.m., and Susan met us at the front door dressed in a white terry robe over pink satiny pajamas. As I looked at her beautiful face, I thought for the thousandth time what a lucky man Neal is to have a woman like her.

"Oh you poor thing!" she said to me in a sympathetic voice that could only come from a mother. "Are you okay? Come in this house right now!"

I said, "Susan, I'm fine. All I need is about a hundred hours sleep, and I'll be right in business."

"Oh, honey! Let's get you upstairs and into bed right this minute! Neal, there's mug of herbal tea I made on the table in the kitchen. Bring it upstairs."

"Yes ma'am," Neal said. "In a minute."

Susan turned back to me and said, "Wait, Coop, before you get in the bed . . . can I fix you somethin' to eat? I've got some baked chicken left over from supper, and squash casserole—how 'bout a chicken sandwich? I know, I can open a can of tomato soup and make you a nice grilled cheese, would you like that?"

"No, no, Susan," I said. "Please don't go to any trouble."

Neal laughed, "Don't go to any trouble? Bud, you must not remember my wife very well. You might as well just sit back and enjoy the ride, 'cause you're in for some heavy-duty pampering."

"Hush, Neal," Susan said, smiling. "You just go get that tea, and bring it upstairs like I told you."

As Neal walked down the hall towards the kitchen, he called back over his shoulder, "Don't fight her when she's in her motherin' mode."

"Neal!" Susan hissed. "You'll wake up the girls!" To me: "You sure you don't want somethin'? Maybe some dry toast with your tea?"

"No, really. You've got enough to do around here, and I just wanna get some sleep. I don't even want the tea, just a glass of water so I can take a couple pills."

She paused and gave me a look of concern. "Okay, hon, if you really don't want anything. I've made up your bed with fresh linens, and there are clean towels in the bathroom. In the mornin', I'll fix y'all a big breakfast and you can tell me all about tonight's events. But now, let's get you upstairs and into bed right this minute."

Susan walked me upstairs and filled a glass with water from the bathroom, and I took the pills. She pulled back the covers, kissed me on the cheek lightly, and said goodnight. The room was nice and cool, the air-conditioning on full blast.

The Feagin home is made possible by Susan's inheritance—no homicide detective in the country could have afforded it, unless of course, Neal had been on the take. It's well over five thousand square feet, and sits on seven acres with a small lake *and* a pool. I looked out the window at the pool, and for a minute thought about diving in. The feeling quickly passed, and I undressed. The bed was just too inviting and the cool air felt like silk.

I slowly got into bed and turned off the bedside lamp, staring at the ceiling fan as it slowly turned, just visible in the moonlight that came through the slightly open curtains of the window.

Shelley's kidnapping played over and over in my head, and each time through, it disturbed me a little bit more. The sounds were so vivid, the feelings still raw. My nerves were shot from all the exhausting activity of the evening, both mental and physical.

Sometime in the middle of the night I drifted off to sleep, and dreamed that Shelley was piloting a plane, and I was riding in the co-pilot's seat. The only problem was that the plane had no nose, and was hurtling through clouds so thick that we couldn't see ten feet in front of us.

I woke up in a cold sweat and looked at the red numbers of the digital clock on the table next to the bed. Twelve minutes past five. I tried unsuccessfully to go back to sleep for another hour, and finally fell into a dreamless sleep. The next time I looked at the clock, it was fifteen minutes past noon.

I stretched in bed for another five minutes, and then went into the bathroom where I spied a neatly stacked pile of my clothes that Susan had brought in and left for me. Looking in the mirror, I saw that my eye looked a little better. At least it was almost open again, and the purple had faded somewhat. Luckily, the bandage on my stitched forehead concealed the ugliness of my stitched wound.

Keeping the water away from the bandage as much as possible, I took a long, hot, shower that helped to ease the aches and pains Hank had inflicted. After gingerly toweling off, I dressed leisurely, avoiding the day and what it might bring for as long as possible. I felt so relaxed that moving was a chore. Another week or two living in Susan's nest and I would be a slugabed for sure.

Walking down the stairs, I could smell the French Roast brewing. Susan introduced me to it way back when she was still just Neal's girlfriend. To this day, I always have it when it's available. I keep a supply of it in my apartment, and often drink a cup before work.

Susan was sitting in the breakfast nook, reading the paper, and Neal and the girls were nowhere to be seen. The place was so quiet and peaceful I felt my heart rate returning to normal for the first time since Shelley's call.

Smiling, Susan said, "Good mornin' sleepyhead. I guess I don't have to ask if you slept all right. Can I buy you a cup of coffee?"

"Oui, mademoiselle, that sounds perfect. Where is everybody?"

"The girls left bright and early for the country club pool—ours doesn't have boys. They said to tell you 'hi' and 'don't leave 'til they get back.' Neal went in to the office for a while, said he'd be back by one. That gives you about fifteen minutes to eat whatever you want for breakfast. And I mean whatever you want. The kitchen is open and ready for business."

"Well . . . in that case, may I have a stack of your famous blueberry pancakes?"

"Comin' right up, cowboy. Sausage or bacon?" she asked.

"Can I get both?"

"You sure can. Sit down and I'll bring your coffee, and you can tell me what in the Sam Hill happened to you last night. Neal left before I could beat it out of 'im."

I told her my saga as she mixed the pancake batter, and fried bacon and sausages. The food smelled so good, and I was so hungry, that it was a struggle to remember all the details of the fun-filled evening. I finished the tale just as the last pancake hit the plate, and Susan shook her head.

"I'm amazed you don't look any worse than you do," she laughed as she headed back for the maple syrup. "Oh, there's Neal now," she said as she looked out the window. "I'll leave y'all alone to talk about business. You call me if you need anything else."

"Thanks for the great breakfast, Susan. This is more than enough," I said as Neal walked into the kitchen through the side door.

"Hey babe," he said, kissing Susan lightly as she left the kitchen. "How you feelin', bud?"

"Mmmph," I said, my mouth stuffed with pancakes. "Mm fnn."

"Yeah, I can see you are. You just get up?"

"Yemph."

"I have some very interesting info that involves Agent Brooke. Lemme get a drink of water, and I'll tell ya all about it."

I swallowed and asked, "Did you talk to Agent Clay?"

"Yep, sure did. He gave me some background on Shelley that might surprise you. Then again, it might not; she's quite a woman."

"I noticed." I took a whole slice of bacon into my mouth. After it vanished, I said, "Agent Brooke is one surprise after another."

He took a bottle of water from the refrigerator, opened it, and asked, "Did you know that her home is in McLean?"

"Yes, she mentioned it. Why?" A whole link of sausage this time.

"Well that's a mighty high-income area. Her father, Stewart Brooke, was a state senator from Virginia for years. He was also a big real estate developer, and there were several times when he was suspected of using his political influence to line his pockets. However he did it, he's a wealthy man, and Shelley grew up on easy street."

I said, "What's her being rich got to do with anything? Are you implying that she's dirty like her old man?" I forked another half a pancake into my maw.

"Only if by 'dirty' you mean 'filthy rich.' I just thought you might wanna know that you're in love with a rich chick."

"Mmm nah nn luff," I said.

"Are too."

After a moment of chewing and swallowing, I said, "Detective Feagin, we've already been through this. Even if I *was* in love with her, which I'm not, I don't stand a chance in hell of ever being with her. And now that we know she's rich on top of everything else, my chances are even less, if that's possible. So just give me the facts, and drop the 'Coop loves Agent Brooke' bullshit. Okay?"

"Ooooooh. Touchy! And you called her 'Agent Brooke' again. That's what you call her when you're tryin' to deny your feelings. It's so obvious that you're in love. Why deny your innermost desires?"

"Do me a favor, doctor. Let me finish eatin', and then you can tell me what you heard. And I'll even let you do your dumbass jokes about me and Agent—Shelley, alright?"

"Okay, partner. It's actually no laughing matter. Hurry up and finish, you need to hear this."

It was clear that he was about to deliver bad news. The fork dropped to my plate. I took a long, slow, drink of coffee to conceal my concern for Shelley. I hoped Neal didn't see the pain in my eyes.

"Tell me," I said.

The picture Neal painted was dark and did nothing to help my frazzled feelings. He had gotten the facts concerning Shelley's kidnapping from Agent Clay, or at least the ones Clay was allowed to give.

There was a ransom note left at her house from a terrorist organization Clay would not name. Though her name was never released to the media, Shelley had been instrumental in bringing more than half of the group to justice. The rest had scattered and sworn vengeance. They were now getting it, and things looked bleak.

The FBI was still keeping a lid on the kidnapping, and the press had backed off once they heard who was involved. Drudge had a story about it on the website, but the Feds had discredited it, saying Agent Brooke was on vacation, and that the 911 call involved another woman named "Brooks." It was classic disinformation, and seemed to be working for the time being.

In addition to the ransom, the group had demanded that their buddies be set free, and that all of them be given amnesty and a jet to whisk them away to whatever cave they inhabited.

The battle was on, and the bad guys were winning.

27

My appetite now completely gone, I tried to digest the information regarding Shelley along with the pancakes. I was staring at my coffee cup when Neal said, "Look. Your ride home is here."

"My what?"

"Susan arranged for your transportation home. When I told her you were goin' home today, she said she couldn't stand the thought of her Coop suffering on a Greyhound, so she made a phone call late last night, or should I say, early this mornin'."

He went and opened the side door, and in walked Penny, dressed in jeans and a red tee shirt, her hair in a ponytail. Penny has accompanied me many times over the years when I've visited the Feagins, and she and Susan became fast friends.

They get together whenever Penny visits her parents, whether I'm with her or not. I could just hear them, talking on the phone this morning about poor Coop, and what a mess he'd made of his life, and how Penny had better get right over here and take care of the unfortunate old fool.

I must admit, it was great to see her, but I still went into my "you shouldn't have done this" routine. Penny wasn't buying it, and came over to inspect my stitches and bruises up close.

She gingerly pulled my forehead bandage up and said, "Dang, Coop . . . did you try and make a move on Agent Brooke?"

Neal laughed, and said, "Naw, Penny, he ran his face into a drunk's fist about three hundred times. But I must admit, the drunk looks even worse."

"Then he must still be in surgery," Penny said, smiling. "Seriously. You okay?"

"Yes, Officer Prevost, I feel better than I look. Shut up, Neal." Back to Penny: "I really wish you hadn't left Gulf in the hands of Adam and Earl. The place is liable to be in the hands of desperate criminals by the time we get back."

"You know they'll be fine," she said. "They don't even have the school crossing this time of year. I think Gulf will survive until we get back, right, Neal?"

"Right, Pen. He's just embarrassed 'cause you're seein' him before he's had the chance to make up a big fat lie about what happened."

They both laughed and I had to smile along with them. A long bus ride home was the last thing I needed. I was lucky to have both of them in my life, and Susan, too.

At that moment, Susan came in and hugged Penny like she was one of her own, and pointing at me, asked, "What are we gonna do with this guy?"

"Well, I can see that you've fed him, so I guess the only thing left to do is to put the widdle baby in his car seat, and dwive him stwaight home."

They both howled, and left the room hand in hand, no doubt going to see whatever new clothes or furniture Susan had bought since the last time they'd seen each other.

"Thanks for the warning, traitor," I said. "How could you let them ambush me like that?"

"Hey, bud, Susan says not to tell, Neal doesn't tell. I haven't lived this long by ruining my wife's surprises. You know I had no choice. Besides, I got a kick outta the look on your face when Penny walked in. You're gonna hafta talk to her about all this soon enough, might as well do it in a nice cool car on the way home."

"I'm just kiddin'," I said. "I'm actually glad she's takin' me home. That bus ride was not something I was looking forward to, especially on a scorcher like today."

Neal got back to business. "I talked to Ron Ferguson, our contact with the Marshals, and he's gonna find out if we can speak with Angeline Devereaux about the Carrabbas day after tomorrow. Does that give you enough time to straighten out things in Gulf and get back?"

"Yeah, that should be enough time," I said. "I hope she heard some juicy stuff."

"Oh. I forgot to tell you. Remember I said that there was something he wanted to say, but couldn't talk about it on the phone? Well, it turns out that Angeline's townhouse had been wired for sound on the night she invited the Carrabba kid over to talk. The dumbass didn't even question why she would want to talk to him. And this the very next day after she shot up his car with his own gun. She fed him a line about not wanting to lose him, got him drunk, screwed him brainless, and got him to talk all night long about what big shots he and his daddy are. The guy's a complete loser. Ferguson said she got him to admit that his old man ordered some hits, and that the kid himself had even been involved. How stupid can one punk be?"

"Obviously, pretty damn stupid. Maybe the breaks are gonna go our way from now on."

"Keep your fingers crossed, bud. The trial is set to begin in a month—a lot can happen in the next thirty days."

I thought of how much had happened to me and Shelley in just *three* days, and said, "With the way things have been goin' lately, I'll be happy if we all just survive the next thirty days."

28

Joey Carrabba hated rising early, but when his old man called, you came on the double. He couldn't resent it much, seeing as how the Don was responsible for Joey's easy lifestyle and never-ending supply of money. Still, getting up at dawn was a huge pain in the ass.

Joseph Carmine Carrabba was the product of the Don's second and current marriage, and his only male child. Joey had four half-sisters, all much older, who lived in different parts of the country. Their mother had died twenty-five years before from lung cancer. There was also another daughter, the youngest, who had been killed at age ten by a drunk driver two years before Joey was born.

The women wanted nothing to do with their father's business, or what they considered his blood money, and that suited Joey just fine. As long as the cash was flowing, he didn't care if it was *covered* in blood, or anything else for that matter.

Those old bitches meant nothing to him anyway. The only family he cared about was the Carrabba Crime Family, and as long as the Don had the bucks to give, he would be there for the meetings. Even the ones slated for eight A.M. At nineteen, he could bounce back quickly.

As he drove his new Lexus across the bridge from his waterfront home on Lake Pontchartrain, he wondered what he'd done wrong this time. These early meetings always meant he was in trouble—otherwise he'd be called out to dinner at the big house. Oh, well, whatever it was, he knew he could skate through it. He always had, hadn't he?

When Vinnie Mandola opened the front door of the Carrabba mansion, Joey felt a shiver run up his spine. The enormous brute always scared the crap out of him, no getting around it. If only a tenth of the stories about Mandola were true, he was to be avoided like the dentist's chair.

"Come in, Joey," the monster grunted. "Your father is waiting for you in his study."

As if I didn't know that, thought Joey.

"Thank you, Vincenzo," he said cheerfully, and walked back towards the Don's office. He knocked at the door, and entered only after the great man invited him.

"Father . . . it's so good to see you. How's the leg? You had us all worried."

"My leg is fine. They got me on some new medicine that truly seems to be helping. But my leg is not the problem, Joseph. Your mouth is the problem," he said, his dark eyes becoming slits.

Joey had seen this look before. If Vinnie scared him, the look on the Don's face terrified him. Instantly he knew he was in much bigger trouble than he had thought.

"What'd *I* do?" he asked with a whine. "I ain't done nothin,' Pop, I swear!"

"You betrayed The Family," the old man said in a quiet voice that frightened him even more. "You betrayed me. You and your whore, you've made things very difficult for me. I want you out of here, and out of this town . . . You will be told where to go, and how long to stay. Do not try to make contact. Keep your stupid mouth shut, and wait for your instructions. Now leave my sight before do I do something that I will regret."

"But Pop, I got no idea what you're talkin' about!" Joey whined. "What whore? How did I betray you?"

"Get out," the Don snarled. "If you were not my blood, you would be dead and buried by now. Had anyone else put me and The Family in this position, I would have killed them personally, and taken great pleasure in making them suffer. To think that I could have sired such an idiot makes me want to hide my face in shame. Now get out of my sight before I change my mind."

"But Pop! I don't know . . ."

"GO!"

Joey backed out of the room like a whipped pup, his mouth still slightly open as he tried to figure out what had just happened. His whore? He knew that the Don had been unhappy when he broke it off with Angeline, so he must've been referring to Becky. But he hadn't even introduced her to him yet. How could she be the whore? Was the old man following him?

Oh no, he thought; that must be it. One of the Don's men must have heard about the crack parties out at the lake, and told him. Oh, shit...what if the cops had bugged his house? Was that it? Did they have evidence that could be used to put him and his father in prison?

After a moment of panic, Joey calmed down and thought, that's not so bad. Like the old guy says, I'll just go away and stay outta sight. Things will cool down in a while, Pop will pay off the right people, and I'll be back before you know it. Not a problem.

Vinnie was waiting for him by a black van, and opened the door for Joey, telling him to get in the back and stay down. Joey did as he was told, and the van pulled out into the street slowly.

It was the last time Joey would ever see his father.

29

PENNY AT THE WHEEL OF HER MIATA, WE WERE SOON PAST NEW Orleans, headed east on I-10. The air conditioner in the little car worked well, especially for a convertible. I gazed out at the scenery, waiting for her to begin the interrogation. I didn't have to wait long.

"So. Tell me about the case. What's the latest on Caroline's background? Do you still think it was a Mob hit?"

"We know that she was involved with them, socially and semi-professionally. Not sure about the motive yet, or even if there was one. It's still up in the air as to whether it was a murder, or suicide. One witness says she was gonna get her life together, and that she was ready to take the straight and narrow. Another says she was depressed about her lifestyle, and in fact, was suicidal. We *do* know that she was pregnant and still using heroin, and that she was turning tricks right up to the time of her death. We talked to her father, and got nowhere. It turns out that he's probably mobbed up as well, and is known to have been involved in illegal gambling and hookers. We might have a breakthrough soon though. Neal set up an interview with the ex-fiancé of the son of Don Carmine Carrabba, the boss of the New Orleans Mob."

"Whew—wait a minute. The fiancé of the son of the whozit? Hunh?"

I smiled and said, "You think *that's* hard to follow? This whole deal is going everywhere and nowhere at the same time. I just wanna get home and lick my wounds and see if I can make sense of it all from a safe distance. How are you gettin' along?"

"Better, now that I know you're alright. Susan's call this mornin' shook me up a little. Especially after what just happened to Adam. I'm so happy that she and Neal were there for you."

"Me, too. Seeing Neal at the jail made me realize for the millionth time what a true friend he is. Maybe next time he comes to

Gulf, he'll go a coupla rounds with a maniac, and I can bail *him* out. Listen, you mind if I take a nap? I promise I'll fill you in on the rest when I wake up."

"Okay. Sorry about bringin' my little ride, but I didn't know whether or not you'd want me to bring a patrol car. Even if you are the chief."

"It's fine, you made the right choice. Besides, after one of Susan's breakfasts, I could sleep in a phone booth, even as beat up as I am. I only need a few seconds, and I'll be a goner. You just drive in a straight line," I said, closing my eyes.

"Roger that," she said, and I settled back, hoping that Shelley would stay out of my mind at least until we got home.

No such luck.

I ran through all the information I had in my mind. The terrorists, the FBI stonewalling the press, the rich-kid lifestyle Shelley obviously still enjoyed, the timing of the kidnapping.

Could it be another Mafia incident? Did she have something on the senator that spelled trouble for the Carrabbas? Did she have something on the Carrabbas that meant trouble for the senator?

Every train of thought led me back to what had now become my new stomping grounds: Nowheresville.

***

After a while, I was finally able to doze off. I woke up about a mile from the exit that leads to Gulf Front. The radio was playing softly, and Penny was humming along. I stretched and yawned, and she asked if I felt better.

"Much better. I can't wait to go to the Colonnade and get a seafood platter. I'm sorry you didn't get a chance to stop. You must be starvin'."

"Are you kiddin'? You think Susan let me leave without a bag of sandwiches and crackers and cookies and Cokes? I probably put on ten pounds while you were snoring away," she laughed.

"Oh, no. Was my snoring that bad? Did it sound like a freight train, or more like a chainsaw this time?"

"Hmmm. I'd say more like a wounded cow, or should I say, 'bull.' Actually, I enjoyed hearin' it again after such a long time without it."

She looked at me for a moment, and I saw the old Penny. The one I fell in love with the first week I met her. I thought back to the day Penny walked into my office to apply for a position as an officer. Then Shelley flashed into my head, and the tender moment evaporated.

"Well, thanks for sayin' that, even if you don't mean it. You know I always worry that my snoring bothers you. I know how hard it must be to get used to somethin' like that."

"Confession time, big boy. The only time you ever snore is after you've had too much to drink. I just used to tease you about it because you're so damn perfect otherwise, that I felt you needed to be knocked down a peg or two."

"Why you, I oughta," I smiled, and got a smile in return. "You mean to tell me that you've been torturing me all this time for a crime I never committed?"

"That would be a ten-four," she said. "Like I said, you don't give a girl a whole lotta things to bitch about. I was just tryin' to even things out a bit. What else is there to use against you?"

"Oh man. I'll take the fifth, and agree with you for once. I'm just the perfect guy, and you'll have to learn to live with it."

"Now what have I done? I take it back, sir, you snore and have bad breath and write bad checks and..." She stopped talking, and looked thoughtful for a moment, before her eyes misted over.

"I really miss you, Coop," she said softly. "I didn't realize just how much until—until you weren't here. I know it was only a few days, but it seemed like months. I just like havin' you in my life every day. I feel safe when I know you're around."

I didn't know what to say to that, so I just stared out the window for that last mile. When she turned onto the main highway that leads to Gulf, we made small talk till we reached the city limits. Then I asked her to meet me at the Colonnade when she dropped me off, and we made a dinner date for eight o'clock.

***

When I opened the door to my apartment, I immediately noticed that things weren't quite right.

The door to my bedroom was closed, which I never close, and

the coffee table in the living room was too far away from the couch. Other things caught my eye as well. One of the couch cushions was upside down, because the red wine stain was visible again. I had turned it over the day after the night I fell asleep with a not-quite empty bottle of burgundy on top of my chest. The stain was not big enough to notice unless you really looked for it, or had caused it to happen. Also, my bedroom closet had things in it that didn't belong, and was missing some things that did.

Clearly, somebody had been in my apartment, and had done a thorough examination of it. My first guess was, of course, gangster types. But, as I thought about it, Feds could have done it, or even a crazier thought, Penny could have been there. I gave her a key for Christmas seven months after she moved to Gulf Front.

I eliminated Officer Prevost quickly. She might be difficult at times, and mad at me a lot, but she's not a sneak. The thought of her investigating my apartment behind my back just didn't compute.

So that left the Mob boys or the government boys and girls, and whoever it was, it felt creepy to know that my space had been invaded. I decided to see if my landlady had seen or heard anything.

I went outside and crossed the parking lot to her door, and rang her bell. A long moment later, she opened it, and her eyes registered the shock of seeing my bruises and bandage. After I assured her that I was okay, she asked me to come in and tell her all about my trip.

As she closed the door behind me, I asked, "Mrs. Wiley, have you noticed anyone coming to see me lately?"

"Well, Coop, let me think a minute." She looked at the floor and scratched her chin. "No, darlin', I cain't say as I have. Were you expecting someone?"

"No ma'am. I just wondered if anyone had been by, maybe Penny, or Adam and Earl."

"Is somethin' wrong, dear?"

"No, no, everything's fine. How you been lately?"

She frowned and said, "Well, I'm still gettin' over the shock of Cecil Harwell bein' murdered. I knew his wife from church—that was a while back—and even though I didn't know *him* all that well, it's still awful to think about. And that poor girl bein' left dead out on the pier! It just makes a body feel terrible thinkin' about how some maniac could do another human bein' like that. What's more, my versitis has been botherin' me, I cain't sleep, and Dr. Brawley says I'm gonna have to have my hip looked at soon. But other than all that, I'm doin' just fine. Listen, hon, you wanna stay for supper? I've got a ham bakin' that Mr. Ross over in apartment nine got for me and him for supper. Would you like to join us?"

Smiling at the thought of being the odd man out on a dinner date with old Mr. Ross and my sweet landlady, I said, "Thank you, but no—I already made plans for supper. Nice of you to ask, though."

I'm pretty sure she was relieved when I declined—those two have been the talk of the laundry room for a couple of months now. A fantastic cook like Mrs. Wiley is in great demand among the older gentlemen of Gulf Front, and there are plenty of fish in her sea. It was hard to leave with the scent of that ham in my nostrils, but I kissed her cheek and went back to my apartment, reflexively looking around to make sure no one was watching.

I decided to keep the break-in to myself for now, at least from Penny. Especially from Penny, because she'd want to stake out my place all night if I told her what had happened, and not necessarily from the outside.

30

PENNY WAS ALREADY SITTING ON THE BENCH BESIDE THE COLONNADE'S front door when I pulled in at seven fifty-five. She said there would be a half-hour wait for a table, and we both groaned, because if they say it's a half-hour wait, it's always more like an hour, if not longer. Since it was such a fine night, we chose to sit outside on the bench and wait to hear John announce that our table was ready on the loudspeaker by the door.

It felt good to be home, thinking about mundane things again. Shelley made a few quick appearances, but Penny's voice chased her away before she could get a grip on my thoughts. The long wait for the table turned out to be just what I needed.

We finally were seated in the restaurant at nine-fifteen. The place gets really crowded during the summer because it's so hot that no one wants to cook. And anyone passing through eats there too, because it's the only family restaurant in town that serves supper. Since fast food hasn't made it to Gulf Front yet, it's the Colonnade or nothing.

My beat-up, bandaged, and still-bruised face drew many stares and glances, and John asked if I was okay as he led us to our table by the window overlooking the ocean. I told him that I was fine, and that I looked much worse than I felt. Three people came over to talk about Cecil and ask about my health during dinner and I told them that the case was still pending and I was fine, and thanks for asking. I guess folks wanna make sure their police force is on the job and able-bodied.

There was no question as to whether or not my fellow officer was able-bodied. Penny was dazzling. She was wearing a pale yellow summer dress that looked great against her dark tan and black hair, which had been down around her shoulders all day, instead of in the bun she wears while on duty.

She was in high spirits, and took my mind off my troubles like she does when our romantic relationship is working. We laughed and talked easily during supper, and my seafood platter was as delicious as always, maybe even a little tastier due to the fact that I was finally back home after such a traumatic trip.

I enjoy my infrequent travels, but Gulf Front will always be home. I plan to live here until the day they spread my ashes a mile out to sea. I actually have that in my will. Some poor schnook, Neal maybe, is gonna have to drive a boat out and dump my remains into the Gulf of Mexico.

I hope the wind blows part of me back to shore, so I can enjoy more than one final resting place. I've always wanted to have more than one residence.

We finished eating, and over coffee Penny suggested a walk on the pier. Since the pier is only a few blocks away from the Colonnade, it sounded like a fine idea to me. We each had another cup, then paid the check—Dutch Treat, like always—and headed over to the pier, walking on the boardwalk when we reached the old sun-bleached planks.

The moon was full behind a group of clouds, and its subdued glow was the perfect lighting for a romantic stroll on the boardwalk. But romance with Penny was the last thing on my mind. I couldn't help thinking how much I wanted Shelley to be there with me, safe and sound, her hand in mine.

We turned onto the pier and headed for the end, passing a family of four and one other couple. We both leaned on the rail and let the sweet summer sea breeze blow in our faces. It had been quite a while since I'd been out to the end of the pier at night, three summers ago in fact.

Going out there is like eating watermelon to me. Every time I have my first slice of the summer, I realize that once again, I've forgotten just how great watermelon tastes. That's how the end of the pier makes me feel. Getting reacquainted with another beautiful thing that I take for granted.

Penny placed her hand on my arm and said, "What happened to us *this* time? Was it my fault or yours?"

I couldn't believe how blind I had been. I was sending her all the wrong signals. Here I was in the moonlight with the woman who had been my only serious relationship, and I was so out of it that I hadn't even noticed. I stalled for a moment, and then said, "I'm sorry, what?"

"Which one of us ran away this time? I swear I can't remember."

"Oh. Well, if memory serves, you called me a child in a rickety old man's body because I wouldn't commit to taking our relationship to the next level, and finally making an honest woman out of you. So, I guess you could say it was both of us, as usual."

She smiled at the memory, and asked, "But didn't I apologize?"

"Yes ma'am, you did, and then you gave me the cold shoulder at work until Valentine's Day, when you brought me a box of those little heart candies that have the sayings on them: 'Be mine,' 'I love you,' 'You have a terminal case of Peter Pan syndrome.' You know the ones."

She laughed softly, and leaned over to speak, her lips on my ear: "They don't print what I really wanna say on those little candies. Unless somebody's makin' an x-rated version."

Penny and I have been off and on now for eight years. She keeps a journal and when she did the math last Christmas, found that we have been apart almost exactly the same number of weeks that we've been together. We're like an old married couple who fight all the time, then make up, only we spend a lot more time apart before we reconcile.

This was the moment I should've known was coming. Whenever we get back together, it's because one of us finally makes a move, and the other responds favorably. This would be the first time that I would have an unfavorable response.

"Penny, wait. I think you're getting the wrong impression here. I just wanted a nice relaxing supper in the company of a friend. I'm not lookin' to get back together. At least, not tonight, anyway."

Her eyes flashed in the moonlight, "In the company of a friend? Excuse me? I'm a *friend* now? You just wanted my *company?* Who the hell do you think you're talkin' to here? I'm not some chick you picked up in New Orleans, ya know!"

Uh-oh. What did she mean by that "picked up in New Orleans" line? Did Susan tell her about—no, Susan couldn't have said anything. Since Neal didn't know anything, Susan didn't know anything, so she couldn't have told on me. Was Penny's female intuition really that fine-tuned, or was she just taking a shot in the dark?

My next words had better be carefully chosen and better than just good.

"Do what?" I asked.

Okay, so I'm no Lord Byron.

I continued the deception, "What in the world are you talkin' about, Penny? I didn't have time to pick up anybody in New Orleans, even if I wanted to, which I don't. Or didn't. Whatever. I was either in the hotel, the casino, freaking jail, the hospital, or at Neal's place. The only pickin' up that went on was when you picked me up at Neal's, remember?"

"Yeah, I remember," she snapped. "Now I'm tryin' to remember why I ever *wanted* to pick up your sorry ass."

She stormed off, and I stood with my mouth hanging open 'til she was halfway to the boardwalk. I trotted after her. This was not the way things were supposed to be happening. I've been in a romantic drought for over six months, and now all of a sudden I've got not one, but two women after me.

Even with all the trouble that surrounded me, such as Shelley, the mob, Caroline's death, my smashed face, I couldn't help but smile at my good fortune in the love department. I stopped smiling as I caught Penny at the entrance to the pier, and took hold of her arm.

"Hey, listen," I said.

"*What?*" she screamed, yanking her arm away.

"I don't know what you're talkin' about, but I'm not after anybody else," I lied yet again. "It's just that everything's been happening so fast lately. I'm sorry if I led you to believe that I'm ready to get back together tonight. That wasn't my intention—I didn't stop to think how this invitation would make you feel, and I'm sorry about that. Forgive me?"

She stared at me coldly. Something had definitely changed in the last few days.

"Forgive you? Sure, I'll forgive you. Now, you forgive *me* when I say I can't stand the sight of you, and that I'm goin' home. Alone!"

31

Angeline Devereaux was in high spirits and ready to travel. The Marshals had placed her in a safe house near Bayou Lafourche, an old fishing lodge about forty-five miles south of New Orleans.

That had been almost three weeks ago, and she was getting a bad case of cabin fever. The area was beautiful, and had a certain rustic charm, but it was definitely not her cup of tea. Her spacious room overlooking the water was fine, but the place was far too secluded.

Still, her plan to bring down that runt Joey and his creepy father was turning out so well, she was the happiest she'd been since she had fallen for the jerk. Of course, now she knew that her former joy was a delusion brought on by the sense of danger, and the lure of the Carrabba fortune, and she was resolved to make the sonofabitch pay for using her like one of his crack whores.

Today was just the beginning. Seeing the Carrabbas in prison would be the big payoff, and Angeline was buzzing in anticipation of what the next few days would bring.

The Marshals had been very accommodating in getting her what she needed, but she wasn't allowed to do anything. You can only play so much gin rummy and watch so much television before you go nuts. She had to get out of the remote lodge before she lost her mind.

The plan was to take her to a motel just outside Metairie, and keep her safe from those Mob creeps until it was her turn to testify. The head guy told her that it might be weeks before she got her turn, but Angeline was ready to wait as long as it took.

No sorry excuse for a man like Joey Carrabba was going to get away with dumping Angeline Michelle Devereaux. It was almost orgasmic when she pictured herself watching him squirm as she took the stand.

Leaving her family and starting a new life in the witness protection program might be difficult at first, but one of the main reasons she'd wanted to marry the little scumbag was to get away from her mother.

Her father's death four years ago had transformed her mom into a bitter, mean-spirited drunk who took out her pain and frustrations on her only child. *Mother could go to hell* as far as she was concerned, *and the sooner the better.* Angeline was the perfect candidate for the witness program, and could hardly wait to see where her next home would be, and find out about her new name and phony background.

She was hoping for a northern destination where it wasn't so damn hot all the time, maybe Colorado or Utah so she could learn to ski. She daydreamed while watching the TV in the safe house greatroom, seeing herself surrounded by snow-covered mountains and handsome ski bums. Colorado would be just the place for an eighteen-year old blonde Southern Belle like Angeline Devereaux. Hopefully, they would provide her with a name as classy as the one her Daddy had given her.

Dan Hester, one of the Marshals who played gin with her, knocked on her door at eleven p.m., and told her to be downstairs in five minutes. The motorcade that was to take her to her new digs had arrived. They were moving out at night so their movements would be harder to trace.

Angeline had packed her things into a single bag hours ago, and breathlessly told Dan she'd be ready in less than a minute. He laughed at the excitement in her voice, and said he'd see her down there.

As she walked out into the humid heat of the evening, she gazed at the nearby well-lit docks jutting into the bayou, and smelled the marsh air and the pine trees—she couldn't wait for her new life to begin. How many people get a second chance like this, she wondered.

Angeline took one last look at the old lodge that had been her home for these past several days, and walked towards the van that sat in the middle of a line of seven vehicles of varying shapes and sizes. She hadn't felt this safe and secure since Daddy died, she thought.

Marshal Andy Moore opened the sliding door of the van for her, winking and smiling as he took her hand and helped her step up into the backseat. She was thinking of snowy Colorado afternoons as Andy climbed into the driver's seat. He looked back and gave her the thumbs-up signal.

When he turned the key, the van exploded in a fireball that sent flames fifty feet into the air, igniting the Spanish moss hanging from the old oaks, and spreading through the branches swiftly. The sound of the blast echoed down the dark waters of the bayou and into the woods.

Smoking debris from the demolished vehicle lay scattered in all directions. The flames from the moss soon ignited the pines, and burning branches cracked and fell on the old, dry roof of the ancient lodge, which caught quickly.

Within five minutes, the entire area was on fire, lighting up the night sky. A brisk breeze blowing in from the marsh fanned the flames, making any attempt to contain them impossible.

No one's training had included firefighting. The only extinguishers were in the now-burning lodge, or in the trunks of the cars. Besides, they would have been useless against the rapidly escalating flames of the inferno.

All the occupants of the van, Angeline, Andy, Dan, and Marshal Glenda Wood, were unrecognizably incinerated. Some of their charred remnants would later be found as far as fifty yards away from the ashes of the van.

Identification was impossible for many of the body parts, so they were bagged and divided equally among the remains that could be identified. The dazed Marshals who were left alive finally recovered their stunned senses, running about trying to escape the out-of-control blaze, and calling for help from every quarter.

The fire raged through the bayou for hours until enough fire trucks could reach the remote area to contain the inferno. Mercifully, rain began to fall not long after the trucks arrived.

32

I WAS GLAD THAT PENNY AND I HAD DRIVEN TO THE RESTAURANT SEPARATELY. The thought of driving her home in the state she was in made my stomach churn.

The look in her eyes was something I had never seen before, and the tone of her voice was too—cold, hard, and mean. The woman who had just chewed me out on the boardwalk wasn't the Penny I knew and loved. This was a completely different lady. Something definitely had changed in the last few days.

Once when we broke up, she drove all night to her parents' house and stayed a week, never even bothering to make contact until she returned to Gulf and called in sick to work. I was so mad at her, I briefly considered firing her, but who was I going to find in town that could do her job as well as she could?

When she finally showed up for work, we both acted as if nothing had happened. That was as mad as I'd ever seen her, until tonight. I wondered if she'd show up for work tomorrow as I turned into my apartment lot, and parked the cruiser.

Inside, the first thing I did was position my gun on the bedside table in case I had more nighttime visitors. Then I made sure everything was locked up tight, and looked in the closets before I took a deep breath and relaxed. A quick check of the bathroom medicine cabinet confirmed my fear that there were no Tums to be had, so I went into the kitchen and got the baking soda out of the fridge. Old soda that's been absorbing all those refrigerator odors tastes pretty bad, but after mixing a half-spoonful with water and guzzling it, my bilious stomach settled down.

The old Lazyboy beside the couch called out to me, and I lay back in it and stared at the ceiling, trying to make sense of the last few hours. Penny had replaced Shelley for a while as my main concern, so that was one positive. If I had been alone in New Orleans, my obsession with Shelley's welfare might have been unbearable. Relaxing in my old chair helped a little.

I thought about the night, ten or so years ago, when I was channel-surfing and came across a TV show about a poor family that lived on a mountain during the Depression. It was a big family, lots of kids and the parents and grandparents all living together.

The son was having trouble with his girlfriend, and asked his father to explain women to him.

The conversation went something like this:

"Pa, I just don't understand why Janie would act this way. Is there a secret to handling women? I mean, what do they want?"

"Son, there's only one thing you need to know about women."

"What's that, Pa?"

"I don't know, son."

That pretty much sums it up.

Another thought that entered my mind was how different things would have turned out if Solly had been there when the intruders came. I laughed at the picture in my mind of my old dog wagging his tail and searching for treats in the interlopers' pockets as they tossed the joint. The only problem they would've had with Solly would be trying to toss the place while he sniffed their pants.

It was way past my bedtime, so after a while I got up and brushed my teeth, debating whether or not to call Penny. I picked up my bedside phone, put it down, picked it up again, and finally placed it back on the receiver before undressing and climbing into bed.

Tomorrow would come soon enough, and I'd be back in her good graces before long.

I hoped.

***

Penny slammed the front door behind her, and stormed into the kitchen of the beach cottage. She stood in the dark and looked out the window at the ocean, at the same moonlight that she had shared with Coop just moments ago out at the end of the pier.

As large clouds moved across the face of the moon, and summer lightning flashed near the house and far out to sea, she hoped for a rainstorm. It always made her feel better when a cooling summer rain came through Gulf Front.

She loved to fall asleep with the steady rapping of raindrops on the tin roof of the small beach bungalow her Uncle Stan had built ten years ago. Uncle Stan had subsequently taken a job on Wall Street and moved to New York City five years ago, and rented the small house to Penny for a ridiculously low price. She never would have been able to afford a beachfront place otherwise. She often thought gratefully of her uncle's wealth and good heart.

However, at that moment she wasn't thinking of how lucky she was to be living by the ocean, or about her uncle's generosity. Her anger diminished as she watched the lightning put on a show, and she thought of trying to live by the ocean without Chief Samuel Cooper in her life.

Penny had never really confronted the thought of losing him forever. Each time they separated, she fully expected to be back together with him soon, and every time she had been proven correct.

But this time seemed different somehow. The look on Coop's face when he had apologized for sending her mixed signals—she'd never seen that look before. It was as if he had already moved on, and she was no longer a part of his future plans. It was a look of pity.

She felt the sadness wash over her, but didn't have the strength to cry. She just stared out at the dark ocean as the lightning flashes filled the tiny kitchen.

33

I SHOWED UP AT MATTHEWS FOR BREAKFAST AS USUAL, AND AFTER fielding a few questions about New Orleans and the murders, found myself the butt of a couple dozen Frankenstein jokes about my disfigured face.

I decided not to tell them that what they really wanted to say was that I looked like Frankenstein's monster—then I would have been the butt of "Professor" and "Genius" jokes as well. It had been a good couple of days for the old boys at Matthews—first Adam's nose, then my face. Like Adam, I took my verbal beating with a smile, finished eating, and left to the loud amusement of all.

At the office, Doreen came out from behind her desk, looked me over, and said, "I heard it was bad, but it looks even worse than I expected. Are you gonna be in shape to give me away? Can I get you anything?"

"No thanks, I'm fine. I'll be ready and able for the wedding. Any calls?"

"No, but I have a request. Or an order, I should say. I got your dress uniform dry-cleaned for you to wear tomorrow. It's hangin' in your office." When she saw my look of disgust, she added, "You're wearin' the thing, so just act happy about it."

Giving away Doreen in my usual jeans and shirt would be seen as rude, not to mention, lead to my death, so I nodded and walked back to my office. To tell the truth, I don't really mind wearing the uniform every ten years or so—I have to keep up appearances, so to speak.

I only hoped it still fit.

Right on cue, Doreen called out, "I had the pants taken out a coupla inches."

I was really going to miss her.

***

Penny had come and gone already, and was patrolling the highway that leads into town. If it was anybody else, I would have pitied the poor soul who got collared by a spurned female officer on that beautiful summer's day. But Penny never lets her personal life interfere with her job, so the only person who would've had a problem with Officer Prevost on that morning was me.

I busied myself by catching up on the paperwork that had piled up on my already cluttered desk while I'd been gone. I despise paperwork, but it was a welcome relief from fixating on Shelley. The only problem was that my concentration wandered and I spilled my entire cup of coffee onto a stack of unfinished papers that were due on the governor's desk in two days. I begged for Doreen, and she came and saved me, assuring me that she had two copies of everything in her file cabinet. Rescued again by my trusty secretary.

As she was digging in her cabinet, line one on the phone rang. I yelled that I'd get it, pushed the button, and said, "Gulf Front police station, Chief Cooper speaking."

Neal asked, "Okay, what'd you do with Doreen?"

"Nothin', man," I laughed. "She's lookin' through her files, savin' my tail again. I couldn't live without her." I felt a pang as I realized that I would be very soon. "What's happening?"

"I got some news," he said.

"Please tell me it's good news this time."

"Sorry," he said. "My contact with the Marshals, Ron Ferguson, called me five minutes ago. Our witness, Angeline Devereaux, was barbecued on the bayou last night. A bomb was planted in the van they were gonna use to transport her to a new safe house, and the fire caused by the explosion completely burned up about five or six acres before they got it under control. The van had been sittin' there overnight, and a remote-controlled bomb must have been put in it. She could just wait safely out of view 'til everyone was in the van, then boom."

"She?" I asked.

"Yeah. Ferguson's convinced that the Carrabbas finally got to one of the Marshals. A young woman who had been assigned to Angeline and was there that night has vanished from the face of Louisiana. There was no way somebody from the outside could've penetrated the perimeter they had set up out there. Obviously, it was an inside job, and this babe's the only one unaccounted for from the group. She's probably in the *Mob's* protection program now, out of the country enjoyin' the money they paid her. Either that—or she sleeps with the gators."

"Very clever line, Detective. How long did it take you to come up with that?"

"Been waitin' years to use that one, bud. Oh, and it gets better."

"Oh, no," I groaned.

"Oh, yes, my friend. Guess what's disappeared from the Marshals' backyard? And guess who had access to it?"

"I don't wanna guess . . . just tell me."

"The tapes that the Marshals made of Joey Carrabba spillin' his guts to Angeline about his and Big Daddy's crimes have turned up missing," Neal said.

"Let me make a wild speculation . . . the same female Marshal who vanished had access to those tapes."

"Bingo."

"Neal, I want you to listen to me now. Stop callin' me unless you have good news. I'm *really* tired of bad news and worse people. Everybody you know is a bad guy. I might as well be back in narcotics."

"Hey, bud, those are the breaks. But honestly, I can't remember a case that had so many problems and dead ends. This is gettin' ridiculous. Speakin' of ridiculous, how's your face? You feelin' any better? When can you come back and help me get nowhere fast with all this crap?"

"You don't need me to get nowhere fast with this crap. You can do that all by yourself. I'm thinkin' about retiring from law enforcement altogether, and becoming a sparring partner for Tyson."

"Well, you certainly have the face for it. Really, when are you comin' back?"

"As soon as you call and tell me that you know who killed Caroline Quitman and Cecil Harwell, and that Shelley's back, safe and sound."

"Oh yeah, about Shelley. You never did tell me why she called *you* the night she got snatched. Why didn't she call the FBI office here, or even me? Why did she call the gray-haired old man from Florida?"

I backpedaled: "She—she said—she said my business card just happened to be closest at that moment. We all exchanged cards and numbers when we met on the pier the first day."

"Oh. I guess that makes sense. What did she want to know?"

"She was just checkin' to see if you and me had found out anything new that we were maybe keeping to ourselves. You know, anything we might've heard on the street. Anyway, until she's found, and Cecil and Caroline's killers are caught, I think I'll just stay here in Gulf and do the job the people of this burg pay me to do," I said.

"You quittin' on me, bud?"

"Yes, Neal, I'm quittin' on you. You don't really need me there. Besides, the mental and physical strain of all this is more than I can handle. It's not like the old days. On top of all that, Penny hates me, I don't have my dog anymore, every part of my body hurts, and my face is all purple and swollen and beat to hell. And, I had to put up with a million jokes at breakfast this mornin' about my new look. It's all drivin' me nuts, and I've reached my limit. What's more, I need to get things here in Gulf back in some kind of order. I didn't leave Tallahassee just to go through this kind of garbage all over again. Somebody tossed my apartment while I was gone, I got the wedding tomorrow, and last but certainly not least, I'm feelin' guilty as all hell about Lucy and Shelley. Joking aside, I'm too old for all this. I just can't take it anymore."

Neal sighed, and said, "Well, I guess you gotta do what you gotta do. Or not gotta do what you gotta not do, or however the hell you say it." He paused for a moment, and then asked, "So...when will you be back?"

"Tomorrow afternoon."

34

After Neal and I hung up, I took the copy of my report from Doreen when she brought it in, and settled down at my desk to finish it.

I was filling out the section regarding requests for resources when Penny called in. There had been a bad accident out on highway 97, involving a tractor-trailer and a new red Corvette. I prayed that it wasn't the Milo Twins.

My prayer wasn't answered.

The Milo Boys were seventeen year-old twins from the wealthiest family in Gulf Front. Rob and Roy were well known for several reasons, reckless driving among them. I had ticketed Rob for driving in excess of a hundred and twenty miles per hour just two days before Caroline Quitman's body had shown up on the pier.

The state patrol had set up a blockade on the old post road that runs parallel to the main drag in town. As usual, the twins were together, so it was actually like ticketing them both, which was the way it always happened.

These would be their last offenses, but you can't arrest dead men. Or boys.

***

When I arrived at the scene of the accident, Penny was talking to a state trooper by the side of the highway. They were standing at the spot where the Corvette had left the asphalt and wrapped around a large pine tree twenty or so feet off the road.

She glanced at me, and went back to her conversation as if I was just another cop on duty. I deserved it, but it didn't make it any easier to take.

I walked over and introduced myself to the trooper, and asked what they knew about the wreck so far. Penny said with a quiver in her voice what she hadn't wanted to say over the scanner, that it was indeed the Milo Twins, and that the bodies were horribly damaged, their faces destroyed.

The state trooper asked about my stitched and bruised face, and I gave him my now standard line that it was not as bad as it looked.

Then he said that the driver of the tractor-trailer had been taken to the county hospital after telling the trooper and Penny that the boys had run smack into him as he came around a curve, bounced off, and left the road. He said it was as if they did it deliberately because the driver—Roy—had made no attempt to avoid him.

In my opinion, the absolute worst part of my, or any other policeman's job, is notifying the parents that their children were dead.

Being that they were the Milos' only children made it even more difficult. I can't imagine what it must feel like to lose a child, much less two, especially when there was no one to blame but the kids themselves.

The twins were also well known for drinking to excess, and three words described their driving style—Speed, speed, speed.

The medical report would later prove that they were both hopelessly drunk; in fact, they each carried three times the legal limit in their now-mangled bodies. That explained why Roy had made no move to avoid the sixteen-wheeler. They never saw what hit 'em. Literally.

Their father, Spencer Milo, is the richest man in Gulf Front, and the entire Florida panhandle for that matter. His grandfather, Franklin Milo, had been one of the first to buy up Florida real estate back when it was practically being given away.

Franklin acquired thousands of acres throughout the state, buying and selling and then buying and selling more, increasing his wealth with each transaction. Franklin Milo could have settled down almost anywhere in the state, but chose the Gulf Front area for his home, declaring it "the finest beach in all of Florida." He was the Founding Father of Gulf Front in 1948, establishing the first businesses and building the first homes. He eventually bought up all the land that makes up our town, and many more acres surrounding it.

By 1964, Franklin Milo was worth almost a billion dollars, a big deal back in those days. When he died of heart failure in 1974, his fortune passed on to Spencer's father, Calvin. Then, early one morning in 1987, Calvin had a stroke while swimming in the ocean, and drowned right in front of the family compound. The fortune then passed on to Spencer, and today he owns everything in sight as his father and grandfather once did.

It's rumored that the Milo fortune has now grown to several billion dollars. One look at the huge Milo beachfront estate and compound and it's easy to imagine the rumors are true.

I haven't had much contact with Spencer Milo over the years, but he seems nice enough. His attorney always bailed out the twins when they got in trouble with the juvenile authorities, or us, which was often. It's actually a wonder that they had managed to make it to the age of seventeen, considering their wild behavior.

Still, they were just kids. The thought of my impending visit to see their parents made me ill, and I stayed a little longer at the scene than I might have, avoiding the inevitable.

The drive to the estate took fifteen minutes, as it is located on the western border of town, and the accident had occurred seven miles east. On the way over, I practiced my speech, even going so far as to speak out loud. It all sounded too pat, too rehearsed, so I decided to just say whatever I felt when the moment came.

One of the few things I know about Spencer Milo is that he's enjoyed poor health for years, and spends most of his time at the compound, so I wasn't surprised to find him on the lawn beside the big main house chipping golf balls.

He looked up when he saw me turn into the drive with the worried yet resigned look of a man who knew what the presence of a police vehicle meant. He watched intently as I pulled up, no doubt preparing mentally for more news that his boys were in some kind of trouble.

"Hello, Mr. Milo," I said as I stepped out of my cruiser.

"Hello, Chief. What in blue blazes happened to your face?"

"It's really nothing sir . . . I . . ."

"What have the boys done now?" he said with a frown, squinting in the mid-morning sun.

"I'm terribly sorry to have to tell you this, sir. They—they were killed in an accident on highway 97 about an hour ago."

He fainted on the spot, crumpling to his knees before falling over onto the beautifully manicured grass.

I called to the gardener to help me, and we carried him into the house, depositing him gently on the leather sofa in his large study.

The stout housekeeper appeared, saw what was happening, and left the room for a minute. She returned with a damp washcloth, and placed the cloth on his forehead as we waited for him to come out of it.

"Does this happen often?" I asked the housekeeper, Clara.

"Yeah, it happens all the time. He has a real weak heart. That's why he plays golf in the yard instead of going to the club. His blood pressure is dangerously high, and the doctor told him he has to take it easy, especially during the hot summer months. The family hardly ever leaves Gulf Front anymore. If you don't mind me asking, did you get in a fight or something?"

"I'm fine. Just a scuffle."

She looked back at Milo, and asked, "What brings you out here today, Chief?"

"I'm afraid I have bad news. The twins were killed in a car accident this morning."

Clara didn't faint. She looked as if she had been expecting to hear those words for a long time.

After a moment had passed, she said, "I always heard that only the good die young. Guess you can't believe everything you hear."

That said, she turned and went back to her duties as if I'd told her that the goldfish was floating upside down in the large glass bowl by the window.

The gardener had also returned to his work, so it was now just Mr. Milo and me in the darkly paneled room. I hoped the lady of the house would take the news better.

As I was thinking of how to soften the blow, Mrs. Milo came into the room, weeping quietly. Someone, probably Clara, had informed her of her sons' deaths.

The former Dawn Dalton of Orlando, Mrs. Spencer Milo was second runner-up in the Miss America Pageant in 1984, representing Florida. Two months after Atlantic City, she was married to Spencer and living in Gulf Front. The twins came along two years later. She's still quite beautiful, and very involved in what there is of a social scene in our town.

"My deepest condolences, Mrs. Milo," I said. "If there's anything I can do, please don't hesitate to ask."

I wished someone would come up with something better to say at times like these.

"Thank you, Chief Cooper," she said, standing straighter as if preparing to walk a runway. "My husband and I appreciate your coming to tell us yourself. It's better to hear this kind of news from someone you know, rather than to hear it on the TV or the radio. I'm sure my husband will . . ."

She ran out of gas, and just stopped speaking and stared at her reclining husband. I don't think she really saw him. She seemed as unconscious as he was. It was truly uncomfortable, but my discomfort was nothing compared to the grief the two of them felt.

Milo finally stirred after a couple of minutes of painful silence, and opening his eyes, asked, "Dawn, why is Chief Cooper here?"

Mrs. Milo turned and walked elegantly from the room without saying a word. If she'd had a book on her head, it wouldn't have moved an inch.

"Mr. Milo, I came because of the accident the twins were in this morning, remember?"

"Oh, God, I was hoping there was some kind of a mistake about that. Did I pass out again?"

"Yes sir, on the lawn. Hector and I brought you in. Are you feeling all right? I mean..."

"Yes, Chief. Physically I'm okay. The boys never came home last night. I was waiting for them outside. I had made a decision to send them away to a military school in Tennessee for their senior year. They were driving their mother to an early . . ."

Now he was out of gas, too.

I helped him to a sitting position and asked, "Is there was anything I can do to help?"

"No, Chief, thank you, but there's nothing you can do right now."

"A glass of water, maybe?"

"No, thank you. Well, perhaps," he said. "Clara—Clara!" he called.

A few long seconds later, Clara appeared at the door.

"Yes, sir?"

"Would you bring a pitcher of water, two glasses, and my heart medicine."

It was more of a command than a request.

"Coming right up, sir," she said in a tone that made me wonder how often she spat in the water pitcher.

I decided to wait 'til later for liquid refreshment.

35

Mr. Milo held his head in his hands as we waited for Clara to bring the heart medicine. I stood by quietly, looking at the floor. I wanted to leave, but felt that I should make sure he was okay first.

Clara entered and put a tray containing the water pitcher, a vial of pills, and two glasses on the table next to the sofa, saying nothing as she turned and left. Milo took a pill with some water, and asked if I wanted a glass. I declined.

"Chief . . . thank you for coming out and telling us. It would have been far worse to have heard it on the news, I don't think Dawn could've handled that."

"Mr. Milo, this is the worst part of my job. Thank you for your kind words. I just hope that in time you and Mrs. Milo can find some peace of mind about this."

Standing, Milo asked, "Chief, can you wait here for a few minutes while I go upstairs and wash my face? I'd like to get your advice on a few things regarding the funeral arrangements and so forth."

"Sure thing, sir. Take your time. I'll be right here."

"Thank you. I won't be a minute."

As he left, my eyes wandered to a grouping of photographs on the wall behind his desk. I walked over for a better view, and was immediately impressed by the people in the pictures.

There was a black-and-white shot of the Milos with President and Nancy Reagan at the White House, the Milos with President and Barbara Bush at the White House, and a color photo of Spencer and Bill Gates playing cards on a huge yacht. Everyone was smiling in all the shots, and it made me sad to think of how long it would be before smiles would be seen around the Milo compound again.

There were more pictures of the Milos with sports stars, Hollywood types, and politicians great and small. I spent five or six minutes looking at them before I came to a photo that took me by surprise—Spencer Milo and the twins, posed with Harry James Quitman and Caroline out on the beach. Their backs were to the huge house, and they all had their arms around each other, the adults leaning down and looking into the camera, everyone with a big smile on their face.

I estimated the picture to be about ten or twelve years old, judging by the ages of Caroline and the boys. I was considering the relevance of the photograph to the case when Milo walked back into the study, wiping his face with a hand towel.

"Dawn makes me put all those pictures up, Chief. Seems to me to be sort of like name-dropping, but I give her what she wants, within reason. I'm sure you understand. Like my grandfather always said, 'You can lose the small battles, but always win the big ones.' I don't know if she can take losing the boys," he said, staring at another photo of the twins standing beside a shark they'd caught.

"Yes sir, I agree with your granddad on that. I try and pick my battles, too."

"You know, I don't believe I've ever met your wife, Chief."

"Neither have I, sir," I said, smiling in an attempt to take his mind off of the twins.

It didn't work.

"Those boys were the center of Dawn's whole world. She's upstairs in bed with the curtains drawn. I expect she won't be much help in making the funeral arrangements, and to tell you the truth, I won't be any help at all. One good thing about having money is that you can pay to have some of the unpleasant parts of life taken care of by other people. I wanted to ask if you think there's a chance we could have open caskets? I don't remember if you said how bad the crash was. In fact, I don't remember much of anything you said before I passed out."

I said quietly, in an attempt to soften the blow, "Sir, they were hit head-on and left the road at a high rate of speed. I'll get back to you as soon as I'm certain, but I think it might be best to have closed caskets." I was already certain. Changing the subject, I asked, "How well do you know Senator Quitman?"

"Oh, I've known Harry James for many years, Chief. Caroline used to baby-sit the boys while we were out on the boat."

The "boat" is a two-hundred-foot yacht that Milo keeps docked at a Pensacola marina. Once owned by Aristotle Onassis, it's one of the finest yachts in Florida, if not the world.

"What did y'all do on the boat?" I asked.

Smiling weakly, he said, "We would sail out past the three-mile limit and play high-stakes poker. That's the reason we never speak anymore."

"I'm sorry. You said you don't speak anymore?"

"Right. I caught him dealing off the bottom of the deck during a hand of five-card stud. I waited 'til the game was over, took him aside, and told him never to show his face in Gulf Front again. That was ten years ago, when that photo was taken. I remember because that summer was the twins' seventh birthday, and seven has always been my lucky number. I know that's a pretty lame choice for a lucky number, but I've never been too original, Chief. What I have comes from being born, not from being original."

I didn't know what to say to that, so I just waited for him to continue.

He didn't. He just stared at the picture of the twins and the shark, his eyes watering until tears began to flow down his cheeks.

I touched his shoulder, and said how sorry I was, before I quietly walked out and left him alone with his bad heart and his grief.

***

Back in the office, I wondered if the connection between Milo and Senator Quitman had anything to do with Caroline's murder, or if it was just a coincidence. Did her body end up on the Gulf Front pier merely by chance?

I also thought about Milo's story of Quitman cheating at cards. Harry James was turning out to be a first-class SOB from all accounts. Cheating at a friendly game of cards? When you're already filthy rich?

I'm a poker player, have been since I was nine, and I play with some friends whenever we can scare up a game. Unlike my days in Tallahassee, that means every couple of months. The thought of one of my poker buddies swindling me out of a pot, no matter how small, made me see red.

I decided that Senator Quitman would go down with all the

other bad guys in New Orleans if I had any say in the matter.

After a few minutes, Doreen came in and said, "Penny called and said she'll be on patrol if anybody wants her."

She looked at me as if she was waiting for me to tell her *I* wanted Penny, but I just gazed dumbly at her until she muttered something under her breath and stomped out of my office.

I smiled at Doreen's attempt to steer me right in the love department, looked out the big windows at the waves coming in, and mentally prepared for the next round of battle in New Orleans.

My resolve strengthened, Cecil Harwell's and Caroline Quitman's killers were in big trouble. Not only that, I was going to find Shelley, or die trying.

Maybe both.

36

IT HAD TAKEN HARRY JAMES YEARS TO TALK HIS WAY INTO THE BIGGEST cash poker game in New Orleans, as the Carrabba Family was very particular about who was allowed to play in it. The game was strictly invitation-only, and there was usually a connection of some kind between the player and the Family.

More often than not the invited guests had done favors of one kind or another for Don Carmine, or knew someone who had, or were being courted by the Don or his capos in order that they might perform a favor in the future.

A few of the players were very rich men who craved the danger and could be counted on to drop huge amounts of currency. There were winners, but as in any organized gambling endeavor, the losers outnumbered them. The Family charged an admission fee and took a percentage of every pot, so it was a very lucrative enterprise.

Many a rich fool had first become heavily indebted to The Don over the years while sitting in at this game, and some had never recovered from the crushing weight of the "vigorish," the weekly interest payment. Businesses vanished, families dissolved, and in more that a few cases, lives were lost due to the inability of the losing player to pay back what he owed. Once you were under the thumb of The Carrabbas, you stayed.

There were three underground Carrabba games in the vicinity of New Orleans, and Harry James had patronized each of them. This, however, would be his first time playing in the biggest of them all.

Three days earlier, as the Senator left his daughter's funeral, a dark-haired young man had stopped him and whispered an invitation. The first thing Harry James did when he arrived in Washington was make a beeline for his bank near the Capitol. There, he withdrew what he thought would be enough to keep him in the game all night, two hundred thousand dollars. His banker, an old crony from back in the days of Harry James's first political campaign, made the necessary arrangements and the tax collectors were none the wiser.

The second thing Harry James did was make an appointment with Louisiana's governor in Baton Rouge, ostensibly to discuss a pet project of the governor's. After flying down for the meeting, he was met after dark and driven to New Orleans for the game in a car supplied by the Carrabba family.

Less than a hundred hours after burying his only child, Harry James Quitman was finally sitting down at the table he had dreamed of for so long. He won the first three pots, each bigger than the last. A straight to the Ace, a set of nines, and a Jack-high flush had won him about three hundred thousand bucks in less than twenty minutes.

The rush he felt was why he had always wanted to play in the "Whale Game." There are big fish, and then there are whales. Harry James knew that only the highest rollers were allowed to play in this game, and his first attempt looked very promising indeed.

Another item that looked very promising was the young redheaded thing that kept coming into the large card room and catching his eye with a devilish smile. Dressed in a little black dress and heels, she couldn't be over twenty years old, he thought.

After the game, win or lose, she was the next thing on the evening's agenda. But for now, a hot streak with these players at this table was a big enough thrill for Harry James.

The game was Texas Hold 'Em, and Harry James showed his best poker face as he looked at his two hole cards and saw a pair of Aces.

Another monster hand!

They might not ever let him come back if he kept raking in every pot, he thought, but a guy has to play the cards he's dealt.

"Open for ten thousand," he said, and tried to keep his voice cool. He didn't want to scare the suckers away.

Only one of the men called the bet, and the dealer dealt the flop.

Three sevens.

That gave Harry a full house. The bastard who had called his bet was now ripe for the picking. The man was a pro from Dallas, and acted like he knew every damn thing there is to know about hold 'em. Well, Harry James was about to deliver a lecture on how the game was supposed to be played.

"Twenty-five thousand," Harry said, trying hard not to smile.

"Raise a hundred thousand," Dallas said calmly.

Harry paused, and checked his hole cards. Still two Aces. Was this clown crazy? Bluffing? Could he have drawn the other two Aces? Maybe the guy had a high pair, too, but Harry James decided that the pro was betting on pressuring him with a bluff, or outdrawing him, so he coolly said, "Call."

Let the guy hang himself, and then clobber him on the last card.

The next card was a King. Harry James bet twenty-five thousand again, and Dallas immediately raised another hundred thousand!

Harry James looked at his cash, which was dwindling fast, stared at the pro for a full thirty seconds, and then called the bet. He now had less than two hundred-fifty thousand dollars left.

The fifth and final card came up, and it was another Ace. Harry knew for sure that his full house was the higher of the two, so he said, "All in."

Dallas smiled, and said, "I call, Senator. Whatcha got?"

Harry James proudly turned over his hole cards and announced, "Aces full of sevens."

The pro smiled again, and turned over the six and seven of spades.

Four sevens.

Harry swallowed hard as he watched all of his money being picked up by the Dallas bastard. Harry James's lecture on poker was finished, and he needed a drink.

Forcing a laugh, he stood up and reached over to shake the hand of the man who had just gutted him like a carp. Dallas smiled and said it was a pleasure to play cards with a senator, and Harry James felt like strangling the smug sonofabitch, but he'd never learned how to fight or use violence.

One thing he *had* learned in his political career was how to handle public humiliation and embarrassment, which came in handy at that particular moment.

He loudly said his goodnights, blustering about "win-some-lose-some," trying his best to act as if losing hundreds of thousands of dollars meant nothing to a man like Senator Harry James Quitman. He then headed for the bar in the parlor, searching out his next objective.

The redhead was sitting on a sofa with her back to the senator, drinking a martini. Harry James ordered a Wild Turkey on the rocks, took a sip, and sauntered over and asked her if he could sit down.

"Why, I'd be honored, Senator Quitman," she said in a pure New Orleans drawl. "How'd you do in the game tonight?"

"Well, darlin', I lost a little money, but I'm sure you could ease my pain." He gave her an oily smile, and without a word, she stood and walked into one of the back bedrooms. Harry James loosened his tie, and followed. No one in the house paid them any attention—the game went on as it had for over forty years. The girls had always been there for the players, and they always would be.

The redhead turned off the overhead light, but left the lamp by the bed on. She slid out of her dress, and stood before Harry James in her bra and panties.

"Damn," he said, pulling off his tie and dropping it on the floor. "You sure make losin' a lot easier to take."

"That's what I'm here for, darlin'," she said huskily, and walked over and began unbuttoning the senator's shirt.

"Lemme help you with that," he said, and soon was down to his boxers and undershirt.

The redhead knelt before him, and soon had control of the situation, her mouth surprising Harry James. The working girls put a condom on him before doing their jobs, but not this young thing.

"Ohhh," said the senator as he felt the tension building. This girl was a pro, and he gave in to the feeling.

She suddenly stood, and kissed him deeply, another thing the other girls would never do; Harry James couldn't believe his luck had changed so dramatically in the last few minutes. "Unlucky in cards, lucky in love," he thought.

He didn't notice the four small video cameras taping their every move and catching every groan.

The redhead slowly drew away from the kiss, and unhurriedly removed her bra. Two small, but perfect breasts made Harry smile and unconsciously lick his lips.

She then removed her panties, and Harry James stopped breathing for a second.

The redhead was most definitely a man.

Stunned, the senator stared at the proof, unable to speak for the first time in years. His first thought was how much his political rivals would have loved to see him mute. Harry James was known for long-winded speeches, and his seemingly boundless capacity for streams of meaningless rhetoric.

Not now, though.

The redhead silently took his hand and led him over to the bed, where Harry James took his first walk on the wild side.

37

THE NIGHT BEFORE DOREEN'S WEDDING WAS NOT ONE TO REMEMBER.

The afternoon had passed without any other remarkable or depressing events, and I left the office early and took home a calzone and a salad from Frankie's. After chow, I tried to watch a couple of movies, but still uncomfortably sore from the bar fight, was unable to concentrate for more than a few minutes at a time, and eventually gave up on them both. Then I spent half an hour trying to write some heartfelt stuff to say to Doreen at the wedding, but came up with nothing.

After that, I obsessed over the details of Caroline's case for a while, which didn't take long since I only had a few details to obsess over. I knew the Carrabba family was responsible for Caroline's death, as well as Cecil Harwell's, but that wasn't exactly a news flash.

I wasted more time wondering if Shelley was dead or alive. I fully expected Neal to call at any moment and tell me that parts of Shelley's dismembered body had been found scattered around D.C., and her severed head had been discovered spiked on top of the Washington Monument. But no one called, and I called no one.

The only good thing about the night was that I didn't have any bad dreams. It's hard to dream when you're staring at the dresser mirror across from your bed half the night like the witch in Snow White.

When my alarm beeped at 4:45 A.M., I found myself between dreams and light sleep, nowhere near ready for the big day. The only good thing about the sunrise wedding was that I'd be able to rent a car and get on the road by eleven at the latest, after the small reception wrapped up. There was going to be some kind of music, and breakfast would be served to the twenty or more friends and family members.

Lying there in the dark, I figured I could keep my eyes closed for a few minutes before getting out of bed. Big mistake. When I opened them again, it was 5:24. I had hoped to leave by 5:30, since Doreen had let me skip rehearsals, and I wanted to be there early enough for her to at least tell me where to stand.

I got up as quickly as my soreness would allow, and having no time for a shower, washed my face and pits and brushed my teeth in a flash. I dressed carefully, not in my dress uniform, which was still taunting me from its hook on the back of my office door, and went to the kitchen where I slammed a big glass of chocolate milk and two cold strawberry Pop-Tarts. It was 5:31 when I forced my cranky and sleepy self out the door and towards the station.

Driving in the pre-dawn moonlight I could see big rain clouds forming out over the gulf. All signs pointed to a dreary day, but I knew Doreen would think it was the most beautiful one on record, and that made me smile in spite of the weather conditions. I rolled down the windows and breathed deeply, trying to get my mojo working, and within seconds, my mood was close to cheerful.

The wedding was to take place on the beach behind the station, and I wondered what a cloudy day meant as far as predicting the success of the nuptials. Losing Doreen had me slightly down, but I was excited at the thought of getting back to New Orleans to work on the cases. Up or down, I just wanted to get through the wedding and reception, and get on the road.

The station was buzzing, the wedding party and guests all showing as much excitement as the early hour allowed. I put on the uniform back in my office— the waist of my pants was a little tight even after being altered—but got rave reviews from everyone but Penny when I came out. My secretary had saved me one final time before heading off into the wilds of matrimony.

The sky never opened, and the dawn was as beautiful as I've ever seen it—yellow, pink, and deep orange, with stripes of light and dark blue clouds. The ceremony went off without a hitch, and Doreen looked like every bride should, that is, deliriously happy. And many in the crowd shed a few tears as she exchanged vows with Mr. Fields.

The Gulf Front Observer sent its only reporter, the lovely young Kelly Ann Rogers, to cover the event. Mike Rogers, Kelly's grandfather, was also in attendance. Mike is the editor of the paper—as well as its only photographer—and I looked forward to seeing Doreen on the front page of the next edition.

Doreen's nephew from Miami played guitar and sang, and after the ceremony, those of us in the wedding party had our picture taken with the sunrise over the Gulf of Mexico as the backdrop. That done, everyone stood around on the beach for a while, talking and laughing as a couple of waiters walked through the crowd serving sparkling water.

Penny, as maid of honor, was stunning in a pale green dress, her hair braided and wrapped around her head like a crown. There were tiny white flowers in the braid, and it was difficult not to stare. Mostly, Penny ignored me, or glared, but one time she looked at me during the vows in a way that made me think she wished it was us standing before the preacher. But that could have been my imagination.

When we all walked up to the station at quarter-till-seven, the group split into smaller ones, and I caught a ride with Adam and Earl. Adam had driven his Jeep Cherokee so we wouldn't have to take the patrol cars. Penny didn't offer me a seat in her Miata, taking Blanche instead, but that was fine. After the other night, I wasn't ready to face her alone just yet, anyway.

The reception breakfast was held at Morrelli's, a seafood restaurant out on the highway twenty minutes west of town. The place doesn't normally serve breakfast, but the owner is a close friend of Doreen's, and opened up especially for her. As a sleepy-looking piano trio played softly in a corner of the big main room, breakfast was served at 7:30.

Even though I was starving, I only ate a moderate amount because I wanted to leave room for a special early lunch I was going to have before leaving town. The food was pretty good, not as good as Matthews, but Morrelli's was a nicer place for a wedding celebration. The band was okay, playing a little bit of everything, and a few couples danced. It was funny to see them yawn and struggle to keep their eyes open on the makeshift dance floor.

Penny was quiet through it all, no longer shooting eye-daggers at me, just ignoring me. It was a little unsettling, seeing as we've always managed to be civil after a breakup, or almost always, and I took her aside.

"What the hey, officer Penny? You ever gonna talk to me again? Or at least acknowledge my presence?"

She scowled for a full five seconds, but was unable to maintain it, and finally a big smile broke out on her gorgeous face, and I knew that things would be okay in the police department, no matter what happened in the romance department.

She said, "I'm never gonna talk to you, or acknowledge your presence, until you admit that weddings can be beautiful."

"Hey, I think weddings are great. I think the institution of marriage is great. In fact, I think anyone who wants to be married belongs in an institution."

Penny punched my sore shoulder, and when I groaned, said, "Oh, I'm so sorry. I forgot."

"Sure you did," I said as I rubbed. "I'm putting you on probation while I'm away."

"So, you're goin' back to New Orleans."

"Yeah, I'm gonna give it one more shot."

She looked at me for a moment and then said, "Say hello to Miss FBI for me when you find her." With that, she turned and walked over to the piano player to make a request.

After breakfast, there were orange juice toasts to the bride and groom. The best man said a few words, Mr. Fields' daughter said a few words, and then it was my turn. I had no idea about wedding protocol, and no speech prepared, so I just spoke from the heart.

I held up my glass, and said, "To the happy bride, or should I say, *delirious* bride: may you be as happy with Jeffery as I've been having you as my partner and guardian angel."

The band struck up "Could I Have This Dance," and the newlyweds took the floor. Doreen locked eyes with me, sobbing as tears streamed down her face.

Either she really liked my speech, or she really hated that song.

***

After the reception, Adam drove me back to my apartment and wished me good luck on my trip. There were now two reasons I had to get back to New Orleans. I needed to take advantage of Neal's position and manpower, because there was obviously very little that

I could accomplish single-handedly in Gulf Front concerning Shelley. Two, I selfishly wanted to be out of town when the Milo Twins were buried. I'd had enough senseless death in the last week to last me for a long while.

The first thing I did was call the only taxi in Gulf Front, and secure its services for later. Then I called Neal's cell, and asked, "Where are you?"

"I'm in my office, where I've been stuck for what seems like forever."

"Sounds like fun. Listen, I'm headin' your way in a while. Will you be there this afternoon?"

"I'll be here most of the day, and into the night. You remember how it works in homicide," he said.

"I almost forgot. I'll see you when I see you."

"Roger and out."

I took a scalding shower, put on jeans and a shirt, and watched ESPN for an hour, waiting for my lunch destination to open. I packed my suitcase and bag again, and locked up when Harold arrived in his salty old sea-battered Ford station wagon at eleven o'clock.

We taxied over to "Big Jim's Bar-Be-Cue," a unique business that rents cars out of the back of a barbecue shack two miles east of downtown. The locals call it "Big Jim's *Car*-Be-Cue."

Big Jim West has five relatively new cars of various sizes that he rents for more than you'd pay at Hertz or Avis, but since the nearest one of those agencies is miles away, no one in Gulf minds paying a little extra. I rent from him every holiday season when I go to visit the Feagins in New Orleans, and since that's where I was heading, it made sense to continue the tradition.

Big Jim is from central Alabama, and his name suits him. He's at least six-feet-five, and I would guess about two hundred and seventy-five pounds, with wild, long, sun-bleached red hair. He's also one of the funniest, nicest people in the world, and cooks the best barbecue I've ever tasted. I can't rent a car from him without also taking out the rack of ribs special. The first thing I always have to do when I arrive at Neal's house is wipe the grease from the steering wheel.

As I entered the smoky, pine-paneled eatery, Big Jim hollered at me from behind the counter in his Gomer Pyle-like voice, "What in the hell happened to yore damn face?"

The dozen or so patrons all turned to look at me, and the ones who hadn't seen me already looked at me with an increasingly familiar combination of sympathy and horror.

"I had a little trouble over in New Orleans," I said, loud enough for everyone to hear. I was completely over any embarrassment I might have felt about my appearance. "Looks a lot worse than it really is."

"By God I hope so," Jim said, and everyone smiled, laughed, or both. "What can I do ye for, Chief?"

"I need a rack and a ride. What's the best car you have available today?"

"Well-sir, I got the two-year-old Buick LeSabre, the three-year-old Ford Taurus, and the brand-new—well, almost brand new—Lincoln Town Car. Take yer pick, they's all ready tuh go."

"I'll take the Lincoln this time. I need some luxury after what I've been through lately."

"Ahh-ite, then," he said, and took off his big sauce-stained apron and placed it on the coat rack next to the cash register. Coming out from behind the counter, he led me down the side hall to the back room where he writes up the rental agreements, and we sat down to business like we had done so many times before. After signing for the Lincoln and getting my usual order of ribs, cole slaw, potato salad, iced tea, and extra napkins, I put my suitcase and bag in the backseat of the Lincoln, and happily headed off for Louisiana, and hopefully, some answers.

38

Penny sat in the rocking chair on her porch, staring at the ocean and listening to the steady rhythm of the waves. Usually the sound of the sea had a calming effect on her, but not today. The reception had turned out to be even more difficult than the wedding, watching Coop and wishing it was their special day. When she had taken off her maid of honor dress, the thought crossed her mind that it might be the closest she'd ever get to being a bride herself. As she gazed at the Gulf, Penny kept seeing the look on his face two nights before when he had said he just wanted the company of a friend.

Her instincts told her that she had already lost him to Agent Brooke, but she refused to believe that there wasn't another chance for them. Even when things had been bad before, they had eventually found their way back to each other, hadn't they?

She went into the kitchen, got a spring water from the fridge, and walked back out and sat on the top step of the porch, sipping slowly from the bottle. She had the next two days off, and was going to take full advantage of her beach house and the wonderful view.

She loosened her braids, and the tiny white flowers fell around her feet. A soft breeze ruffled her long hair, soothing her as she listened to the wind chimes playing their tune in time to the waves' gentle tempo. Coop had given her the chimes as a housewarming gift, and had hung them for her on the side of the porch. Their soft music usually cheered her, but today they only reminded her that she was spending another day without him.

What she really needed was to talk to Coop, to get his advice on her problem as she always could when they were together. The only trouble was that he was the problem.

She had been debating with herself all morning about whether or not she should secretly follow him to New Orleans again, and at that moment, sitting on the step in the ocean breeze, she finally reached her decision: Penny Prevost would never put herself in that humiliating position a second time. She would stay home and forget about the two of them completely.

Besides, if Coop really wanted to have a relationship with Shelley, what could she really do about it? She decided to let him go to New Orleans without her following him like a damned puppy, and if it turned out that he didn't come back to her, well…

Maybe they were never meant to be together after all.

39

Don Carrabba sat alone in his study, sipping his favorite brandy from a crystal snifter, and smoking a huge, hand-rolled Cuban.

Since they no longer had a live witness or taped evidence, the Feds had dropped all pending RICO and murder charges, and he could relax for the first time in weeks.

Joey's crazy ex-fiancé was out of the picture, and the Don's wife had accepted the fact that she would not be seeing her son for quite some time. Don Carmine regretted that he had made Gianna unhappy, but was relieved that his troublesome son would be out of his hair, temporarily at least.

The brandy relaxed him, and as he gazed at the blue clouds of smoke, his mind wandered back to the day that sealed his fate.

The morning long ago that led to his becoming a member of La Cosa Nostra.

He was twenty-three years old, just three years removed from Sicily. Carmine Carrabba would live up to his town's fearsome reputation. In fact, he rose higher in the ranks in America than any other man from his area. He took great pride in the fact that he was the only head of a crime family to come from his hometown.

Unable to speak a word of English, he had arrived in New York City on a steamer after a long tedious voyage. Fifty-two American dollars in his pocket, he gazed happily at his new country for the first time from the deck of the ship on a hot, humid, steamy summer's day.

Carmine had a job waiting in New Orleans, and arrived there three days later after hitchhiking and sleeping in the cheapest motels he could find along the way. He worked in his uncle Giovanni's fish market, and lived in a small apartment down by the docks. Other more lucrative and illegal jobs slowly came his way as he became a familiar figure around the area, and he made contacts with the criminal element that frequented the harbor district.

The morning of his most momentous day, he rose before dawn, put on his only cheap suit and tie, and hurried out of his grimy apartment, too excited and nervous to even consider eating anything.

As he stepped out into the foggy darkness of the waterfront, he ran over the plan in his mind for what seemed like the thousandth time. Everything was in order, it was just a matter of following through, and doing what needed to be done. Take a man's life, and get away with it.

The target, a state judge, had betrayed the family Carmine soldiered for by sending two capos to the Louisiana State Penitentiary at Angola after promising that he would set them free.

The fact that he deserved to die made it theoretically easier to kill him, but the young Sicilian still had to actually do it, and anxiety had the bile rising in the back of his throat as he hurried to meet his accomplice.

The dense fog still lay on the dark streets as he reached the corner where he was to be picked up and driven to the judge's neighborhood. He had been to the house four times, riding the bicycle that he used to make deliveries from the fish market. He covered more than ten miles round-trip each time he went on his trial runs, but his legs were strong from making his living on the bike, and with each mile he knew he drew closer to his dream of being a made man in the largest crime family in the South.

Three long years of hijacking trucks, stealing cargo from the docks, and breaking fingers and legs for Mob loan sharks was about to pay off for the young ruffian. He had never felt so powerful.

Angelo, the driver, picked him up at the appointed time and place, and they rode to the judge's house, talking about jobs they had pulled, women they had known, and places they wanted to see—anything but the matter at hand. They both knew the significance of the act, and didn't want to jinx it by speaking of it.

Carmine intended to shoot the two-faced bastard at seven A.M. as he left his home for the drive to the courthouse, and then meet back up with Angelo, who would drive him across the state line to a safe house in Texas.

No one, not even a judge, could be allowed to double-cross the

Family, and the importance of his target assured that young Carrabba would "make his bones" with this killing.

In typical Cosa Nostra style, the order to murder the judge had come down a full year after he had passed sentence, giving him a false sense of security.

Carmine would change all that.

Angelo dropped him off at a newsstand, run by a blind man, three blocks from the house, and Carmine walked slowly down the street in his suit and tie, as if he belonged in the neighborhood. In his left hand he carried a newspaper he purchased for camouflage.

Dawn was slowly lighting his path now, pink streaks appearing in the sky through the old trees as he came to the judge's short driveway. Without slowing his pace, he turned and walked up the drive to the small freestanding garage he had chosen on previous trips for his hiding place. He crouched behind two shiny new garbage cans, and waited for his mark to come out the back door and open the garage.

He knew the judge was a widower with no children, so the only possible witness in the house was the housekeeper, a slight black woman of perhaps forty. If things went bad, and she saw him, he would have no problem killing her as well. The fact that she was a woman would not trouble him in the slightest.

The sun had driven away the darkness completely by the time Carmine finally heard the screened backdoor squeak loudly as his target opened it. The judge stood on the step, yawned, rubbed the sleep from his eyes, and walked towards the garage.

Carmine silently counted to five, and stepped around the garbage cans, raising his gun and aiming directly at the startled judge's face, no more than three feet away from him. He pulled the trigger and the gun jammed.

The now alert judge turned to run, and Carmine lunged and caught him by the arm, bringing the weapon down hard on the back of his head, driving him to his knees. As the judge tried to call out for help, Carmine hit him again, harder this time, rendering him unconscious. The judge now lay facedown and motionless on the scraggly grass of the small backyard.

Carmine put the gun behind the judge's ear, and pulled the trigger again.

Nothing.

Momentarily frantic, his eyes darted around the yard looking for something he could use to finish the job. He spotted a rusty gardening spade in a bucket next to the garage. He seized it, raised it above his head, and plunged the old blade into the judge's neck and head repeatedly until the man was a bloody pulp above the shoulders.

Less than ninety seconds after starting the attack, his suit spattered with blood, Carrabba coolly tossed the spade aside, and walked down the drive and up the street back to the newsstand.

He said goodbye to the blind proprietor, and got into the front seat of the waiting car. Angelo congratulated him with a nod of respect, and drove him to safety in Texas.

The furor over the judge's heinous murder died down after a few months, and Carmine Carrabba was brought back to New Orleans to be initiated into La Cosa Nostra. The initiation ceremony took place in the home of the Boss, whom Carmine would later have killed, in order to take over the Family and rename it after himself.

Several jokes were made before the ceremony about the use of the spade as a tool for murder, and for a time, Don Carmine was known as The Gardener. However, as he rapidly rose through the ranks of the Family, the nickname was soon forgotten, and no one dared use it anymore.

The Don smiled at the memories of his early years as he took his last sip of brandy, and gently extinguished the Cuban in the green marble ashtray on his desk.

40

I POLISHED OFF THE LAST RIB ABOUT TWENTY MILES OUT OF TOWN, AND settled back for the ride to New Orleans. The big Lincoln rode like a dream, and the air conditioner made the Florida heat evaporate. I found a great radio station playing classic jazz, and set the cruise control to sixty-two.

Driving through Florida during summer, it's not unusual to be in a torrential downpour for three minutes, blazing sun for five minutes, and then back in the rain. After my fourth rain shower in thirty minutes, I thankfully had clear sailing the rest of the way to Neal's.

Shelley was still at the forefront of my thoughts. Even Miles Davis couldn't make me forget her predicament, but I made a conscious decision to concentrate on something else. I decided to think about my imminent visit to the Feagin household, and reminisced about the times I had spent with Neal's daughters.

The girls are all so smart and beautiful that's it's impossible for me to have a favorite. Each has her own personality, and I love them as if they were my own. All three are blonde and blue–eyed like their father, and sweet and caring like their mother.

Julie is a typical oldest child in that's she's very dependable, and is the clear boss of the other two. What makes her unique is that she's also the comedian of the family, a position usually claimed by the baby child.

An exceptional student all her life, at age twenty she's in pre-med at Tulane University in New Orleans, with plans to become a neurosurgeon. She's still at home for now, as Tulane is in the downtown area, and Susan won't allow her to get her own place yet.

I have a standing two-dollar bet with Neal that Julie will be the first self-made millionaire in the Feagin clan. He thinks that he'll be the first, due to his ability to shoot high-stakes craps, but I think Susan's inherited millions will have to do for Neal.

The middle child, Jill, was born with an extra dose of sex appeal, which I can say because she's eighteen, and a high school graduate. Jill was a gawky, ugly duckling as a young girl, all legs and elbows, but when she hit her teens, she blossomed into a real beauty. She's had a steady stream of suitors following her since the day she entered high school, but has yet to pick one out from the crowd. She's going after her real estate license when summer's over, and is also staying at home for the time being, which once again makes her mom and dad quite happy. She'll give Julie a run for her money, literally, in the race for the first million bucks. She should be able to sell the average man any piece of real estate.

Then there's Joy, the wild child of the family. At age sixteen, she's already been through an alcohol and drug rehab program. Vodka and Ecstasy were her poisons of choice.

There was a time when we all feared that we would lose her to drink and drugs, but she's turned her life around and is making good grades in school and staying out of trouble. Joy is a combination of her sisters, smart and cute and funny. She's not sure about her life's goals, but I have no doubt that she will be just fine, whatever she chooses to pursue.

When she was at her wildest, in and out of a juvenile home, Neal told me that if he could manage to keep her out of prison until she was twenty-one, he would feel as if he'd done his job as a father, but no one in the family worries about her future anymore. Susan told me that Joy's friends always tell their problems to her, so maybe she'll end up becoming a psychiatrist one day.

Joy is also the one who came up with the Feagin family motto. I'll never forget the first time she spoke the words.

It happened the Christmas after she had just turned three years old. Her birthday is December 22, the same as my Mom's, which is why I remember it. We were all together on Christmas Day, opening presents after the girls had come downstairs in the much smaller house that Neal had bought when he was promoted to detective in the years before Susan's inheritance.

As usual, I had brought toys for the three girls, including a popular doll for Joy that I had seen on TV. I had made a special trip to Pensacola in order to purchase it. Susan was helping her unwrap it in the middle of the cozy living room while the other girls were ripping open packages and oohing and aahing over their gifts, running back and forth showing Neal and I what they had gotten from Santa.

When Joy saw the large doll, she squealed gleefully and squirmed as Susan took it from the box and placed it in her tiny arms. The shiny new doll was almost as big as she was. Joy looked like a little blonde Chubby Checker as she twisted back and forth, hugging the doll to her chest, and kissing it all over its doll face.

It was at that moment that the motto was born.

She held the doll up for all to see, and at the top of her little lungs, bellowed, "Life is *GOOOOOOOD*!"

Susan, Neal, and I were all so surprised that we just looked at each other for about ten seconds, finally laughing as Joy toddled off to show her siblings her prize.

We tried to figure out where she could have heard those words, or if maybe she had seen someone say it on television. We never did find out where she heard it, but since that moment we have been using the expression on special occasions.

The interesting thing about it is that no one has ever misused it. Even when they were very young, the girls seemed to sense that it was not to be used except at the right moment. To this day, it has to be applied to a particular situation.

The most special time I remember it being said was when Joy came home from rehab for the final time. It was the day before Thanksgiving, and I was already with the family for the weekend, and rode along when they went to pick her up. As she stepped into the fresh autumn air and freedom, she said it with more feeling than any other family member ever had, or has. Neal, Susan, the girls and I agreed, each of us with a tear or two.

Sometimes, you just have to acknowledge the good in life.

***

I was nearing the Florida-Alabama state line when Shelley came crashing back into my thoughts. Luckily, I spotted a way to avoid dwelling on her predicament coming into view.

There's a Welcome Center about a quarter-mile past the state line, and I often stop there on my way to Neal's to use the facilities and stretch my legs. It's well maintained, and a good diversion when the road gets a little boring. Needing the distraction more than usual,

I decided to pull off, take care of business, and relax for a while. The sun had broken through and burned away the clouds, leaving the sky a clear and brilliant blue.

As I left the interstate and took the exit ramp to the Welcome Center, I noticed a large old dog behind the restrooms, sniffing around, looking for lunch. I couldn't help but think of Solly, and decided then and there to get a new hound as soon as the current craziness came to its conclusion. The pound in Pensacola was added to my agenda, and I felt better just thinking about looking for a new furry pal.

I got out, locked the car and stretched my back and legs. As I walked up the path to the men's room, a gaggle of five or six boys of varying ages and sizes almost barreled me over on their boisterous way back to the parking lot. A bedraggled mother of thirty or so trailing along behind the group mumbled an apology, and walked slowly after them, yelling names and orders to the boys, who acted as if they didn't hear a word she said.

They continued running, fighting, and causing a ruckus, getting louder, if anything. I envied them, and felt sorry for her. I thought for the millionth time how great it must be to grow up having brothers around to punch and chase, and how hard it must be on mothers, regardless of how many children they have.

The men's room was cool and dim, and as I splashed cold water on my face, noticed in the mirror that it was slowly returning to its normal state. The bruising and swelling had lessened, and the redness around the stitches was fading. I still looked slightly monstrous, but at least I was healing.

That cheered me a little, and I walked around the grounds for a few minutes, breathing deeply. The pack of boys had found the old dog, and they fed him under the picnic table as their mom was setting up lunch, and she yelled at them to leave the grubby beast alone. The father of the brood sat at the end of the table reading a map and ignoring the lot of them.

I decided to relax for a while, so I walked over to a picnic table in the shade set apart from the others. I lay down on top of it, closed my eyes, and stretched the stiffness out of my body. The shade hid the worst of the sun's heat, and it felt good to breathe the fresh air and relax. The drone of the cars and trucks on the interstate soon had me nodding off, and within a few minutes I was sound asleep.

41

Shelley sat naked in the darkness, tied up at the ankles, her arms secured at the wrists behind the chair with duct tape. A single light bulb suspended from the ceiling illuminated her body and formed a circle of light around her chair.

Her prison seemed to be some kind of warehouse in a secluded area, as there was no sound coming from outside the building. She couldn't tell how many guarded her, but from the sound of it, there were plenty. She strained to listen to their voices, but could make out nothing of what was being said. Still, she showed no fear, and glared in the general direction of her tormentors, almost daring them to get on with the rape and torture that she knew was to come.

The men laughed and spoke amongst themselves, enjoying the show. The blonde FBI bitch that had caused the humiliation of their comrades was now fair game for their pleasure, and it was only a matter of time before the fun would commence. Shelley stared at the dark shapes, trying to get comfortable by adjusting her position on the hard wooden chair.

Increasingly louder laughter from the men filled the room and Shelley tensed at the sound of it. Rivulets of sweat began to trickle down from her forehead into her eyes, and she shook her head in an attempt to keep it away from them.

The large bearded leader of the men suddenly strode forward and slapped Shelley hard in the face, almost causing her to lose her balance and fall. The rest of the animals cheered and jeered, moving into the light so that she could see them clearly. They all carried AK-47s slung over their shoulders, and wore military fatigues. Shelley hung her head when she realized that there were more than two-dozen of the bastards.

The man in charge asked her in broken English how it felt to be in their custody, and if maybe now she could see how their brothers-in-arms felt when she had helped to capture them. He called her every filthy name in English that he knew, and then continued in his native tongue, the others joining in. He spat on her and grabbed and pinched her bare breasts, leaving bruises wherever he roughly touched her. Others from the group came up and joined in, spitting and pinching, laughing as they saw her panic.

The leader then stood directly before Shelley, grabbed her by the hair, and forced her face into his groin, which brought shouts of derision and encouragement from the others. As he backed off, laughing, another man drew his knife and quickly kneeled before her, slicing the rope that secured her ankles. He then reached behind the chair, cut the tape from her wrists, and Shelley was free of her bonds.

She leapt to her feet, and in a flash, turned to run. The other men grabbed her before she got ten feet, laughing as they punched and slapped and groped her. They all fell to the floor in a pile, Shelley at the bottom, at their mercy.

42

"HEY MISTER!"

The voice sounded as if it came from a distance. I opened my eyes and saw the gang of boys gathered around the picnic table. I had been dreaming, and Shelley wasn't really in a truly horrible situation with the terrorists. Not that I knew of, anyway.

The biggest of the boys said, "You were like, moaning, real loud. We heard you, and you were like, moving around and stuff. We were like, 'What's he doin'? What were you dreaming about?"

"Was I 'like' moaning, or was I *actually* moaning?" I asked, sitting up and rubbing my eyes.

"Hunh?" he asked.

"Nothing," I said. "I was dreaming that my friend was in a lot of trouble and, like, never mind."

"You been in a wreck?" he asked.

"Yeah, somethin' along those lines."

He studied my face for a moment, and then said, "Well, my mom is like, waiting for us, so we gotta go. Take it easy!" With that, the gang was off and running again, the old dog following and barking. What a great life. A carefree existence with mom and dad nearby.

Despite having been in the shade, I was covered in sweat after my dream, and my clothes were sticking to my body. I checked my watch, saw that it was 12:25, and closed my eyes as I had done earlier. And, as I had done earlier, I fell back to sleep. When I woke up, my watch showed that I had been out for almost three hours, and since I still had more than three hours of driving before hitting New Orleans, I hurried over and unlocked the now-boiling Lincoln, started it, and cranked up the AC. I noticed a piece of paper under the passenger's side windshield wiper, like one of those flyers that people leave on your windshield in parking lots. I got out and pulled the paper out from under the wiper blade.

A hand-written note read: *Please do not continue to look for trouble in New Orleans Chief Cooper. You will be safer and so will your friends. There is nothing to find except bad things. Take this as a warning and go home.*

I looked around the Welcome Center, but all I saw were children and parents. Whoever left the note was long gone, or so I hoped. I knew the odds of fingerprints being on the paper were slim, but I carefully picked it up by the corner, and reached inside the car for one of the clean napkins that were lying on the dashboard. I wrapped the note loosely, and put it in my shirt pocket.

I got back in the car and headed back to the Interstate, watching the rear view mirror closely. A little *too* closely as it turned out—I almost rear-ended an old Volvo from Rhode Island that was crawling out of the exit. Luckily, I slammed on my brakes and avoided it, waving my apology to the elderly couple inside.

They both scowled at me as I passed them once we were on the freeway, and I could swear that the old lady gave me the finger. But maybe that was just paranoia stemming from the fact that I knew I was being watched.

But as someone once said, 'Just because you're paranoid doesn't mean they're not out to get you.'

The nap at the Welcome Center had rejuvenated me, and I spent the next fifteen minutes or so driving and listening to a radio station play rock and roll oldies.

The simple, steady beat of Fats Domino and Little Richard and some groups I couldn't name had me singing along to the ones that I recognized. Those old songs will probably be around until the sun stops shining, or the planet freezes, whichever comes first.

Music once again helped me to forget the problems waiting for me in New Orleans, and when I set the speed control for sixty-two mph, the big car seemed to drive itself.

Chuck Berry was chugging along, asking Maybelline why she couldn't be true, when I looked in my rear-view mirror and spotted a black van a few car-lengths behind me in my lane. I didn't have a good view of the driver, as the visor was pulled down. All I could see was the bottom of a face, and dark glasses. I assumed it was a man, but the gender of the driver really made no difference when the van sped up and headed directly for the back of my car.

It closed to within a foot or less of the Lincoln, and stayed there for a full minute or so, causing my heartbeat to veer into overdrive. I couldn't see anything in the rear-view mirror but the front of the van. I gritted my teeth and waited for impact.

I didn't have to wait long.

The van slowed for a second before speeding back up and tapping the left side of my back bumper, causing me to swerve and lose control of the big car for a few seconds. Police pursuing a perpetrator often use the tactic—the light tap on the side rear causes the targeted vehicle to veer out of control without damaging the police car.

I crossed into the other lane and almost ran off the road, fortunate that there wasn't another car anywhere near mine. I was strangely calm as I got it back under control, braking slightly, and then slammed my foot on the accelerator as hard as I could once I was heading straight again.

The Lincoln roared and slowly pulled away from the van. Within ten seconds or so, I was starting to put some distance between us, and I realized that my heart was almost back to normal. Maybe all the adrenaline that had been pumping through me the last several days had made me immune to danger, I thought, then smiled at such a ridiculous notion.

After all I'd been through, I was just too tired to remain excited about anything at that point. Knowing my gun was in the back seat made me feel better, but it had been so long since I wore it regularly, it hadn't even crossed my mind during the wild bump and chase. Maybe that was a good thing, because if I had tried to get the gun and drive at the same time, I probably would've shot myself in the ass.

I checked the mirror again and saw that the van was still following me, but was now a half-mile or so behind. I took a deep breath and brought my speed back down to slightly less than seventy, and reset the speed control. I assumed that the driver of the van or an accomplice was probably the one who'd left the threatening note on my windshield, but I wasn't too keen on the idea of waiting for them to catch up again so that I could ask them if my assumption was correct.

I was somewhat surprised that they didn't make another attempt at running me off the road, or worse. The only thing I could figure was that their orders were just to mess with me a little, instead of killing me outright.

I noticed my hands weren't shaking or sweaty, but were relaxed and steady on the wheel. I thought to myself that any sensible person would've been shaking uncontrollably and crying and simpering after such an experience, and that caused me to actually giggle out loud. No doubt about it, I was losing my mind, and I needed to get to Neal's office before it actually happened.

I've always wondered about the process of going insane. Does a person know the last moment when they're still sane? I mean, one second you're okay, and the next you're a raving lunatic, is that how it works? Or do you slowly go batty until they get the net and take you away?

I remember reading that Edgar Allen Poe once said that he was insane, with terrible fits of sanity. That makes sense to me sometimes, but I wonder if that's a good thing.

43

NEAL WENT BACK AND FORTH ABOUT WHETHER OR NOT TO ATTEND THE funeral service for Lucy, but he couldn't shake the feeling that he was responsible, and finally decided he had to show up. He took a cab to the church so he wouldn't have to park, and could walk away quickly if need be.

He took a seat alone on the very last row of pews in the old church, and evaded eye contact with people who wanted to know why a white man was at Lucy's funeral. The last thing he wanted to do was distract anyone from paying his or her respects. After a few curious glances, the small crowd of mourners ignored him, and he looked around the church.

He noted that neither Ray-Ray nor any of his henchmen were there and had mixed emotions about it. Surely the bastards could take half an hour and pay their respects, but then again, maybe it was best that they didn't show their ugly faces in the church. Lucy would probably be happy that they didn't show, he thought, looking at her closed casket down front and thanking God yet again that he hadn't seen the mutilation of her young body.

The small number of people who had come to mourn Lucy saddened Neal. There were less than a dozen, and none of them were crying. It was as if they all knew that this sad day would come, and had already resigned Lucy to an early grave. He could only imagine how devastated he would be if any of his daughters were to meet a similar end. He said a silent prayer for his girls and Lucy, and sat up straight in the pew.

The small choir sang a beautiful, quiet rendition of "Swing Low, Sweet Chariot," accompanied by a sweet, mournful organ. It struck the perfect note for the beginning of the service. After the last notes died away, the preacher, a stocky gray-haired black man of about fifty, walked slowly to the podium and began to speak. Neal barely heard a word, as he was thinking for the hundredth time that he was the one responsible for Lucy resting in the casket, and how different things would be if he had never let her get into his car.

The few words that he did manage to hear soothed him to some extent. The preacher's strong faith in God and His forgiveness made Neal wish that his own faith were stronger. Maybe he should look into attending church more often with Susan and the girls. His wife's bond with God was something she often spoke to him about, but he never really listened. Maybe now would be a good time to start.

He could sure use some forgiveness after what he had let happen to the pretty young woman whose life had ended so violently. He just wasn't sure if he would ever be able to forgive himself for putting her in the position to lose her life. The sadness he felt might never leave him, he thought, and he deserved every bit of it. Lucy would never feel sadness, or happiness, or anything, ever again.

***

The rest of the drive was quiet, yet slightly nerve-wracking, as the van kept following me. But when I finally saw the New Orleans skyline I felt relieved and energized, ready for anything. And fortunately, the van stopped following me as soon as I got off the interstate.

I drove downtown, pulled into Neal's police precinct lot and found a parking spot in the visitors' section. Still slightly paranoid, I strapped on my gun, and smiled at the thought of arming myself before going inside a police station. I pulled a light jacket out of the suitcase, put it on, and headed toward the building.

There was a commotion near the entrance as a couple of uniformed officers struggled to bring a filthy, long-haired, homeless guy under control as they pulled him kicking and screaming from their patrol car. He was shouting something about cardboard lightning and pubic dolphins, and though I wanted to stay and hear what that was all about, I made my way around them and went inside.

Detective Feagin was again out of the office, so I nodded to a few of the folks who recognized me, and went in and took a seat in front of his desk. Everyone had all heard about my fight with Hank, so there were no questions to answer about my mug.

I closed my eyes and stretched my legs out in front of me as I sat waiting for Neal. Five minutes passed, then ten, and I got up and looked around the big outer room, but all I saw were very busy people working, moving here and there. No one seemed to have enough time, and like me, all looked as if they needed a good night's sleep.

I thought again how lucky I am to live and work in Gulf Front, and returned to Neal's office. I noticed something about the size of a playing card on the floor next to the desk. I picked it up, and saw that it was a newspaper obituary clipping that had been laminated and given to the mourners at Lucy's funeral. The name of the funeral parlor was on the back, along with a verse from the Bible, Ecclesiastes 12:7.

The obituary read:

Lucy Lynn Ellis passed, and is now safe and happy in the arms of The Lord.

She is survived by her brothers: Ted Ellis, and Lairy Ellis; her sister, Wanda Ellis; and her twin nieces, Tedmeekia and Lairteesha Ellis.

Lucy Ellis worked as a restaurant hostess in New Orleans, and was a graduate of The Southern Louisiana School of Cosmetology.

Her Home-going Ceremony will be held tomorrow at Oakhurst Baptist Church at 1 P.M. The Right Reverend Malcolm Pittman, Jr. will preside.

Her closed casket may be viewed tonight at Dansby's Funeral Parlor, 1222 Blake Street. Visitation hours are 6-10 P.M.

She will be truly missed by all who knew and loved her.

Neal came in at that moment, and said, "Isn't that a pitifully small amount of words to describe a beautiful, young woman's entire life?"

"Yes it is. Pitiful's the word, all right. I take it you went to the funeral?"

"Yeah. I wasn't sure if I should've been there or not, but I finally decided that I owed her at least that. Damn, it was sad. There couldn't have been more than fifteen people. The old church was so empty, the sound of the choir had a little echo to it. I was hopin' they'd do a real old-fashioned *New Orleans* funeral, you know, with the band marchin' through the streets, and people dancing for joy, celebrating Lucy's life and all. But it was just a depressing, short service with few mourners, and even less emotion. Broke my heart, man."

"Well, like I told you, you need to let this thing go, and stop beating yourself up about it. You can't save everybody. The way her life was goin,' it probably would've happened sooner or later."

Neal sighed. "Maybe it would have happened a lot later if I had been on my toes. Lucy's gone too soon because of my actions. That's somethin' I'm gonna have to live with for the rest of my life."

"Okay, live with it, but don't let it take over your life. Besides, I almost got killed drivin' over here."

"What?" he asked, forgetting Lucy for a moment.

"Somebody in a black van tapped me from behind on the interstate, and almost drove me off the road. I'm tellin' ya, bud, things got pretty hairy there for a few seconds. They followed me all the way until I got off the interstate and hit downtown."

"You have any idea who it was?" Neal asked.

"Couldn't see much, but they left a note on my windshield at the Welcome Center tellin' me to back off the Quitman case, so I assume the van was connected to whoever wants me to go home." I reached in my pocket and pulled out the wrapped note. I put it on Neal's' desk, and said, "I'm pretty sure there are no prints on it, but you can have it checked out for laughs."

Neal looked down at the note, and said, "I'm sure you're right, but I'll check it out anyway. Be right back."

He took it outside, called a young officer over, and handed her the note. He talked to her for a minute, then came back in and said, "I've got a way we can keep you around without anybody knowin'."

"Do tell."

"Come home with me after work. You'll be safe out at my place for the duration."

"Not this duration, no damn way. I'm not draggin' Susan and the girls into this, and don't you even think about arguing with me about this, Detective. I'm gonna get a room at the cheapest, sleaziest motel I can find. They won't think to look for me in some out-of-the-way dump. Besides, it'll be nice to be alone for a while—no ex-girlfriends, no neighbors—I'm actually lookin' forward to it."

Neal knew that when I said no arguing, I meant it. He took

Lucy's funeral card from my hand, and said, "Just don't get yourself killed before we find the bastards who got Lucy."

"Well, if you insist, I'll live for at least another week or so."

"Good. Now, the best place for you to hide would probably be out on the Airline Highway, in Jefferson Parish. There are plenty of cheap motels along there."

"Sounds good," I said.

Neal pointed to the map of New Orleans on his wall, and said, "Check that out while I draw you some directions."

I did as I was told, and after a minute, Neal handed me a crude map. "Head out of here like you're going to my house, and follow this to the highway. Get yourself checked in, and call me as soon as you do. I'll call down and get you a car from the station pool. I don't think it's a good idea for you to be drivin' around town in a car the bad guys are familiar with. There's a back way out that you can take to pick up the ride just to be sure nobody sees you. I don't know what the hell I'm supposed to tell Susan, though. She thinks I'm bringin' you home with me tonight. You got a good story I can tell her?"

"No, I don't. Use your natural husbandly lying ability. I'm sure you can come up with a good falsification."

"And you also know Susan won't believe a word of it, too, don'tcha?"

"Of course I know she won't believe a word of it, but it's for her own good. Besides, misery loves company."

Neal paused for a few seconds, and then asked, "What misery and what company?"

"Well, after she gets through with you, I won't be the only one with a miserable lookin', beat-up face. I'll have company, see?"

Neal closed his eyes, rubbed his temples, and said, "My head is pounding, and you're not helping. Get outta here and call me when you're settled."

44

I MADE MY WAY THROUGH LONG HALLS TO THE CAR POOL AT THE BACK of the building, and was given a fairly new green Ford sedan, which didn't look like a typical cop car. I felt safer immediately as I pulled out of the underground parking garage. I waved to the guy manning the booth at the exit, and he returned my wave and went back to reading his paper.

I headed toward Airline Highway, checking the map Neal had provided as I drove along in the late afternoon traffic. The car handled pretty well, but I missed the luxury of the Lincoln. I quickly got over that feeling when I thought about how easy it would have been to spot. One thing I didn't need was more attention from the jacklegs trying to scare me off.

Hungry again, I decided to look for a diner or a fast food place off the main roads. It was a strange feeling to be constantly checking the rear-view mirrors for anyone or anything suspicious, but just about everything that had happened to me lately had been a strange feeling. I wanted normalcy more than anything at that moment, and stuffing myself on greasy diner food sounded pretty damn normal to me. In fact, it sounded wonderful.

After driving for ten minutes, I spotted a classic old diner built like a railroad car. I pulled into the large lot and parked my hopefully invisible green Ford. I took a look around to make sure I wasn't being followed as I locked it, and felt sure that I was not. The hair on the back of my neck stood up as I realized that Neal and I had felt the same way the night Lucy was murdered. I took another long look around and decided it was my imagination that was making me so uneasy.

At the entrance of the diner I held the door open for an old guy who was on his way out. The inside of the eatery smelled terrific—burgers, fries, coffee. Everything a starving man could want was mere minutes away from my stomach. If the immediate future wasn't going to include Susan Feagin's home cooking, this was the next best thing. I walked over to the counter and sat down.

A redheaded waitress of about forty with "Rita" embroidered on her pink outfit brought me a menu she plucked from a stack by the register, and asked if I wanted something to drink.

"I'd like the biggest Coke you have, please."

She nodded and grabbed a big glass from the counter and filled it with ice before placing it under the machine that began to dispense the Royal Crown Cola. Like any other place in the South, Coke means whatever cola you happen to serve. Actually, RC is one of my favorites, and out of habit I asked her if they had any Moon Pies for sale.

Turning to face me as she continued to fill the large glass, Rita said, "No, I'm sorry, but we don't serve Moon Pies. Don't know why they won't get some; I know we could sell a whole lot of 'em in here if they'd just give 'em a shot. You're about the millionth customer who's asked for 'em. I tried to tell him he's missin' a bet, but he won't hear of it. You just cain't change some people's minds, I guess."

"I guess," I said, and took the glass she placed before me and took a long drink.

"Looks like you needed that," Rita said, smiling.

"You have no idea how much," I said, smiling back. "What looks good today?"

"Well, if I was a hungry man, I'd get me the meat loaf sandwich plate. It comes with fries, slaw, and your choice of our homemade pies. Today we got coconut crème, lemon meringue, and the best butterscotch pecan you ever put in your mouth. Can I order you a plate?"

"Sounds perfect. Can I get Russian dressing on the sandwich?"

"You sure can, hon. What kinda pie you want?"

"I can't resist the butterscotch pecan. Bring me the fattest slice you have."

She wrote my order in her ticket book, and said, "Comin' right up."

As Rita placed my order, I swiveled around on my stool at the counter and checked out the diner. It was maybe half full, and no one was taking any notice of me. I relaxed and watched the cook through the opening to the kitchen as he readied my order. The bell above the door jingled as more customers came in, and Rita went to seat them in a booth by the window. After about thirty seconds, I glanced in their direction, and my heart stopped for a beat.

Shelley was sitting in the booth with her back to me!

Her hair was loose and on her shoulders. I'd know that beautiful blonde hair anywhere!

I jumped from my seat at the counter and was at her booth in a flash. I took her shoulder and pulled her to face me, and saw—that it was not her.

In fact, the woman in question looked more like Duane Allman than Special Agent Shelley Brooke of the FBI. I stammered an apology to her and her lady friend, saying I mistook her for someone else, and slunk back to the counter where I finished my RC in one long gulp.

I must have scared the poor woman half to death with the passionate way I grabbed her shoulder, not to mention the fact that my smashed face would be enough to scare anyone half to death, whether I grabbed them or not.

Rita came back in a minute or so, and asked, "You alright, hon?" My jacket had fallen open, and she'd spotted my gun. "You in trouble of some kind?"

I pulled the jacket closed, and said, "No, nothing you need to worry about. I'm a police officer."

"Oh, that's good, I got a soft spot for cops." She paused, and then said, "Another thing, I didn't wanna ask, but about your, um, your..."

"Face?"

"Yeah, that's it. Are you feelin' okay? Do you need me to call somebody?"

"No, Rita, thanks. I'm fine; I've just had a rough week. I'm sorry if I caused any trouble. Maybe you should pack my plate to take out. I just seem to be causing problems wherever I go these days."

"No, now don't you worry about a thing, hon. That lady is a regular customer, and she ain't upset with you at all. In fact, she said she wished she *was* the woman you was lookin' for." Rita patted my hand. "You just sit right there and let Rita take care of you." The order bell dinged, and she said, "See there? Your order's ready."

She set the plate down in front of me. It smelled great, and I knew I wasn't going anywhere soon.

Rita put her hands on her hips, and said, "You take your sweet time now and eat ever' bite of this good food. That's an order."

45

DON CARRABBA SMILED AT HIS VISITOR AND LIT HIS CIGAR—THIS was going to be fun. The older he got, the more he enjoyed wielding his power. Unlike most of his adult life, the need for sex no longer drove him, and with more money already than he could spend, forcing his will upon others had become the main motivation of his golden years.

The visitor took his usual chair in front of the large antique oak desk, and felt his stomach tighten as it always did when he was summoned to the mansion. Only this time he felt he had the upper hand.

"Don Carmine," Harry James said, "What was the big idea of you shootin' up my house? All that glass bein' busted up like that cost a bundle to repair."

"That was simply a reminder to you that we still have a connection, even though, sadly, your lovely daughter is no longer with us. I wanted to make sure that you remember that fact, Senator. My men were given the strictest orders not to harm anyone."

"Well, it didn't feel like it was just a 'reminder' when I was shakin' like a wet dog after all the damn bullets stopped flyin'."

"I understand your concern, but it was something that I felt had to be done. It was just business. By the way, did you enjoy your poker game?"

Harry James said, "I'm sure you know I didn't, Don Carmine."

The Don smiled. "Well, to the matter at hand. I have a favor to ask, and it is very important to my business interests, so do not fail me. There are laws on the books in this state that are preventing me from searching for oil on some property I have recently purchased. I would like for you to use your influence in Louisiana and Washington to change this situation. I know you will do this for me, yes?

Harry James paused for a moment, and said in his earnest politician's voice, "Don Carmine, if only you had come to me sooner, I would happily have been of service. When I was here the day after my daughter's death, I let you convince me that nothin' had changed in our relationship. I was so accustomed to being in your debt that I just put my tail between my legs like I always do, and crawled out of here like a whipped pup. But in the past few days, I've had a chance to really think about our relationship, and well, I realized that things *have* changed, Don Carmine. Like I said that mornin', now that Caroline is no longer with us, your power over me is diminished to the point that I will not be working for you again. I'm sure you understand."

Don Carmine said, "No, Senator, I don't understand. Please enlighten me."

"Well, it's like this. You and I have had a long and productive friendship, but I feel it's time that I distanced myself from you. My reelection campaign is in full swing, and I can't be at your beck and call as I have been. Surely you can see my side of this, Don Carmine. It's just impossible for me to help at this time." He smiled at the old man, feeling he was finally free of the Boss's grip. Harry James had been dreaming of this day for well over twenty years, and it felt better than he had imagined.

The Don puffed on his Cuban. "Senator," he said, "my old friend and colleague. Surely you would not want to deny me your services at such a difficult time, especially with your reelection nearing. I'm sure you don't want me to talk to the newspapers about your distasteful personal life. That would only bring you heartache and trouble. Do this favor for me, and we will continue our mutually beneficial arrangement. You will be making an old man very happy," Don Carmine said, smiling like a grandfather trying to persuade a stubborn child.

"Well, sir, to be blunt, I'm through bein' your lap dog. It took me a while to see it clearly, but you no longer have the upper hand with me. Now, I'm not a man who normally resorts to threats, but if you say one word to the media, I'll tell them how you used my daughter for all those years, and you don't want your wife to know about that, do you? Sure, you could say that I used my influence to help you in business ventures through the years, but I'm willin' to bet that you won't, because you don't want all the publicity that would follow such a revelation. The way I see it, you no longer control the situation. We both have something on each other, so I'll just go about my business, and you go about yours. Simple as that." Harry James returned the grandfatherly smile, sure that he had the old man right where he wanted him.

"Senator, must I remind you of what happened regarding your wife? Do you not think that that would pose a problem for you?"

"Don Carmine, I think that what we have here is a good old Mexican standoff as far as wives are concerned. In order for you to tell what you know about my wife, you'd have to expose yourself to scrutiny from the law. I don't know why I let you get away with bullying me all these years, but I've had it with your orders and demands. I intend to change things between us, starting right this minute."

The old man sighed heavily, and said, "I had hoped that we could come to an agreement on this matter without my resorting to unpleasant pressure, but if you insist on being difficult, Senator, I will have to play my card, in a manner of speaking."

"And what card is that?" a suddenly uneasy Harry James asked. What was the old sonofabitch trying to pull? Harry James's mind raced and he tried to smile, but his lips stuck to his teeth, and the grin was more like a grimace.

"Surely you know the card I speak of, Senator."

"No, Don Carmine, I don't, but whatever it is, I'm not worried about it. All you can hold over my head is that I gamble a little and that I've been a womanizer. Recent events in Washington make me believe that the people of this great nation don't give a rat's ass about what a man in office does to get his rocks off these days. On the other hand, I think your wife would be very upset with what *you've* been doing sexually all these years, don't you agree, Don Carmine?" Harry James couldn't help but smile again at the old man. It was nice to be in control.

Don Carmine returned the smile, and called Vinnie Mandola into the large room.

"Vincenzo, would you please play the tape for the senator. After all this time, he seems to think we're on common ground."

"Yes sir, Don Carrabba," Vinnie said, grinning at Harry James as he obeyed his instructions.

"What is this?" Harry James said. Air in the room suddenly seemed to be harder to find.

Don Carmine said, "The people of this great nation may not give a rat's ass about how a man gets his—what did you say—'rocks off'? But I think they might care about who he gets them off with, if you catch my meaning. Vincenzo? When you're ready."

At first, Harry James didn't recognize himself as the star of the production, because the camera was filming the action from above and behind him and due to the dim lighting, his white hair appeared much darker. It looked more like a low-budget porn.

"This is very interestin', Don Carmine, but I don't see what this has to do with our conversation."

The view switched to another of the cameras hidden in the room, and suddenly Harry James could see himself clearly, being serviced by the redheaded freak he had come to know as "Scarlett". He understood what Don Carmine had meant when he said he would play his card. He looked down at the beautiful antique Oriental rug beneath his feet, but averting his eyes didn't help, as the sounds of his pornographic debut filled the room and drew loud laughter from Vinnie and the Don.

Harry James realized that in all the years he had known Don Carmine, he had never once heard him laugh, and now that he heard the evil tone of the old man's guttural amusement, he wished he never had.

The action continued on the screen, as Harry allowed the redhead to do things to *him* that he had never let a human being of either gender do before.

Laughing at the action and at Harry James's obvious agony, Don Carrabba continued the torture, "It is difficult to tell from watching this remarkable love-making. Do you play the part of a woman for a man who is really a woman, or do you play the part of a man for a woman who is really a man? You receive pleasure, and then you drop to your knees and give pleasure. You are the master, and the slave also. It is very confusing, Senator, yet extremely entertaining!" Don Carrabba laughed louder, the sound even more wicked than before.

"Vincenzo?" the Don continued, "What did you say an animal such as this is called?"

"A 'she-male,' Don Carmine," Vinnie grinned, looking at Harry James, who still stared at the rug as though he might crawl under it.

"Ahhh, yes, yes," the old man said. "I can see the headline now. 'The Senator and the She-male.' Don't you think that would make a wonderful story for the reporters, Vincenzo?"

"Yes sir, it would be a really great story, maybe even a movie or somethin' like dat." To Harry James, "Youse could even play yourself in the movie, Senator, seein' as how you ain't gonna have a job in Washington when dis gets out."

"A wonderful idea, Vincenzo," Don Carrabba chuckled. "How does that sound to you, Senator? Do you wish to go to Hollywood and seek your fame and fortune? All you need to do is say the word, and Vincenzo will hand-deliver copies to the appropriate people."

Harry James sighed deeply as he realized that he was right back where he'd started, under the Boss's thumb. In fact, Don Carrabba had always been in control.

"Very well, Don Carmine. I'll try to work out your oil situation when I get back to Washington."

The Don glared and said, "Do not '*try*,' Senator. Do." His stare relaxed into a smile and he said, "I knew you would not deny me your support in this matter. Please have a safe trip back." He dismissed Harry James with a wave of his hand and turned back to watch the lurid action on the TV screen.

46

THOROUGHLY BEATEN BY THE OLD MAN, HARRY JAMES LEFT THE OLD house meekly. He got into the back seat of his large gray Mercedes after Douglas, his driver of twenty years, opened the door for him.

As they drove off into the dusk, Harry James wondered what had possessed him to confront Don Carmine. He was lucky that the old man hadn't ordered Vinnie to kill him on the spot. He resolved never to try and pull such a stunt again, and as the big car quietly made its way through the streets, he remembered the night when he had fallen completely under Don Carmine's control.

Heavy rain, stiff wind, and tremendous thunder and lightning had pummeled New Orleans that evening, the kind of storm that always accompanies problems.

His wife had just returned from the hospital after giving birth to Caroline a few days before. Though she wasn't due home until the next afternoon, Amelia Thibodeaux Quitman was never one to follow rules, and she left the hospital early, impatient to resume her hectic social life. The baby was to follow the next morning.

She caught Harry James and his latest paramour—that's what Amelia called his other women—going at it in the big bed that her aunt had bequeathed to her in her will. This wasn't the first time she'd been made personally aware of his infidelity, but it was the first time he'd had the unmitigated gall to do it in her own bed.

The bed, however, meant more to Amelia than Harry's fidelity, coming as it did from her beloved aunt's estate in Fort Lauderdale. She calmly told the two lovers they had one minute to get out of her sight, or she would shoot them both. They believed her, because she was aiming the shotgun she usually used for skeet directly at Harry's most treasured apparatus.

The other woman, a call girl for one of the Carrabba escort services, grabbed her clothes, ran stark naked down the stairs, and drove away as fast as her fancy little convertible could take her. No one observed her departure, just as no one had seen her arrive, and that would prove to be fortunate for Harry James. The usual house staff consisted of a butler, a housekeeper, a cook, and a personal maid for Amelia in those days, and all four were on vacation while the lady of the house was in the hospital.

Once they were alone, Amelia coolly said, "Harry James Quitman, this is the last time you'll ever embarrass me with one of your whores. Tomorrow I'm takin' the baby and goin' to my parents' house in Baton Rouge. I've always known this day might come, but I had hoped the baby would make a difference in your behavior. Obviously, it hasn't. Daddy's attorneys will contact you about our divorce as soon as I can make the necessary arrangements, but I still want you out of my house tonight. Do you understand me?"

"Amelia, honey, listen to me for a minute. Just let me explain. This didn't mean a thing, it's just that it's been such a long time since we—"

"A long time?" she screamed. "You've been screwin' around on me since the first week of our marriage, you sorry sonofabitch! You haven't gone without the whole time I've been pregnant! Hell, I think you've been gettin' *more* these last nine months!"

Amelia suddenly became quiet as her eyes began to water, and she said, "Well, this is it, you bastard. You've finally done it, and in Aunt Dora's bed, too. How could you? I don't wanna see your face or hear your lies ever again. Get out and leave me alone."

She broke down the shotgun, and laid it on the bed, a little too close for Harry James, and he quickly got up and pulled his pants on, not taking his eyes off her for a moment.

"Darlin', now listen to me a minute."

"Shut. Your. *Mouth!*" she shouted finally, and turned and walked from the bedroom out to the upstairs landing.

Harry James knew that if she left she would take everything. The Quitman money he had inherited was almost all gone, due to his whoring and gambling. They lived off of the millions Amelia had inherited in a trust fund from her maternal grandfather when she'd turned twenty-one. And with Harry James's first run for the Senate coming up soon, he literally could not afford to lose Amelia.

He hurried after, and took her arm, but she slapped him hard and pulled away. Harry James saw red, and with a growl leapt at her, grabbing her by her thick blonde hair, and slammed her into the wall. She tried to fight back, but he was crazed at the thought of losing everything he possessed, and her blows had no effect. But even weakened by her recent childbirth, Amelia managed to stay on her feet as he struck her again and again, and somehow got out of his grasp and ran for the stairs. Harry James Quitman would pay for the next moment for the rest of his life.

He darted after her, and grabbed her arm to try and pull her to him, but she lost her balance and went over the railing, falling to the hardwood floor below with a sickening thud.

Harry James stood frozen to the spot, unable to will himself to look over the railing. The silence of the old house often had a calming effect on him when he had the place to himself, but the events of the last few minutes had changed everything.

He walked down the stairs like a condemned man, knowing that he was about to face the end of his political career instead of his life. His misdeeds flashed before his eyes. Gambling, drinking, the whores in the Carrabba brothels—his hands shook slightly as he came to the bottom of the grand staircase.

He stood on the bottom step and looked at Amelia's body lying on the old, hardwood floor, and suddenly he knew what he had to do. He slowly walked over to the phone that sat on the small table in the foyer, making sure not to look at his wife's body.

He dialed a number he had committed to memory, the number that Don Carmine had given him when they had met at a charity auction several months ago. So far, their relationship had not progressed beyond a few contributions to Harry James's senatorial campaign channeled through some of the Carrabba family's legitimate businesses. So far, he hadn't used his friendship with the Don for anything other than the most trivial of matters, for fear that he might become indebted to the old man, but he was resigned to the fact that his only hope now was to ask for the mobster's help.

Within two minutes of placing the call, Harry James was talking to the beast, Vinnie Mandola. Vinnie listened as Harry James told him of the situation, that he was alone and that no one had seen Amelia fall. Vinnie told him to turn out all the downstairs lights and draw the curtains, and that he would bring a clean-up crew to the Quitman mansion directly.

Harry James's heart rate slowed considerably after he hung up the phone. He closed his eyes, and, with his back to his wife's body, he attempted to pray for the first time since he'd been an altar boy. This proved a problem for him, as he couldn't remember any prayers pertaining to beating your spouse, until she fell over a railing to her death.

As though in answer, Amelia groaned loudly and tried to raise herself into a sitting position.

Harry James turned around quickly and stared in shock at his wife. Amelia was too weak to sit up, but lay on the floor, moaning and calling for help in a barely audible voice.

He was momentarily relieved that she was not dead, but then quickly realized that if Amelia lived, his political career would be over before it began. Fighting to remain calm, he ran to the parlor and grabbed a big decorative pillow from the sofa, and returned to the foyer where Amelia now mumbled and called for her daddy.

Harry James knelt down beside her, placed the pillow over her lovely face, and pushed down with all his might.

Amelia struggled violently, kicking her legs wildly and trying to push the pillow away. He threw his knees over her, pinning her shoulders to the floor, applying more pressure to the pillow. Amelia kicked and bucked, trying desperately to reach the oxygen that would save her, but she couldn't budge her desperate husband.

Harry James couldn't believe how long it took to kill her. The clash continued for well over two minutes as Amelia slowly lost the strength to fight him off.

She finally stopped struggling, but he didn't remove the murder weapon until a full five minutes had passed. Harry James wasn't going to remove the pillow until he was sure that Amelia would never rise again.

Exhausted and covered with sweat, he finally tossed the pillow aside and slowly got to his feet. He looked at his dead wife with a mixture of regret and relief.

Seeing Amelia's hooded stare, Harry James suddenly felt sick, and he ran back to the kitchen where he vomited forcefully into the sink. He rinsed the sink clean, washed out his mouth, and splashed some cold water on his face before going around and drawing all the curtains in the downstairs rooms. He turned out all the downstairs lights except for the small lamp in the foyer where Amelia lay, and sat down on the bottom step of the staircase to wait for Vinnie and his crew.

***

Twenty minutes later, a knock at the door brought Harry James quickly to his feet, and he opened it to let Vinnie and three other men into the mansion, out of the storm, which still raged wildly outside.

The smallest of the men had a big professional-looking camera, and immediately began taking pictures of Amelia's body. He also snapped shots of Harry, and the foyer. He pushed the senator into the frame with Amelia, and caught the dazed look on Harry James' face as he stared back into the lens.

The two other men had pairs of muddy shoes in their hands, and when Vinnie nodded at them, they headed for the back of the house, leaving Harry James alone with Vinnie and the photographer.

"What're the pictures for?" Harry James asked.

"Insurance," Vinnie said, and with a nod towards the door, dismissed the cameraman.

"Insurance for what? Oh, I see," Harry James mumbled. "What's with the muddy shoes?"

"Don't choo worry 'bout nuttin'," the beast said. "The shoes is so it looks like somebody else was in here besides you, ya know? They're gonna put on shoes a coupla sizes too big, so's it'll look like some really big guys did it. Then they'll jimmy the back door and make it look like they come in from there. With muddy tracks all over da place, it'll look like a honest-to-God burglary. And, just so you know, Don Carrabba wants to talk to you after all dis dies down. He gave me the story that he wants you to tell everybody about wha' happened."

Harry James stared at him dumbly, his mouth slightly open. "What story does he want me to tell?"

"Well, it goes like dis. You was sleepin' when you heard some awful racket what woke you up. You hear the wife outside your room screamin' bloody murder, so you come runnin' outta the bedroom, and hear a guy beatin' her up then throwin' her over the railing. You say you hear this happening, because you can't see on accounta it's so dark, unnerstan'? Then, before you can react, somebody lets you have it right in the gut, then the mush. You fight back pretty good, but this really big guy rears back and knocks you out cold. Tell 'em she was on her way down to the kitchen or somethin' like dat, and they caught her by surprise, and slapped her around and tossed her over the railing down to da floor. If they ask you what you seen, you tell 'em you ain't seen nothin'. It all happened so fast, and it was too dark for you to see anything anyhow, is what you tell 'em. The boys is gonna take some stuff, too, ya know, silver and jewelry and whatnot, and make it look real good, so nobody will have no doubts that it happened just like you say it did. Only thing is, I'm gonna hafta really letchoo have it so it looks believable, so we need to go upstairs and take care'a dat. C'mon, let's go up now."

"But, wait a minute! Is all that really necessary?" Harry James asked, now alert as Vinnie took his arm, almost lifting him off his feet, and led him towards the staircase.

"Yeah, I'm afraid it is, Mr. Quitman. Sorry, but I got my orders. I'm gonna need a coupla your neckties too, so's I can tie you up. Don Carrabba even wants me to bust a few ribs so it looks like you really got creamed. That'll play better for sympathy, is how he looks at it, ya know? If you hafta spend a little time in bed gettin' well, maybe the papers and the TV will leave you alone, is what he said. Let's just get it over wit'. The boys and me will make all your troubles disappear, and before ya know it, this'll all be forgotten."

As it turned out, the Don was right about everything. The police bought the story that Harry James fed them when they arrived the next morning after being summoned by Hensley, the Quitman's butler. He'd found Harry trussed up like a hog in some very expensive neckwear on the landing outside the bedroom. Vinnie had spent several minutes picking out just the right ties for the occasion, and even took the three finest ones for his own collection. If Harry James had been a bigger man, Vinnie would've taken his best shoes, too.

The spoil from the phony robbery was given back to Harry James as a gesture of goodwill by Don Carrabba, and was immediately sold off through Family fences by the grieving widower, making the evening even more profitable. Amelia's estate naturally went to Harry, so he became a very wealthy man and a very *single* man on one memorable stormy night.

Vinnie took special care to leave the murder weapon in the pouring rain behind some shrubbery so the cops would find it. No prints could be taken from a wet pillow, so there was no way to prove who had suffocated Amelia. And how could poor Harry James have tied up himself?

The next few weeks were some of Harry James's best days ever, especially politically. All the publicity generated by the murder, and the contributions to his campaign from Don Carmine swept him to an easy victory with a tidal wave of sympathy votes. Harry James Quitman of Louisiana won the senatorial election in a landslide, and he marched into Washington like he owned the place. Within a year, he'd learned the game and used his ever-growing influence to help his new best friend, Don Carrabba. The partnership was a boon to each of them, as money flowed in and fattened each of their bank accounts considerably.

When she was old enough to understand, Harry James told Caroline that some very bad men had hurt her mommy, and he had tried his best to stop them, but God wanted Amelia in Heaven. Caroline accepted the lie, and learned to live a sheltered life without her mother. She rarely ever left New Orleans, seeing her father only on holidays or when he had time to come home, which seldom happened.

With each passing year, the Don's leash tightened on the junior Senator from Louisiana, but the kickbacks and gifts of money and women that Don Carmine bestowed upon Harry James made it all worthwhile.

The life of a United States Senator, with all its perks and privileges is as close to royalty as one gets in America, and Harry James took full advantage of his position. Add to that his hometown connections and acquaintances, and it was a very sweet life indeed. At least on the surface, and that's where Harry James Quitman had lived each and every day of his life.

***

Harry James heard Douglas ask him something, but couldn't make out what he'd said.

"What did you say, Douglas?" he asked.

"I asked if you want to go home, or if you have some special place in mind that you would like to go."

"No, let's just drive around for a while, I'm not ready to go home just yet."

Douglas met Harry James's eyes in the rear-view mirror and said, "That's what I thought, Senator. You look like a man with something on his mind."

"That I am, Douglas. That I am."

47

"DO YOU STILL HAVE THE FLORIDA POLICEMAN UNDER SURVEILLANCE?" Don Carmine asked Vinnie.

"Yes, Don Carmine. My boys been followin' him since they bumped his car on the freeway. I got a call from 'em just before the Senator showed, and they said the cop left the police station and is gettin' some dinner. We found us a new kid, who put some kinda gadget on the cop's new car while he was eatin' so's they can follow him without having to be right behind him. You know, track him wherever he goes. Kid says we don't even hafta be anywhere near 'im, that this thing is the same gizmo the Feds use. I told Alberto that as soon as the cop is on the move again, to follow him and pick 'im up as soon as possible, like you said. We got a plan all worked out."

"Excellent. I want this man taken care of tonight, or tomorrow at the latest, capeesh? I'm going to bed early, so don't bother me tonight, but I wish to be informed of your progress as soon as possible in the morning. Now leave me and do what you must."

"Yes, Don Carmine," Vinnie said, bowing customarily as he backed out of the room. Vinnie didn't believe that the police chief knew anything, but he had his orders, and he was always ready for the opportunity to demolish a human being.

Vinnie's cell rang as soon as he left. It was Alberto, telling him the Florida cop was on the move again, and that the crew was ready for him.

Vinnie said, "Just make sure you don't hurt 'im 'til I get there. I know you know your business, I'm just sayin'. Okay, okay—I'll meet up wit' you as soon as I can."

Vinnie hung up, and as he walked to his car, whistled an old tune his Sicilian grandmother had sung to him back in New Jersey when he was a small boy.

Nothing like a new assignment to put a song in your heart and a little pep in your step.

48

I PAID MY CHECK AT THE REGISTER, AND LEFT RITA A TEN-DOLLAR TIP, which she tried to give back. I told her that her services went beyond the meat loaf, and that she'd restored my faith in humanity. She came out from behind the counter and carefully gave me a kiss on the cheek.

"You take care of yourself, and come back real soon, hon," she said, beaming at me as I headed for the door. The woman I had mistaken for Shelley turned and waved coyly from her booth, and I sheepishly waved back as I opened the door and stepped outside.

It looked like there was about a half hour of sunlight left as I got back in my new ride, and looked at the map to make sure I was still on the right track. I pulled into traffic, checking to see if I was being followed. Once again, it seemed that there was no one behind me who had any interest in me whatsoever. I hoped and prayed that it would stay that way.

Traffic was heavy, and the angle of the sun made things difficult as I looked for Airline Highway. When I finally spotted it, I was lucky enough to be in the correct lane to make the left turn. It would have been hell trying to get across three lanes of traffic at that time of day.

The area was seedy, which was exactly what I wanted. I figured that anybody looking for me would be more likely to search the downtown hotels. I was sure that I had been followed ever since I was seen at the police station that first day. How else would they have been able to put a note on my windshield and ram me on the interstate? I didn't just believe I was being followed, I was totally convinced. And totally full of meat loaf.

The names on the motel signs were already turned on, shining works of neon art in the fast-dimming late afternoon haze. Almost all of them were missing at least a letter or two: "Pirates Cove" became "Pirate Co," "Creole Hideaway" was now "Crole Hidey," "French Quarter West" was "French Quart West," but my favorite, "Al's," had all its letters. I parked in front of the motel office.

There was a greasy-haired guy of about thirty behind the desk, reading a hard cover book, which surprised me. I expected him to be flipping through a dirty magazine, not an actual book. He didn't look up as I walked in to the accompaniment of a loud door buzzer.

The lack of interest was a relief after all the stares my face had been getting. He said, "Thirty-nine ninety-five a night, plus tax. I'll need a credit card and some ID. How many nights you be here?"

"Charge me for two days, and we'll see how things go."

"Whatever you say."

I pulled out my Visa and my driver's license, and placed them on the desk. He wrote me up, handed me a key to room 12, and went back to his reading.

Turning to leave, I asked, "Could you have someone call and wake me at seven tomorrow morning?"

"Phones ain't workin' right now. I'll leave a note for the day clerk and have him knock on your door at seven if the phones ain't fixed by then."

"Thanks."

"Yep," he said, his nose still in the book.

I parked the car in front of my room, and looked around to see if there was anything suspicious going on in the motel parking lot. The only thing I saw was a bird pecking at something on the concrete walkway a few doors down. It looked like I was safe for the moment, so I unlocked the door to my room, went inside, and turned on the light.

Two huge roaches scurried across the filthy orange shag carpet, headed for the bathroom. I made a mental note to be on my toes during my before-bed shower. I thought for a minute that maybe I should've gone to a nice hotel after all, but figured a couple of bugs couldn't kill me. Rough me up a little maybe, but not kill me.

I tossed the jacket on the low dresser, put my gun and holster next to it, and slid the chain on the door. The ancient air conditioner by the window roared to life when I pushed the button, and I looked around for the television remote. There wasn't one to be found, so I turned it on manually and sat down on the garish paisley bedspread.

A local commercial for a car dealer was blaring at me, so I quickly got back up, turned it off, and sat back down on the bed. I loosened my belt, unzipped, and took off my shoes. I lay back on the bed and stared at the door, trying my best to relax after another bizarre day.

It was still early evening, but the desire for another nap suddenly came over me. Doreen's sunrise wedding had knocked my sleep cycle completely out of whack. I closed my eyes and listened to the noisy hum of the air conditioning unit. A nice snooze would have been great just about then, but, weary as I was, my nervous system had other ideas.

I remembered how nice the guestroom at Neal and Susan's house was, and how great it would be to spend another night sleeping in it. The only thing that kept me from driving straight there was the fact that I could never in a million years put the Feagin family in even the slightest bit of danger. The motel was a complete pigsty, but there was nobody at risk there but me, and I felt fairly certain that no one knew I had checked into Al's.

All I needed to do was figure out how to make it through the night. I turned on the TV again, checked around the dial until I found a familiar face, and settled back to watch the news. Maybe, by some miracle, I'd find out that Shelley had been released by her kidnappers, and was safely back at her home in Virginia.

And maybe there would be a story about a compassionate IRS agent, a sincere politician, or an intellectual supermodel.

49

Alberto Prizzi didn't particularly care for the young techno-geek who had supplied him with the piece of equipment that enabled him to follow the nosy Florida police chief, but he definitely liked the fact that he didn't have to worry about being seen as he trailed him.

It was even fun in a way, to watch the monitor that the geek provided and follow the cop's car on the screen as it moved through the traffic up ahead. And he knew that the real fun would start later.

He dropped the techno-kid off at a bus stop, and continued driving the van through the traffic, staying a minute behind and making all the indicated turns until he found the designated motel. He pulled in the parking lot, and there was the green Ford the geek had bugged while the cop was in the diner.

Alberto slowly cruised the parking lot looking for the right spot to park the van and start the evening's festivities. He backed into a slot that was directly across from room eleven, and turned off the ignition. He wasn't sure which of the rooms held his prey, but the Ford was parked in front of room twelve.

Holly, a buxom, bleached blonde who was Vinnie Mandola's latest conquest, whimpered from the back seat of the van, "How long before I can go to the ladies' room? I really gotta go *bad.*"

Her whiny voice had been irritating Prizzi ever since he'd picked her up at her apartment an hour before; he had no idea how Vinnie could stand the grating bleat of the stupid blonde whore. He grunted, turned around to face her, and gruffly said in his Sicilian accent, "Shut up your mouth, and wait to do as you are told."

She immediately averted her eyes, and shut her mouth. Alberto Prizzi scared the living daylights out of her. The discomfort she had been feeling suddenly didn't seem so bad.

Her partner for the evening's job, a thickly muscled biker called Shack, wasn't scared of anything or anybody, but even he wouldn't talk back to Prizzi. Shack just wanted to get on with it. He'd been in the van when they had picked up Holly, and was tired of the cramped back seat and the company of the other two Mob guys who sat in the middle seat of the van.

He closed his eyes and envisioned the long ride to California after the evening's work was accomplished. He was leaving for the coast as soon as he could get back to his place and pack his gear. With the bread he was making for tonight's job, he could live pretty damn well for six or eight months out there. Maybe even stretch it out for a year if he hooked up with the right crowd.

That was Shack's plan, but Vinnie Mandola had other ideas for Shack and Holly.

***

The national news was more of the usual. The stock market was up and down all week, before finishing down slightly. A woman in North Carolina had taken five people hostage at her job because her boss had fired her best friend the day before. The President was addressing the United Nations, and the main suspect in a big murder case out in California had attempted suicide in his jail cell.

I thought: I'm glad I don't own any stock, at least I wasn't a hostage in North Carolina, the President has a crummy job, and although I couldn't actually do it, I was beginning to understand why some people tried to kill themselves.

Then I remembered that I was supposed to call Neal and let him know where I was staying. Looking around the room, I realized I'd left my bag in the car.

Still slightly drowsy, I put on my shoes to go out to the car and get the bag. I slid the door chain from its slot, opened the door and stepped out into the bug-infested light of the walkway that fronted the rooms. Just as I did, to my left I heard a woman scream, "Stop! I'll call the police!"

I looked three or four doors down to my left and saw a man and woman standing in the parking lot a few feet out of the light, wrestling and shouting. I immediately went into cop mode, pulling my badge so it would be ready to show. Jurisdiction or no, a quick flash of a police badge might end the situation before it escalated.

I flipped my badge, but the woman broke away and ran into the breezeway that housed the refreshment area, the man close behind. Following at a run, I made my way around the corner just in time to see the short but very muscular man slap the hell out of the woman, a blonde who was dressed in the uniform of a street hooker. She wore a ridiculously short and tight leopard-print skirt, a silver bra that barely held her massive, artificially enhanced breasts, and silver shoes with high heels and pointy toes. She screamed as the man struck her, and cowered back against the ice machine.

I reacted like I always do in a situation like that. "Hey! Police officer!" I yelled, as I held out my badge and flashed it at the muscleman.

He was dressed in a denim shirt with the sleeves cut off, greasy jeans and motorcycle boots. He was either a real biker or a convincingly dressed wannabe. I made him out to be the real thing, and decided to try and settle the matter with diplomacy instead of force, which was a good decision since he could have killed me easily with the knife he was holding to the blonde's throat.

When he saw the badge, he immediately backed off and put his hands up. He dropped the knife and said, "I don't want no trouble man. This bitch just ripped me off for fifty bucks. That ain't right."

"How did she happen to do that?" I asked, keeping my eyes on both the biker and the knife.

"Let's just say she took my money, and didn't deliver the service that she was paid for," he snarled, glaring at the blonde.

She stood up straight, and came back loudly, "You wouldn't deliver no service neither, if you knew what he tried to get me to do. I been workin' for five years, and I ain't *never* heard nobody say they wanted *that!* There ain't enough fifty-dollar bills in the fuckin' *world* to get me to do what he wanted, the pervert-ass bastard!"

The biker dude went after her again, this time trying his best to get his hands around her neck. She screamed even louder, and fell back against the ice machine.

"Okay, okay, that's enough!" I shouted as I pulled the guy away from her. He calmed down and backed off again, muttering about what a whore she was and what she should do to herself. I didn't think even half of what he said was anatomically possible, but I let it pass.

"Calm down, you two, or I'm gonna hafta call in some back-up," I bluffed, hoping that my badge was enough to keep the situation in hand. It seemed to work as they moved away from each other again and became silent.

Keeping my eyes on them, I put my badge away, picked up the knife, and placed it on top of the ice machine where I could keep track of it.

I said, "Okay, now if you two stop all this squabbling, I think we can forget about takin' a ride downtown. Can you both promise me that this is the end of the fighting for tonight?"

I really didn't want to have to call Neal and get him to come make a legitimate arrest. I was hopeful that they would walk away thankful that there was no jail time involved.

But the biker dude continued to scowl at the blonde, who was standing with her hands on her hips daring him to come after her now that the threat of incarceration was in the air.

I turned to her, and she kicked me squarely in the groin, and I doubled over in a world of pain unlike any I have ever experienced.

From the darkness behind me two guys appeared and drove me to my knees. They duct-taped my mouth and pulled a hood over my head while nearly breaking my arms as they pulled them behind me to tape them, too. My ankles were wrapped with tape in a few more seconds, and I was picked up like a trussed hog and put in a vehicle that had screeched to a halt directly in front of the breezeway.

I couldn't tell for sure, but it seemed as if only the two duct tape guys got in with me. The biker and his babe must have stayed behind. They had performed their parts to perfection, and the final act had caught me completely by surprise.

The van eased out of the motel lot and into the flow of traffic; less than a minute had elapsed since the blonde had put the boot to me.

One of my captors said, "Okay, give it to 'im."

I felt a needle jab my arm, and within seconds I began to nod off.

The last thing I remember thinking was "these guys are really good at their jobs."

50

SHACK RETRIEVED HIS KNIFE FROM THE TOP OF THE ICE MACHINE AS Holly's cell began its musical ring. It played "Zippity Dooh-Dah," and Shack rolled his eyes as Holly opened it and said, "Hi, Vinnie!" in that stupid, excitable, Jersey girl voice of hers.

As soon as they got paid for their little acting job, he was off to California in search of beach babes. He was glad that this was the last he'd be seeing of Holly—she was such a pain in the ass, she was one of the only good-looking chicks Shack had ever seen that he would take a pass on even if the offer was made.

Her voice went straight to his spine, like a little yapping dog. It would be worth all the trouble as soon as he got paid, but not until then. If he didn't get his payment and get away from her soon, he might just bash her head in and forget about the money, just to shut her damn mouth.

Holly continued her conversation, squealing every once in a while, and doing a little hopping dance of excitement.

He paced up and down the sidewalk in front of their corner room next to the breezeway, and waited for Holly to calm down and tell him their next move. After another minute or so, Holly shut her cell and turned to him with a huge grin on her face.

In her high-pitched, excited voice, she said, "Vinnie's sending a car to get us in an hour or so, and he said to wait in the room out of sight, and like, be real quiet so nobody notices us. This is so exciting! Did you see the look on that cop's face when I kicked him in the nuts? These shoes are just perfect for kicking, I mean, the way the toe is so pointy and sharp, and everything. Could you believe the look on his face! I thought he was gonna die! That was like, such a rush! I think I could really get into this acting thing. I mean the guy totally fell for it! You were really great, too, dude, I mean, he didn't have no idea that we were playing him! I've never had so much—"

"Okay, okay, Holly, calm down. Let's go in the room like your boyfriend wants us to," Shack said as he took the blonde by the arm and led her towards their door. "We done enough actin' tonight to last us for a while, so let's us just sit back and lay low like the man says."

Holly said, "Oh, okay sure. I'm ready to go in the room and hang, but wasn't that just like, the best thing you ever done? I mean, it was like—it was just like being in a movie!"

Shack steered her into the room, and said, "Yes, it was just like bein' in a movie. Now, if the money comes through, we'll be just like the movie stars, loaded down with cash. That's what *I'm* talkin' 'bout."

"Oh, you don't hafta worry about Vinnie paying us. He always takes real good care of me, and like, keeps plenty of cash around. You'll have your money real soon, don't worry about it. You know what? I'm gonna buy me a new car! Something real *fast*. What are you gonna do with your money?"

"I'm goin' up north and visit my sick mother," Shack lied. You could never be too careful with people like Holly and her boyfriend. The less they knew about his whereabouts after tonight, the better.

***

Vinnie Mandola checked the tools he kept stashed in a townhouse near Storyville—chainsaw, surgical tools, electrical equipment, butchering knives, and other assorted instruments of torture.

Over the years he had accumulated quite an assortment of utensils to make a person's last hours—or days—on Earth a living, dying, hell. He sometimes came over to the out-of-the-way place just to handle his paraphernalia, feeling all the pieces and remembering the exciting ways he had used them. It was reassuring to know his collection was right there waiting for him whenever he needed it.

Vinnie had also tape-recorded every one of his victims' screams of agony and pleadings for their lives right from the beginning. When video cameras became accessible to the general public, he'd been among the first to buy one.

He now had quite an extensive library of horrific sights and sounds, and loved to watch and listen to them when he was by himself in his hideout. However, he was not alone on this particular evening.

He excused himself when his cell phone rang, answered it, and looked out the window at the deep darkness of the street as he gave orders to the young woman he had recruited to handle the Florida cop.

After talking with Holly, Vinnie wrote the address of Al's motel along with her room number on a piece of paper and handed it to the young man who had just arrived in the States the week before. The guy had come from his hometown of Palermo, Sicily to begin his career working for his grandfather's oldest friend, Don Carmine Carrabba.

He already had four eventful years under his belt as a made member of the Sicilian Mafia. His name was Aldo, and he was eager to do anything to draw the attention of Don Carrabba.

Vinnie gave him his first assignment: "When they open the door, go in and shoot 'em as soon as you can, capeesh? Shoot the bitch first, 'cause I don't want her to have a chance to scream. *Marone,* what a voice dis one has. She can wake the dead, so blow her mouth off before she knows what hit 'er. The guy is pretty strong, so go for a head shot wit' him, too—just start blastin' and don't stop 'til they both ain't movin' no more. The piece has a silencer, so don't worry 'bout nobody hearin' it. You'll find it in the desk behind ya. Get outta there quick, and call me when it's done. You unnerstan' what I'm sayin'?"

"Yes, boss," Aldo said, fetching the gun from the desk drawer. "I can know everything you say and I do a great job for you and Don Carrabba. I call you whenever the job has been."

"Close enough," Vinnie said. "You do good tonight, an' I got plenty more work for ya. Screw it up, and we got trouble. Take the white car dat's parked out on the street, and leave it at da motel. Call me when the job's done and just say 'It's done.' You'll get my voice mail. Do you know what voice mail is?"

"Yes," said Aldo. "It is machine."

"Right, a machine. After you call, go to another one of them motels down around there and check in. Call me in the mornin' and I'll have somebody pick yuz up tomorrow. You got everything straight in your mind?"

"Straight?" Aldo asked, puzzled by the use of the word.

"I mean, you unnerstan' what you're gonna do, yes?"

Aldo beamed, "Yes, boss, I have to know everything I will do."

"Yeah, okay." Vinnie smiled at the broken English, but felt that the kid would pull off the job. One look into Aldo's dark eyes, and he could tell this guy was a killer.

Now that Holly and the biker would soon be out of the picture, Vinnie began to think of exactly how he wanted to take care of the Florida cop. It was getting more difficult with each new victim to be original in his occupation these days. With the number of killings mounting, he was running out of ideas.

As Aldo said goodbye and headed out into the night, Vinnie watched him from the window and had an inspired thought regarding how to tackle the night's job.

Originality has its place, but sometimes a guy just has to go old school.

51

NEAL AND SUSAN WERE SITTING BY THEIR POOL IN LOUNGE CHAIRS enjoying the warm night, sipping iced tea and listening to a country station on the radio. Neal knew the topic of where Coop was and what he was doing would come up sooner or later, but had so far managed to dodge it successfully.

He had asked Susan every question concerning their daughters that he could think of, and Susan had been more than happy to tell him all the latest concerning the girls. If he asked about one of the girls' boyfriends, he knew the answer would go on for several minutes, leading to other topics as they entered her mind. After listening to several lengthy answers, he was running out of questions. When he asked what Jill's shoe size was, Susan looked at him as if he had two heads, and asked, "Why in the world do you wanna know that?"

"Well, um, I don't know, I just thought—"

"You just thought that if you keep me talkin' all night, maybe I won't notice that Coop isn't here and hasn't called, and you won't have to cook up some lame excuse to cover for him, am I right, big boy?"

Neal looked away and said, "Well, he's not comin' here tonight, and don't ask me why, I promised that I would keep his whereabouts a secret." Looking back at her, he said, "He's not doin' anything that you need to know about, but I *am* a little concerned that he hasn't called. Fact is, though, he's a full-grown man and doesn't hafta check in with me and tell me every little thing that he's doin'. Anyway, I'm sure he'll call before it gets too late."

"What's he doin' that I don't need to know about? Is he in some kinda trouble? If he comes in here with his face all busted up again, I swear—"

"Susan, settle down now, it's just stuff concerning the Quitman girl, and you don't need to know about it, that's all. He's not in danger, or anything," Neal lied, his eyebrows rising for just a second.

"I saw those eyebrows go up, Neal Feagin. You know you can't lie to me, so why don't you just tell me what the deal is?"

"Now, look, baby—"

"Don't you 'baby' me, buster brown. Tell me what the problem is. Right this minute."

Neal sighed, resigned to his fate, "Okay, it's like this. Coop met a girl when he was stayin' downtown at his hotel, and he's shackin' up with her, and he doesn't wanna face you, 'cause he knows you'll figure it out somehow, and tell Penny about it. Are you satisfied now?"

Susan said nothing for a moment, unsure whether or not to believe this bit of information. Deciding to, she asked, "Have you met this woman?"

"No, but he's really got the hots for her, and I promised him I'd keep his secret. You know that he and Penny have been on the outs lately."

"Yeah, I know," Susan said, studying her husband's face for rising eyebrows or facial tics. Still skeptical, she asked, "That's the truth, the whole truth, and nothin' but?"

"Yes, baby, it is. Now, promise me you that you won't tell Penny—it'd break her heart. You know how she feels about that boy."

Susan started to speak, but Neal's personal cell phone rang, a number known only to family and close friends. The hot line. Neal kept it with him at all times, and knew that when it rang, there was a friend or a family member on the other end. No one in the police department had the number, so he knew the call wasn't regarding police business.

"Hello?" Neal was silent for ten seconds. "Oh, hi Coop," he said, looking at Susan and winking. "Oh, okay—sure, I can come get you. No, not a problem. Susan and I are just sittin' out here by the pool." Twenty seconds passed with Neal saying nothing. "Okay, I'll call the department tow truck, save you a few bucks. No, don't worry about it; I'll be there as soon as I can. Okay—later."

Something about the tone of her husband's voice and the long silence in the middle of the call made Susan feel uneasy. She sat silently, searching Neal's face again for a moment, trying to decide whether to question him about her feeling.

"Was that really Coop? Is one of the girls in trouble, and you're tryin' to hide it from me?"

Laughing softly, he said, "No, Susan, it wasn't one of the girls. Coop's got car trouble, and he wants me to come help him get him and his new babe back to her house. I'll handle it just as soon as I can, and be back before you know it. Go on up and go to bed, and have a little faith in your husband."

"That's just it," she said, grinning. "I have a little faith in my husband. Very little."

"Cute," Neal said. He got up and drained his tea glass, bent down and kissed her cheek, and headed for his ride. He tried not to hurry until he was out of sight of the pool area, but as soon as he was, he sprinted to his truck.

He knew he had to move fast, or this night would haunt him forever. He had to find help before it was too late, and it was going to be tricky to pull it off in time.

Susan listened as he started the pickup and drove off, before she rose, picked up the glasses, and headed inside. There had to be something on TV that she could watch, maybe an old movie or a home decorating show. She knew she wouldn't be doing any sleeping until her man was back home safely in their bed.

***

Vinnie drove carefully on the way to the Carrabba meetinghouse, set on fifty wooded acres just west of New Orleans' city limits. Don Carrabba's predecessor, Carlo "Fat Charlie" Mazzone, had built the large house of imported Italian stone in 1959. It was often used for meetings, and parties. Vinnie had used the dungeon-like basement on many occasions to take care of the Family's problems. Including enemies who needed to be tortured and killed, or poor souls who had to be executed because they happened to be at the wrong place at the wrong time, and saw things that they shouldn't have.

He was always extra cautious when driving with his trunk full of his beloved instruments. Explaining why he carried scalpels and saws and electrical equipment might prove difficult if he were ever pulled over by a police officer.

Besides, he liked to get his mind right before he performed his duties. The leisurely pace at which he drove helped him to focus. And, the fact that torturing a man to death was the task at hand just made focusing a pleasure.

When he turned on the dirt road that led to the Carrabba property, he phoned ahead to inform the guards that he was nearby. As he pulled up to the gatehouse, two guys manning the entrance waved him through, and then closed the iron gate behind him. He saw the van that Alberto had used to bring his victim to the house, and he smiled as he pulled up and parked next to it in the gravel parking area.

This was going to be fun. He'd brought along something especially for this cop. A special something he hadn't used in years.

52

When the effects of the drug wore off, I found myself lying on my back on a concrete floor. I was in what appeared to be a makeshift jail cell, a sort of chicken-wire cage that looked like a storage room of some kind. There was a filthy toilet in the back corner, its seat long gone, with a couple of sheets of an old newspaper next to it on the floor. For a moment I felt relieved, thinking that somehow I had been arrested again and placed in a drunk tank, but no such luck. As the drug fog dissipated, I realized that wherever I was, it wasn't a place run by the city.

There was a light source coming from outside my new digs that kept it from being totally dark. With considerable difficulty, I sat up and tried to take stock of my latest weird situation. My head throbbed in rhythm with each pulse of my heart, and I wasn't sure if I could stand up without falling back down, so I remained sitting as I tried to figure out where my abductors had brought me.

From the musty smell of the place, I deduced that I was in a basement. It was unusual because of the height of the ceiling, which looked to be at least twenty feet high. It was more of a dungeon than a basement, and the fact that it had its own sort of jail cell didn't bode well. The only positive thing I could think was at least I'm alone. I would have been an easy target for one or more prison types in my foggy condition, and probably trapped in a loveless marriage within a matter of minutes.

Finally, after a while spent sitting on the cool concrete floor—which actually felt nice after the heat of the Louisiana night—I crawled over, grabbed the chicken wire, and pulled myself slowly to my feet. Feeling steadier than I expected, I looked out into the basement toward the light. It was at the opposite end of the dungeon, behind a partition that only stretched halfway to the ceiling.

After a few seconds I heard voices and realized that I was under surveillance when a man's voice said in accented English, "Our guest is awake and on to his feet. You want I should go and bring him to the operating room?"

Operating room?

Whatever the hell that meant, it couldn't be good. It was now clear to me that wherever I was, Vinnie and his pals had me right where they wanted me.

My life didn't flash before my eyes, but I did begin to think of missed opportunities—Shelley, poorly handled relationships, Penny, my father, hopes and dreams that were soon to be dashed, again, Shelley—and then places that I would never see—Scotland, Hawaii, Paris.

A resigned depression fell over me as I realized that the thing I now wanted most was to simply get it over with as quickly and painlessly as possible. It also occurred to me that quickly and painlessly were not words in the vocabulary of Vinnie Mandola.

For the first time in my life, I wished that I was already hurtling through the long, dark tunnel, headed towards the pure white light.

"Yeah, bring 'im to da room," another man said, and what I assumed to be the first guy I'd heard stepped from behind the partition and began walking across the basement floor towards my cell, a ring of keys in his hand.

He was a pretty big gentleman, two hundred and fifty pounds or so I guessed, and in my foggy state I had no chance of overpowering him and making my escape. Hell, on the best day of my *life* I had no chance of overpowering him and making good my escape. So, I moved back as he unlocked the door and opened it.

"Come with-a me, please," he said. As he opened the door wide, he smiled so graciously that if I hadn't've known better, I might have assumed he was taking me to someplace quite pleasant, perhaps leading me to the drawing room for a dinner party. One look at the gun in his waistband convinced me that we weren't going to any place that could be described as pleasant.

One look at his sneering, pockmarked face also convinced me that wherever he was taking me, it was most likely the last place that I would ever see.

As we walked towards the partition wall, the other guy stepped out from behind it and into the light, and I recognized him immediately. He was the titan I'd bumped into the night that Shelley and Neal and I had been in the casino—the man with the shiny shoes and the beautiful suit.

He was dressed very differently now, wearing a gray jumpsuit, the kind that you see mechanics wear. Only I was pretty sure that the stains on this garment were not from grease and oil. I shuddered involuntarily at the thought, and wondered if anyone ever shuddered voluntarily. Funny the things that run through your mind when you're scared out of your wits and looking squarely at death.

So Vinnie Mandola had been at the casino that night also, no doubt keeping an eye on me and Shelley for his boss. My already shaky legs weakened further as I stumbled and shuffled across the floor towards what was surely the Operating Room.

Trying out a little bravado, I asked, "So, how's your luck been runnin' lately?"

"Better than yours, my friend," he said. "Allow me ta introduce myself; I'm Vincenzo Mandola."

"How do you do, Mr. Mandola?" I said, hoping my voice didn't crack. "I'm so glad we're finally getting properly introduced. It's so nice to see you again. And, it seems you're correct about my luck. Looks like it's run out completely."

"You got *dat* right, pal," he said, and he and his buddy guffawed like psychopaths rolling loaded dice.

53

ALDO PULLED INTO AL'S MOTEL AND SMILED AT THE AMERICAN VERSION of his name on the neon sign. It was a good omen that his first job for Don Carrabba was to be in this place, he thought.

He checked the paper that Vinnie had given him, and located the room that held his targets. He parked the car, got out quietly, and started his approach towards the door, looking around to make sure he wasn't being watched. No one was visible in the parking lot, so he pulled the gun from inside his lightweight suit jacket, and screwed the silencer into place. He had never held such a fine weapon, and it made him feel that he'd made the right decision in coming to New Orleans. The gun was solid and balanced, and felt good in his hand. He put it back inside his jacket, looking around again to make sure he wasn't seen.

This was not Aldo's first contract killing. He had killed nine men, and a woman and a small child, although they were an unavoidable accident. They had walked in unexpectedly as he gunned down the husband and father of the pair. He regretted having to do it, but the killings were the price that all three had to pay for the man's disobedience. None of them would be dead if only the man had upheld the bargain he had made with Aldo's boss. But all that was part of his other life, and his first American job was what he needed to concentrate on now.

He made his way across the lot and stood at the door and listened for a full minute. He could hear a woman's high-pitched voice, and the gruff lower voice of a man responding.

He knocked on the door, and when the blonde woman asked if Vinnie had sent him, he smiled and nodded. She shook his hand and invited him in, closing and locking the door behind him.

Her muscular partner remained by the bed, silent while the blonde kept up a steady stream of rapid-fire conversation. She was still rattling on when Aldo pulled the gun from his jacket and quickly shot her twice in the mouth before turning to shoot her startled partner dead center between the eyes.

The heavily muscled man dropped where he stood, and the woman fell back onto the bed, still alive and gurgling as thick blood filled her mouth. Her legs convulsed so violently that her left shoe flew off and hit the ceiling, bouncing back down to land on her enormous breasts.

Aldo calmly put another bullet in her forehead, and she finally lay still. He then put two bullets into the back of the muscleman's head.

He stuck the still-smoking gun back in his jacket, and as he walked out of the room, pulled his handkerchief from his pants pocket and wiped the doorknob clean.

Leaving the car in the parking lot, he walked over to the next motel where there was a public phone near the entrance, and called Vinnie's number.

When he got the voice mail, he said, "It is doing," and hung up. His first job for Don Carmine had gone smoothly, and he couldn't wait to call his grandfather back home in Palermo to tell him all about it.

Aldo went inside the motel, smiled at the pretty desk clerk, and paid for his room with cash and a fake ID. He chatted with the young girl as she signed him in, using his heavy accent to his advantage. American girls had always fascinated him, and he felt that he would do well with them if her enthusiastic reaction was any indication. Aldo said goodnight, and headed out the door, turning to give her one more smile.

Love for his new country welled up inside him, and he could barely keep from dancing as he headed for his room.

***

"Come right dis way," Vinnie said genially, and gestured towards the partition.

I walked behind it into a brighter part of the dungeon. There were several saws, and large knives, lots of electrical equipment, and ropes and pulleys—a state of the art torture chamber.

Two tall iron poles about twelve feet apart held a third between them. It was probably eight feet or so off the floor with chains and shackles attached. The poles were the only things that looked permanent in the room. The other stuff was in boxes or bags, probably brought from somewhere else.

My false bravado gave way to terror as I imagined what the coming hours would bring. I wish I could say that I was brave and ready to spit in my captors' eyes, but the truth is, I began to tremble like a Chihuahua.

Unless you've faced death by combat, or been captured and held hostage by terrorists, or maybe had someone hold a loaded gun to your head, there's no way you could understand the feeling of utter helplessness that came over me.

My last hours on Earth were to be spent in agony without hope of escape. I simply could not believe that this was the way I was going to die. I had been in Gulf Front minding my own business a week ago, and now I was about to be tortured to death by a subhuman brute.

Vinnie told me to take a seat in a metal folding chair that was positioned in the middle of the large room, and I remembered my dream of Shelley being held by the terrorist organization that may have already killed her. The other man asked Vinnie something in Italian, disappeared briefly, and returned a moment later with a canvas duffel bag that looked like something a sailor might carry. He set it down and crossed his arms over his chest, leaning against the wall and smiling at me.

Keep them talking as long as possible, I thought, and pray for the kind of miracle that you know isn't coming.

Vinnie was oiling a handsaw, and testing its sharpness when I began my stalling tactic. "It seems you guys know a lot about me," I said. "I mean, you saw me at the casino, and your friends have obviously been followin' me. I figure I should know a little about you before you do your um, job. Only fair, right?"

He paused for a few seconds. "I guess so," he said, smiling.

"So. How did you get into this line of work?"

He chuckled and put the handsaw down. "So you wanna know how I got my start, hunh?" Then to his partner: "Should I tell him how I got started, Alberto? Should we send him off wit' my life story fresh in his head?"

Alberto said, "Shoo, why not. It ain't exactly like he gonna tell nobody, si?"

"Si," Vinnie laughed. "He ain't gonna be doin' any testifying in court when I get through wit' 'im." He looked at me and said, "Okay, here goes. I come down here from New York about twenty-two, maybe twenty-three years ago, Chief. I was a young tough guy with the Gambino Family in them days, and got into a little trouble with—" He paused. "Well, let's just say I hadda leave because I done somethin' maybe I shouldn't have, ya know? Anyways, Don Carrabba takes me in and gives me my first serious job. You always remember your first time, hunh, Chief?"

"Yeah, I would think so," I said, just hoping that he would keep talking forever, if not longer.

"What happened, see, this fag hairdresser from New Orleans got drunk as only a fag can get, and killed Don Carmine's youngest daughter, Francesca. She was ridin' her bike on the street where they lived, and the queer just runs her over. Then he crashes head-on into a tree and knocks himself out cold. Don C hears the crash, comes running out and finds his little girl dead in the street, and just loses it. She was his favorite, a real beauty, and smart as a tack. Anyways, Don Carmine gets his boys to grab the faggot and take him and his car off before the cops get wind of it. They brought him out here, as a matter'a fact. I'll never forget the punk's name—like I say, you always remember your first time. David Gregory Fontaine. It was a real pleasure wastin' the prick bastard."

He continued with a smile on his face, "In fact, youse two have a little somethin' in common, Chief. Not that I'm sayin' you're a fag or nothin'. Hand me my bag, Alberto, lemme show the Chief here what I'm talkin' about."

Alberto handed the bag over to Vinnie. I knew this was going to be real bad, if it related to the murder of a hairdresser in this hell-hole, and I was right.

Vinnie pulled what appeared to be a giant fishhook out of the bag, and held it up for me to see. Grinning, he said, "This is a honest-to-God meat hook, Chief. The Don used ta own a meat packing plant near that college downtown. Whassit called, Alberto?"

"Xavier," Alberto said.

"Yeah, dat's it, Xavier. Anyway, after they get the fag out here, the Don wants to give him special treatment, know what I mean? So, he sends his boys down to da plant and tells 'em to bring back a meat hook. Dis one I'm holdin' here, in fact. When they get back, Don C calls me in and tells me he wants this faggot to suffer like he ain't never suffered before, and lemme tell ya, I done one helluva job on dis freak. Don Carmine took me aside, and told me later, he says, 'Vincenzo, seein' that worthless fuck in pieces was the only thing dat helped me get over my heartache.' That really made me feel good inside, ya know?"

Attaching a chain to the hook as he talked, he went on with his narrative, "The boys stripped 'im naked, and I put this here hook up inside the queer where he usually *liked* to have stuff up inside him, know what I'm sayin'? Only I don't think he liked it so much this time—he was screaming like a whatta-ya call, ban-chee, or somethin'. Anyways, we hoisted him up and he's hangin' on dat pole you scc right over there, with this hook all the way up inside 'im, musta hurt like hell, and I'm goin' at 'im pretty good, sawin' over here, takin' a little skin off over there, twistin' dis, breakin' dat, you know, doin' a real number on this piece'a shit. He don't even look like a human bein' no more." He paused before saying "But I gotta say dis for the rat bastard, he stayed alive, bleedin' and losin' body parts and skin and stuff, and screamin' through the gag we finally hadda put in his mouth to shut 'im up, and he stayed alive on dis hook I'm holdin' right here for *three fuckin' days*, Chief. Can you imagine dat? It was absolutely the most amazin' thing I seen in my entire life. That's why I remember it so good, 'cause it was fuckin' unbelievable! I mean, you can't make dis shit up."

Surreal is the only way I can describe the situation. The man was telling me how he tortured another human being to death as he was preparing to torture me in the same manner.

I almost laughed when the thought crossed my mind that this was a moment I would remember for the rest of my life. The very short rest of my life, that is. Like Vinnie said, you always remember your first time.

The only thing that seemed real to me was the fact that I had to keep him talking. It was my only chance, slim as it might be.

I said, "That really *is* amazing. Three days? That's gotta be a world record. I hope you don't wanna break the record on me."

Vinnie chuckled and went back to telling me how he killed the hairdresser, but I didn't hear what he was saying.

I didn't hear him because suddenly a truly chilling thought scuttled into my head. What if he started torturing me, sawing here, and skinning there, and twisting this, and breaking that, and then someone *did* come to my rescue? After Vinnie had been going after me for hours. What if all that remained of me to be rescued was a mutilated, broken, twisted torso with a still-living head attached?

As much as I wanted to survive the situation, as much as I wanted to make it through the night without dying, I came to a particularly horrifying realization.

There are worse things than dying.

54

OUTSIDE THE CARRABBA MEETINGHOUSE, THE TWO MEN ASSIGNED TO watch the big iron gate at the entrance were back to their gin rummy game. The game had been interrupted twice during the evening—once when Alberto drove the van in, and again when Vinnie arrived. The men were always glad to see Vinnie because he sometimes stopped to talk and joke with them, unlike the sullen Alberto. Vinnie would sometimes bring them drinks or food, and occasionally he even tipped them a few bucks.

The two guys who had been helping Alberto left as soon as they took all of Vinnie's bags and boxes to the basement of the large old stone house. They didn't say a word as they left, or acknowledge the guards' presence in any way. They were nobodies in the Carrabba Family.

The small guardhouse next to the gate had seen many a game between the two gin players through the years. There was not much else to do during the long nights. If there had been a meeting or a party, there would have been many more of them for security. But there was no need for more than the two of them when only the basement was being used.

The smaller asked, "What's the name of the game?" as he laid down his winning hand.

As he was marking the tally on a tattered notepad, his partner said, "Hey, a car's comin'."

The car slowed as it came up the dirt road, passed the gate, and came to a stop about twenty yards up the road. The engine was then turned off, followed by the lights. Since there was a full moon, it could be seen clearly even from the guardhouse.

"You recognize it?" the bigger one asked.

"Nope. I never seen it before. We better check it out. You go first, I'll stay outta sight 'til we know who it is."

"Okay. And no stackin' the deck while I'm out there."

"Shaddup and go," his partner said as the big one drew his gun and walked out through the open door of the guardhouse.

As he stood behind the gate, he said in a low voice, "Whoa. There's a chick gettin' outta the car, and she ain't wearin' nothin' up top. Looks like she's drunk, too. Whatta we got *here?"*

He put his gun back in his shoulder holster without taking his eyes off of the welcome sight.

The topless woman stumbled drunkenly towards the gate, her breasts clearly visible in the bright moonlight. The smaller man came out at the mention of a half-naked female, all thoughts of staying behind now forgotten.

The bigger man said, "Hey there sweet cheeks, you lost or somethin'?"

"Not if this is the Carrabba place," she said, slurring her words. "Your boss called me and told me to come take care'a you guys. Said he shouldn't be the only one havin' fun tonight. Everything's been paid for already—alls you gotta do is sit back and let Dixie take care'a ya," she said, smiling and trying to focus her eyes.

"Vinnie sentcha, hunh?" the big one asked. "Maybe I better call 'im and check you out."

"Fine by me," Dixie said. "Just means there'll be less time for me to give head and take orders." She was swaying slightly as she took hold of the gate.

He turned to the guardhouse, but his partner took hold of his arm.

"Wait—she's right," the smaller man said. "Besides, Vinnie don't like bein' bothered while he's workin', and he's doin' us a pretty nice favor here. Open the gate and let's get the party started."

His partner looked at him, then back at the naked breasts, and decided they were both right.

"Okay, sweet cheeks, come on in," he said, and hit the button that opened the gate.

***

Vinnie was still fastening the chain to the meat hook when he turned to Alberto and said, "You better tie the Chief here to his chair. We don't want him gettin' no ideas about makin' a break for it. There's some new rope in the bottom of the bag."

Alberto got the rope and tied me to the metal folding chair. When he finished, he patted my head and said, "You all tied up pretty good now, Chief. I hope you good and comfortable."

I didn't say anything in response. I just wondered why he felt the need to pat me on the head.

Watching Vinnie working on the meat hook refocused my drifting mind. I returned to my plan of keeping them talking until my miracle appeared.

"Why me?" I asked.

Vinnie stopped working on the chain, looked me in the eye, and asked, "'Why you' what?"

"Why do you guys have such an interest in me? I'm just a cop from Florida with absolutely no interest whatsoever in what happens in New Orleans. So, why me?"

"Oh. Okay. Well, I'll tell ya, it's like dis. I don't really know why Don Carrabba has such a hardon for you. He don't like nobody knowin' about his business. He's really a very complex individual, ya know? All I know is dat I take my orders from him. And his orders are to pump you for information before I—how shall I put dis—put you to sleep. So, dat's what I'm gonna do." He smiled and began working on the chain again.

Unwilling to give in just yet, I said, "You know, the thing is, there's really no reason to do *anything* to me, if you're lookin' for information. I mean, I'm aware of a few things, but I really don't see how any of what I know could hurt your boss. In fact, everything I know about him seems to be common knowledge." Stalling for all I was worth, I asked, "Would you at least tell me what Don Carmine is so worried about me knowing?"

Vinnie paused for a moment, apparently deep in thought. Or at least as deep in thought as he was capable of being.

He looked at Alberto, then back at me before saying, "Sure, why not?"

As scared as I was, there were a few things I wanted to know. "Okay, where do I start . . . One thing I've been wonderin'—is there really a connection between Don Carrabba and Harry James Quitman?"

"You wanna know about Senator Shitman?" Vinnie said.

This got a laugh from Alberto, and I nervously joined in. Maybe a little too enthusiastically, but I was trying my best to make them see me as a human being rather than as just another job that had to be done. Pretty lame idea, but I was running out of options.

Vinnie said, "Okay, Chief, I guess I can tell ya about their connection. And actually, it's a kinda interesting story."

I didn't really care if the story was interesting or not. I just once again hoped that it would be lengthy.

"The first time they met, as I remember it, was at some kinda charity deal," Vinnie said. "You know, one'a dem big society-type parties where everybody's rich, and shit. They hit it off pretty good dat night, but what really connected 'em was what happened to da Senator's wife a coupla months later."

"What happened to his wife?"

He laid the meat hook and the chain on the workbench and asked, "You mean you really don't know? I figured you and your detective pal woulda known all about dat. Goes ta show ya. Anyways, it's like dis—the Senator killed his wife. By accident, he says. Maybe it *was* an accident, I dunno, but anyways he calls me right after it happened and I go over to his house and make it look like somebody broke in to his house and did da wife. I brung my crew and made it look like a break-in; stole all the silver and whatnot, roughed him up, ex settra. Had one'a my guys take pictures of da whole deal for blackmailin' purposes. I even tied the Senator up wit' his own neckties so's it would look good to da cops."

"Nice touch," I said.

"Thanks, dat's what I thought. Anyways, Don Carmine's got da Senator in his hip pocket from that night on, and it's been a long and very whatta-ya call, 'lucrative partnership.' Don C needs some help in Washington, da Senator's his guy. He's done a lot down here, too, ya know, helpin' change laws or just gettin' around 'em. Oil deals, introductions to da right people, whatever. Quitman's come through for Don Carmine for a lotta years and of course, Don C saved the Senator's ass."

"So Harry James had a little trouble with his wife, hunh?" I said.

Vinnie smiled, and started to speak, but stopped and looked at something behind me.

At that moment, I felt a light hand on my shoulder.

"Well, well, what've we got here? Looks like that hot shot detective, Chief Cooper."

I would've known that voice anywhere.

55

SHELLEY RAN HER FINGERS THROUGH MY HAIR, AND TUGGED GENTLY AS she slowly walked around me and brought her face down to mine.

The exquisite face I had been dying to see was now inches from mine, her blue eyes brilliant. She was dressed in a plain white tee shirt, jeans and sneakers, her hair loose on her shoulders. She sported a deep tan, which accentuated her eyes, and made her seem even blonder.

The scent of her perfume instantly brought back every memory of that extraordinary night: The moment in the casino when she let me know that we would be spending the night together, the sexy slow dance in the dimly lit jazz club, my first glimpse of her perfect naked body as she stood by the bed, and the fantastic lovemaking that followed.

Goosebumps formed on my arms as she softly pulled my face to hers and touched her lips to mine.

That beautiful blonde hair fell against my face, and I felt dizzy as my mind struggled to make sense of the mixed feelings overwhelming me. The surreal nature of the situation had taken another unbelievable turn.

There she was, my dream girl, now a player in my bizarre nightmare.

Her lips still inches from mine, she said, "Guess you didn't expect to see *me* here tonight, did you Coop? Have you been waitin' for me to call? Did you miss me?"

I could only stare.

She went on, "I guess you're wonderin' about my 'kidnapping,' hunh? Worried about that mean old gang of bad guys holdin' me for ransom? That was sheer genius, if I do say so myself." She laughed. "Those terrorists are some bad mofos, aren't they? They made my life a livin' hell down in Key West the last few days. Made me drink margaritas and lay out on the beach all day long. Yep, I gotta tell ya, Coop, fightin' the war against terrorism can make a girl real thirsty."

I stared.

She leaned in and rubbed her nose on mine, and said, "And in case you're wonderin,' that was Agent Clay doin' all the cursin' and smashin' in my house that you heard over the speakerphone. We're sort of a team, if you get my meaning, loverboy. We've been on the Carrabba payroll for quite some time now." She leaned her head back. "Sounds kinda sleazy when you say it out loud. But, the money is worth it, wouldn't you say so, Chief?"

When I didn't answer, she slowly stood up and studied my face for a full thirty seconds, inspecting my bruises and stitches. I continued to stare dumbly, unable to think of a single word to say. It was all too much to comprehend under the circumstances.

Shelley didn't seem to have the same trouble. "I heard all about your little ruckus in the hotel bar. Sounded like you were lucky you weren't killed. I was really worried about you, Coop. I hated to hear that someone had damaged that adorable face of yours, but you seem to be healin' up just fine. Wish I coulda been there to take your mind off it." She put her hands on her hips, and did a stripper's bump and grind. "Think I'd look good in a tight little white nurse's outfit? Or maybe out of a tight little white nurse's outfit? In or out, if I'd been there, I could've kissed it and made it all better. Let Nurse Shelley show you what you've been missin'."

She bent back down and tenderly kissed each bruise, all the while delicately tracing the stitches on my forehead with her finger.

I hate to admit it, but I wished it could've gone on forever. And not just because it would have extended my life, but because nothing had ever felt so good to me, ever. I could feel myself blushing from the shame I felt. This woman had played me like a kazoo, and there I sat, still responding to her touch.

I've always considered myself to have an above average intelligence, but I take the most pride in my ability to perceive. I can spot a phony a mile away, and liars usually don't stand a chance with me.

But Shelley had duped me so utterly and completely that I was beginning to question whether or not I was so perceptive after all, and my pride wasn't the only part of me that was going to suffer tonight.

Shelley stood back up, put her arms on my shoulders, and slowly lowered herself down, so that she was straddling me, her face again just inches from mine. Then she locked her fingers behind my neck exactly as she had done in her hotel room the night that we had been together.

The last time I had seen her.

The night that had haunted me every minute since.

"Don't you have anything you want to say to me, Coop? Surely you've been dreamin' of this moment."

The mocking tone of her voice made me feel even more like a fool. Her eyes had a coldness to them that I had never seen before.

Had they always been that way?

A few hours ago I would've killed to see those stunning blue eyes again, would have done almost anything to look into them just one more time. But at that moment, I wished only that I had never seen them, that we had never met, that I had never fallen for her like some lovesick schoolboy.

After days of praying and wishing for a miracle, I was back in Shelley's arms. Hog-tied to a metal chair.

Some miracle.

Shelley said, "Anyway, I heard you ask Mr. Mandola here, 'why you'? You know, it seems obvious to me, but maybe you're not as sharp as I thought."

She looked at me as if she expected a response, and when I said nothing, continued. "Mr. Carrabba is a businessman, and like any good businessman, he likes to cover his bases. And like any *crooked* businessman, he likes to stack the deck in his favor whenever possible. The deck was already stacked with the N.O.P.D., and naturally, with the FBI through myself and Agent Clay—but you? You were a wild card. Who knew that you would turn out to be so much trouble? Meeting with that pimp, snoopin' around, and bringing your clean detective friend onboard. With your experience, that made *two* homicide detectives who weren't under Mr. Carrabba's control. That was two too many, Chief." She shook her head, and made the night even worse. "Now, your best buddy Neal will have to be dealt with after you're gone."

I hadn't thought I could have felt worse at that moment, but I was wrong. The thought of Neal suffering through what I was going to go through made my heart sink even more.

"Maybe the boys *are* goin' a little overboard with you," Shelley said. "I mean, Vinnie could simply put a bullet in your pretty little head, and be done with it, but the Don is an old-timer, and sometimes he likes to send a message rather than just take someone out. The message here being: don't cross the boss. The others on the pad here in New Orleans will think twice about getting in Mr. Carrabba's way after they see what's left of you. All in all, better safe than sorry. You were just too dangerous to leave out there in the mix."

She paced silently for a moment before she came close again and continued, "You wanna know what the worst part about this is? The reason I was originally called in by Don Carrabba was to simply make this all go away. To make sure that whatever happened, he wouldn't become part of the FBI investigation into Caroline Quitman's death. Unfortunately, a murder was committed in your jurisdiction, and you got frisky after all these years of sitting on your cute ass in Florida. So, a new job was added. To make *you* go away. You were just part of my job, but I really did have a great time with you that night. I wasn't acting in my bed, like I was with the kidnapping thing. *That* acting job was to make you so worried about finding *me* that you would forget about Caroline and your old guy. It almost worked, too, but then you had to come back and get involved again. If only you had gone back and stayed in Gulf Front, none of this would have been necessary. It's such a damn shame."

I opened my mouth to speak, but she quickly put her fingers on my lips, and said, "On second thought, maybe it would be best if you don't say anything, Chief Cooper. I wanna remember you as the man you were, rather than the problem you've become."

She began to run her hands through my hair again, scratching my scalp sexily, but having no effect on me whatsoever for the first time since the moment I'd first laid eyes on her. It wasn't hatred that I felt, just numbness.

I had moved straight from rekindled lust to indifference in a matter of minutes, the worst minutes of my life and likely the last.

"Agent Brooke," I said, unwilling to honor her request for silence, "I guess this pretty much kills any dream I had of you and me livin' happily ever after."

Fixing her eyes on mine, she laughed coolly, and said, "Life is always better as a dream than as reality."

With that said, Shelley stood up and placed the palm of her left hand on my cheek. She looked down and I thought she was going to leave me with more words to remember her by. Instead she just let her hand drop to her side and motioned to Vinnie to take over and get back to business.

She left in the opposite direction from which she'd come, never turning back as she walked into the darkness and out of what remained of my life.

56

VINNIE WENT BACK TO WORK ON THE CHAIN AND SAID, "SO, CHIEF. Looks like you and the FBI babe had a little fun dat night I seen yooz two at Harrah's. Was there a little fling or somethin'?"

"Well, let's just say we spent one memorable night together. I guess that's one good thing about dyin' tonight. I won't hafta live with that memory for very long."

Vinnie turned to Alberto with a grin on his massive face. "See? There's always a silver lining." To me, he said, "Good for you that you can take your last hours like a real stand-up guy instead'a whinin' and cryin' about it. I gotta give ya respect for dat, Chief."

I said, "Gee whiz, Vinnie—may I call you Vinnie? That really means a lot to me."

That got a good laugh, and he said, "I like you, Chief. It's a shame dat you play for da wrong team. I could really use a guy like you."

"You could, hunh? Hmmm, I'll tell you what, Vin. You let me go, and I'll be the best mobster I can be."

Laughing again, Vinnie said to Alberto, "Ya gotta love dis guy!" He smiled and shook his head before saying to me, "But, we got work to do here. Ya know, Chief, I'm sorry we gotta put a man like you through all dis. And I ain't never apologized to nobody before, trust me. I mean, every other time I was doin' the world a favor, get-ting' rid'a some asshole what deserved it. But wit' you, it just don't seem right, Chief. It's not somethin' I'm gonna enjoy. But, like I said, I got my orders." He looked at his watch.

"Now, you wanna tell me what you got on Don Carrabba? And dat detective buddy of yours, Feagin, right? What has he told you, you know, about Don C and the Family?"

I said, "Vinnie, listen to me. I can't give you information that I don't have. Lemme say it again. I don't know anything that can hurt your boss. I swear to you, God as my witness, not a single, solitary *thing*."

Vinnie put the chain down for what seemed like the hundredth time, and said, "Ya know what, Chief? Da bad part is I believe you. I really do. But, now you know about me, you know about Alberto over here, all kindsa stuff I told ya about Senator Quitman and Don Carmine, and so forth. So now you really *do* hafta die. It's—it's—whatta-ya call it when somethin' happens dat you didn't expect ta happen?"

"Ironic?"

"Yeah, dat's it! Ironic." He shook his head again. "Shitty way to go out, 'ironic.'" He rubbed a spot on the chain for a moment before saying, "Well, it's been nice talkin' to ya, Chief. Really, I mean dat. Now, I better get to work and get this damn chain hooked up right. We gotta get started here."

I gave it one last desperate shot. "No way I can talk you into just letting me go?"

I thought he'd laugh, but he looked at me with a serious, almost compassionate look on his face.

"Like I toldja, Chief, I'm really sorry about dis whole thing." He looked to Alberto, and said, "Help me get da chain hooked over dat bar."

I realized that my time was up. I closed my eyes and began to pray silently, the way my mother had taught me to before bedtime when I was a six-year old.

I asked God, if it was His will, to somehow save me from this monstrous death. I asked one last time for a miracle. I asked in Jesus' name, amen.

My eyes still closed, I heard the sound of the chain rattling as the two psychos tried to put the meat hook into position on the bar between the poles.

I heard Vinnie cursing when the chain clanked on the cold concrete floor.

I heard Alberto apologize for dropping the chain on Vinnie's foot as he withstood Vinnie's foul-mouthed verbal assault.

Then I heard another voice I'd know anywhere.

57

"*Freeze!*"

I opened my eyes to see the shocked looks on my captors' faces and the new most beautiful sight I've ever seen: Penny with her Glock, in the classic shooter's stance, both of the monsters under her control.

She asked, "Coop, are you okay? Did these bastards hurt you?"

Tears of relief forming in my eyes, I managed to say, "Penny, I can honestly say I've never felt better in my life. I'm totally and completely fine. They haven't gotten around to hurting me yet."

"That's lucky for them."

I asked, "How in the hell did you find me?"

Penny said, "I'll explain everything, but hold on a minute, I kinda have my hands full right now."

"Yeah, I guess you kinda do."

She then barked at the two men, "Both of you. Put your hands on your head."

When they hesitated, she screamed, "*Now, you motherfuckers, or I'll blow your fuckin' heads off!*"

I had never heard Penny use either of those words, and I was a little shocked, but, under the circumstances, I was willing to overlook it.

Vinnie and Alberto put their hands on their heads, conceding defeat. I'm sure they were as stunned as I was to see a beautiful woman holding a gun on them, especially since Penny was not in uniform. She was wearing shorts and a halter-top. Her black hair was down, and she looked damn fine. In fact, I've never seen her look more beautiful.

Penny continued her orders, "Okay, down on your knees."

They didn't hesitate this time, and the smile on my face grew wide as Vinnie's eyes met mine. He looked like a scared little kid, albeit a gargantuan one. Alberto looked utterly menacing, and if looks could kill . . .

My smile widened even more.

Penny said, "Coop, sit tight. I called Neal and he's on his way. I'd cut you loose, but I don't think it would be a good idea to take my eyes off these birds for even a second. Can you sit like that for a little while longer?"

"Penny, I can sit here and look at this beautiful sight for days. In fact, I could probably do it for *three* days, right, Vinnie?"

He didn't smile, or acknowledge me in any way. Alberto, however, glared at me with as evil a look as I've ever experienced. I couldn't have cared less. I wasn't going to die! My prayer had been answered, and my miracle had arrived.

After a couple of minutes of tense silence, I couldn't stand it any longer, so I asked, "Penny, how in the world did you find me? Don't get me wrong, I've never been happier to see you in my life, but what the hell?"

Penny smiled broadly, and said, "All will be revealed in due time, Chief Cooper, all in due time. But for now, just relax and—"

She was still talking when I saw Alberto's hand rapidly descend to the gun hidden in his waistband, the one I had forgotten about.

"Penny! *Gun!*"

She turned her Glock on him as he pulled the gun and raised his arm, and pumped three bullets into his chest before he could get off a shot. Alberto crumpled, dropping his gun as he hit the floor. The echo from the blasts bounced off the high ceiling and walls. The sound of the gun discharging was deafening, actually a little painful. It was a glorious pain.

Vinnie's eyes were big as saucers as he watched his comrade fall. When Penny aimed at him, he squealed, "Hey! Don't shoot, I ain't got no gun!" He looked to me, pleading, "Chief, tell her I ain't packin'!"

Holding back a laugh, I said, "He's tellin' the truth, Officer Prevost. All he has are chainsaws, butcher knives, and meat hooks. But he doesn't have gun one. In fact, Mr. Mandola is a real pussycat. A big, fat, greasy, enormous pussycat."

Vinnie looked at me as if my words had actually hurt his feelings. Like I said, it was a surreal night.

Penny took control again. "Okay, pussycat, lay face down flat on the floor, and keep your hands together behind your neck. We're all gonna sit here and wait for detective Neal Feagin of the New Orleans police department."

I took a deep breath, let it out, and rolled my neck to alleviate some of the stress that had been choking me ever since I woke up on the basement floor. As soon as I was slightly relaxed, I said, "All that time you spent at the shooting range really paid off. It sure is nice havin' an expert on the force. But I need some answers. So, Ms. Prevost, you have done your duty and saved my wretched life. Now it's time to tell the Chief just exactly what the hell is goin' on. You obviously followed me here. Just exactly how long have you been followin' me?"

Penny took a moment before she said, "Now, don't get all mad about it. I followed you all the way from Gulf Front."

"You what?"

"I followed you all the way from—"

"I heard you the first time!" I snapped. "Why didn't you call me and tell me what was happening?

Penny said, "I tried to call you, but—"

"You *tried*?" I yelled. What in the hell does *that* mean?"

"Well, it means that I couldn't get—"

Before she could finish her explanation, I struggled to stand up and move out of the way, because Alberto had picked up his gun and was aiming it at me as he lay dying on the floor.

SEVEN DAYS EARLIER

On the last night of her young life, Caroline Quitman decided that she needed to take a bubble bath before she went out. She had big plans, and wanted to look her best when the time came to implement them.

She turned on the hot water in the big black marble tub, poured in a little French bubble-bath liquid, and lit several stout scented candles all around the mirrored room.

After several minutes, the tub half-filled, she undressed, put her favorite Billie Holiday CD in the built-in player by the door, and slid into the welcoming water. Melancholy music filled the dim room, and time seemed to slow down as it always did when she listened to the old tunes. No one sang like Lady Day. The pain in her voice touched Caroline like no other singer ever had, because it seemed to be a match for the pain she felt everyday.

After a long soak, she dried off and dressed in her favorite pink nightie and black stiletto heels, and daubed her signature scent on both wrists and at the base of her neck.

She checked herself in the full-length mirror of her bedroom, turning this way and that. I won't have trouble with any man tonight, she thought.

Then she took a small slender box from her top dresser drawer, and put it in the pocket that she had gotten Marina to sew into the lining of her summer raincoat. She put the raincoat on over her nightie, tied the belt around her waist, and looked at the clock by her bed. 11:52 P.M., it would be twenty-five or thirty minutes past midnight when she arrived, the middle of the midnight hour.

Perfect.

It was another hot steamy night in Louisiana, and the waxing moon shone through the huge old trees as she drove her black Jaguar convertible to the large house outside of town that served as headquarters for the Carrabba Family.

Caroline knew from experience that the trip would take no more than twenty-five minutes. She'd been there several times in the past six months attending parties with Vinnie Mandola.

The powerful car drove there almost without her conscious thought. She didn't remember making the turns when she pulled up to the open gate of the big house and came to a stop next to the small guardhouse.

The bigger of the two guards was called Nico, and he smiled at her as he leaned into her open window, enjoying the view and her scent. Another man stood behind him, scanning the dark dirt road.

"Hello there, Nico," she purred, opening her coat a little to give him a better look at her breasts. "Is Vinnie here yet?"

"Yes he is, gorgeous. The old man's having a hundred or so special guests over. Tonight's the anniversary of the Don's arrival in New Orleans. Mrs. Carrabba is away at the beach house in Florida, so the mouse is playing a little bit tonight. Are you one of the anniversary presents?"

"You know it, sweetie. You can't have a party without the presents. I have a few tricks up my sleeve that I think the fellas will enjoy." She smiled and winked at the other man who stood behind Nico in the darkness.

"Oh, I think they'll enjoy 'em too, doll-face. In fact, I *know* they will," Nico said. "You mind stepping out of the car so's I can pat you down?"

"Only if you promise to pat all the right places."

"My pleasure, baby," Nico said, opening the car door.

She stepped from the Jag and he pawed her all over her naked body under the nightie, leaving the pocket in the raincoat lining untouched.

Caroline smiled as she rubbed up against his hands, confident her secret was safe.

***

Inside the big stone house, the Don's anniversary party was warming up, getting louder and rowdier by the minute. A band was playing classic rock in the large high-ceilinged meeting room, and a small Dixieland ensemble was strolling around the backyard.

There were over a hundred male guests in attendance, and if all the police and political cronies on the Carrabba payroll had shown up, that number would have been larger by half. Those who couldn't be seen attending a party for a mobster had sent gifts, which made an impressive pile by the large rented stage. The rock group had been brought in from Dallas without being told their employer's real name or line of work. This insured that they wouldn't be too intimidated to rock and roll.

A dozen strippers from the family's several clubs were performing in front of the band, in varying stages of undress. One particularly wild young woman was on the stage trying to get the singer as naked as she was. He was laughing and singing and trying his best to stay clothed, to the amusement of the crowd. When she finally got his pants down to his ankles, he managed to break free and hobble behind the drums, knocking over a cymbal, which crashed to the stage.

The crowd cheered and applauded wildly. The stripper took a deep theatrical bow, and went after the bass player. He didn't run, and soon his pants were down around his ankles, too. That caused several inebriated guys in the crowd to drop their trousers and jump up on the stage. They all went after the stripper, who happily allowed them to hoist her above their heads and be paraded back and forth in front of the band to the beat of the music.

All around the house, inside the upstairs and downstairs bathrooms, in dark corners of the big room, and outside on the patio and in the bushes, twenty working girls were taking care of the guests' needs.

Two girls were putting on a show together on top of the large glass table in the center of the patio, kissing and pawing. A crowd formed around them, cheering them on. They were both so bombed they didn't even notice, as they tore off each other's clothes.

After several minutes, they were finally naked, and they went at each other like a pair of wildcats, which sent the men around them into a frenzy of hooting and hollering. The Dixieland band stopped playing and gathered around the girls, except for the banjo player, who went into a spirited version of "She'll Be Comin' 'Round The

Mountain When She Comes." He was the only one who got the joke, as everyone else was spellbound by the wild performance on the table.

One brave soul tried to join the girls on the table, but they got rid of him by slapping and scratching his face until he left them alone. The rest of the men took the hint, and the girls weren't bothered again. They resumed their activities with even more enthusiasm, which caused the men to hoot and holler even louder.

Booze was pouring out of bottles as fast as it could be guzzled, and since drugs weren't allowed on the grounds, the bottles were emptying quickly. Everyone knew the penalty for possessing drugs anywhere near Don Carrabba, and all of them knew of one or more persons who had paid the ultimate price for being caught. The Boss was more than happy to take his share of the profits from dealing drugs, but he was not about to go to jail for them. So booze was all that was available, but there was enough to keep everyone partying for days.

The only person who was not partying was the man himself. Don Carmine was in his office in the back of the huge house, on the phone with his wife. He was far enough away from the action that Gianna heard nothing unusual from her end. The only sound she could have heard was the music of Vivaldi coming from the stereo speakers in the office.

He listened as she complained about the help at their south Florida mansion, a familiar tune that the old man could have sung himself without missing a note. There wasn't enough this, there was too much that, blah, blah, blah. How could anyone be unhappy in a big, fine house in the elite section of Key Biscayne?

He listened for another minute, then told her that he was going to bed, and that he would take care of all her problems in the morning. This worked as it always did, and they hung up.

He lit one of his beloved Cubans, poured himself a brandy, and settled back in his leather swivel chair, finally able to relax after spending the evening pretending to enjoy the company of fools and whores.

***

Caroline parked her Jag in the gravel parking area next to the fence that separated the yard from the pasture. The house had originally been a fifty-acre horse ranch, and still had trails and fences.

Fifteen or twenty limos were parked inside the pasture near the fence, their drivers all standing around talking and smoking.

When they saw Caroline get out of her car and head to the house, they all teased her good-naturedly, and she smiled and waved. She had to concentrate to be able to walk on the gravel in her heels. On her first visit to the house, she had ended up on her rear end. This night was no time for anything like that, and she made it to the wide front porch without any problem.

Three young guys who were not yet members of the family were standing guard on the porch, and she smiled at them as she went into the house. The guards would spend the next few minutes talking about how hot she was, and what they would do to her if given the chance.

There was no one in the front of the house, but she could hear the din coming from the big room. She checked her watch and saw that it was twenty-five minutes after twelve.

Right on time.

Caroline had partied at the house several times, and had learned from Vinnie that Don Carmine always left the gathering between midnight and twelve-thirty and retired to his office in the back of the house. There he would change into his smoking jacket and have a cigar and a snifter of brandy. She had always detested the smells of cigar smoke and brandy, but she could stand them one more time. Especially since it would be the last time.

She looked to her left and saw that the long hallway was dark and empty. She headed down the hall, her heels clicking on the hardwood floor, and walked until she came to the right turn that would lead her down another dark hallway to the old man's office.

The light was on under the big oak door, and she could hear classical music playing softly. She took a deep breath and knocked twice.

"Come," said Don Carmine, and she opened the door and paused for a moment in the doorway before making her way across the large room to the high-backed chair in front of his desk.

"May I sit?" she asked.

"But of course, my dear. What a lovely surprise to see you."

Caroline said, "I'm sure it is. Do you mind if I take off my coat? It's a little close in here."

"You must forgive me, the air conditioning makes it too cold for my old bones, so I use it very little. Please, make yourself comfortable."

She took off the coat and lay it at her feet in front of the large antique mahogany desk, sat down in the chair, and crossed her legs.

Don Carrabba smiled and said, "Well, your choice of apparel will surely meet with everyone's approval. My, my, you are still quite beautiful after all these years, aren't you my dear?"

She stared at him for a few seconds before saying, "I didn't think you'd notice. After all, I'm old enough now to—what is it they say? 'Old enough to bleed, old enough to breed'? You couldn't possibly find me attractive *now,* could you?"

The hatred in her voice matched the loathing in her eyes, and the old man swiveled sideways in his chair to avoid seeing it. He tried to blow a smoke ring, but failed. His second effort sent a perfect blue-gray ring several feet into the air before it broke up and disappeared.

He puffed on his Cuban a few more times and said, "Caroline, I know you didn't come here to see me for no reason at all. What is it that brings you here?"

Again she waited before saying, "I thought you should be the first to know, Don Carmine. I wanted to share my happiness with you and see the joy on your face when I told you the wonderful news. You see, I'm pregnant. Don'tcha just love that? And the thing is, any one of the animals you surround yourself with could be the father. Or, sperm donor, I should say."

He turned his chair back and looked at her blankly.

"And what do you expect me to do about it?"

"Not a damn thing. I just wanted you to see for yourself what your years of abuse have caused. A junkie havin' a baby."

He put his cigar in the marble ashtray, scratched the back of his head, and said, "So you have come here to bring up the past and punish me, is that it? You have become a junkie on drugs who is now with child, and somehow this is *my* fault? You know, Caroline, if you feel that you must blame someone, blame your father. If not for his weakness, I would never have had the opportunity to—to act out my—my 'sexual preference.'"

"Sexual preference!" Caroline shouted. "You call stealing my virginity at nine, and raping me for six years afterward a preference? You sick, demented bastard! You ruined my life, you and my 'dear' father. Do you know that I didn't start my period until I was almost fifteen? Well, of course you knew, what am I saying? That's when you stopped comin' around! But what *I* didn't know was why my girlfriends had all gotten their periods, and I hadn't. My doctor said it was because of stress, probably from too much homework, or the pressure of trying to live up to being a Senator's daughter. Maybe I should've told him it was because I was being *raped three or four times a week by a perverted old Mafia Boss, who was doing it with my father's blessing!* Maybe I also should've told him that my daddy told *me* that if anyone ever found out about the little secret that we shared with uncle Carmine, that daddy and Caroline would both be killed, and we didn't want *that* to happen, now did we! Think I should've told my doctor? Think he still would have diagnosed my problem as stress?"

At that moment, Caroline wanted to bash his skull in with the heavy ashtray, and claw his eyeballs out of their sockets with her long red fingernails. She also wanted to weep for her lost childhood, for the little girl who suffered through all those terrible nights. But she knew she had to remain focused and finish what she had come there to do.

So she sat back and calmed herself. It was time to set the wheels in motion.

"No, Don Carmine, I don't want to punish you for your past. I'm going to punish you right here in the present. I'm going to bring you and your entire Family down, starting right now."

This brought a hearty chuckle from Don Carrabba, and he picked up his cigar from the ashtray, swiveled sideways in his chair again, and blew another smoke ring, successful this time on the first try.

Before it could dissipate, he said, "A sweet little thing like you? You're gonna bring *me* down? What, you gonna go on the TV news and tell them about bad old uncle Carmine? How I make you into a junkie whore who got herself pregnant?"

"No, I'm not goin' to the media and tell them about you—you'd just have me killed if I tried to do that. No, my way is much more subtle. The beauty of it is, you won't ever see it comin'. But mark my words, I'm takin' you down."

Don Carrabba turned his chair back, smirking, and said, "Well,

I suppose I will have to deal with it when it happens."

"Yes, you will."

He puffed on his Cuban as they looked at each other, and then said, "My dear, if you don't mind, I am growing tired, and wish to go to bed soon. Why don't you go join the party and have some fun? I know Vincenzo will be happy to see you. Tell him he might be a father soon, see how he likes the idea. Perhaps he will wish to marry you, and you can forget about all this nonsense, these dreams of vengeance. Go and be with the other young people. Have some fun."

Caroline sat up straight in her chair, stretched, and said, "Actually, that sounds pretty good right about now. But—these shoes are killin' me. Mind if I take 'em off and rub my feet for a minute or two?"

"Not at all, my dear. Please, take a few moments to relax. I'll just sit here and enjoy the music."

"Thanks. I won't be a minute."

Leaning down, she said, "Oh, it feels so good to rub my poor feet. I oughta have my head examined for wearin' these things."

Now out of his line of vision, Caroline reached into the coat at her feet, located the slender box, and opened it. She took out the syringe she had already loaded with a lethal dose of heroin, and slowly injected herself between the big toe and the second toe of her left foot.

Almost immediately, she slumped over, and then slowly slid out of the chair.

Caroline Quitman was dead when she hit the floor, the sound of her fall muffled by her raincoat.

***

After a minute of relaxing to the music, Don Carrabba said, "You know, maybe having this baby will be a good thing for you. Maybe Vincenzo will make an honest woman out of you." He chuckled and puffed on his cigar, then asked, "What do you think would be best, a boy who looks like Vincenzo, or a girl who looks like her mother?"

When he got no response, he said, "Caroline. Are you all right?"

He stood and looked over his desk, and saw that she was on the floor. He rushed around and got down on one knee beside her, and pushed at her lifeless body. Frantic, he turned her over on her back, checked her pulse, and realized she was dead.

He stood and paced as he tried to figure his next move, all the while slinging Sicilian curses at Caroline under his breath.

A jaunty Vivaldi tune was the background music for his pacing. Nothing could have been a worse choice for that particular moment. He went over to the old-fashioned turntable, took the vinyl disc off, and started to smash it before he realized that that wasn't such a good idea. He needed the office to look as if nothing unusual had happened there, and he would never be able to explain destroying one of his treasured recordings.

After pacing for another minute, he was ready to put his hastily formulated plan into action. He had decided to have Vinnie take Caroline's body to the tiny town of Gulf Front, Florida, a place he had heard about from Senator Quitman. How perfect it would be. The Senator's daughter found in a town in which her father had connections.

Perfect.

Feeling better now that the shock of Caroline's actions had worn off, he was ready to implement the second part of his plan, and there was someone he needed to call immediately.

He found a phone number in his desk drawer, and dialed Special Agent Shelley Brooke. After less than two minutes, everything was in order. Agent Brooke assured him that she would be in Gulf Front before anyone else. He hung up and took a moment to slow down and catch his breath.

Now as relaxed as he could be under the circumstances, he opened the big oak office door, and checked the hall. Finding it empty, he wrapped Caroline's body in her raincoat, and put the syringe back in the box. He slid the box under his desk for the time being. There would be plenty of time to dispose of it later.

Still strong despite his age, Don Carmine picked her up and quickly made his way down the hall that led to the back of the house. When he got to the door that led outside, he put down Caroline's body and slowly opened the door to check if the partygoers on the back patio could see him.

Certain that he could not be spotted, he took the body down the steps and through the darkness alongside the patio wall, then placed her on the grass just a few feet outside the halo of the backyard lights.

The crowd on the patio was making a lot of noise, gathered around the big glass table cheering and whistling at something that Don Carmine couldn't see. He was thankful for the diversion, and silently made his way back to the house. He hurriedly retraced his steps back to his office and closed the door.

He opened the vault concealed behind the portrait of Caruso that hung on the wall beside his desk, planning to hide the box that held the syringe inside it. After a moment, he changed his mind and shut the vault. It was too risky to keep it there, so he got down on his knees and retrieved the box from under the desk, and put it in the pocket of his smoking jacket.

He turned off the office light and quickly made his way up the back staircase to his bedroom. Once there, he undressed, picking up his book from the bedside table so he could pretend to be reading when someone found the body and came to notify him.

After a few minutes, he realized that the evidence was still in the pocket of his jacket, so he leapt from the bed, got the box, and slipped it under his pillow. Now all he had to do was wait until someone found Caroline's body and came upstairs to alert him.

The old grandfather clock in the corner loudly ticked off each second. When it sounded the hour at one A.M., he nearly jumped out of his skin. It continued its relentless march for what seemed like ages, but was in reality less than fifteen minutes.

Finally, he heard footsteps heading up the stairs to his bedroom. He sat up straight, holding the book out in front of him as if he were reading it.

He heard a knock on his door, and said, "Come."

The door opened and Vinnie Mandola walked quickly to his boss's bedside. "'Scuse me for botherin' ya like this, but we got trouble, Don Carmine. *Big* trouble," Vinnie said breathlessly, winded after his quick ascent of the stairs.

Don Carrabba calmly laid down his book and asked, "What kind of trouble, Vincenzo?"

"I just found Caroline Quitman in the grass near the patio. She's dead."

Doing his best to appear shocked, the old man said, "Oh, no. I didn't even know she was here." He paused for a moment, and then asked, "Did anyone else see her?"

"We got lucky there, Don Carmine. The only other person what seen her was Alberto. He stashed her body under da back stairs in dat closet. He's keepin' a eye on her now."

"How did she die?"

"Dat I don' know. There ain't no marks on 'er, and no blood or nothin', so she wasn't shot or knifed. Maybe she was strangled?"

"Did she have marks on her throat?"

"I really couldn't tell ya, it was real dark and everything."

Don Carmine rubbed his chin and said, "Well, how she died is not important now. What's important is getting rid of her body." He pretended to think for a while before saying, "I want you to get her out of town, out of the state. Steal a car and take her over the state line."

Confused by the order, Vinnie said, "All respect, Don Carmine, but why do youse want her out of the state? We could just bury her, or take her to da swamp, or whatever. I could take her apart and—"

"I know what we *can* do, Vincenzo. I'm telling you what we are *going* to do. I want her body found. I want her father to see what he made of her. I want to rub his face in her death. I want the news people to hound him, and that will help take the spotlight off of us. And most important, if you take her body across the state lines, the FBI will be brought in, and I have plenty of influence to use to make sure this goes away fast. Do you see my meaning now?"

"Yes, sir. Forgive me askin'. I shoulda known you was way ahead of the game."

Don Carrabba said, "Good. Now, here's what I want you to do. Take Alberto, steal a car, and leave the body out in a public place where it will be found soon. Get rid of her car, too, and make it fast."

"You want I should take her to Texas?" Vinnie asked.

"No, definitely not Texas—too many friends of ours are there. Take her to a small town in Florida, Gulf Front to be exact. It is near Pensacola, I believe. Find it on a map. *Gulf Front*, capeesh?"

"Gulf Front. Got it," Vinnie said.

Don Carmine asked, "You have a man who can get rid of the car tonight?"

"Absolutely. We got a guy runs a pretty big chop shop not thirty minutes from here. I'll get one'a the young guys to take care'a dat. Her car will be scattered all over the South by tomorrow afternoon. And no problem with gettin' a ride, me and Alberto can get a car in no time. He's a expert at boostin' cars."

"Excellent. Get on the road immediately, and report back to me tomorrow at a reasonable hour. It will be best if I go home tonight. Meet me there late tomorrow afternoon."

"It's a done deal, Don Carmine. Rest easy, you can count on me to take care'a everythin'."

"I know that I can, Vincenzo. One last thing. Get a clean-up crew here to remove any traces of the girl. Clean the house from top to bottom, and outside as well. By the time you get back, she will be someone else's problem. We will look back on this as nothing but a bump in the road."

58

When I opened my eyes, the first thing I realized was that I had tubes in both nostrils, but I calmed down when I saw that I was in a hospital bed. I could hear a beeping sound, and my left index finger was in a monitor. I wasn't on a respirator and I took that to be a good sign. Breathing on your own is pretty much always a good sign.

There was a bandage on my head that wrapped around and covered the top of my head down to my ears, and my right shoulder felt stiff and very sore. It was also bandaged, but not as heavily as my head.

The clock on the wall across from the bed read one fifty-two, and I could tell by the light filtering in through the closed blinds that it was daytime. The room was silent, I was the only occupant. I was impressed that for once I had my own room. I hated the times I spent in hospital rooms with other people. It's bad enough just being in one, much less having to listen to someone snore, or rattle on about how they see the world, or cough continuously, or just exist in your space. I like to have power over who I allow in my space, or at least have the option to walk away, which is difficult with a tube in your arm, or your nose.

As my eyes adjusted to the light, I checked out my surroundings. To the left by the door was a thing that's like a chalkboard, but it was white. You can write on them with a magic marker and then erase it. Whatever they're called, it read, Your Nurse Is on the top, and written in magic marker below was Karen. August 20 was also written under her name, and it seemed that I had lost track of time, as it was about three weeks or so later than I thought it should be.

I lay in bed and stared at the clock on the wall, trying to clear my head and remember why I was there. After ten minutes or so, my memories caught up with me. Being shanghaied at Al's motel, being scared out of my wits by Vinnie Mandola in the Operating Room,

Shelley appearing like a ghost in a bad dream, and Penny coming to my rescue. I closed my eyes for a few more minutes, and thanked God that I was still alive.

When I finally felt ready, I found the nurse call button and pushed it.

In about twenty seconds a nice-looking nurse came hustling into my room with a chart in her hands. She looked to be about thirty or so, and seemed genuinely happy to see that I was awake.

"Chief Cooper!" she said excitedly as she came and stood by the bed, "Welcome back from la-la land! How do you feel?"

"Well, Karen, I'll tell you. I have a slight headache, but other than that, I feel pretty good. Have I been much of a problem for you guys?"

"You've been an absolute pleasure, Chief. I like the strong, silent type," she said with a smile. "You sure do have a lot of nice people who think the world of you. I can't remember anybody having such loyal friends. In fact, last night was the first time somebody didn't sleep here in your room waiting for you to wake up. One really pretty woman, Penny, I think her name is, spent the whole first week in that chair over there. She's been so worried about you, I just know she's gonna go nuts when she finds out you're back among the living. And that nice detective and his family have been here every single day in one grouping or another. Those beautiful blonde girls took turns reading to you. See, beside your bed? That's a copy of 'Lonesome Dove' they've been reading to you. They said it's your all-time favorite book, so that's what they brought. And their mother read to you from the Bible a lot, too. You're a very lucky man to have such wonderful people love you like that, Chief. Now, what would you like? Water, or juice? You've been fed by an IV for this whole time, and I'm not sure when you can have solid food again, but I'm sure you can have something to drink."

I said, "I'd really like a glass of ice water to start, and maybe somethin' for my headache?"

"No problem. I'll be right back. Do you want me to call anyone for you?"

"Yes, please, Call Detective Neal Feagin if you would."

Karen fluffed my pillow, and said, "I have his number at the nurse's station. I'll call him right this minute, and bring you some water and Tylenol. How's that sound?"

"Sounds perfect. I'll be right here when you get back."

"You better be. I don't wanna hafta come lookin' for you."

I said, "Thanks for everything, Karen."

"My pleasure. I'll be back in a jiffy. You just lie back and relax. It's really nice to meet you," she said as she headed out the door.

"Nice to meet you, too," I said.

After what I'd just been through, it was nice to meet anybody.

59

LESS THAN FIVE MINUTES AFTER KAREN HAD LEFT, FEAGIN CAME INTO the room carrying a plastic cup of ice water and two Tylenol capsules, a big goofy smile on his face.

"Look who's back from the dead. Chief Cooper, my favorite vegetable. Don't you worry about a thing, Veggie Man, Nurse Neal is here and I'm gonna take real good care'a you."

"Lord, help us all. The first face I recognize, and it has to be yours? Why can't you be Susan, or one of the girls?"

"Don't worry, bud, they're all at the new mall that just opened out near the house, and when I call and tell 'em you're back, you're gonna hafta to spend hours with each and every one of 'em. They'll probably fill up this room with presents for their second-favorite man. I'm just glad I have a rich wife."

"Me too," I said. "Where's my good-lookin' nurse?"

"I bushwhacked her and stole your drugs—just happened to be walkin' in to see your sorry butt when she told me the good news. It's great to have you back, partner."

Seeing Neal made me realize that I really was back, and that everything was going to be all right after all. I had to struggle to keep my emotions in check.

But I wasn't about to tell him that.

I said, "Before we get into the particulars of my hospital stay, I need to know somethin'."

"What?" Neal said as he handed me the pills and the water. I washed them down and handed the cup back to Neal.

"I wanna know how Penny found me, and why she followed me, and how come she didn't call me?"

"Okay, let's start from the beginning. She followed you because she loves you, and didn't want you to get yourself killed."

"How could she have followed me without me seein' her? I

could spot that little red car of hers anywhere."

"Ah," Neal said. "That's just it, she didn't follow you in her car. She rented a big Mercury Marquis in Pensacola the day before you left. She knew you'd spot her Miata, or any of Big Jim's rides, so she got a car you'd never recognize."

"Okay, that makes sense. But if she was followin' me from the time I left Gulf, how come she didn't call me and tell me about the goons at Al's motel?"

"That was *your* fault, numbskull. When you changed cars at the police station, you left your suitcase and the bag with your cell in it behind. We found the phone and the suitcase when Big Jim called and asked me to get his car back to him."

"Okay, I'm an idiot, I'll give you that. But why didn't Penny just call my motel room?"

"Because the phone line was down for about eight hours that day."

"Oh, yeah, I remember now. The clerk told me when I tried to get a wake-up call. That's pretty convenient. Did the mob boys have anything to do with that?"

Neal said, "Actually, no. The line had been down for a coupla hours before you ever got there. It was just one of those things, bud."

"Okay, but if she couldn't call, why didn't she just knock on my door and warn me?"

"Boy, you are one slow individual. Are you sure you're not still comatose? Maybe I better call your nurse," he said.

"What?"

"If she had come knockin' on your door, brainless, then both of you would've ended up in that hellhole. As usual, the woman made the right decision, and saved your rear end."

I saw that he was right, and that Penny was, too. How could I have left my stuff in the car at the police station, I wondered. Then I remembered all that had happened that week. I said, "With all the stuff goin' on in my life at that time, I was lucky I didn't forget my name."

Neal said, "You're also a lucky man to have made it through all this alive. Most guys don't have a babe like Penny backin' 'em up."

"Besides havin' Penny, I don't see that I'm so lucky."

Neal rolled his eyes and said, "If you don't see that, maybe I really *should* call the nurse."

I laughed a little, which made my head pound, then said, "What I mean is, I busted a guy once in Tallahassee for selling cocaine, and he did his time in one of those 'country club' prisons. You know the type, low-security, tennis courts, decent food, and no hard work. Well, when he got out, I saw him one night and told him how lucky he was to have been sent to a relatively pleasant place. He said, 'If I was really lucky, I never would've been caught selling cocaine.' I guess it's all in how you look at it."

"You're an idiot," Neal said.

I chuckled, and my head pounded a little more. I had more questions, so I said, "Detective Feagin, please take a seat and fill me in on some more of the missing parts to this equation."

He pulled the chair over from the corner next to the bed.

"Ask away."

"Okay, I know that Penny followed me from home, so she saw me at the rest stop, and at the police station, but, how did she know what car I was driving when I changed to the green Ford?"

"Well, I'm sorry to say that the Carrabba Family had guys working for them in the department. In fact, four of 'em have already been arrested. The fifth is in the wind. Anyway, to answer your question, Penny was smart enough to keep following the bad guys instead of you, and they got the word from inside that you had changed cars. She's really somethin,' ya know?"

"Believe me, I know. Okay, that takes care of that. Now. How did she end up in the basement without being seen?"

"Oh man," Neal laughed. "This is the best part of the whole deal, by far. You're not gonna believe this. Okay, she follows the guys who grabbed you at Al's motel out to the Carrabba meetinghouse."

I stopped him, "Is that where I was? The meetinghouse? I was drugged at the time, so I have no idea where they took me."

"Yeah, it was the Carrabba house. It's on fifty acres just outside of town. It used to be a horse ranch in the old days, still has trails and stuff, which I'll get to in a minute, but let me tell ya about Penny. It's unbelievable. Man, I love that woman."

I said, "Shut up and tell me, already."

"I'm gettin' there, I'm gettin' there. Don't rush me. This is just too good. Okay. Penny sees the van turn onto the dirt road that leads to the house, so she cuts her lights and follows 'til she sees it enter the gate. Then she puts the Marquis in reverse and backs it down the road to figure out what her next move will be. Then she calls me on my hot line, and me and Susan are sittin out by the pool, just hangin' out, listening to music. Then, while Penny's talkin' to me, who should she see turn onto the road but a big, fat guy in one of those huge old white Lincoln Continentals. She doesn't know who he is, but I sure do, so I lie to Susan and run to my truck and call Penny back. Only fat guy I know who would be goin' there in an old white Lincoln is—"

"Vinnie Mandola," I said.

"Correct. So, I tell her how dangerous he is, and to wait for me, that I was gonna get a warrant and come out there with sirens screamin.' She says, 'okay, I'll wait,' and I head for my office to roust a judge who'll get me a warrant. Only thing is, Penny is not goin' to wait for me to get there, when she knows her boy is now in the hands of that murdering bastard Mandola. This is where it gets good. Damn, I love that woman!"

"Will you get to the point, you're killin' me. My head is gonna explode."

"Okay, bud," he said, a huge grin on his face, "Picture Penny, topless under a full moon."

I closed my eyes, my headache throbbing, and was silent for a few moments.

"Coop?" Neal asked. "You okay? You want me to get the nurse? Is your head all right? Coop?"

I made him wait another moment before saying, "You told me to 'picture Penny topless under a full moon.' That's what I'm doin'," I said, smiling.

"Very funny, moron. Stop foolin' around."

"Sorry, it was just too easy. What in the hell are you talkin' about, 'Penny topless'?"

"This is so brilliant. Penny pulls up past the gate to the house and parks. She takes off her top, and stumbles up to the guards like she's drunk, and tells 'em their boss has sent her. She acts like she's a hooker Vinnie called to come service these two idiots, and they buy it! She's just too much!"

"Will you please just get on with it?"

"I'm *tryin'*," he said, laughing. "So these two geniuses let her in, and here's Penny, tits in the breeze, acting like a drunk whore, and these guys think they're gonna have a little party on the boss's dime. When all of a sudden, she pulls her Glock out of the back of her shorts, takes their weapons, and locks 'em in the trunk of her rented Mercury! I mean, is she unbelievable, or what?"

I needed a minute to process the information before I could speak. A smile slowly grew from ear-to-ear as I thought of how sexy Penny must have looked in the moonlight, on her way to save my life.

I said, "You're right, bud. Damn, I love that woman."

Neal laughed, and said, "I don't care what it takes, Coop, you have got to get Penny back. If you don't get down or your knees and beg her to marry you, I'm gonna personally beat your ass. And if I can't get the job done, believe me, Susan can."

"Slow down now, what makes you think she wants me back?"

"Uh, duh, well—let's see here. She follows you all over the southeast, uses her body to break into a mob house, and takes on two psychotic Mafia murderers to save your life. Gee, I don't know why in Heaven's name I would think she wants you back."

"Well, we can discuss the wedding later. But, you're right, Penny is absolutely amazing."

Neal said, "No kiddin'. So, now that I got your attention, there's some other news you might enjoy hearing, although nothin's gonna top Penny's measures. But let's see, where's a good place to start?"

"What happened to Vinnie?" I asked.

"Good question. Well, your old pal Vincenzo is in Witness Protection. He's given the Feds enough on Carrabba to put the old man away forever. They have him in custody as we speak. Don Carmine is finished, and most of the family is under indictment, or in jail, or has left town. Vinnie is gonna bring the whole lot of 'em down before he's through talkin'. Oh—he said to tell you 'no hard feelin's, and he hopes you get better real soon.' What a nimrod."

"You know," I said, "The thing is, he was actually pretty nice to me. Except, of course, for the intended torturing and killing part."

Neal looked at me seriously, and said, "It scared the hell out of me thinkin' about you at the mercy of that sick bastard. All the way over to the meetinghouse, I was seein' pictures in my mind of what he might be doing to you." He looked at his hands. "We found out Vinnie had recorded every one of his murders. The first few were just sound recordings, but then he started videotaping them. He told the Feds the location of the townhouse where he kept all his stuff. I couldn't watch any of 'em, but one of my guys told me he had videotaped Lucy. He said the sounds were as bad as the pictures." He paused again, and then said, "Oh, another thing—Vinnie copped to killin' your guy. Cecil Harwell? He said the old man saw them make the body drop. Anyway, the Feds gave Vinnie partial immunity in exchange for his testimony. He's gonna hafta do some time, but not as much as he deserves by any means. I can't believe that fat sonofabitch isn't gonna get the death penalty, but it looks like he won't." He stared at his hands again. "When I think about what he would've done to you."

"Stop thinkin' about it then, and get back to the rest of the players in this movie. What about Harry James, what's gonna happen to him?"

"It already happened. He took his late wife's shotgun, and swallowed it. They found him in the foyer of his mansion here in town, his head splattered all over the wall. Vinnie says it's the exact spot where his wife died. It was quite the scandal."

"Wow. The hits just keep on comin'. Looks like I missed a lot while I was away. What happened, did Vinnie tell the story about Harry James' wife, and the cover-up?""

"Yep. He didn't have much choice, seeing as it was on the videotape he made of you. Oh yeah, I almost forgot," Neal said, starting to laugh. "There's one thing on the videotape that got the same response from everyone who saw it. Every single person, male or female, asked if you and Penny were married, or said that you and Penny should *get* married."

"Why?"

"Because right before Alberto shot you, you were yellin' at Penny about why she followed you, and why she didn't call you, and she was tryin' to explain, and you were yellin' louder. Think about it for a minute: You're tied to a chair, about to be tortured to death, she's holding a gun on two Mafia killers, and you two are *arguing*. If that wasn't typical behavior of an old married couple, nothin' is."

I couldn't help but laugh, too, and that made my head throb harder. It's the only time I've ever enjoyed having a headache.

After Neal finally stopped laughing, we sat quietly for a few minutes, and it felt like we were out in the boat, fishing the bayou. I still had questions, so I brought us back to shore.

"What about the biker and the hooker who tricked me at the motel, no pun intended?"

"None taken. We found them at Al's in a room near yours. They'd both been shot, execution style. Well, maybe a little more overkill than execution style. Turns out, she wasn't really a hooker—name was Holly DaSilva. She was just down from Jersey, and was Vinnie's latest flavor-of-the-month. The biker really was a biker, though. Alberto hired him off the street downtown somewhere. The shooter used a silencer, so no one heard any shots. Nobody saw anyone go in or out of the room, either. We got his name outta Vinnie, but the guy is in the country illegally, so we have no idea where he is right now. The FBI is on the case, so we'll see what happens with that."

"That Holly girl had really sharp shoes," I said.

Neal chuckled, and said, "Yeah, Penny told us about how she, uh—disabled you."

"Boy, did she ever."

"Well, that should teach you a valuable lesson. A man shouldn't be doin' good deeds outside of his jurisdiction," Neal said.

I asked, "Speaking of that, did anybody bother to get my gun?"

"No, sorry, it was stolen from your room, evidently. I know you loved that old relic. I mean, you got it when—your patrol days?"

"Yeah, I've had it for over twenty years. In the old days, I never would've confronted those two without my piece, but I'm rusty after being in Gulf Front for so long. Besides, like I said—I was out of it at the time. I'll miss that old gun, but I'll trade it for being alive any day."

Neal agreed, "Yeah, that's a pretty good trade, all right. Now, enough about all that. What else you wanna know?"

"How did I end up in a coma?"

"Well, Penny said that you were trying to stand up just as Alberto shot you in the shoulder, and the force of the gunshot knocked you backwards. Your big head hit the concrete floor pretty hard. In fact, you fractured your skull, but the doctor says you'll be okay. Or at least as okay as an ultra-maroon such as yourself can be."

"Har, har. So—did Penny kill Alberto?"

"Oh, hell yes," Neal said. She just about blew his head clean off. After he nailed you, she put five more in his head to go with the three she'd already put in his chest. It was a really tight cluster, too—in the chest, I mean. Her hands had to have been completely steady when she fired to get a cluster like that. What a babe. Don't mess with a woman who's defending her man. When we came in, she was sitting on the floor cradling you in her arms with her gun aimed at Vinnie's head."

I thought to myself, *Damn, I really do love that woman.*

Reading my mind, Neal said, "You gotta marry Penny."

"Shut up. Were you able to get a warrant to search the house before you got there?"

Neal said, "No, I wasn't, the two judges I contacted turned out to be owned by Carrabba, so they gave me the runaround, and wouldn't give me the go-ahead. Obviously, I couldn't just sit there and wait, so I went out to the Carrabba house with a few of my boys that I trust, and—well, let's just say I'm in a little hot water. Technically, the search may be bad, but since Penny was there, who knows? I don't know what's gonna happen, but I'm on suspension until further notice. The fact that I tried to get a warrant from two crooked judges who are now under indictment might make a difference. Anyway, the department lawyers are handling it. Now that they have Vinnie's testimony, it should all come out in the wash, but to be honest with you, I'm not really too concerned about it. This may turn out to be a good thing for me in the long run, whatever happens. So, I've just been takin' it easy, bringin' the girls over here to see you in a coma, talkin' about you bein' in a coma, admiring your bandaged head in a coma. All in all, it's been a fun three weeks, no question about it."

"Yeah, man, I'm at my best in a coma."

"You said it."

"So you're basically a bum with a rich wife is what you're sayin'. How bad can that be? Is Susan gonna make you get a job, or is she resigned to the fact that she'll be carryin' you the rest of your life?"

Neal said, "Actually, I don't know if I'm gonna go back to the department, whatever happens. Susan's been talkin' about movin' back home to Atlanta. There's a lot of open land thirty or forty miles outside the city limits, and I may just become a gentleman farmer, or at least a country gentleman. I'm also entertaining the idea of becomin' a private investigator. Feagin, P.I. Whatta-ya think?"

"I think you'll miss the gambling, and so will I. How will I be able to afford losin' at Harrah's without your wife's money?"

"Hmm. That's a real problem. But, we can always go straight, give up the life of crime," he said. "Besides, New Orleans is a short flight from Atlanta. We can still go. In fact, we can fly off to anywhere out of Atlanta. We can be in Vegas or Atlantic City in no time."

"You know I hate to fly. But the P.I. thing is not a bad idea. I've always thought it would be great to open an office in a big ritzy shopping mall. Think of the walk-in business you'd get from all the rich women hiring you to follow their husbands and catch 'em with their girlfriends. You could make a fortune on divorce cases alone."

Neal said, "That actually might work, two ex-homicide cops going into business together. Feagin and Cooper Investigations. Has a nice ring to it. And don't try and change it to Cooper and Feagin, I'm the one with the rich wife. Speakin' of wives, lemme go outside and call Susan, tell her you're awake. See how long it takes her and the girls to get here. She's just gonna wet her pants."

Neal came back in ten minutes and sat back down in the chair by my bed. While he was gone, I thought about what other questions I needed to have answered. I had been avoiding the subject for as long as I could, but I finally had to know.

I couldn't look Neal in the eye when I asked, "So, did Penny or any of your guys see Agent Brooke that night?"

An awkward moment passed, and then Neal said, "You fell pretty hard for Shelley, didn't ya, bud?"

Keeping my gaze downward, I said, "Neal, we had this conversation once before, remember? More than once, now that I think about it. When are you gonna realize that she's outta my league?"

He said gently, "Coop, I think you're forgetting somethin'. Remember about Vinnie and his videotapes?"

"Yeah, I remember, but what has that got to do—"

That's when it dawned on my fresh-from-a-coma brain. Neal had seen Shelley humiliating me on videotape. I shut down completely for at least a minute, and Neal never said a word. It took me that long to be able to look in him in the eye again.

Finally, I asked quietly, "Does Penny know?"

"Not to my knowledge. Only a few people in my department saw the tape, and the FBI has copies, of course. Unless she has contacts that we don't know about, she has no way of knowing. Naturally, I didn't tell Susan. I'm sorry as I can be, bud. I know it must be killin' you."

"I can't lie, Neal. I was in love with Shelley. Big time. But when she showed up in that basement, it was obvious that I've never been so wrong about anyone or anything in my life. I convinced myself at the time that I didn't care about her anymore, but I'm not so sure about that right now. It's gonna take me a while to get over her, that I'm sure of. I'm gonna need some time."

Neal said, "Well, one thing we know for sure is that Penny will be there when you're ready. I know you two can work out whatever problems you may have."

"That's the last thing on my mind right now. Besides, it wouldn't be fair to Penny. I'm a wreck right now."

"Okay, so take some time off. You can come stay with us at the house. But get ready to be spoiled rotten. The treatment you got the last time you were there will be nothin' compared to what Susan and the girls will lay on you this time."

I smiled at the thought of being pampered and spoiled by four gorgeous women before saying, "No, Neal, as great as that sounds, I think I'm gonna go home when I get outta here, and just take it easy for a while. Maybe catch up on my reading."

"You? Reading? What kinda reading are we talkin' about?"

"Anything but detective mysteries," I said.

Neal smiled, "I get your point."

"Speaking of mysteries, what's the deal with Shelley? Did they arrest her, too?" I asked.

"That's another interesting story. She went out through the underground tunnel, and disappeared completely. She'd parked on an old side road, and got away clean as a whistle. Nobody has any idea where she is."

"Wait a minute, the 'underground tunnel'?"

Neal said, "I know, it sounds ridiculous, but here's the scoop.

You ever heard of Apalachin, New York? The big Mafia meeting back in the Fifties?"

"Yeah, I remember somethin' about that. Didn't the Feds nail a bunch of Mafia bosses at a house near there, or somethin'?"

"That's the place," Neal said. "Anyway, Carlo Mazzone, the guy who had the Carrabba meetinghouse built, swore that nothin' like that would ever happen to him or his friends. He used to have big meetings there with bosses of families from all over the country in those days—New York, Chicago, Kansas City. So, when he built the place back in 1959, he had an underground tunnel dug that led out of the basement to an old horse trail about two hundred yards behind the house. Shelley was one of the few outsiders who knew about it. Whenever she needed to meet with Don Carrabba, she'd park on the old side road and take the tunnel to the basement. That night, she took the tunnel out, and drove away without being seen. She could've been driving off as Penny was arriving, or she could've already been gone by then, we don't know. What we do know is that she vanished. The FBI traced her to Key West a day before she showed up in that basement, but the trail went cold there. She'd cleaned out all her bank accounts, too. So she has plenty, and I mean plenty, of money. She literally could be anywhere in the world."

"Just as long as she doesn't show up in Gulf Front, I don't care where she goes," I said, trying to convince Neal and myself that I meant it. I think he bought it, but I'm not so sure about me.

Neal said, "The sooner you forget about her, the better."

"Forget about who?"

I only had one more question.

I needed an answer to the question that had led to all the killing, and to Shelley.

"So. Who killed Caroline Quitman?"

Neal stood up and walked over to the window. He opened the blinds halfway, and sunlight poured into the room. He walked back, stood by the bed, and cracked his knuckles. He looked me in the eye, shrugged his shoulders, and said, "Nobody knows."

"Nobody knows? You gotta be kiddin' me. Didn't Vinnie tell who did it? I mean, if he has immunity, what does he care? Why wouldn't he confess, or rat out the killer?"

"Vinnie swears he doesn't know, he even passed a polygraph. He admitted to finding Caroline's body outside of the meetinghouse, and leavin' her body on the Gulf Front Pier, but he swears up and down that he has no idea how she died. And, like I said, the polygraph backs him up. Don Carrabba says he doesn't know how she died, and also said that even if he did know, 'Omertà.' And that old bastard won't be takin' any lie detector tests, believe me. I realize that this is not a perfect end to this little adventure, but—I guess we'll never know how Caroline Quitman died."

EPILOGUE

I WENT TO GET A NEW DOG TODAY.

It's been three months since I was released from the hospital. I spent one conscious week rehabbing and healing there before they let me go.

Susan made all the arrangements for my return trip to Gulf Front, and as usual, she went overboard. She rented a bus from a company in Nashville that supplies country music stars with their touring buses, and let me tell you, it was amazing. It was like riding down the highway in a really nice apartment. Ridiculously expensive, downright unnecessary, and completely appreciated. Neal, Susan, all three Feagin daughters, and Penny came along for the ride. We had food from a New Orleans caterer, beer and soft drinks, music, even a little dancing. The dancing was difficult, especially for me, but we all gave it a try. We drove a couple of hundred miles past the Gulf Front exit, then turned around and drove back. We rode that bus all day, and half the night, luxuriating all the way. It was a special excursion, and one I'll never forget.

Of course, I also made the front page of our local newspaper, the second time I've been so honored. The first was when I took the job as chief of police. So, now there's another framed, front-page picture of me on my office wall, thanks to Doreen. I haven't returned to work yet, but miraculously, the town is still standing, again thanks to Doreen. She's back on the job and in charge again after missing only a week. Neal had kept the news from me when we talked in the hospital after I came out of the coma because he thought I had enough to think about at the time.

Doreen and Mr. Fields had been in Paris on their honeymoon, when on the second day, she woke up and found him unconscious on a sofa in their suite. He never woke up, and died of a brain aneurysm two days later in a Paris hospital. Doreen came home to Gulf Front and reclaimed her job before a replacement had been found, and is trying to get on with her life, sad as it is.

Adam, Earl, and Doreen call me about a hundred times a day, and Penny has been coming over three or four nights a week since my return home. She's been a joy to be around, and hasn't mentioned Shelley's name even once. I've thanked her so many times for saving my life that she's given up saying that I don't have to thank her, and now just says, "You're *WELCOME!*"

We're taking things slow, day-by-day, but I predict we'll be on-again in the near future.

That is, as soon as I quit mooning over Special Agent Shelley Brooke. I think I'm almost over her for good, but I wanna make sure. I still can't believe that she fooled me so easily and completely, but I guess I'll just have to accept it and move on. The problem is, I don't know if I can, or even if I want to. One thing I do know is that I need to quit thinking about what might have been.

Easier said than done when you've lost what you thought was your dream girl.

Neal was completely vindicated and has his job back, but is still making noise about moving to Atlanta to become a private investigator. If I had to put money on it, I'd bet on him making the move. Susan wants to, but the girls don't, so we'll just have to wait and see.

I think of Caroline Quitman most days, and wonder if I'll ever know what really happened to her. It's strange to think that after all the time and effort Neal and I put into her case we're no closer to the truth. Just another thing I'll have to learn to live with, I guess.

Anyway, I decided it was time to go get another dog. Friday was the chosen day. I got up early and headed to an animal shelter in Pensacola where I hoped to find a new canine pal.

The drive over was especially nice, since it was the first time I'd been outside the city limits since coming home from the hospital. Simply being out of the apartment was a huge lift to my spirits.

It was a perfect autumn day in the Florida panhandle, seventy degrees, low humidity, and dazzling sunshine from a brilliant blue sky. The ocean looked like it had just found its way to the Florida shore that very day. A picture-perfect morning. All I needed to accompany it was the perfect dog.

I had looked in the Yellow Pages and found that there were two animal shelters in Pensacola, and I was headed for the smaller of the two. I figured they needed my help more than the big one, and they were closer. I still missed Solly, but was excited by the thought of a new pup just minutes away.

I found the shelter with no trouble. It was a freestanding building, one story high, and looked like it might have been a gas station at one time. There was a big sign on the face of the building with a great painting of a cat kissing a dog. The dog looked enough like Solly that I knew I'd come to the right place.

Five minutes after they opened, I was the only client in the joint. There was an older, white-haired gentleman standing behind the front desk with his back to me. He was writing in what looked like a checkbook, so I waited for him to finish. He closed the book, turned and looked me over, and asked, "What kinda dog you lookin' for?"

I laughed and said, "Is it that obvious that I'm a dog person?"

"Yep. You're too rough around the edges to want a cat or a bird, no offense. Besides, it's better than a fifty-fifty proposition that anyone that comes here is lookin' for a dog."

I smiled and said, "Yeah, I guess that's right. I'm definitely in the market for a dog, but not just any dog. I recently lost the best dog that ever lived, and it won't be easy to replace him. In fact, he can't be replaced, so let's just say I need another dog, and let it go at that."

"Fine. Follow me back to the kennel, and we'll find you a good one, I guarantee it. There's a pretty dang good selection today. I think I got twenty-two or three back there, puppies and full-grown. I betcha I know the exact dog you'll choose, too, but I'll let it come as a surprise to ya. That way, you'll think it was your idea."

I smiled again, and as we walked to the back of the building I said, "My name's Coop, what's yours?"

We shook hands, and he said, "I'm Mac Beatty. Nice to meetcha, son."

"Same here, sir," I said, and meant it. Mac made me feel even more certain that I'd come to the right place.

As we made our way to the back, we passed cages filled with cats and kittens of all types and colors. There were probably thirty or more, and one litter of kittens didn't even have their eyes open yet. There was a cage holding a big bird, a cockatoo, I think, and another cage with an iguana that must've been four feet long from his nose to his tail.

I stopped in front of the Iguana's cage, and said, "Wow, Mac, do you think you'll ever get somebody to adopt that thing?"

"Don't need to. That's Felipe, and he belongs to me. At least as much as an iguana can belong to any human. Don't judge this book by its cover, he's a lot nicer than he looks."

"I hope so."

"I bring him to work with me 'cause he likes to watch the bird and the cats."

When we entered the kennel area, the dogs went nuts. They'd been barking since they heard me ask about Felipe, but now they were in full voice. It was a great racket, and I wanted to open all the cages and set them free. But, I'm a lawman, and I know we can't have packs of stray pooches running wild. So I just petted them as I came to them, and touched as many of them as I could.

I was on my sixth cage when I saw two beautiful young German Shepherds in a large cage under one of the windows. One of them was so much bigger than the other that they almost looked like different breeds.

I walked over to them and the big one sat up straight with the most alert dog face I've ever seen. The smaller one backed off and lay down in the straw that lined the bottom of the cage.

"Mac—what about this guy?"

"Dang," he said. I shoulda bet you five bucks. That's the dog I *knew* you would fall for. The smaller one there is a female. They're brother and sister, come from the same litter."

"You can't be serious. He looks like he's twice her size."

Mac said, "He's a big fella, all right; and notice how proud he is? He looks like he knows where he comes from."

"Where *did* he come from? Was he born in a nuclear reactor, or somethin'? He should be in one of those Sci-Fi movies: 'Attack Of The Fifty Foot German Shepherd.'"

Mac snorted. "I don't know if he was ever exposed to radiation, but I do know his background. That pup you see before you, my friend, is the son of a champion. In fact, he comes from some of the finest breeding stock in the country. And, if they ever make that movie, it has to be 'Attack Of The Fifty Foot German Shepherd *Dog*.' That's the official name when they're champion show dog types: 'German Shepherd Dog.'"

"How old is he?"

"He's six months, I believe," Mac said.

"*Six months!* He's enormous for that age, isn't he? I mean, look at the feet on this guy. And that *head*...it's ridiculous!"

"I hafta agree with ya, son. I don't remember ever seein' a bigger Shepherd pup."

I said "So, tell me about his background."

"It's a kinda interestin' story, Coop," he said. "See, there's a woman who lives near here, or should I say, lived near here, she passed away last week. Anyway, her name was Eleanora Mendelbright, and she was one of the foremost German Shepherd Dog breeders in the country. She had more champions come out of her kennels than anyone in the South. In fact, no one even came close. She was worth more than a hundred million, from what I hear, and had been married several times, but she always kept her maiden name of Mendelbright. When she died, she left all her money to charities, and cut her last husband off completely. She hated him from what I've been told, and didn't leave him even one of her dogs. There were about seventy-five dogs and pups living in her kennels when she passed, and in her will, she left most of 'em to family and friends. The rest she willed to us here at the shelter. We received eighteen of her dogs on Tuesday, and these two are the only ones left."

"Wow," I said. "So, these two are from a long line of champions, hunh? Well, I'll tell ya somethin' Mac, it's easy to believe. You only need to take one look at these pups to know they're special. They are both absolutely beautiful. I wish I could take both of 'em, but I just don't have the room."

"You don't hafta worry about the little girl there, Coop. She'll be gone before lunch. You take the big fella and give him a good home. He'll make a wonderful replacement. I mean, he'll be another good friend to you, just like your other guy was."

"It's a done deal. How much do I owe you?"

Mac said, "Well, he's already had all his shots and so forth, so you make a fair donation and you got yourself a dog."

"How's three hundred sound?"

"You're playin' my song," Mac said.

I laughed and reached in the cage to pet my new pal. He smelled my hand and licked it as I petted his big head.

"You know, Coop, you ought to go ahead and sign the registration papers. You might wanna breed him someday."

I pondered the idea for a moment, before saying, "I don't think so, Mac. I don't know if I'll ever be interested in doing that. Sounds like a lot of hard work. I think I'll just retire him before he gets started."

"Suit yourself," he said. "But I insist that you register him and give him a fancy name, like all the other show dogs. Got the papers up front, won't take a minute."

"Okay, that might be good for a laugh. I've never owned a show dog. Got any suggestions for a name?"

He thought for a moment, and asked, "What was your last dog's name?"

"Solly, short for Solomon."

"I like that. Officially, they usually give these dogs some long fancy name, then they have a call name, which means just what it sounds like, it's what you call the dog. For example, you might name him somethin' like: 'Lord Chauncey's Chesterfield,' and call him 'Chester.' Or maybe: 'Southeast Golden Coast,' and call him 'Goldie.' Make it somethin' about where he's from, the way he looks, or the way he makes you feel. See what I'm sayin'?"

"Yeah, I think I do. Let's take 'im up front and sign the papers, and I'll think of a name while we're doin' that."

"Good idea," he said, and got the key to the big puppy's cage off of a nail on the wall.

When he opened the door, the pup calmly walked out and stayed beside me as Mac relocked the door.

The three of us made our way up to the front, setting off another round of raucous barking from the other dogs. The big puppy sniffed at a few cat cages, but was otherwise a good boy.

When we got up front, I remembered something from my

childhood that gave me an idea as to what I might call my new companion.

"Mac," I said. "I think I have a name for this big guy."

"What, somethin' like 'Solly's Shadow'?"

"No, nothin' like that. Remember how I said the puppy looks like he was born near a nuclear reactor? That he's atomic?"

"Yeah," Mac said.

"Well, when I was in the third grade, my best friend was Chris Folsom, and his great-grandfather lived with him and his parents. I was over there all the time, and I got to know his great-grandpa fairly well. He was pretty old, maybe ninety or ninety-five, and was a real hillbilly from East Tennessee. For some reason, he was obsessed with the Russians, and was convinced that they were gonna drop an atomic bomb on us at any moment. It was practically all he ever talked about. 'Them damn Russkies.' The funny thing to us was, whenever he mentioned the bomb, he would pronounce it 'bum,' with that hillbilly accent of his. We used to bring up the Russians just so we could hear him say 'atomic bum.' Thinkin' of that gave me the idea for a name."

Mac said, "Good, now we're getting somewhere. Okay, then. Put all your personal information on the registration paper, and put the name down where it says 'Registered Name.'"

I filled in all the required spaces on the papers, and when I came to the line for his official name, I wrote 'Solly's Atomic Bum.' I left the line for his call name blank.

Mac read it, and said, "That's nice, you're gonna use 'Solly' for his call name. Good choice."

I said, "No, I'm not gonna call him 'Solly.'"

"What're you gonna call 'im then?" he asked.

I smiled and wrote his new name on the line:

"Bum."

Mac chuckled, and said, "Now *that's* a good name for a retired stud."

"I think so, too."

We finished up the registration papers, and I wrote a check for three hundred bucks. After I shook hands goodbye with Mac, Bum and I headed out the door.

When we got to the patrol car, I opened the driver's side door, and he jumped in and took his place on the passenger's side like he'd been doing it all his life. He sat up straight and didn't object when I took the shoulder strap and buckled him in place. I scratched his head and got another lick on my hand.

I backed the car up and Mac came out and waved goodbye. I waved back and slid into traffic, headed for the interstate.

I changed my mind on the way and took the back roads until we came to the old highway that runs along the ocean. I wanted Bum to get a good view of the Gulf.

After we were away from all the city traffic, the big puppy started to press his nose against the window, so I rolled it down halfway, and he pushed his face into the wind, savoring the sea air.

We had traveled five miles or so, when out of the corner of my eye, I noticed that he had pulled his head in and was staring at me. I turned and looked at him, and saw that he had that expression on his face that dogs get when they want to tell you something.

"Woof," he said.

I knew exactly what he was trying to say: "Life is *good.*"

"Woof," I replied, and drove my new buddy home in the Florida sunshine.